The Preacher's Bride

The Preacher's Bride

JODY HEDLUND

BETHANYHOUSE
Minneapolis, Minnesota

Published by Bethany House Publishers
11400 Hampshire Avenue South
Bloomington, Minnesota 55438

Bethany House Publishers is a division of
Baker Publishing Group, Grand Rapids, Michigan.

Printed in the United States of America

Library of Congress Cataloging-in-Publication Data

Hedlund, Jody.
 The preacher's bride / Jody Hedlund.
   p.   cm.
 ISBN 978-0-7642-0832-4 (pbk.)
 1. Young women—Fiction. 2. Clergy—Fiction. 3. Orphans—Fiction. 4. Great Britain—History—19th century—Fiction. I. Title.
 PS3608.E333P74   2010
 813'.6—dc22

                                                                2010016350

To my mom

For pedaling beside me up and down all the hills,
always encouraging, always believing.

JODY HEDLUND is a debut historical romance novelist who was a double finalist in the 2009 ACFW Genesis Contest in Historical Romance. She received a bachelor's degree from Taylor University and a master's from the University of Wisconsin, both in social work. Currently she makes her home in Midland, Michigan, with her husband and five busy children.

Chapter
I

BEDFORD, ENGLAND
MAY 1659

*T*he babe's crying would rip her heart to shreds if she had to listen to it one more minute.

Elizabeth Whitbread shoved open the parlor door and barged inside.

"We need a wet nurse or the babe will die," she said, meeting the startled gazes of the women surrounding the deathbed of Mary Costin.

"Exactly what do you think you are doing?" Mrs. Grew dropped the long winding sheet and started toward her. "Get out this instant. You are not permitted in here."

"The babe's been crying all morning. He needs help." Elizabeth moved toward the low rocking cradle shoved into a corner of the small room. "I'll hold him and attempt to comfort him."

Mrs. Grew stepped in front of her, intersecting her path. She held her shoulders straight and her chin high. "No one is welcome in the parlor for the laying out. Only those of our congregation specified by Sister Costin herself before she died."

"I won't disturb your preparations, to besure." Elizabeth nodded at Sister Norton and the others who had stopped washing the body to stare at her. She'd participated in laying-out rituals before—on her own mother. But the work of preparing the dead body didn't interest her now.

"I only want to help with the babe."

"We do not need any assistance."

"The crying must be a distraction. I'll take him into the other room of the cottage—"

"Sister Whitbread," Mrs. Grew said louder, "we can do nothing more for the child. He will tire himself eventually."

Elizabeth spotted a wooden flask on the floor next to the cradle. "I'll try feeding him."

"Each of these women, including myself, has already attempted to suckle him from the bottle. What makes you think you can succeed where no other has?"

"He won't take it, the poor dear," Sister Norton said. She clucked her tongue against the roof of her mouth. "The poor, poor dear needs his mother's milk, and it's long gone."

Elizabeth's gaze trailed to the face of Sister Costin, the pale skin draped over sharp bones. She followed the length of the arm hanging over the edge of the bed, the whiteness of the skin broken by the long dark cut from the bloodletting.

The parish bells of nearby St. Cuthbert had ceased their tolling only a short time ago, but Mary Costin's life had been counted as dead for more than a fortnight, ever since she'd birthed the babe and caught the fever. Few women survived childbed fever—even fewer newborns lived without their mothers.

Elizabeth faltered and tucked a stray wisp of hair back under her coif. Did she think she could calm the babe when none of these experienced Puritan matrons could?

His cries tore at her heart again. "The babe is in desperate need of a wet nurse."

"We are quite aware of that," Mrs. Grew replied. "Do you hold us in such low esteem to think we would not have begun the search by now?"

"Then why hasn't one been found? In all of Bedford there must be many nursing mothers."

"You do not know anything about these matters. Moreover, they are not your concern. You must leave the room immediately. Your presence is entirely inappropriate."

She *had* overstepped the boundaries of propriety by entering, but she'd only thought to help. 'Twas not a punishable offense to offer one's aid, was it?

Mrs. Grew regarded her with narrowed eyes and pinched lips, her body tight with displeasure.

She supposed to a woman of Mrs. Grew's high social standing and wealth, rules took precedence. But this time couldn't she make an exception and let her stay? "I'm sorry, Mrs. Grew. 'Twasn't my intent to disrupt you. I don't have your great experience or your natural way with infants. But I thought perchance I could be of service in some small way."

"Your service would be better spent outside with the others in fasting and prayer." Mrs. Grew's glare moved from her to the door.

Elizabeth glanced at the cradle. How could she go back outside and pray with the infant's wails echoing through her head? She had failed to focus before. Over and over she had asked the Lord to provide someone to help the babe. Finally, she'd decided the Lord would have *her* be that someone.

"Come, my dear." Sister Norton left the bedside and approached Elizabeth. "Mrs. Grew is right. You ought not be in here." The tall widow tugged on the white falling bands at her neck and then scratched at the red ring left by the collar. Her look pleaded with Elizabeth to cooperate with Mrs. Grew, whose husband was not only the town alderman but also an elder, one of the founding members of their congregation. They all knew Mrs. Grew was not the sort of woman one should offend.

"Very well. But I don't understand why you won't let me try. I can't make matters worse than they already are."

Mrs. Grew drew herself up. "I have always thought highly of your father. I had believed him to have respectful and obedient daughters." She turned to the body and picked up the winding sheet. "Perhaps I have been mistaken in my view."

Sister Norton touched Elizabeth's elbow.

Elizabeth swallowed her response; she didn't want to bring dishonor to her father.

"I'll escort Sister Whitbread out." Sister Norton tugged Elizabeth toward the door.

Elizabeth followed. The babe's cries clung to her, begging for her attention.

"My dear," said the older woman, once she had closed the door and they stood in the cramped main room of the Costin cottage, "Mrs. Grew has done all she can to help that baby. She's sensitive about the situation."

"What harm could come from holding the babe? Even if he continues to cry, at least he'll know some measure of care."

"You would have done no harm except to wound Mrs. Grew's pride, to chance your succeeding where she has failed."

Elizabeth shook her head in frustration. She glanced at her father with his baker's bow-legged stance and cane and then at the other men of the congregation as they now talked quietly amongst themselves. Of what consequence was the woman's pride when the babe's life was in jeopardy? Surely God cared more about the babe. Surely the men would too.

Most of the men stood and a few sat on the sparse furnishings, their doublets unbuttoned, their broad-brimmed hats discarded in the stuffy warmth of the room. They styled their hair the same— long enough to reach their shoulders but short enough for them to have earned the nickname Roundheads by fashionable Royalists who wore their hair much longer, with curls and lovelocks.

She didn't spot the dark copper flame of Brother Costin's hair. It usually lit a room like a torch, just as his presence, the fire of his spirit, sparked the room with energy. Wherever Brother Costin went, whatever he did, people flocked to him and vied to speak with him. She couldn't remember seeing him without a crowd surrounding him. She'd heard that even throughout the other small boroughs and hamlets of the Bedfordshire countryside, his preaching drew multitudes. Some said he was even beginning to attract people from London—at least three days away by carriage.

Of course he had never drawn *her*. She concerned herself with people in need—the poor, the sick, the helpless—not important preachers who had equally important friends.

"They began the search for a wet nurse two days ago," Sister Norton said in a hushed voice.

"They haven't found one yet?"

"Not one of our kind. Margaret Bird has green sickness. Agnes Leith is weaning. Sister Smythe is newly expecting and has lost her milk. No one else meets Mrs. Grew's standards."

"But the babe won't last the day if something isn't done. All of the women are saying this."

"Ah, ah. Poor, poor baby. The women are right. He'll soon join his mother."

The cries of the babe drifted under the parlor door.

Did Sister Costin, on the brink of paradise, look down on her neglected babe? Was she listening to his hungry wails, her heart breaking as she watched him starve to death?

"Can we do nothing else for him?"

Sister Norton stretched her long neck and peered around before leaning into Elizabeth. "Perchance *you* could find a wet nurse."

Elizabeth met the old woman's gaze. "Are you suggesting I defy Mrs. Grew?"

"No, no, my dear." Sister Norton shook her head. "Not defy. *Convince.* Surely you must know a nursing woman among the poor who would be grateful for the work?"

Elizabeth's mind raced among the possibilities of the women who lived in cottages and above warehouses near the River Ouse.

"If you found someone and brought her here, I'm sure you would be able to *convince* Mrs. Grew into letting the poor woman suffice as wet nurse until a more permanent arrangement could be found."

"I'm not sure I could convince Mrs. Grew of anything."

"You have a way with words, my dear. If anyone can do it, you can." Sister Norton squeezed her hand. "It's worth a try. And if we fail, then we are no worse off than we are now."

⌒

Elizabeth picked her way through the slops that littered Calts Lane. In the heat of the May afternoon, the putrid smell of rotting food combined with the acrid stench of urine from the nearby ditches. She breathed through her mouth to avoid gagging.

During the late spring and early summer months the smells worsened. While Bedford was the largest village of the county, it was still small enough that any time the wind swelled, the rankness of the open sewage pit overpowered the scent of baking bread at her father's bakehouse on High Street across town from the Saffronditch.

"I don't understand how this is going to help matters." Catherine followed her through the muck, her petticoat bunched in her hands.

"I should've brought Anne with me," Elizabeth said. "She doesn't complain."

"I wouldn't need to complain if this place wasn't so filthy and smelly."

"You wouldn't need to complain if you stopped thinking about yourself all of the time."

"Forgive me for not being a saint like you."

Elizabeth bit back a retort. Sparring words with her sister would only lead to sin. The girl had grumbled the moment Elizabeth pulled her away from the women of the congregation who'd gathered to pray. Since the bells tolled Mary Costin's death, the women had resorted to more talking than praying—especially Catherine.

"No one can be as good as you, Elizabeth. You're practically the perfect Puritan."

Elizabeth stopped at the bottom of one of the warehouses and glanced up the steps. In places, boards were missing. Those that remained were thin and sagging.

"Stay here and be quiet."

"I don't know why it was necessary for me to come with you if you're going to abandon me."

"You'll be safer out here, unless, of course, you wake Fulke with all your whining."

Fear flitted across Catherine's delicate features.

Elizabeth started up the steps and began praying. She was sure Lucy Clarke wasn't the type of poor woman Sister Norton had in mind, but the others she'd visited had either been too sick or drunk.

At the top she stopped before a door hanging from the upper hinge and crooked in its frame. She put her ear to the crack and listened. The silence that greeted her was a good sign. It meant Fulke was sleeping off a stupor.

She pushed the door wide enough to squeeze through. A sliver of light stole between the room's only shutters, and it illuminated

Fulke, who was sprawled on a boarded bed. The shallow wooden box had broken and fallen to the floor. Straw spilled out of wide holes in the mattress.

"Lucy?"

A woman on the bed shuffled.

"Lucy, it's me, Elizabeth Whitbread."

The woman extracted herself from Fulke and sat up. She straightened her bodice and pulled down her petticoat.

Warmth rushed through Elizabeth's cheeks, and her gaze darted to the children sleeping under tattered blankets, to the broken stool in the corner, to the cracked mug by her foot—everywhere but to Lucy and the bed.

Lucy's bare feet padded almost soundlessly across the room. The woman brushed past her and maneuvered outside.

Elizabeth followed.

In the sunshine Lucy squinted and raised her hand to shield her eyes and hide the black laceration on her forehead. The sleeve of her bodice shifted to reveal greenish purple patches on her arm.

Elizabeth hesitated. Not only was Lucy battered, she was dirtier and more disheveled than she remembered. Her long red hair hung loose and tangled. Sweat smeared soot on her cheeks, and brown drops of dried blood dotted her gray petticoat.

What would Sister Norton and Mrs. Grew think of such a ragged woman? But what about the baby and his ever weakening cry? What choice did she have?

"Lucy, I need a wet nurse."

"You, miss? Didn't know you had a baby. Didn't know at all."

"It's for Brother Costin. His wife died this morning. Her babe, not even three weeks old, will die too if you don't come feed him."

"Me, miss?"

"His life depends on you, Lucy. You must come with me right away."

Lucy scratched her head, her scalp festering with sores from lice.

"The babe needs you."

"But Fulke's home—see? An' he won't take kindly to finding me gone."

Elizabeth didn't have to imagine what Fulke was capable of doing to this woman. Once he'd beaten Lucy with the broad side of a shovel because she'd been visiting a neighbor instead of being home to greet him.

She didn't want to put the woman in more peril. Lucy already had enough.

And yet, the babe's life was at stake. Perhaps if they were quick enough . . .

"Fulke is sleeping off last night's drunkenness," Elizabeth said. "If we hurry, you'll be able to return before he awakes. And besides, how could he object to the extra earnings you'll bring him?"

Lucy scraped her scalp again. "Mayhap he don't need to know about the earnings."

"I don't think it would be wise to hide earnings from him. If he finds out, he'll vent his anger on your head again."

"I'll be careful. And it'd be more for the children—see?"

Elizabeth nodded. The hungry look in Lucy's eyes was always magnified in the children's. Each Sabbath morn when she distributed the stale loaves that hadn't sold, Lucy's children and others of the neighborhood clamored around her for anything she would give them. Elizabeth couldn't deny they would benefit from more.

"Let's make haste." Elizabeth started down the steps.

Lucy trailed after her. "I'll need to get back before the children awake."

"Then we'll run." 'Twas no secret Lucy gave her children a sleeping cordial when Fulke was home. It contained the increasingly popular opium poppy mixed with spices and dissolved in wine. Many of the poor used it and not just for their children.

When they reached the bottom, Catherine stopped fidgeting with her coif and the loose tendrils she was curling around her fingers to form ringlets by her cheeks. "This is to be Thomas Costin's wet nurse? You cannot be serious."

"I'm sure you remember Lucy Clarke?" Elizabeth narrowed her eyes.

"How do you do, miss?" Lucy fixed her gaze on the street and bent her head in deference.

"She is not appropriate. Not in the least."

"Lucy has a nursing babe. She has milk. She *is* most certainly appropriate."

"She's utterly filthy. Her condition is deplorable."

"For shame, Catherine," Elizabeth said. "We cannot all lay claim to your beauty."

Catherine smoothed a hand over the spotless apron covering her petticoat. "There are some who don't even try." She looked pointedly at Elizabeth's smudged apron.

"There are *some* who shun vanity."

"It's not vain to take care with one's appearance."

" 'Tis entirely vain to be thinking of the outward appearance of this woman at a time when the babe's life doesn't depend upon it in the least."

As usual, her response left Catherine sputtering, unable to find a suitable retort.

"Now, shall we go?" Elizabeth smiled at Lucy.

The woman didn't smile back. "The others won't like me either, will they?"

" 'Tis no matter. You're desperately needed to save this babe's life. Remember that."

Chapter
2

Surely Mary wasn't dead.

John's muscles tensed with the urge to go back to her bedside, unwind the cloth, and shake her until she awoke.

He stabbed the tip of his knife into the roasted hen on the platter and ripped off a chunk. With his elbows resting on the table, he stared at the blade and the meat, twirling it around.

She'd been sick and weak all the months she carried the baby, but he had assumed once she gave birth she'd recover. . . . He never imagined she would die. . . .

"John, the women are done with the laying out."

He nibbled the hen, tasting nothing. He had no appetite, but the elders had insisted he partake of the meal their wives had prepared. They sat with him at the table and tried to engage him in the discussions he usually loved. But today he couldn't find the energy or passion to be distracted, even by talk of his favorite, Martin Luther's *Commentary on the Epistle to the Galatians*.

"John?" Vicar Burton stood beside him and laid a hand on his shoulder.

John's preaching had demanded more time over the past months. He hadn't neglected Mary, had he? If he'd been home more, could he have kept her alive somehow?

"John?"

He sighed and shifted his gaze to the vicar.

"The women are done with the laying out. They'll leave the body on the bed overnight."

"Then I'll sit with her." Maybe there was still hope she could revive during the night. If he watched her hard enough, maybe he'd see some sign of life.

Vicar Burton squeezed his shoulder.

John dropped his head and fought the ache in his throat. He'd held her cold hand between his all morning. He'd watched her chest rise and fall for the last time. When he'd kissed her thin blue lips, the stillness of death had greeted him.

"What shall be done with Thomas?" Vicar Burton asked.

"Thomas?"

"Your son. The baby."

"Methinks there is naught to be done." Without Mary, it was only a matter of time before the baby died. That was reality, and he couldn't begin to think about the baby when his heart was breaking over the loss of the woman he loved.

Vicar Burton coughed; his stooped shoulders shook with the effort.

John took another bite of hen and tried to chew it.

"You'll need a housekeeper, John. The children will need someone to look after them—"

"No." He made an effort to swallow, but the meat stuck in his throat.

"Plenty of young women in the congregation would be willing—"

"No." He couldn't—wouldn't even fathom the idea of another woman being in his home.

A sudden commotion by the door drew his attention.

"Exactly what do you think you are doing?" Mrs. Grew's voice boomed through the room and commanded silence.

From his position at the table John could see a disheveled, poverty-stricken woman holding a baby. She had tugged aside her bodice and the stained shift underneath and had pushed the crying infant to her breast.

"Who is this foul woman? She is nursing the baby? Who gave her leave to do so?" Mrs. Grew's tone turned shriller with every question. "I say, stop this instant. Stop at once."

A young woman standing near the vagabond stepped in front of her, as if to shield her. "I brought her here, Mrs. Grew—to wet-nurse. And as you can see, she is succeeding where we've failed."

The poor woman nursed the baby with her tangled hair falling over her face. In the quiet of the room, the infant's greedy gulps had blessedly replaced his cries.

"And just what, may I ask, do *you* know about selecting a wet nurse?"

"To besure, I don't have the wisdom you have in these matters—"

"*To besure*, indeed. You do not have the slightest idea what election ought to be made in this regard—her religion, lineage, countenance, behavior, milk, and her child. All must be carefully considered. This is not a decision to be made lightly."

"Perhaps 'tis true under different circumstances. However, there's not time—"

"The very soul of the baby is at stake. Everyone knows the milk is nothing but blood whitened. This woman is not of our religion or even our congregation. She is depraved. That depravity will be transmitted to the child by the milk. Wherefore, the child will be forever tainted with bad blood."

"We're all born depraved, Mrs. Grew. We all have bad blood. Thus, we all have need of the cleansing blood of the Savior."

"Amen," called Vicar Burton.

Inwardly John echoed the vicar. He'd always counted himself as the most depraved sinner of all, especially in the days before coming to know Christ's saving power.

"I have seen enough wet nurses," Mrs. Grew continued, "to know that to produce a sufficient milk supply they must always be of a middle stature. This woman is too little and much too lean. She will not be healthful enough to keep up with the baby's demands."

"Whatever milk she has to spare will be better than nothing."

The girl held her head level and spoke evenly, as if she made an everyday occurrence of battling important matrons of the church.

"If this babe were mine, I'd be grateful for anyone, anyone at all who was willing to preserve him. Nothing else would matter— not stature nor countenance nor anything else. Only saving the babe."

"Why save his life only to lose his soul?"

"Let us worry about his life now and place his soul in the Almighty's hands for safekeeping." The young girl's voice sounded clear and convicting in the silent room.

"Amen," Vicar Burton said again. "She has some very good arguments."

John raised his brow.

The vicar leaned toward him. "One of Brother Whitbread's daughters."

John nodded. He didn't have the energy to care except to admit the girl was skillful in her arguing.

Mrs. Grew slapped her hands on her hips. "This woman is

simply unfit. Who knows what kind of sinful life she leads? What kind of morals? Moreover, she is filthy and battered."

"Then she is in need of our kindness and charity all the more—"

"Worst of all, this woman has red hair. The experts agree a wet nurse ought never to have red hair."

The Whitbread girl didn't respond. Instead her eyes flipped to John, to his hair. The others followed her gaze.

Mrs. Grew turned until she discovered what had captured their attention.

If the circumstances had been different, if everyone had been there for any other reason, John would have enjoyed playing along with the Whitbread girl's method of litigation. As it was, he could only manage to comb his fingers through his hair, hoping to embarrass Mrs. Grew into silence. She'd taken charge of the laying out, and for that he was grateful, but now she'd overstepped her bounds.

"Red hair is not grievous of itself," stammered the woman. "It is merely undesirable in a wet nurse—"

"We shall keep the woman." John pushed away from the table. What did it matter if they had this wet nurse or another? The baby was already weak and would die soon too.

Besides, he was weary. He'd had enough of Mrs. Grew's prattle. And now he wanted to escape. "Methinks when one is sick, one cannot be choosy with a physician. Nor when one is drowning can one afford to send away the rescuer with the rope."

Feeling like a judge delivering his verdict, he stood and strode to his study. He scraped the door shut and barricaded himself into the closetlike room, away from the rest of the world. He wished he could as easily block out the pain that wracked his body.

Elizabeth nuzzled the sleeping babe in her arms. His silky reddish hair tickled her lips.

"Ah, the poor dear." Sister Norton tucked the edge of his cloth tighter. "This is probably the first time he's ever had a full belly."

The babe's lips puckered with dreams of suckling. He had resisted the strange scent and texture of Lucy for only an instant before latching on.

"I'm afraid I've made an enemy of Mrs. Grew."

"She was none too pleased with me either. But for the present, this is the best solution, until someone more suitable can be found."

"My Elizabeth, my daughter," her father called from his chair by the hearth. "Time to be going home, my daughter. The bread cannot wait any longer."

How could she relinquish the babe now that she had him? What would happen to him if she left?

"My daughter, my Elizabeth," he called louder, thumping his cane on the floor.

Sister Norton held out her arms for the babe, but Elizabeth turned away from her and started toward her father. She couldn't hand him over—not yet.

"Father." She nodded at him.

"Gather your sister and let us be on our way."

Elizabeth glanced around the room, still crowded with members of their Independent Congregation. She didn't spot Catherine, who was likely outside flirting with the young men.

Vicar Burton approached them. His breathing was wheezy, as though he struggled to catch his breath. Whenever this happened, his shoulders hunched further, and his chest sank inward like a bowl. "Your daughter Elizabeth has a persuasive way with words, Brother Whitbread."

"Yes, Mr. Burton, that she does. She has attempted to persuade me many a time."

"She is not only gifted at caring for the baby, but she is a natural-born lawyer as well."

"A lawyer, ye say? Too bad she is a girl, then." He gave a half-hearted laugh, sadness turning his gray eyes cloudy. The lines on his face deepened, and Elizabeth knew he was thinking of his only son, murdered by the king's soldiers during the English Civil War.

If only she had been a boy. Or if only she had died instead of Robbie. Her father wouldn't have cared about a daughter, especially because he had seven of them, plenty to spare. But losing his only son? He could never replace his son.

"Too bad she is a girl," her father repeated.

"Come now, Brother. God gives abilities to everyone, even to women. And he does not bestow those abilities without expecting us to use them for Him."

"Right ye are, Mr. Burton. But this daughter of mine will never be a lawyer. Who's ever heard of a woman becoming a lawyer? She would serve herself better by focusing on the talents that will make her a good wife and mother."

"If that is how you feel, Brother Whitbread," the vicar wheezed, "then perhaps you will not object if I beseech Elizabeth to take on the housekeeping for the Costins."

Elizabeth straightened. Housekeeping for the Costins? Her?

Her father settled both of his big hands on top of his cane. "Housekeeper, ye say?"

Vicar Burton nodded. He glanced at the closed door of the study. "John will need help. He can't continue his preaching without someone to care for the children."

"I'll do it, Father."

Her father shook his head.

"I want to help."

"Ye have a good heart, my daughter. But I fear such a position will interfere with the plans we are making with Samuel Muddle."

"Surely a good man like Samuel will understand." At least she hoped he would understand. He had become insistent over the past weeks, especially since he had finished his cooper's apprenticeship.

Her father shook his head and deepened his frown. "Could ye make use of another daughter, Mr. Burton? I have my Catherine and my Anne. They are younger than my Elizabeth but are good workers too."

"Elizabeth has already proven herself today." Vicar Burton coughed.

Sister Norton stepped in. "No one else knows the wet nurse the way Elizabeth does. She should be involved, at least until we can find another."

Her father said nothing.

"This may be a calling from the Lord, Father. Haven't you said, along with Vicar Burton, every man and woman receives a calling from the Lord, that the Great Governor of the world has appointed to everyone a proper work, wherein we should spend most of our time so we may glorify God?"

The vicar nodded and smiled.

"If God is calling me to help the Costins during this time of need, how can we say no?"

Her father was silent, thumping his cane against the floor.

"At least for a while. It would not have to be forever."

"John would certainly be grateful," added the vicar.

Her father gave a last thump of his cane. "Fine. Fine. My Elizabeth may be housekeeper for the Costins. It is a losing battle, arguing against my Elizabeth." The twinkle in his eyes softened his grumble.

Elizabeth smiled and hugged the babe closer to her bosom.

"But only," Father continued, "if Samuel has no objections to waiting. The fellow has been persistent of late. It would do my Elizabeth no good for him to get tired of waiting. It would do her no good at all."

Chapter
3

No." Samuel stood in the middle of the bakehouse. His body filled the space and left little room to maneuver. "If Elizabeth is busy as a housekeeper, then she'll not want to settle down with a husband."

"I hear what ye are saying, Samuel. I hear ye." Her father's fingers worked briskly as he shaped the pastry cases before him on the brake. He had already floured the table with its long-hinged roller used for kneading dough, and now the table served as his work space for the more delicate confections of his bakery.

Henry, her father's helper, had broken away the mud seal on the oven and removed the stone slab covering. With sweat dripping from his face, he used a long-handled peel to remove the loaves that had baked during the night. They would sell most of the bread that day, but a few loaves belonged to cottagers like Samuel's aunt, who prepared her own dough and paid a small fee to use the bakehouse oven—one of the few in Bedford.

The beehive oven was built into the thickness of one of the bakehouse walls. Even after an entire night, a considerable quantity of heat still radiated from it. Father and Henry would use the leftover heat to bake the other goods that required a lower cooking temperature.

The door of the bakery was open, but the warm breeze wafting inside didn't give any relief to the heat of the oven or the fresh-baked loaves.

Elizabeth had whisked the sweet egg and milk mixture that would serve as the custard filling, and now she was as hot and soggy as if she had been weeding the garden in the sun at noonday. Her bodice stuck to her back and her petticoat to her legs.

"I don't understand why *I* may not serve as the Costins' housekeeper," complained Catherine, lingering at Elizabeth's side after delivering more milk and eggs.

"The children need someone who is concerned about their well-being," Elizabeth said. "Not a vain young girl whose only interest is in making a good impression and winning herself a husband."

"He'll have to remarry eventually. It wouldn't hurt to let him know I'm available and interested."

"He has need of a housekeeper, not a housewife."

"I am the better choice for both." Catherine dipped her finger into the bowl of custard filling.

"We have already gone over this." Elizabeth swatted Catherine's hand. "Vicar Burton requested me."

Catherine licked the sweet mixture dripping from her finger. "But I am free of obligations—"

"Enough." Their father cut in without breaking the rhythm of his work. "For now, my Catherine, ye must assume Elizabeth's tasks here where ye are needed. This is a great responsibility in itself."

The look in Catherine's eyes made clear she didn't think their father's ruling was fair. But respect took precedence. She dipped her head. "Yes, father."

Their father had assigned her the task of caring for the younger children, including Jane's. Their oldest sister had always carried a heavy work load in the bakery, since their father had not taken on another apprentice after Henry.

"I understand that Vicar Burton has asked for Elizabeth to do the housekeeping," said Samuel. "However, I don't think he's aware of the situation."

Elizabeth sighed and peered out the door, seeing the first light of dawn. She smoothed her coif and tucked in stray wisps of hair, ready to be on her way to the Costins'.

"I'm a master cooper now. I have the cottage next to Uncle's. I am ready to be married. I've waited long enough for this time to come."

"Samuel, my boy," replied her father without looking up from the pastries he was shaping, "I understand ye have waited these many years to complete the terms of your apprenticeship and to afford a proper home of your own. But if it is Elizabeth ye want, then surely ye would be willing to extend your courtship."

Samuel pulled up his breeches, which had the habit of slipping below his protruding belly. He hitched them high above his waistline, as if to give them plenty of sliding room.

The first chore she would undertake after they were married would be sewing points into his breeches so he could lace them to his doublet and keep them from perpetually falling down.

"How much longer, Brother Whitbread?" Samuel asked.

"We have barely begun our courtship, Samuel," Elizabeth cut in. "We must finish our courtship, trothplight, post the banns. These things all take time."

"How much time?"

"Jane and Henry courted for two years."

Beneath his scruffy beard and scraggly hair, Samuel's face blanched.

She ought to mention that Jane and Henry hadn't had a choice. Henry's apprenticeship had delayed them. But 'twould not help her cause to bring that to light. "Don't you agree we should help the Costins during this terrible time of need? Surely you cannot prohibit my offering them charity."

"I don't prohibit charity—"

"Would you have me leave the poor motherless children to fend for themselves?"

"No, of course not—"

"Then you cannot object to postponing our plans in order to extend a gracious hand of service to the Costins during this hardship."

"I guess I can't object."

"Everyone will understand why we must postpone, and they'll be grateful. They'll laud you for your sacrifice."

Her father cleared his throat and leveled a frown at her, a warning that she'd gone far enough in her efforts to convince Samuel.

"If ye are agreed, Samuel, my boy," her father said, "then my Elizabeth will marry ye at summer's end."

"That's more than three months." Samuel plucked at his beard.

"Elizabeth must be ready by then."

Her father's statement was directed at her.

"I will be ready." Would she, though?

"You will promise this?" Samuel asked.

Could she promise?

For the space of a few seconds she didn't know if she could make such a promise. Then she shook off the notion. Samuel was a good man, even if he wasn't handsome. He was like the big barrels he crafted—round and hefty. But she was nothing special to look at either, with her stocky bones and wide girth, her hair the color of bread crust, and her eyes plain and gray. Compared to Jane or Catherine, or any of her other sisters, she had missed inheriting their mother's beauty. No wonder a man like Samuel Muddle had chosen her—she was one of the few he bargained he could win.

"Will you promise?" he asked again.

The scraping of the peel against stone echoed in the room as Henry finished taking the last brown loaves out of the oven.

"Very well. I promise."

"Let there be an agreement betwixt us. At summer's end, you'll finish your housekeeping, and we'll make haste to take our vows before the magistrate."

"Agreed."

"Only until summer's end."

"Summer's end. I promise."

⌒

Breathless, Elizabeth stood on St. Cuthbert's Street before the Costin cottage. She had hoped to arrive before Lucy. From the sound of Thomas's hungry cries, she guessed she had achieved her goal. She prayed Lucy would be faithful to wet-nursing or be lured back by the prospect of more money.

Elizabeth shifted the warm bread loaves under her arm and knocked.

She heard nothing but the babe crying. Was Brother Costin gone? Could he not hear her knock above the baby's cries?

After another long moment, she pounded the door with her palm. "Brother Costin?" She listened, then pummeled harder. "Brother Costin? Are you home?"

At the sudden sound of crashing and a grunt of pain, she shoved the door open.

In near darkness, lying on the floor, tangled under an over-turned trestle was Brother Costin. Platters and mugs littered the ground around him, along with the bones of last night's meal.

"Brother Costin, are you hurt?"

He grunted.

She crossed the room and bent over him.

Blood ran from his nose across his mustache and dripped from his chin.

"You're bleeding."

Brother Costin touched the blood.

Elizabeth grabbed the nearest rag from the floor and shoved it against his nose.

"Ouch!" He squirmed.

"You must be still."

"And you must stop pressing so hard."

"Forgive me." Elizabeth loosened her grip.

He held his head still.

She couldn't keep from scanning the weary outline of his face. Even sprawled on the ground, his shoulders dwarfed hers, and the magnitude of his presence tugged at her long-held awe of him.

"My nose. It's broken." His voice was low. "Though 'twould not be the first time."

In all of the years she'd known Brother Costin, she'd never had reason to speak to him or seek him out. He had joined their Independent Congregation five years prior. At that time, she'd been a girl of only twelve, and he'd seemed so much older, someone she respected, like Vicar Burton.

But she wasn't a girl of twelve anymore, and he suddenly didn't seem so old. Rather, he was very much a young, vibrant man. At that moment she was in a closer proximity to him than she'd ever been with any man—he was at her fingertips, with the heat of his breath brushing her wrist.

The impropriety of their predicament slapped her in the face.

She jerked her hand away and stumbled backward. Her legs bumped against the trestle, and the force of her body pressed it down onto Brother Costin.

He groaned.

She scrambled to get off, but her feet tangled in her petticoat, putting the bulk of her weight on the bench and on him.

"I think you're killing me now," he said through clenched teeth.

With a jerk of her petticoat, she fell off the trestle and landed in an ungracious heap.

He lifted the bench. Then with a wince he got to his feet and rubbed his side. "Methinks you would have been satisfied breaking my nose. It would have been most kind of you to leave my ribs alone."

She cringed. How was it she'd only just arrived and was already failing to make a good impression?

He wavered then braced his hands on the table.

"Shall I send for the physician?" she asked, pushing herself up.

"I'm tired, is all. It was a long night. And I must have finally fallen asleep at the table." He rubbed a hand across his eyes. "The beating on the door startled me."

Elizabeth struggled to her feet and smoothed down her petticoat and apron.

He combed his fingers through his disheveled hair, but it only stuck up more. "You're here too early."

Thomas's pitiful cries drew her attention. "It seems to me I'm late."

"We won't be departing for St. John's until midday."

"But you'll need me before then." In a dark corner of the room, Elizabeth spotted the cradle.

"I won't have need of anyone. And I'd prefer to be left alone. Come back later when the parish bells ring."

"That wouldn't be wise." Had she misunderstood Vicar Burton? Hadn't he instructed her to begin housekeeping this morn? "*You* may not need anyone. But the babe most certainly does."

He listened. Then he rubbed a hand across his eyes. Weariness stooped his shoulders with its weight.

What could she say to ease his grief? She hesitated, but the babe's hoarse cries beckoned to her and dragged her across the room.

"Ah, little one," she cooed when she reached him. His swaddling bands were unraveled and his dress in disarray. His thin arms and legs flailed at the air. She scooped him against her chest. His sourness assaulted her, and the moisture from his soiled clout pressed against her arm. Likely no one had shifted him since she'd done it the previous evening.

"You're the wet nurse, then?"

"Would that I was." She slipped her finger between Thomas's lips and pressed it against the roof of his mouth. His crying faltered, then he began sucking. The trick would only soothe him temporarily. If only Lucy would arrive before he realized he wasn't receiving nourishment from her finger.

"I'm Elizabeth, the daughter of Robert Whitbread, the baker."

"Then you were the one who argued with Mrs. Grew over the wet nurse?"

" 'Twas I."

"You have a skillful tongue."

The compliment caught her off guard with warm pleasure. "I don't think Mrs. Grew was impressed."

"Then you're here to fetch the wet nurse?"

"I'm here to work as your housekeeper."

He was quiet for a long moment. "I don't need a housekeeper, nor do I want one."

Heat infused her cheeks. She took a step back, grateful for the early morning shadows. It would seem Vicar Burton had been anxious to hire her but hadn't been so anxious to tell Brother Costin the important information.

"I'm only a tinker. I can hardly afford a wet nurse. And now a housekeeper too?"

"Money or no, you have *need* of a housekeeper."

"*Need* or no, I don't want a woman in my home."

The pain in his voice bridled Elizabeth's quick response. How could she argue with a man in the depths of grief, the scent of the decaying flesh of his wife setting in?

On the other hand, how could she ignore this calling from the Lord to serve? And how could she allow this man's despair-ridden reasoning to dictate the situation? Surely if she walked out the door as he wanted, she would leave the babe to certain neglect and death.

"Where are your other children?"

"They are in Elstow—with family."

"They'll be back today, won't they?"

"To besure. For the funeral."

"Who will care for them when they return? How will you look after them *and* labor to provide for their well-being? 'Twould be a most difficult task."

"Mary is nigh eight. She's old enough to help."

"To help, perchance. But not old enough to shoulder the responsibility of the others, especially the babe." She would refrain from mentioning that the major obstacle was not Mary's age, but her blindness.

"Family and friends will surely aid," he said, although his tone lacked conviction.

"You have no family in Bedford. And Elstow is not close enough for the daily supervision the children will require."

He tilted his head back and gazed at the ceiling.

"If you can't pay me what is due a housekeeper, then I shall accept whatever you can afford."

Lucy barged through the door, breathing in heavy gulps. Her footsteps faltered when she saw Brother Costin, but then with eyes to the floor, she skirted around him and rushed to nurse the babe. Her movements were short and jerky, her hands trembling, her feet tapping while she hurried Thomas through his feeding.

"Feed 'im pap," she said as she pried the sleeping infant from her breast after he'd filled his belly enough to lull him into an exhausted slumber. With shaking hands, she nearly dropped him when she handed him back. "If I can't get here for his next meal, then make 'im pap—a paste of bread and water, thinned with milk."

Elizabeth nodded. "Be careful, Lucy."

Lucy didn't respond. Straightening her bodice, she headed for the door.

"Lucy, wait."

She glanced over her shoulder, her eyes sad and tired.

Elizabeth handed her a loaf of bread. "Don't forget this."

The woman took it and rushed out the door.

As Elizabeth turned to face the disordered room, she released a breath of relief. Brother Costin had disappeared into his closet, and she could begin her housekeeping duties without the worry of his sending her home—at least for now.

Chapter
4

*B*y midday friends from all over Bedfordshire had gathered in front of the cottage for the funeral procession. John forced himself to leave his study and dress in his meeting clothes. He could hardly make his hands and feet move with the heaviness of his sorrow.

The men of the congregation had laid Mary's body in the parish's reusable wooden coffin and then loaded the simple box onto a wooden bier to transport her body from the place of death to its final resting spot. After draping the coffin with a black hearse cloth, John assigned his family and closest friends the job of carrying it. They lifted the bier by its handles onto their shoulders and led the procession from the cottage.

In a blur he followed the coffin, stumbling along with his children and other family members.

The funeral procession in Puritan style was simple and silent.

In the days before the war, when the king ruled, the Anglican Church had dictated customs, and funerals had been ostentatious. But when Cromwell came into power, the Independent Puritans had eradicated much of the frivolity and pomp of the old traditions. The changes hadn't always been easy for John, but today he received the solemnity with gratitude.

Vicar Burton met them at the stile and accompanied the coffin to the grave. The sexton had already dug a deep spot in an area without recent burials to avoid the probability of digging up the remains of another. Mary's grave would be unmarked except the disturbance of earth.

The men gingerly lifted Mary's body from the coffin and lowered it into the ground. Wrapped in a winding sheet, the outline of her delicate form was all that distinguished her. He wanted to shout at his friends to stop and unwind her, that she was only asleep. But he had sat at her side most of the night. She'd nary moved.

The women of their Independent Congregation had done all they could for her, but it had been a losing battle from the start. For over a fortnight she'd languished with fever and sweat, then skin dry and burning, pain in the head and back, vomiting, and swollen belly until she could not bear the lightest covering.

John gazed into the gaping hole in the earth, at the clods of dirt that had fallen onto the smooth white linen. His chest constricted.

He finally had to admit: the beautiful woman he'd wedded ten years past would never smile at him again.

Johnny's small hand wound through his fingers. "Where's Momma?"

John shifted his gaze to his son. The eyes peering up at him pooled with confusion. "Me want Momma."

The ache in John's heart pulsed outward. How could he begin to explain to this child that he would never see his mother again? How could one so young understand just how much he had lost?

Tears welled in the boy's eyes.

John reached for him and swallowed him in an embrace against his chest. He breathed deeply of the boy's soft hair. "I'll be here, Johnny. I won't leave you."

Even as he whispered the words, a sliver of concern pricked him. How could he be there for his children in place of Mary? Over the past year, his preaching duties had slowly taken more of his time. People hungered for the true Gospel and were coming to hear him in greater numbers. He couldn't pull back now, not when the harvest was so ripe.

John held the boy tighter. He numbly reached for a handful of dirt and sprinkled it on top of the woman they had loved.

"Earth to earth," Vicar Burton spoke quietly, "ashes to ashes, dust to dust, in sure and certain hope of resurrection to eternal life."

Somehow, they'd have to survive without her. But how?

~

Elizabeth's eyes stung with tears when young Johnny Costin, with his wide eyes and solemn face, tossed earth onto his mother. She could almost feel the moistness of the soil, the coarseness of it slipping through her fingers down onto the shrouded figure of her *own* mother.

She blinked back tears. Her mother had died during childbirth, along with a baby girl who would have been the eighth Whitbread daughter had she lived. 'Twas no secret her mother had hoped to give their father another son, one to replace his firstborn. 'Twas also no secret she had blamed herself for Robbie's murder. No matter how much Elizabeth's father had reassured her and had taken the blame upon himself for not having been there to protect his family, her mother had died with the regrets.

Thomas squirmed in Elizabeth's arms with the grunts and fusses of hunger. 'Twas past time for another nursing. She'd instructed

Lucy to meet her at the church. But it was becoming apparent this time she'd have to search for the woman if she wanted Thomas fed. He couldn't survive on pap.

"Let's go, Anne," she said.

Anne, the more willing of her sisters and most like-minded, followed her as she made her way around the church, past the rectory that had been a hospital in ancient times. She glanced over her shoulder as they started up St. John's Street, half expecting Brother Costin or one of his kin to come after her and accuse her of stealing the babe.

But amidst the large gathering no one had noticed their disappearance. She could only hope that grief kept them from showing an interest in the babe rather than a conviction he would die.

Their walk back over the River Ouse to the north side of Bedford was a short one. Past businesses and the homes of tradesmen like her father, they made their way into the area of town where the poor laborers lived.

When they approached the warehouse, the voices of children playing under the steps turned to stony silence. The children stared, the whites of their eyes too big against the dirt that covered their faces.

"Nick," Elizabeth said, picking out Lucy's oldest from amongst them. His matted hair still had enough red visible to set him apart from the rest. "Is your mother home?"

The boy nodded and his eyes darted to the upstairs door.

"Is she awake?" She jiggled the increasingly unhappy Thomas.

Nick shrugged his bony shoulders. None of the others said anything.

She listened a moment then started up the flight of steps.

"Mum said not to disturb 'em," Nick blurted, taking a step toward her, his scrawny body tightening. "Or Fulke'll beat our backs."

"I'll be quiet. I promise."

When she reached the top, her neck prickled, as if someone was watching her. Of course half a dozen pairs of eyes from the children below were fixed on her. But the strange feeling didn't originate with them.

She glanced over her shoulder, down the street, past the row of dingy cottages packed tightly together. There on the corner across from the school, not far from the poultry market, stood a man with a tall black hat. It shadowed his face, and she saw nothing but his short beard.

She may not have given the man a second thought—only to consider him a curious onlooker—except that when he realized she had spotted him, he ducked his head and limped away, almost as if he wanted to keep his identity hidden from her.

For a moment she watched the corner around which he had disappeared. Why would anyone be interested in her doings? She could think of several lame men in Bedford who had sustained injuries either during the war or in the course of their work. But what reason did one of them or anyone have to stalk her?

She shook off the unease. 'Twas likely a passerby who had stopped to wonder what a woman like herself was doing down Calts Lane.

Elizabeth pushed open the door. "Lucy," she whispered to the dark room.

When her eyes adjusted to the dimness, she saw two couples—one on the bed and one on the floor.

"Lucy," she whispered again, louder.

The woman on the floor sat up and pulled a ragged blanket against her. Even in the darkness, Elizabeth could tell the woman was naked. She averted her eyes as the woman stood up, wrapped herself in a thin blanket, and made her way to the bed.

Elizabeth hoped it wasn't Lucy's homeless sister, Martha. If so, Lucy was asking for more trouble.

Of late, the ordinances had grown stricter. Many parishes didn't want to support the poor who didn't belong to their towns, and the churchwardens had made new rules to keep them out. No one was permitted to house someone from another town without the consent of the mayor. Elizabeth doubted Lucy had presented a request or received permission for Martha to stay with her.

The woman shook Lucy.

"I have the babe," Elizabeth whispered as Lucy raised her head. "He needs to nurse."

Lucy didn't move.

"Please, Lucy. I can pay you."

Finally she nodded.

~

At dawn the next morning, Elizabeth hesitated outside the Costin cottage door. Brother Costin had insisted he didn't want a housekeeper. But she was sure she could convince him of his need if she got the chance.

With firm set of her shoulders she pushed open the door and stepped inside. She stopped short when Mary staggered toward her and held out the wailing Thomas.

"I've been waiting for you." The young girl stared past her with unseeing blue eyes. She cocked her head to one side, golden curls dangling across her face. "Thomas has been hungry and crying."

Elizabeth took the babe from the girl and slid her finger into his mouth. He latched on to it and sucked with greedy gulps. "I'm sorry to disappoint you, Mary. But I'm not the wet nurse. I'm the housekeeper."

"I know. The wet nurse is the one who smells like the chamber pot, and you're the one who smells like fresh-baked bread."

Elizabeth smiled. Indeed, Mary was perceptive to have gleaned so much when she had scarcely been near her or Lucy yesterday. After the funeral most of the congregation, along with family, had returned to the Costin home, where matrons of the congregation had assembled a modest feast of roasted lamb, bread, cheese, biscuits, and ale. In her efforts to help with the meal and cleanup, as well as tend to Thomas, she'd had little opportunity to seek out the other children.

"Momma." Johnny's broken wail tugged at Elizabeth's heart. "Momma. Me want Momma."

The young boy sat at the table, and tears trickled down his cheeks. Betsy hunched next to him, nibbling a piece of leftover cheese. She stared at Elizabeth with wide, scared eyes. At two and four, Johnny and Betsy wouldn't understand why she, a stranger, stood there in place of their mother.

"Mom-ma!" he wailed louder.

Mary turned and, with outstretched arms, shuffled to the table, feeling her way toward him. "It's all right, Johnny."

Elizabeth saw the mug and Mary's hand gliding toward it but only had time to say "Take heed—" when the girl bumped it. The liquid rushed into Betsy's lap.

The girl squealed. Johnny began to wail louder. Mary tried to calm them and clean the spill, but in the process knocked over another mug, this time drenching Johnny.

Elizabeth shook her head at the chaos that had erupted in a matter of seconds. She strode to the cradle and placed Thomas down. However, without her finger to suck on, he started crying again—piercing, hungry cries.

Mary plopped onto the floor and burst into tears too.

"What has happened?" The door to the study banged open, and Brother Costin stumbled out, rubbing his eyes.

Elizabeth caught only a glimpse of him before shrieking and yanking her apron over her face to shield her vision. Heat rushed to her cheeks. Brother Costin was immodestly attired—from his breeches upward, his chest was bare and his broad shoulders exposed.

'Twas embarrassing to happen across the immodesty of another woman, as she had with Lucy from time to time, but to see a man unclothed, even if only partially, was altogether horrifying. 'Twas not decent nor appropriate for her, a young unmarried woman, to be anywhere near such a man.

"With all of the crying and screaming, methought the house was afire or someone was hurt," he bellowed above the squalling. "But it's only a woman with an apron over her head scaring my children."

" 'Tis the housekeeper," Elizabeth called through the white linen.

"I don't have a housekeeper."

She'd never in her life seen a man in such a state of undress, not even her father. She squirmed and prayed he would disappear.

"All was calm until you arrived."

She saw his form through the material as he moved across the room toward the children. He hoisted Johnny into one arm and Betsy into another and murmured soft words in their ears until they ceased their crying.

Even through the apron she could see the thick bands in his arms expand to hold the weight of both children.

She squeezed her eyes shut and tried to block him out. "I'm only here to help."

"Help?" He snorted. "You were the one who broke my nose yesterday, weren't you?"

"And a few of your ribs. But 'twas an accident. I promise it won't happen again."

"Reassuring. I suppose this was all an accident too? Frightening my children?"

"No. I mean, yes. What I mean to say is that I didn't frighten them—not intentionally."

"Then why are you holding your apron over your head?"

"Because of you."

"Me?"

She nodded, heat scalding her cheeks again.

"You don't wish me to see you?"

"No. 'Tis the other way around. *I* do not wish to see *you.*"

For a moment the room was silent except for Thomas's pitiful cries.

Elizabeth cracked open her eyes and strained to see him through the fabric. He stood motionless, his head tilted to one side.

"If you do not wish to see me, then why are you here?"

This was going poorly. For once her words had deserted her, and she could speak nothing but nonsense. "I do wish to see you. But I don't wish to see you this way."

He shook his head then set Johnny and Betsy down. "Woman, you are making about as much sense as a vicar reading the *Book of Common Prayers* in Latin." He began walking toward her.

"Stop. Let me explain."

But he didn't stop. He came toward her until her back was pressed against the door, leaving her no escape from his overpowering presence.

"What exactly are you hiding?"

"Nothing. Really. Only mine eyes." She was in the most indecent of predicaments, and she couldn't think straight to get herself out of it.

"What is wrong with your eyes that you must hide them from me?"

Her chest rose up and down rapidly. "Nothing is wrong with my eyes. Indeed, they are working altogether *too* well this day."

He reached a hand out and fingered the edge of the apron.

Through the veil of linen, her gaze followed the path of his strong bare arm to his wide shoulders, and then down his smooth chest to his navel. "Oh, this is terrible! Most terrible! You must go away. Please leave. You must leave!"

"Go away? Leave?" He gave a light tug on the material. "Methinks you are forgetting something important here."

His face loomed closer.

Her breath drowned in her chest.

"You're forgetting this is my home, and if anyone is to be doing the leaving, it will be you." With his final word, he yanked the apron and pulled it from her grasp, forcing it down, so that she stared eye level at his well-defined chest.

With another shriek, she pinched her eyes shut. "I only meant that you must clothe yourself."

He was quiet, as if finally understanding the impropriety of the situation.

She half-opened her eyes and prayed he would see the error of his ways.

He gave her a lazy, lopsided grin. Then he slapped his chest and rubbed his stomach before finally lifting his arms into the air.

She couldn't stifle her gasp. "Brother Costin!"

He gave a short laugh. "I haven't long been a part of the Independent Congregation. And there are still many things a former rebel and chief of sinners such as I must learn about Puritan ways."

"Apparently so. Modesty and prudence are virtues of great worth."

"In my youth it would have been a strange occasion for a maiden to hide her eyes from the sight of me thus unclothed. The maidens I once knew were much less chaste."

" 'Twould seem that way." She was glad he didn't have to know that she had looked at him—not long to besure—but it had been enough time to give herself an education in the male physique. "Now, Brother Costin, I must say it again—this is a most awkward situation—"

"Say no more." He turned away from her. "I promise I'll clothe myself, if you promise not to scare the children again."

Elizabeth couldn't help smiling. He had a charisma about him that made him easy to like. She could understand now why he was winning many souls for the Lord—and why he was winning the favor of all of the eligible young women. Not that *she* was one of those women—she wasn't weak enough to let a man's charm sweep her away.

She waited until he crossed the room to his study, listening to his heavy steps retreating before she opened her eyes. However, she was a second too soon. As he entered his closet, she saw his back.

She sucked in a breath. If the front of him was a sight of physical perfection, then his back was the opposite. Patches of purplish red skin marred the expanse of muscles.

She cringed at the thought of the amount of pain he had experienced to receive such scars.

"For all of the fuss you made about not looking at Father," Mary said, "you sure are taking advantage of every opportunity to stare."

Elizabeth jumped. She hurried across the room, took hold of the crying Thomas, and comforted him. She tried to ignore the bright blue eyes that followed her every movement even though they were blind.

Elizabeth realized that for one who was sightless, the girl could see more than most.

Chapter
5

*S*hould I call you Momma?"

Elizabeth sat back on her heels and dusted the dirt from her hands. She peered out from the brim of her wide hat at the little girl kneeling in the herb patch next to her. Betsy's face was smudged and her hands caked with soil. Her efforts to help prune the herb garden had evolved into the concocting of mud biscuits and weed soup.

"Since I don't have a momma anymore, could you be my new one?"

Elizabeth smiled at the upturned face and brushed at a streak on the girl's cheek. She was flattered the children had quickly grown to like her. Yet she was at a loss to answer such a question. How simply a four-year-old mind worked—thinking she could gain a new mother merely by the asking.

Elizabeth lifted her gaze to the forge to the outline of Brother Costin on his bench, illuminated by the brazier within. With his narrow tinman's hammer, he shaped a piece of tinplate over the stake in front of him. The tapping echoed out the door and over the cottage plot—a pleasant, comfortable sound.

For a man grieving over the woman he'd lost just over a fortnight past, finding another wife was likely the furthest thing from his mind. Besides, he was a busy man. When he wasn't gone preaching or locked away in his study, he labored in his forge, repairing kettles and pots and anything else the locals needed him to fix.

She'd hardly had the chance to speak with him, which had worked to her advantage. She wasn't avoiding him—exactly. But he'd never officially given her permission to stay, and she didn't want to give him the opportunity to send her home.

Elizabeth glanced to Mary under one of the apple trees with Johnny snuggled on her lap. He sucked the thumb of one hand and with the other fingered the edges of Mary's curls. Thomas slept near Mary on a bed of blankets, quiet for the moment. Her gentle lilting voice rose and fell with the drama of David and Goliath—the story Johnny always asked her to tell.

"Momma is a good name." Betsy stood so that she was at eye level. "Don't you agree?"

"Oh, Betsy, *Momma* is a wonderful name." She brushed her hand against the girl's cheek. "But it can only belong to the woman married to your father."

Betsy's eyebrows furrowed.

Did a mind as young as Betsy's even comprehend marriage? Elizabeth stroked her cheek trying to think of another way to explain.

"So if you marry Father, then I could call you Momma?"

"Well, yes, but 'tis not that easy—"

"Then you must marry my father." Betsy shook the dirt from her skirt. "I shall go ask him this instant."

"Oh—no, no, love." Elizabeth jumped up and grabbed Betsy's arm before she could dart away. " 'Tis much more complicated than that."

"I shall make it easy." The girl squirmed under Elizabeth's firm grip. "I promise."

"Let me tell you about marriage." Elizabeth lowered herself back to the ground and pulled Betsy onto her lap.

The girl settled herself and peered up at Elizabeth with wide eyes.

" 'Tis like this." Where did she start?

Her gaze wandered around the garden with its freshly turned soil and tiny sprouts showing in places. She had planted her own family's cottage plot more than a month ago but was only now bringing order to the Costins'.

To besure she could plant a garden. But she was not the most qualified candidate for giving a marriage lecture. She was only a maiden and would herself benefit from such a talk.

" 'Tis not easy to explain."

Betsy's eyes didn't waver from hers.

She must do this or have the girl run to her father proposing marriage betwixt them. "The Bible says a believer is not to be yoked to an unbeliever. This is the most important consideration."

"You're a believer. Father's a believer."

"But there must also be the weighing of character—two people who share values, virtue, and godliness."

"You're godly. Father's godly. You see, there's nothing to stop you from marrying him. I shall go tell him this is what he must do."

Elizabeth wrapped her arms tighter around the girl. The conversation wasn't going as planned.

"No, love. You mustn't go to your father about this. There must also be a mutual consent, a willing partnership of both the woman and the man, a liking of one to the other."

At this Betsy was silent.

"Notwithstanding, I'm already courting another man."

The girl studied Elizabeth's face, as if trying to comprehend the magnitude of this revelation.

Thomas's whimpering turned louder, the sign that his belly needed the nourishment she struggled to provide. Mary deposited Johnny and picked up the babe. She was proving to be a greater help than Elizabeth had anticipated.

"Do you love him?"

"Love who?"

"Do you love the man you will marry? I know my mother and my father loved each other. I heard 'em say it."

Did she love Samuel Muddle? She'd never pretended to feel anything even near attraction for the man. Theirs was a practical match. That was all. She didn't have dreams about gaining a man's love or attention. That was reserved for pretty women like Jane and Catherine, whom men watched and admired—or a woman like Mary Costin, who had gained the adoration of John.

"Well," the girl said, "do you love him?"

"No, I don't love him. He's a good man, and perhaps with the passing of years we'll learn to have affection for each other. But love isn't always something that accompanies marriage vows. Sometimes marriage is more like a partnership."

Betsy smiled and squirmed out of her arms. "Then it will work after all. You don't need to love my father to marry him. Nor does he need to like you."

Elizabeth lunged forward, but the girl dashed beyond her reach.

"I'll go tell my father."

"No, Betsy. 'Tis much too soon for your father to be thinking of such things."

She skipped along without turning back.

"Come back, Betsy." She couldn't let the girl play matchmaker. It would only end in embarrassment for everyone. "Stop."

Thomas's cries rose in the morning air, becoming more insistent. Lucy had come at daybreak to nurse and rarely made it for two feedings in a row. At least once a day, Elizabeth walked over to Calts Lane to find the woman, often with that strange feeling of someone watching her.

Perhaps Mrs. Grew had been correct. What did an uneducated commoner like herself know about choosing a wet nurse? Maybe she'd made a mistake selecting Lucy. Lucy's whole way of living was fraught with peril.

And she feared what would happen if the authorities learned that Lucy was harboring her homeless sister. Lucy had begged Elizabeth not to tell anyone about Martha. The woman's husband had run off, and she didn't know where the man was or even if he was still alive. Martha had nowhere to live and no way to support herself or her three children. She'd resorted to begging, moving from place to place to avoid the Bedell of Beggars, whose official duty was to track down poor beggars and then arrest and whip any who didn't belong to their town.

Elizabeth rose and brushed the weeds and dirt off her petticoat. "Betsy! You mustn't disturb your father."

Already at the door of the shed, the girl smiled and then stepped inside.

The tapping of Brother Costin's anvil stopped.

Elizabeth watched the doorway for a moment. Should she follow Betsy and make sure he knew none of this was her idea?

Thomas's wails drew her attention back to Mary. The girl rocked and bounced him and sang to him, but his cries only escalated.

"I shall make him pap," she called to Mary.

"He's ready." The girl stared in her direction, her forehead creased with anxiety.

Elizabeth stepped through the rosemary and sage.

"Johnny, you shall have milk and bread too." When she reached him, she smoothed a wind-tossed lock of his hair. "You were a good boy to patiently wait for me. Did you like Mary's stories?"

Smiling, he nodded. "Giant. Killed."

Elizabeth planted a kiss on his head.

Once inside the cottage, Elizabeth prepared the pap while Mary jiggled the crying babe. She mashed the bread with the back of the spoon and pressed it into warm water and milk—the milk and bread she had brought from her father's house.

"Mary, with little mouths to feed, I must question why your father doesn't have a cow."

At first Mary didn't reply.

Elizabeth paused and lifted her gaze. Had the girl failed to hear her above Thomas's wail?

Mary's chin dipped low. "We did have a cow," she finally said. "But it got loose and wandered off. Mother was too weak to look far. When Father returned and learned it was gone, he was too late. He found the cow dead almost to Newnham, her carcass about cleaned out."

Elizabeth shook her head. A laborer like Brother Costin wouldn't earn enough wages to easily replace a cow.

" 'Twas a difficult time after Thomas's birth." Guilt crept into Mary's voice. "Mother couldn't milk the cow anymore. And Father sometimes forgot. I tried to help. . . ." The girl's face constricted.

The door of the cottage banged against the wall.

Elizabeth's hands jerked and splashed pap onto the table.

Brother Costin stood with feet straddled and arms crossed. "Methinks you have too much ambition, using my own daughter to arrange a marriage. It's appalling when my wife's been gone less than a fortnight."

"Here we go," she murmured, whisking the pap as if her life depended on it. Apparently, he had not taken favor to Betsy's plan.

"You've quite the nerve forcing yourself into my household

day after day under the pretense of housekeeper, when all along you've been biding your time until you can weasel your way into marriage."

Elizabeth slopped half of the pap into another pewter bowl and pushed it in front of Johnny. " 'Tis not the case."

Betsy peeked around one of her father's legs and her lips quivered. Elizabeth narrowed a frown at the girl.

"And to encourage my daughter nonetheless."

" 'Twas Betsy's idea entirely." She lifted Thomas out of Mary's arms. "I had nothing to do with it. I tried my best to discourage her."

"Methinks a four-year-old cannot know so much about arranging marriages unless someone has instructed her."

Elizabeth's cheeks grew hot. She *had* said too much to Betsy.

She tucked a rag underneath Thomas's chin and sat on the bench next to Johnny. She positioned the baby in the crook of her arm and spooned pap into his mouth. His tongue pushed it out, and she rushed to scrape it off his chin before losing a drop of the precious mixture.

"Well, what do you have to say?"

What should she say? How could she defend herself when she sounded guilty even to herself. "I did instruct her," she finally said. "But only to try to help her understand that 'tis a complicated matter in choosing a mate."

"Say what you want, but I've heard the whispers and seen the looks. The maidens and their mothers are planning who shall become my next wife. You thought to be the winner—you wanted to get to me first and hook yourself a husband."

"That's not true." It *was not* true that she wanted to *hook* him. But 'twas certain the young women of the parish were speculating about him. Her own sister Catherine had been amongst the gossipers.

"You may deny it. But it's obvious. It's entirely obvious you want to marry me." He uncrossed his arms and began walking toward her.

Was he growing just a bit presumptuous? Did she hear arrogance in his tone? Elizabeth tried not to squirm when he stopped in front of her.

"Why else would you come here and work without pay unless you wanted to entrap me?"

"Entrap you?" She suspended the spoon of pap in midair and looked up at Brother Costin towering over her.

His eyes sparked.

If she'd been a weaker woman, she may have cowered. But she didn't consider herself of frail caliber, and the sparks that flew from his eyes ignited her own ire. "Brother Costin, you're puffed up with yourself to imagine that any and every maiden would entrap you into marriage."

His eyes widened and he hesitated. "It's not inconceivable—"

" 'Tis quite inconceivable from me. Believe it or not, I'm interested in serving God and doing the work He sets before me rather than fawning over a man puffed up with himself."

Again he paused, as if unprepared for the frankness of her words. "Nevertheless," he fumbled. "I must ask that this be your last day of service as housekeeper."

Betsy, who had wheedled her way into the room, burst into tears.

Elizabeth rose from the bench, ignoring Thomas's angry cries at having his meal disrupted. She straightened her shoulders and faced Brother Costin. "Let me clarify this misunderstanding—once and for all. I have no intention of marrying you. None at all. Not now. Nor ever."

"And I have no intention of marrying you either—"

"I'm courting another man, and I'm planning to marry him."

He opened his mouth but then drew in a deep breath. "You're already getting married?"

"We are not betrothed yet. But I've given the man my promise to marry him by autumn."

Brother Costin studied her face.

"She's telling the truth," Mary spoke quietly. "I overheard her conversation with Betsy."

Betsy hung her head, and tears rolled down her cheeks. "She didn't want me to go to you. I did it because I miss my Momma and thought maybe I could have a new one."

Brother Costin let out a low whistle. Then he crammed his fingers into his hair, tilted his head back, and glared at the ceiling.

Finally, with lines etched across his forehead and eyes overflowing with sadness, he crossed to the door and left without a glance back.

Chapter 6

*W*ho will come on the morrow to help?" Betsy picked up a stick of gorse and added it to the basket Elizabeth had made with her apron.

"I'm sure your father will locate a very capable person." Elizabeth forced cheerfulness to her voice.

The girl had asked the question at least a dozen times since Brother Costin left. And each time Elizabeth had tried to reassure her, even though she struggled with the same concern.

Elizabeth had wanted to stay angry at Brother Costin for his unfair accusations. But now only heaviness weighed upon her heart—and guilt. She'd let her tongue get the better of her once again.

She glanced to the gray clouds that hung low in the sky. She'd spent the afternoon trying to understand why she longed to stay when Brother Costin didn't want her there—had, in fact, never agreed to a housekeeper.

She believed God had called her to help the Costins. If He was ending her service there, then shouldn't she accept His will? Wouldn't He have something else for her?

Taking a deep breath, she filled her lungs with the damp scent of rain. She tried to push aside the thought that maybe God wouldn't have anything else for her, that maybe it was time to marry Samuel.

Johnny plodded beside her on one side and Betsy on the other.

Her apron overflowed with gorse. The Costin cottage, situated on the edge of Bedford, bordered the meadows that stretched toward Newnham and gave them a steady supply of fuel.

"Buf-fly." Johnny pointed to a fluttering among a cluster of thistles.

Elizabeth followed the direction of his finger. A flicker of orange-pink danced in and out of the ironweed and thistles. " 'Tis a painted lady."

She tiptoed closer.

The children imitated her.

"See the four small black spots on the bottom wings that look like eyes?"

"Why do they need four eyes?" Betsy walked closer.

"They're false eyes—a wonderful design God gave this butterfly to protect it. Birds and other attackers are fooled by the false eyes and scared away. Therewith the butterfly is safe."

Johnny pounced at one of the painted ladies, but it fluttered away, easily escaping the boy's chubby fingers.

"God also gave them speed and agility to protect them from young children who want to catch them." She smiled at Johnny's attempt to chase the butterfly, thinking back to the days before her mother had died, when she'd done the same thing.

A splotch of rain fell against her nose, then another against her coif. "Time to turn back home, children. We'd best hurry before we get a soaking."

The children began to run through the field ahead of her toward the cottage. Their squeals drifted through the increasing gusts of wind. She followed and watched their abandon, seeing in them the little girl she'd once been.

As much as she admired butterflies, she had not turned into one. She'd grown up to be a moth—plain and unadorned, practical and useful, but certainly not eye-catching or graceful.

If she'd been more pleasing to behold, would Brother Costin have relinquished her so easily?

By the time she reached the cottage, the splatters of rain had changed to a steady sprinkling. She ducked into the dark gloom of the interior, where the high shuttered window begrudged little light.

"Good day."

Elizabeth halted. Unease slithered through her.

Her gaze scanned the shadows and landed upon a tall man standing in front of the hearth. He caressed the edge of his hat, and when he stepped into the low glow of the fire, one glance told her that he was not one of their kind. Everything about his attire spoke of a lavishness foreign to a Puritan—from his pointed doublet finished with a narrow sash to his loose breeches tied with ribbons.

"I'm here to meet with John Costin," he said. "The blind child insists he is not hereabout. But I was told he would be home today."

Mary stood against the wall holding the sleeping Thomas, her head cocked as if she was using her perceptive sixth sense to take in all that she couldn't see. Johnny stood on one side of Mary and Betsy on the other, each clutching the girl's petticoat, their eyes wide.

"She's correct." Elizabeth stepped further into the cottage. "Brother Costin is presently away on business."

"Business?" His voice had a hint of sarcasm. "What kind of *business* did he say he was about today?"

Her unease pattered harder, keeping tempo with the beat of the rain on the dirt street outside the door. She narrowed her gaze on him. He looked familiar, a Bedford resident, most likely a Royalist who had weathered Oliver Cromwell's sequestrations enough to live comfortably.

Even though most citizens of their small town had complied with Cromwell's Puritan laws, there were many staunch Royalists who had remained loyal to the exiled king and his church.

What kind of dealings would such a man have with Brother Costin?

As if sensing her discomfort, he sauntered toward her. In his narrow face, his eyes were too big, too brazen. His gaze roved over her, taking her in from head to toe.

"Has Costin taken himself a mistress? Or has he more than one wife?"

Heat flamed into Elizabeth's cheeks. "Neither. I'm the house-keeper."

"The housekeeper? Oh, I beg your pardon." He stared at her bosom. "It would be devastating if someone overheard me. Indeed, it would be quite a detriment to Costin's reputation." He lifted his gaze and met hers. "Would it not?"

His eyes glinted like the blade of a knife.

"I don't understand." She was tempted to take a step backward, but she didn't want him to know he was beginning to frighten her.

"I think you understand. Call it what you will. Housekeeper. Maidservant. But we all know it's more than that. It would hurt Costin for word of this to get out. It would hurt your reputation too. Don't you agree?"

"Perhaps. Were it true." The heat in her cheeks seeped into her blood and spread to the rest of her body. "But 'tis not true. Not in the least."

"Ah, but how do we know that?"

"On my word."

His lips turned up into a cold smile. "Do you really think people are going to believe *your word?* You, a mere maiden?"

She swallowed a knot of panic. "I can assure you, I'm nothing more than housekeeper to Brother Costin."

He gave a short laugh. The glint in his eyes grew sharper. "Fortunately, I can help."

"How can you *help?*"

"I can help ensure no one knows about your indiscreet relations with Costin."

"You can't help me with it because no such relations exists."

"Let me make myself clear." His tone took on an edge. "If you help me, I'll make sure no rumors are started. If you don't help me, then I cannot guarantee anything. So you see, you help me, and I help you."

Anger started to mingle with her fear—anger that she was helpless to stop this man from saying whatever he wanted and ruining both her and Brother Costin's good names.

"Exactly how am I to help you?"

He glanced at the children. Her gaze followed. Their eyes glistened with fear.

He leaned close to her. "I want information. Watch Costin. Report what he's doing, where he's going, what he's writing."

His foul breath fanned over her face, and she took an involuntary step back. Was his soul as rancid as his breath? For surely only someone with a rotting black heart could manipulate this way.

She wouldn't tell him his manipulation was useless, that after today she wouldn't be around to do what he was asking. "Brother

Costin is a good man," she whispered, darting a glance at the children. "Why would you want information about him?"

The man's features hardened. "John Costin is a blight on the security of true religion."

Elizabeth knew by *true religion* the man was referring to the Anglican Church and its ritualistic ceremonies that had dominated England for over a century.

Elizabeth shook her head. Puritan preachers like Brother Costin were hardly a blight. They were sharing the truth of salvation and bringing hope to those long held in bondage to empty traditions.

"John Costin presumes too much." The man's tone was condescending. "He is an unlearned, simple, poor tinker with no training or calling, and therewith he is taking liberties with the holy Word of God."

"Liberties?" Her head told her she would be safer to agree, but her heart demanded that she defend Brother Costin. "I've heard Brother Costin preach many times and can't think of anything he's ever said that contradicted the Bible."

"Only a man with an education in the Scriptures and with the years of required and proper training ought to preach and teach." His voice rang with conviction. "Anyone else who does so endangers the soul of Christianity, interpreting and twisting Scripture until it no longer resembles the truth."

"Brother Costin might not be educated, but he knows the Bible as well as any ordained preacher."

"Are you educated?"

Like most girls, she could neither read nor write, but that didn't mean she couldn't think or reason. "My father has taught us from the Scriptures every day and has helped us to memorize—"

"You're a stupid wench. You know even less than Costin."

Words of rebuttal sprang to life, but the anger in his eyes stopped her. The war had been over for many years, but the tension between the Royalists and the Independents had only increased. And now, apparently Royalists in Bedfordshire were growing to dislike the increasingly popular John Costin.

"You must do what I've asked. That's all." His gaze slid over her again, leaving an ugly trail. "And if you help me, then you can rest assured, I'll keep your secret."

Protest rose within her, but before she could speak to defend herself, he grazed her upper arm with the back of his fingers. The shock of the touch cut the words off her tongue. She jerked away from him. Her eyes clashed with his, and the carnality within them sent alarm racing through her.

"Perhaps when you're finished as Costin's housekeeper, I'll make you mine." He grabbed her wrist and rubbed it with his thumb in a circular pattern.

Repulsion swelled through her stomach, and she stumbled backward. The linen of her apron slipped from her fingers, and the heavy load of gorse clattered to the floor onto the man's feet.

He cursed then kicked at the twigs.

Elizabeth pushed the sticks around with her foot. She was innocent in the ways of men and ways of the world, but she sensed enough to know this man could easily let his lusts take control of him, making him the kind of man with whom she would never want to be alone.

"I'll be back." He slammed his hat onto his head and adjusted it so that the long plume slanted outward. "When I come, you must have the information I've requested."

Chapter
7

*E*ventide was the worst part of the day.

John hesitated in front of the cottage door. Rain dripped from the brim of his soggy hat into his soaked cloak. He was chilled through to his skin and had been since he'd started home from south of Harrowden.

He'd always loved returning home after a busy day. Mary's gentle eyes would light up, and she'd slip her slender arms around his waist and bury her face against his chest.

But Mary wouldn't be there tonight or any night hereafter. And that thought alone was enough to propel him away from the cottage, back into the oncoming night.

The ache in his chest pulsed. With a grunt he dropped his tool bag and pulled out a chisel. He scraped at the thick layer of mud on the bottom of his boots.

Darkness was approaching, and he'd put off the inevitable long enough. He had to go inside, as he did every night, and face the emptiness.

With a stomp of his boots he pushed open the door and ducked into the cottage. A sweeping glance told him the children were abed. The wet nurse suckled the babe, and the Whitbread girl mended by the light of the hearth.

At the sight of him, she arose and began folding Johnny's breeches. "Good evening, Brother Costin."

He nodded at her and tried to push aside a nagging guilt that his late homecoming would force her to walk the narrow streets of Bedford in the dark. "You must hurry home now."

He slipped out of his dripping cloak and hung it on the peg on the wall beside the door. Then he shed his hat and shook his head, flinging his hair back and forth like a dog shaking its fur, spraying water in all directions.

With a final shake, he dug into the pouch at his waist and retrieved a tuppence. As he turned to toss it onto the table, the Whitbread girl shifted her gaze away from his wet hair and began refolding Johnny's clothes.

"Two pence for the wet nurse." He wasn't sure if that was enough, but he'd only earned a shilling himself that day and couldn't afford to give her more. Actually, he didn't want to give her more. What was the use? The baby would soon die.

The wet nurse pried the baby loose, her eyes upon the coin.

John started toward his study and stopped long enough to retrieve a candlestick and light the candle's wick.

"I've kept the pottage warm for you, Brother Costin," Sister Whitbread said breathlessly after him.

"You must go." He'd already detained her overlong. "I'll see to it myself."

She didn't respond.

He stopped in the doorway and glanced at her. "My thanks anyway, Sister. Now no more dawdling."

He closed the door and placed the candle on the small shelf above his desk. In the overcast evening, the light threw long shadows. The room hardly afforded him space to turn around, especially amidst the discarded clothes, scattered papers, sermon notes, and pamphlets.

He unbuttoned his doublet, peeled off his shirt, along with a plain wide linen collar, and dropped them to the heap on the floor. He stretched both arms above his head, wishing he could ease the ache in his heart as easily as he could the ones in his body.

"Brother Costin?" Sister Whitbread rapped against the door. "May I speak with you?"

He stifled a sigh. Hadn't he told her to go?

Crossing his bare arms behind his head, he sat back in his chair. It creaked under the weight of his body. "Sister Whitbread, the hour is late. Make haste and be on your way."

He waited for a long moment, and upon hearing nothing more, he sat forward and reached for his latest tract.

Not only had God gifted him with a preacher's tongue, but he'd also given him a skillful pen. Lately, the words had flowed onto paper as effortlessly as when he preached.

Of course, the Royalists didn't like either his preaching or his writing. He'd heard increasing criticism from the nobility and the displaced clergy. They were no longer curious nor amused about the tinker turned preacher. Even some of the wealthy Independents, those he'd considered friends, had begun to mumble about his popularity, about how he was rising above his position.

He leafed through the pages of his pamphlet. He was nearly finished writing it. Too bad his adversaries couldn't understand God had called him to mend souls, not just kettles. It was a divine appointment—not one he'd sought, but one that had come to him shortly after his conversion not too many years ago.

Didn't they see how God was working through him?

"Brother Costin, if I might speak to you for just a moment."

He tossed the paper back to his desk. Was she still there? "Sister Whitbread, did I not send you home?"

"This cannot wait."

Something in her tone set him on edge.

"We had a most frightening visitor today after you left."

"Visitor?" He grabbed a dry but wrinkled shirt from the floor. "What kind of visitor?"

"He didn't give his name."

John stuffed his arms into the sleeves and yanked open the door.

Sister Whitbread gave a gasp and spun away.

He tugged at the shirt but it stuck to his damp skin. "What did he want?"

She kept her back to him. "He said he wanted to meet with you. But I'm not so sure that was his true intention."

"What do you mean?"

"He made threats."

Apprehension rippled through his gut and he squirmed to unravel the fabric at the base of his shoulders. "Did he threaten the children?"

"No. Not the children." She continued to face the opposite way. "But he insinuated he would spread rumors about you."

"What kind of rumors?" The pressure around his middle cinched tighter.

Red crept up her neck. "They were . . . very distasteful rumors—"

So those who opposed him were planning to attack him now? Did they really believe they could connive against him and somehow force him to stop his preaching?

With a last pull, his shirt finally fell into place. "The man—did he tell you his name?"

"If he did, I don't remember it." She spoke over her shoulder, finally taking a peek at him and then pivoting to face him. "He appeared to be gentry. Royalist. Narrow face. Big eyes."

John's mind whirled over the long list of Bedfordshire Royalists. "Your description could fit any number of men."

"He was most certainly not a friend to our Puritan ways nor to your preaching."

"Well, whether he likes me or not, there is nothing he can do to stop me." Not when Cromwell, the leader of their country, was himself a Puritan and gave all men the freedom to share the Gospel. "On the morrow I'll ask the neighbors if they saw anyone."

"Speaking of the morrow—"

"No more speaking tonight, Sister Whitbread. Time to go home." He reached for the door. "Surely your father will be worried about you."

She stepped forward and braced it open with her foot. "Did you locate someone to replace me?"

"Of course not."

She faced him squarely. "You said this was to be my last day of service. The children have been worried about who will come to help them in my stead, and I want to make sure you're prepared before I take my leave."

His mind flashed back to that morning, to the sorrow in Betsy's voice when she'd declared that she missed her momma and wanted to have a new one. The words had pierced him like a sword through flesh. She wanted a new momma when her natural-born mother had narry been in the grave two weeks? How could she?

He shook his head, feeling the pain again. Deep inside he knew Betsy did not wish to replace her mother. She'd expressed her yearnings and sorrows in her childish way.

But still, her request seemed disloyal, even traitorous, to ask for a new momma so soon. His own mother had died shortly before he'd joined Cromwell's army. He had despised his father for taking a new wife within a month's time and had vowed if he ever lost a wife, he wouldn't do that to his children.

He couldn't imagine he'd ever want to remarry—he would never desire anyone but Mary. Besides, God's call on his life had only grown stronger over the past years, and it left little room or time for the cares of the flesh.

"Brother Costin, if you need me to come one more day while you find someone else to care for the children, I will."

Had he really told her today was to be her last day of service? If he had, he'd been a fool.

"Have you given thought to a new caregiver?"

"No."

She sighed. "Brother Costin, while your children are well trained, I don't believe they're capable of independence. They need a caretaker."

He sat back in his chair and crossed his arms behind his head. He didn't disagree with her. As much as he resented the presence of any woman in his home who was not his wife, he'd begun to realize it would be nigh impossible to accomplish his work, especially his preaching, without help.

The fact was he needed Sister Whitbread to stay.

What he needed to do was confess his pride, apologize to this woman for his wrong accusations of earlier, and then ask her to remain his housekeeper, for he certainly did not want the trouble of finding someone else.

"My children are in need of a caretaker. You're correct, Sister Whitbread. But no, I don't want you to come one more day while I find someone else."

She sighed louder.

He twirled his thumbs around each other behind his head. Then with a deep breath he forced the words out. "I would like you to come not just one more day, but every day—if you would, please."

She was silent.

"I ask your forgiveness for my accusations earlier this day. They were presumptuous and unfounded, and I am sorry for them. Especially since you have shown nothing but kindness and self-sacrifice in your efforts to help."

Her gaze swept across the untidy closet.

He spun his thumbs faster. "Well?"

"I forgive you. And I'll return on the morrow and thereafter—until summer's end, when I'm wed."

He stopped fidgeting and dropped his arms, resting them on the sides of his chair. "Very well. Then you may reassure the children of this." All was settled. He reached for his tract. "Now would you please close the door on your way out?"

"Actually, Brother Costin, all is not *very well.*"

The terseness of her tone forced his focus back to her face.

"If I am to stay, then I must have the means to care for the children."

"I am but a poor tinker. And I have just given the wet nurse more than I can spare."

"I'm not concerned for myself." Her clear gaze met his and didn't waver. "But the children cannot survive without the proper provisions."

Was she insinuating he wasn't taking care of his children?

"The food stores are nearly depleted," she continued. "We are scavenging for roots until the garden grows. But 'tis not enough."

He stared at her in surprise. This woman was bold—rebuking him this way.

His gaze skimmed over her. She was neither tall nor short of stature. Her build was round and full, her face pleasant but plain, and the hair that had come loose from her coif was dark blond, almost brown. She was quite ordinary. In a crowd, she would blend in, would give no one cause to search her out.

She cleared her throat. "I understand that late spring and early summer are always a hungering time . . . the time when the gleanings are either gone or rotten." Her tone was matter-of-fact, but the red splotches on her neck couldn't hide her embarrassment at his perusal.

No doubt about it, she was a Puritan maiden—the epitome of chastity.

But she was right—the children should not go hungry.

A tap on the cottage door propelled him to his feet. He reached for his candle and made his way toward the door.

"Who's there?" he asked.

"I'm looking for Sister Whitbread," bellowed a voice outside.

" 'Tis only Samuel Muddle," said Sister Whitbread behind him.

"Brother Muddle, the barrel maker?"

She nodded.

"Why is the barrel maker seeking you at this hour? Surely you don't need barrels repaired at this time of night."

"He . . ." She hesitated. "He's the man I'm intending to marry."

"Samuel Muddle?" John raised his brows.

Her cheeks were pink, and John couldn't tell if the color was left from his earlier appraisal or if she was embarrassed again.

"He's a good man."

"There's no doubt of that. But he is rather big—"

"Surely we should invite him in?" Her face *was* redder.

"Surely." He grinned and then swung open the door.

Samuel Muddle held an oiled cloak like a tent above his head, a useless attempt to keep his bulging middle and lower half dry.

"Brother Costin." The man nodded in greeting.

"Come in, Brother Muddle." John backed away and gave the man room to enter. He didn't know Samuel Muddle well, but the man's uncle had been a long-standing member of the congregation and had apprenticed Samuel when his parents had died.

Samuel shuffled through the door and lowered his cape, making a puddle on the floor around him. His eyes sought Sister Whitbread. She met his gaze straightway, but John didn't see any gladness or eagerness in her expression, such as would befit someone on the verge of marriage.

"It's nigh dark." With one hand Samuel hefted at his breeches, which had sunk low enough that another few inches and they would be slipping all the way to the floor.

He half hoped they did. Then Sister Whitbread would really have cause to hide her eyes in her apron.

"With the evening growing late, your father and I began to worry. We thought it best I walk you home. We didn't want you out alone under these conditions."

"Thank you. 'Twas thoughtful of you both." She reached for a straw hat on the table. "But you shouldn't have troubled yourself. 'Tis not altogether too late nor the distance too far."

"It will not be long until curfew." Samuel nodded to the gloomy evening outside the door, illuminated by the dim light of John's candle. "No maiden should be abroad at this hour. It's not safe. Not in the least."

She looked as if she were about to argue with him further, but then she nodded curtly. "Very well."

Out of the corner of his eye, John saw a movement in the crack of the parlor doorway. Mary was awake. She had been sharing the room with the babe to tend to his needs at night, whereas he had taken to throwing a pallet on the floor in front of the hearth. The thought of sleeping in the room he had enjoyed with his wife sent him into despair. Letting Mary take over while he slept on the floor had been no hardship.

Samuel cleared his throat and once more pulled up his breeches. "Brother Costin. I must ask that you allow Sister Whitbread to leave her duties as housekeeper much earlier in the evening."

John wanted to say he wished the maiden would leave much sooner too, but he held his rudeness in check. "Methinks I will certainly encourage her to leave earlier from now on." He raised his brows at her.

Without breaking his gaze, she put on her hat and began tying it underneath her chin. "Perhaps if Brother Costin will arrive home from his daily absences at an earlier hour, then I'll be at leisure to depart sooner."

Her response was like a well-placed parry. Instead of backing away, she'd deflected his, which only stirred his craving for a battle of words. He stepped forward, ready to place another measured strike. "Thus when I'm late in homecoming, as will occasionally unavoidably happen, perhaps Sister Whitbread shall be all the hastier in taking her leave."

He grinned at his quick, witty response.

Her eyes took on a spark. She too stepped forward, meeting his challenge with a strike of her own. "If Brother Costin is only *occasionally* late, he would know what his children need without his housekeeper having to stay late to inform him."

His grin widened. She was good. Even if arguing with him as her elder and as a man *was* out of line for a godly Puritan woman, she was adept with her words.

As if realizing she was overstepping the bounds of respect, she turned and reached for a small jug on the table, but not before he caught sight of the red creeping into her cheeks. "Shall we be on our way, Samuel?"

Samuel nodded, his mouth agape, as if he had wanted to join in their parley but had not had the slightest chance of getting a word in.

She trudged to the door.

"We are agreed, then?" Samuel tugged his dark beard. "You will let her leave earlier from now on—"

"Of course, Brother Muddle," John said. "I've never prevented her from coming or going. She seems to have a will of her own—"

"My will is only to please God." With her eyes still sparking, she gave one more sword swipe. "He has called me to help your children during this time of need, Brother Costin. 'Tis not *my* will. 'Tis *His* calling."

Her words threw him off guard. He could think of no good response, no quick thrust back. He could only stand speechless at the conviction of her words. He could no more argue with her about her calling than the Royalists could argue with him about his.

"Let us take our leave." As if knowing she'd had the last word, the wounding strike of the battle, she turned and stepped out into the rain. Samuel bustled after her.

When they were gone, John stared unseeingly at the door.

"She is quite convincing."

He turned.

Mary stood in the half-open doorway in her shift with a night coif covering her plaited hair. She was a miniature of his wife, and the sight of her, as usual, brought a pang of fresh pain. She stared at him with her beautiful blue eyes. He learned long ago that while she wasn't able to look at anything in the physical sense, she could see everything, sometimes even clearer than he.

"I cannot remember a time when anyone left *you* without the last word, Father."

"Methinks you should be abed."

"Will she come back?"

"I asked her to." He sighed and stuck his fingers into his damp hair, combing it back.

"I think she will. She likes us. She likes you."

"She would rather see a rope strung about my neck."

Mary just smiled.

Chapter
8

"If His Majesty King Henry VIII had not purged England of its abbeys, you would have made a perfect nun." Catherine jerked a ladle through the mead, and it sloshed over the side of the kettle.

"You're just upset at me because I confronted you on your irresponsibility." Elizabeth swept the last of the crumbs out the back door of the bakehouse. She drew in a deep breath of the cool dawn air with its lingering scent of woodsmoke and freshly baked bread.

"Not everyone can be as godly as you."

"I'm only trying to please God through my work." Elizabeth turned back into the room. "You would be wise to do the same."

A last glance told her the kitchen was finally tidy, a duty Catherine had ignored along with many others. "I'm tired of coming home every night to find that you've been neglectful of your duties. I shouldn't be required to take care of two households."

"Then maybe you should stay here, and I'll go to the Costins'." The pale light of the hearth fire cast an angelic glow over Catherine, highlighting her slender yet supple body.

Elizabeth smoothed a hand over her stomach. The stoutness of her own form rose up to mock her and stir a twinge of unexpected envy. What would it be like to have just a fraction of Catherine's beauty?

She pressed her lips together and gave herself a mental shake. She was wasting time by dwelling on vanity. "I'm taking my leave to the Costins'." She bustled to the table and tucked her hair into her coif. "And because of your negligence, now I will be late."

Catherine sniffed. "I didn't ask for your help."

"You must take your responsibilities seriously. 'Tis practice for managing your own home someday." If only Catherine had ben-efited from more guidance from their mother before she'd died.

"It's not fair. It should have been me. I'm the more likely choice, since you're already courting Samuel."

"We've discussed this before and 'twill do no good to discuss it again." Elizabeth retied her apron and turned her gaze from the yellow stains and streaks of dirt that covered it.

"I don't understand why you get to go. He'll never be interested in you."

"I don't care in the least if he's interested in me. This is service to God. Nothing more."

"He won't look at you. But he'll certainly notice someone like me."

Elizabeth shrugged off the sting of the girl's words and reached for her basket. "The only thing he'll notice is your lack of responsibility."

Catherine breathed an exaggerated sigh. "Here I stand, wasting my youth and my beauty, when I could be winning the affection of a man—a well-respected and handsome man."

"The job is not a position in which eligible young maidens flaunt themselves before Brother Costin, hoping he will choose them. 'Tis really a housekeeping job, Catherine. 'Tis hard work. You wouldn't like it."

"He'll have to remarry someday. Why shouldn't he choose me as wife?"

"Perhaps one day you will be the next wife of Brother Costin." Elizabeth reached for the loaf of bread and tall jug of milk and tucked them into her basket. 'Twas possible. Catherine turned the eyes of many a man. "But for now, you must focus on becoming responsible. A careless young woman won't make any man a godly wife."

With Catherine's complaints following her, Elizabeth started out in the faint light to the Costins'. The short brisk walk gave her time to clear her mind of her self-doubts and refocus on what was truly important—her service to the Lord.

When she arrived at the cottage, she hesitated outside the door. Her parting words of the previous evening echoed through her mind and made her heart lurch. She had overstepped proper boundaries in her exchange with Brother Costin. What must he think of her now?

First chance she had, she would make amends. She squared her shoulders and braced herself to face him. Then she pushed open the door and stepped inside.

"You're late." Brother Costin's stern voice greeted her. The children were perched on their benches at the table, and Brother Costin sat in his chair at the head, his Bible open in front of him.

She was late? All thoughts of overstepping her bounds evaporated. She placed her basket on the floor and slanted Brother Costin what she hoped was a censuring look. Was he truly accusing *her* of being late—he who was always tardy?

"Father told us he will allow you to remain our housekeeper." Betsy's dimpled smile lit her face, and she looked up at her father with wide adoring eyes.

"Allow me to remain?" Her gaze snapped to him. Surely he was growing a tad presumptuous again.

Even though his face was a mask of seriousness, his eyes had the hint of a sparkle. He pushed back from the table and stood. "Since you're now officially in my employ, I must ask that you arrive promptly in the mornings."

"I beg your pardon, Brother Costin, but I hardly think you are the one to demand promptness."

He ambled toward her and didn't stop until he stood directly in front of her. "Hold out your hand," he said softly. "I have something for you."

The gentle crinkles in the corners of his eyes made her stomach dip low. She held out her hand.

He lifted his hand to hers and pressed several coins into her palm. Then he bent her fingers closed around them. "For the market. Today."

For a moment she couldn't tear her eyes away from his weathered fingers against hers.

"You were right. The children need more," he said.

She lifted her gaze to his. Her heart skipped ahead of her tongue.

One of Brother Costin's brows cocked, and a grin played at his lips. "Methinks I'm now having my turn at tongue-tying."

⁓

"Father is still very sad, isn't he?" Mary asked as they sat in the shade of the apple trees behind the cottage, trying to keep cool during the hottest part of the day.

Elizabeth's fingers grew idle among the folds of Johnny's shirt, pausing in their feeble attempts to lengthen the linen and make room for his growing body. Her gaze trailed over Mary, who was resting on her back in the grass, to Thomas, swaddled and asleep next to her, then finally to Betsy and Johnny, playing near the hedgerow, heedless of the heat, lost in their make-believe world of knights battling dragons.

"When Father is home, he doesn't want to be here."

Elizabeth glanced at the empty forge. The darkness of the small shack surely reflected the emptiness of Brother Costin's heart. " 'Tis only natural that your father is still grieving over losing your mother." Two weeks had passed since Brother Costin had asked her to stay as their housekeeper, but just because he had agreed to her presence in his home didn't mean he was nearly finished grieving his wife.

"I miss her too." Mary's voice wobbled.

Elizabeth lifted her needle and looked at the girl. Mary hadn't cried once over the loss her mother—at least not that she'd seen. Johnny and Betsy still had bouts of crying and missing their mother. But Mary had been the strong one, the one who comforted the others, the one who tried to make everyone else happy.

A tear slipped out of the corner of Mary's eye.

Elizabeth's heart swelled with a sudden ache. She dumped her sewing onto the grass and reached for the girl.

Another tear trickled down Mary's cheek.

"Oh, love." Elizabeth drew the girl up and wrapped her arms around her.

Mary wound her thin arms around Elizabeth and pressed her face into Elizabeth's chest. Silent sobs shook the girl.

Elizabeth hugged her tighter and kissed the top of her head. "Oh, love. Oh, love." She held her and rocked back and forth, watching Johnny and Betsy wave sword sticks in the air as they fought an imaginary creature. They shrieked, and then Betsy led a retreat, with Johnny eagerly mimicking her every move.

Mary's sobs diminished until she lay still in Elizabeth's arms.

Finally she gave a loud sigh. "Sometimes I think Mother's death is my fault."

"You do?"

Mary nodded.

Elizabeth pressed another kiss into her curls. "Oh, love, 'tis not your fault. 'Tis not anyone's fault. Only our sovereign God determines the number of days we have."

"But if I wasn't blind, I could have helped her more—"

"Here they are, Sister Spencer," a voice clucked behind them.

"I told you," came another voice, louder and brasher. "Didn't I tell you they would be in the back keeping cool?"

Elizabeth glanced over her shoulder. Sister Norton and Sister Spencer were making their way past the garden toward them, the one tall and thin like a Maypole and the other short and round like a large kettle.

"Seems we have guests," Elizabeth murmured to Mary. She kissed the girl's head one more time, and then pushed herself off the ground.

"Good day, Elizabeth." Sister Norton took one long stride to three of Sister Spencer's choppy ones. "We've just come from market and have good news for you."

An empty basket swung at Sister Norton's side. The two widows supported themselves by selling eggs, butter, and garden produce at the market square, as well as the bone lace they spent long hours sewing. The earnings were meager, and the women could hardly afford the rent of the small cottage they shared. But it kept them from having to live at the bridewell.

Sister Norton ducked into the shade of the tree. She hunched her shoulders to keep from bumping her head against the tiny apples beginning to swell in place of the blossoms that had fluttered away.

"It's actually good news for the poor baby Thomas." The taller

woman tugged the collar at her neck and peered down at the sleeping infant. "Ah, ah. Poor, poor baby."

His face was pale and lean. Lucy's wet-nursing was irregular,
and the babe survived on less mother's milk than he needed. But
he was still alive, and for that Elizabeth was grateful.

Sister Norton bent closer to Elizabeth. "Sister Bird's baby died
yesterday morn. She agreed to wet-nurse Thomas to ease the discomfort of having an abundance of milk but no baby."

"Truly?" Elizabeth looked from Sister Norton to Sister Spencer.
A bud of hope pushed to the surface of her heart.

Sister Spencer gave several nods; her cheeks jostled from the
motion. "She came to market this morn and said as much herself."

" 'Twould be very helpful." Elizabeth's mind began to spin.
She didn't know Sister Bird well, but perhaps the woman would
be willing to come at the times Lucy could not.

"They had the funeral for the babe last eve." Sister Norton
spoke in hushed tones. "Ah, poor, poor wee one. Healthy one day,
gone the next."

"They had the poor baby wrapped in a winding sheet and
ready for burial before anyone even knew he was dead," Sister
Spencer added.

Thomas began to squirm, and his face scrunched into the beginning of a cry. Elizabeth reached down and picked him up. "When
can Sister Bird come?"

The two women glanced at each other sideways.

"*Come*, my dear? Did you say *come*?" Sister Norton straightened,
bumped her head on a branch, and then slumped again. "Ah, Sister
Bird cannot *come* here to wet-nurse. She has five other yonkers to
tend. We must take the baby to her."

Elizabeth nodded. She could do that. She often took the babe
to Lucy. 'Twould make additional work. But if it would help him,
then it must be done. "I'll take him to Sister Bird during the parts
of the day that Lucy isn't able to make it here."

"Oh no, no, no," Sister Spencer said. "Sister Bird made it very clear the beggared woman wasn't to continue wet-nursing in any way. Already the child has received bad blood and has been exposed to all manners of depravity. Sister Bird doesn't want any further contamination."

"Lucy was only a temporary help. You knew that, my dear," Sister Norton said more gently. "Now we've found permanent arrangements."

Elizabeth pressed the tip of her finger into Thomas's mouth. He latched on and sucked it hungrily, finding from it a small measure of comfort during his constant waiting for nourishment. With her other fingers she caressed his pale cheek. Every day he grew weaker and more listless. Was it just the natural course of never having a full belly? Or was there truly something bad about Lucy's milk that was hurting the babe?

"I shall have to dismiss Lucy, then?"

Sister Spencer nodded. "This is for the best."

Elizabeth wasn't sure if it really was for the best, but it seemed like the most logical way at present to get the babe the milk he needed. "Did Sister Bird say what times of the day she wants me to bring Thomas?"

"*Tisk. Tisk.* I see that we've not been very clear, Sister Whitbread," Sister Spencer said. "We must take the baby to live with Sister Bird."

Elizabeth's gasp echoed Mary's. "Send the babe away? I can't do that."

Sister Norton's eyes filled with compassion. "Ah, my dear. I know this is all very difficult. But I'm sure you understand this is the way of things."

Elizabeth swallowed her protest. Not many wives could leave their families and responsibilities to wet-nurse, unless it was for the nobility.

Her chest tightened and an ache formed at the back of her

throat. She looked down at Thomas. Even though his tongue and lips were moving, he'd fallen back asleep.

Despite his fussiness of the past three weeks, she'd grown to love him, and the thought of letting him go into someone else's care was as unthinkable as sending away her own baby. But even as her arms tightened around him, she knew she would have to let him go.

"We cannot send Thomas away," Mary said, as if she had been able to hear the agony clamoring in Elizabeth's head. "We'll keep Lucy. She may not be exactly what he needs, but having her is better than sending him away."

Elizabeth reached for Mary's hand and grasped it. Her heart agreed with what Mary said, but her reasoning prevailed. Thomas needed more than he was getting, or he would dwindle away to nothing.

"Ah, ah, you poor dears." Sister Norton smiled sadly. "This will be much easier for the baby than for you. He's young and will adjust to a new home—especially one where his belly is full."

"He won't like it." Mary's thin body tensed. "He'll miss us."

"*Tisk. Tisk.*" Sister Spencer frowned; the deep folds of her face added severity to her countenance. "Even if he doesn't like it, he'll be better off. He'll get the milk of a godly woman."

Mary's arm trembled against Elizabeth's. She squeezed the girl's hand. "Before we can agree to such an arrangement, we must ask Brother Costin for permission—"

"It's already done," Sister Spencer said. "Mrs. Grew herself approached Brother Costin after the funeral and made all of the arrangements."

Mrs. Grew? The name slugged Elizabeth and threw her off guard. As one of the wealthiest and most prominent women of their congregation, no one would challenge Mrs. Grew's efforts to assist Brother Costin in the care of his children. Elizabeth had already defied the woman once. She didn't dare do it again.

"Mrs. Grew needed only to confirm Sister Bird's willingness to help today, and now that she has agreed, there is naught else to be done but take her the baby. That's why we're here."

"You're taking him today?" Elizabeth struggled to catch her balance.

"It's not fair." Mary's voice rose in pitch. "Then we're not allowed a say in the matter?"

"Ah, I am afraid not, my dears." Sister Norton shook her head. "It's already been decided."

"You can't take him."

"Ah, ah, poor child." Sister Norton clucked softly. "Think about the good it will do for thy brother. It may save his life."

"It won't save him to be away from the ones that love him!"

"Let's be on our way." Sister Spencer gave the girl a disapproving look—one that may have put the girl in order had she been able to see it.

Sister Spencer grasped the babe in such a way that Elizabeth knew she meant to take him and wouldn't accept no as an answer.

Elizabeth bent her head to the baby's soft brow. She nuzzled a final kiss. Then she extracted her finger from his mouth and let the older woman take him from her arms.

"No!" Mary's sobs filled the air.

Tears stung Elizabeth's eyes. She reached for Mary.

Betsy and Johnny dropped their sticks and watched the unfolding drama.

The baby, having lost his sucking comfort, began to cry.

The wails wrenched Elizabeth's heart.

Sister Spencer hefted him in her arms. "Come along, Sister Norton. There's no sense wasting any more time," she said as she strode back the way they'd arrived.

Sister Norton ducked out from the shade of the apple tree into the bright afternoon sunshine. "Try to remember, even though this is difficult for you, it will be good for the baby. Perhaps he'll have a chance to live."

⟶

"Now I see what goes on when I'm away."

A whisper startled Elizabeth. Her eyes flew open.

Brother Costin towered over her. The branches snagged at his coppery hair, overlong and wind-tossed, which added to the roguishness he couldn't shed no matter how conservative he tried to appear.

She blinked. Had she dozed?

He wore a lopsided grin. "Methinks a housekeeping job would suit me just fine—if I could nap the afternoon away too."

Heat rose from her neck into her cheeks. " 'Tis not what it appears."

"Certainly not. It only appears you are napping, when really you're very hard at work thinking or pursuing some other intellectual activity." His eyes crinkled at the corners with humor. The bright blueness was dyed the same color as the sky.

"We've had a difficult afternoon." She carressed Mary's tear-splotched cheek. The girl had cried herself to sleep on her lap, and Johnny and Betsy had fallen asleep next to her in the grass.

"I have just the thing to make life easier. I've brought home a cow." He nodded in the direction of the forge.

She glanced to the shed, to the dilapidated overhang. There stood a petite white cow with burgundy splotches concentrated at its head and rump. Its udder hung low and full—a young heifer to produce good quantities of milk.

"She's a fine one," he spoke softly. "One of Colonel Okey's Ayrshires."

"She looks fine."

"I've put in a week of repairs at Ridgmont in Ampthill for the Okeys, and I owe him another two. But he said I could take her today." His gaze came back to hers and searched for her approval.

" 'Twill be good for the children to besure." She couldn't help thinking of Thomas and how it would be of no use to him now.

Mary stirred. "Father?"

"I'm here, Mary." He reached down and cupped the top of her head.

"Father, how could you?" Anguish radiated from each word.

"It's only a cow, Mary."

Betsy and Johnny opened their eyes and scrambled to sit up.

"A cow?" Johnny stood. At the prospect of seeing a cow, his two-year-old mind could easily forget the tragedy of losing his brother. "Cow? Where cow?"

"Over there." Brother Costin turned the boy's face in the direction of the animal. "Isn't she a beauty?"

"No!" Mary pushed off the ground and stamped her foot. "I don't care about a cow!"

Brother Costin's forehead scrunched into a mass of lines. "What is it then, Mary?"

"How could you, Father?"

"How could I what?"

Mary's breath caught on a sob.

Brother Costin dropped to one knee in front of the girl, dwarfing her with his body.

"You let them take Thomas!" Her sobs rushed out in heaving gulps.

His brow furrowed deeper, and he turned questioning eyes to Elizabeth.

"Sister Spencer and Sister Norton came this afternoon." Elizabeth tried to keep the tremor out of her voice. "They took Thomas away to Sister Bird for wet-nursing."

"Mm-hmm." He folded his arms, and his eyes pierced into

Elizabeth as if he were reading something written in the depths of her soul.

" 'Twas so sudden, so unexpected. We weren't ready for this."

"Why?" Mary demanded through her sobs. "Why did we have to lose Thomas?"

Brother Costin lifted his hands in a helpless gesture. "Mrs. Grew said Sister Bird was available to wet-nurse the baby. I gave my consent to it."

"You gave your consent?" The pitch of Mary's voice rose with every word. "How could you?"

Brother Costin jabbed his fingers through his tousled hair.

"How could you give him away so easily? Don't you love him?"

"It has naught to do with love. It's the reality of living in a sinful world—death comes to us all. And for some it comes sooner—especially babies."

"You think Thomas is going to die?"

"Methinks there is little chance for a baby without its mother. I haven't known many to survive."

"But he's lived thus far. Sister Whitbread and I have been helping him. We've worked ceaselessly to care for him. Why can't we continue?"

"It's best for you not to become too attached. His loss will be easier to bear that way."

"I'm already attached. I love him."

"All the more reason for him to be gone."

Elizabeth watched Brother Costin's face, the tautness of his jaw, the muscles straining in his cheeks. Suddenly she understood: *he* did not want to grow attached to the infant and chance losing another whom he loved. If he sent the baby away, then he wouldn't love it only to lose it as he had his wife.

Brother Costin reached for Mary, but she jerked away from his touch. "It's altogether best for the baby to go to a wet nurse. He has a better chance of surviving there than here."

"But he already has a wet nurse. If you let us have Thomas back, Lucy said she'll try to come more oft."

Lucy had come shortly after the Sisters had taken Thomas. Elizabeth had been trying to comfort the children, and in the midst of the chaos, she'd had to explain to Lucy what had transpired. And Lucy had insisted she would come back, she would do better, she would come more often. She couldn't understand Elizabeth had no say in the matter. She'd finally left, pleading to let her have another chance at wet-nursing the babe, anxious for the small amount of money it had paid.

Brother Costin shook his head and pushed himself up until he was standing under the branches. "The decision is already made, Mary. As hard as it will be, you must accept it."

He backed out from the tree until he was standing at his full height.

The hard set to his shoulders made it clear he wouldn't change his mind—not even for his favored blind daughter.

An ache of disappointment lodged inside of Elizabeth. Only then did she realize how much she'd hoped he would sympathize with Mary and bring the babe back to them—even though she knew having a full-time wet nurse was in his best interest.

"We must go on now, Mary. And pray that the Lord's will be done." His words were a command, not a request.

Mary stood rigidly and said nothing.

He blew out a frustrated breath then turned and strode away.

"I already know the Lord's will," she murmured. "And I intend to see it done."

Chapter
9

$\mathcal{E}$lizabeth heard Thomas crying.

She scrunched her eyes and chanted the metrical psalm with the rest of the congregation.

Even through the singsong voices, Thomas's high-pitched, hungry wail reverberated in her head as if he were in the church instead of outside in the rectory garden with one of Sister Bird's young daughters.

She longed to stomp out of the building into the garden and take him away from the girl.

The staleness of the air swarmed around her, and the hard back of the pew pushed against her body, urging her to go. She hadn't found any of her usual joy in the simple Puritan worship service that morn. Instead, the prayers and Vicar Burton's long sermon had wound her nerves tight until her entire body had become a board about to snap.

If only she hadn't heard Thomas crying when the Birds had walked up the path leading to St. John's. If only Sister Bird had lovingly taken the babe to the garden herself instead of wearily hefting him into the arms of a girl hardly big enough to hold him.

Catherine's arm brushed against Elizabeth's, and she flinched. She cracked open one eye and peeked at her sister.

With eyes closed and head bent, the girl was pinching her cheeks.

Elizabeth watched rosy pink spring to life in Catherine's cheeks. Her mind scrambled to understand why her sister was intent upon abusing herself. Then a sudden burst of dismay and irritation raced through her.

She poked her elbow into her sister's side.

Catherine's eyes flew open, and a soft protest slipped from her lips.

Elizabeth narrowed her brow and shook her head.

Catherine smiled and gave her cheeks a last pinch before darting a glance across the aisle to the men's side.

Elizabeth couldn't keep her gaze from following and landing directly on the bent head of Brother Costin. The terseness of his wide shoulders and the clasp of his folded hands declared the fervor with which he worshiped.

Certainly a zealous preacher like Brother Costin should have his own congregation by now. But week after week he sat under the teaching of Vicar Burton, carrying out his own preaching at odd hours and in various places throughout the countryside.

Elizabeth's gaze drifted to Samuel, further behind Brother Costin. With his eyes closed and his lips moving in chant, his face held all the reverence of a godly man. He was a good man, but why did his presence not command her attention the same as Brother Costin's?

She couldn't help but look again at Brother Costin, to his large hands folded in front of him. Her stomach tumbled in a warm circle at the remembrance of the way his eyes sparked with anger one minute but crinkled in mirth the next.

Catherine's elbow dug into her arm.

Elizabeth jerked her head away from the men and slid a glance at Catherine. The girl shook her head and frowned, mimicking the rebuke Elizabeth had just given her, only her eyes held a mocking gleam.

Heat rushed to Elizabeth's cheeks. She closed her eyes and tried to force her mind back to the words of the psalm. She certainly wouldn't have looked at the men if Catherine hadn't tempted her. She never made a practice of gazing at the men like many of the young women did.

What had led her to such vanity? She squeezed her eyes tighter and chanted louder. The Sabbath was supposed to be a day sanctified for the worship of God, a day entirely set apart to the hearing of God's Word, to praying and meditating. It was not a day for idle activities *or* for wayward thoughts.

She'd heard others grumble about the Sabbatarian laws, that they'd grown too strict during the years of the Protectorate, that now, after a long week of work, they had no time for amusements. But since Elizabeth had been an infant when King Charles I had surrendered his throne to Cromwell, she could remember no other way of keeping the Sabbath than giving it wholly to the Lord.

Usually she relished the special worship focus of the Sabbath and had no trouble keeping her mind from straying to worldly matters.

Her thoughts flashed to Brother Costin's bent head, and just as quickly she gave herself a mental shake. She was having trouble staying focused this Sabbath because she was worried about Thomas.

Once again she strained forward to listen. She was certain she could hear his cries outside; the wails resonated through her head and ripped her heart. It had been less than twenty-four hours since Sister Norton and Sister Spencer had taken him away, but it felt more like twenty-four weeks.

As soon as Vicar Burton recited the Apostolic Blessing and dismissed them, she sprang to her feet. Relief swirled through the driving need to find Thomas and make certain the crying had only been an illusion of her anxious imagination.

"Don't leave too soon." Catherine grabbed her arm. "*Someone* is on his way over here."

Elizabeth's heart gave a loud thump with unexpected hopefulness, and she followed Catherine's gaze.

"Oh," she muttered. Samuel Muddle lumbered with a jolting side step along the length of his pew, his eager eyes fixed upon her. What had she expected? That Brother Costin would seek her out? She flushed at her own foolishness. Why would such an important man ever give her a passing glance?

"Catherine, I need you to detain Samuel for a moment."

The girl's eyebrows arched high and revealed a surprised glimmer.

"I don't have the time to make small talk with him." Elizabeth edged backward down the pew.

Catherine glanced at Samuel working his way out of the narrow pew, his wide stomach making his steps cumbersome. "I can't remember when you've ever had time for the man."

"I have plenty of time. Just not today. Not now." She narrowed her gaze on the back of Sister Bird still sitting in her pew with the matrons in their place of honor close to the communion table.

Why wasn't she rising to leave? Didn't she have even the tiniest sense of urgency to check on the babe placed in her care?

"I think you should take at least a moment to speak with Samuel." The genuineness of Catherine's tone was lost in a smirk. "You certainly can't afford to spurn the attention of the first man who's ever shown you interest."

"I'm not spurning him." She backed to the end of the pew and slipped into the aisle. "I just have something more important to do."

"I'm sure you're off to save the world, as usual." Catherine's sarcasm trailed after her.

Elizabeth shook off the girl's words and the niggling of unease they stirred within her. Instead, she wound her way through the congested aisle toward the door.

As she stepped outside, dismal low-lying clouds greeted her and touched the gray stone tower of the church. Heavy moisture filled the air, and a light mist had begun to fall. She took a deep breath of the coolness that had blown in and replaced the late June heat.

She hoped Sister Bird had swaddled Thomas warmly.

Elizabeth peered past the towering canopy of branches to the rectory garden. There the Bird girl swung from a low branch of a mulberry tree, kicking her legs back and forth in merry abandon. Elizabeth couldn't see Thomas, but his faint, unceasing cries beckoned to her.

All the worrying over the past hours and the heartache of losing him pooled in her chest and rose in a tight, aching cry that begged for release. She took a step forward.

"I say, where do you think you are going?" Mrs. Grew's voice and a tight grip on her shoulder stopped her.

Elizabeth swallowed the ache in her throat and turned. "Good Sabbath, Mrs. Grew."

The woman stood tall and straight. Her ruffled white collar rose out of her bodice and touched her chin in a fashionable style. The rich chestnut color and fine linen of Mrs. Grew's meeting gown spoke of wealth and prestige. In comparison, Elizabeth's best meeting clothes, remade from Jane's, were dingy and faded.

"I asked where you are going." The woman's disdainful expression clearly communicated that she had not forgotten Elizabeth's defiance when she'd brought Lucy to wet-nurse Thomas.

Elizabeth hesitated. Her mind scurried for excuses but finally landed on the truth. "I was on my way to check on the Costin babe. He's crying—"

"Stay away from him."

Her mind warned her to acquiesce to someone of Mrs. Grew's status. But Thomas's cries called to her as if he were her own baby, her very own flesh and blood.

"He needs attention." Surely the woman couldn't fault her for wanting to help. "He's cried for overlong now and should have attention."

"He is no longer your concern."

"I shall make him my concern if no one else does."

"You no longer have any say in matters regarding that baby—not that you should have had any say in the first place. His care is now in more capable hands and will stay that way."

"I beg your pardon, Mrs. Grew. But it doesn't appear he's in anyone's hands at present." Elizabeth took a deep breath to calm herself and to keep from saying anything she might regret. "I merely wish to comfort him until Sister Bird is available."

"You shall do no such thing. It is precisely your meddling and coddling him that has made him so whiny and difficult. You have indulged him these past weeks. And only the good Lord knows what corruption the baby has suffered at the hands of that beggar you pulled from the ditches. It will take much time to undo what you have done."

"The source of his fussiness has chiefly to do with his lack of nourishment. Loving and nurturing him have only served to sustain him—especially during the times of insufficient feedings."

Mrs. Grew took a step closer to Elizabeth, her chin high and her eyes cold. "You have asserted yourself far above your status as a poor, unmarried girl."

Elizabeth wanted to cower, but she squared her shoulders, determined to help Thomas even if she made an enemy of this woman.

"Your work with the baby is terminated." Mrs. Grew lowered her voice. "If I had my way, you would be done with the Costins altogether. But as it is, you are finished with the baby. Do not go near him again. Do I make myself clear?"

Silence stood between them. Thomas's cries echoed through Elizabeth's head.

"I'm truly sorry, Mrs. Grew. I don't wish to disobey your command. But I can't do what you ask. My conscience before God will not allow me to stand idly by."

At that moment Elizabeth caught a glimpse of Mary. Somehow the girl had made her way from the church to the garden and was stumbling through the arch of branches. Her fingers guided her along the wall until she disappeared around the corner.

She didn't doubt Mary was just as desperate to get to the babe as she was, perhaps more so.

"Excuse me. I must see to Mary—"

Just then Sister Bird stepped past them. She bowed her head in deference to Mrs. Grew.

Elizabeth caught a glimpse of the dark circles under the woman's eyes. Was Thomas the source of the fatigue, or was the woman still grieving the loss of her babe?

Mrs. Grew nodded her head impatiently, and the woman hurried past, keeping her eyes focused on the ground.

Sister Bird crossed the churchyard with choppy steps and snapped at the girl swinging from the mulberry tree. The girl dropped to the ground and disappeared with Sister Bird into the garden. It was only a moment later the crying ceased.

Elizabeth released the pent-up breath she hadn't realized she'd been holding.

"If you know what's good for you, you'll stay away from him." Mrs. Grew's hard tone had an unspoken threat to it.

"God shall guide my conscience, Mrs. Grew. Rest assured, I shall do no less than He asks of me."

～

John halted in front of the small cottage his brother rented. Surrounded by long grass and weeds, it stood at the entrance to Elstow on the main road south of Bedford. John had lived in the cottage with Mary before they moved to Bedford. The sight of the timber and pebble building with its gabled roof and tiny dormer windows surrounded by thatch stirred painful longings in his heart.

Why did reminders of Mary chase him everywhere he went?

The mist had slowly but thoroughly soaked John during the long hike back from Stevington, where he had preached that afternoon. Thankfully the drizzle hadn't dampened the number of people who'd come out to hear him. God was moving powerfully through his words, bringing men and women to repentance, and nothing—not the weather nor his critics—could stop the hand of God.

Without knocking, John pushed his way into his brother's cottage. He stepped down into a low dark room, its large fire the only source of light in the dismal late afternoon. He took off his hat and wiped his eyes. The tangy scent of bean soup set his stomach to rumbling, reminding him he hadn't eaten since dawn.

"Father!" Betsy and Johnny scurried across the dirt floor toward him. For an instant he thought they would fling themselves upon him with hugs. Instead, when they reached him, they stopped short and peered beyond him out the door.

"Children." He patted each of their heads, dripping on them and onto the straw that covered the dirt floor.

"Do ye have Mary?" His sister-in-law stood in front of a large kettle. Her gaze searched the doorway behind him. The worry in her voice snagged him and set his body on edge.

John surveyed the room. "She's not here?"

In the commotion of the room he struggled to distinguish amongst the children. The older three were born of Sarah's first marriage. The others, with Costin red hair, had come along after she'd married his brother. Willie, as kindhearted as ever, had taken in the young widow with her children in an effort to save her from having to live at the bridewell. The workhouse for the poor had a reputation for being a sentence of death. If overwork and hunger didn't claim the vagrants consigned there, then rampant disease often did.

John had discouraged Willie from the match. He hadn't understood why Willie would want to marry a woman simply to save her life. She was plain and the years had not been kind to her. He was sure she was younger than his nine and twenty, but she had the coarse hair and skin of a much older woman.

"Mary weren't with us when we got back here after the morning service," Sarah explained. "We was hoping she'd gone with you."

"She isn't with me." He'd left with Brother Smythe after the service at St. John's. He'd never taken one of the children before. Why would he start now? "Wasn't she at the meetinghouse with you when you left?"

Sarah's shoulders slumped and the lines in her face had the deep crevices of someone who had known much trouble. "I'm truly sorry, John. Truly I am. As surely as it rains, it's my fault. Amidst the other families that walked with us, I didn't check when we left Bedford to see if everyone was present."

John's mind whirled with all of the possibilities of what could have happened to Mary. Panic swirled through him and rose in his throat like bile.

"Usually Eleanor walks with Mary, holds her hand, guides her. But Eleanor claims she didn't see Mary at the meetinghouse before we left."

He followed Sarah's gaze to Eleanor, the youngest of her

daughters, close in age to Mary. The girl had always seemed responsible and had shown a kindness toward Mary that most did not.

"She weren't nowhere around. Nowhere 'tall," the girl whispered, eyes alight with fright.

"We don't understand what could've happened," Sarah said. "Mary never wanders off. She always stays right by me or Eleanor."

"Betsy, Johnny, do you know what happened to Mary?" John's voice was sharper than he intended.

Their eyes filled with tears, and they shook their heads.

"Did she tell you anything? Did you see her go anywhere?"

Again they shook their heads.

His thoughts returned to the visitor who had made threats to Elizabeth and the children earlier in the month. He'd checked with neighbors; none of them had seen anyone unusual in the neighborhood. And as he'd expected, he'd gotten nowhere in discovering who had visited.

The criticism against him was growing daily. He could easily picture a number of men as the culprit—especially Royalists who would do whatever they could to undermine the Puritan cause.

Had one of them finally resorted to the ultimate intimidation—using his children as a way to force him into complying? Was Mary even now abducted and held captive by someone who wanted his silence?

"Willie has been out looking for her most the afternoon," Sarah said. "He's worried sick to death about her."

John's stomach clenched, and he took a deep shaky breath to keep himself from getting sick.

"We'll find her." He slapped his soggy hat back on his head and hoped his words didn't ring as hollow as he felt inside.

He turned to leave, but then stopped and glanced from Betsy and Johnny to Sarah.

"You go on." Sarah waved at him with her dripping ladle. "They'll stay with us here."

He gave her a curt nod before he turned and bounded out of the cottage.

He'd lost his wife and had given up their newborn baby for dead.

How could he survive if he lost his daughter too?

Chapter
10

*J*ohn swished through the long grass. Mud clung to his boots and slowed him down. The familiar run between Elstow and Bedford was usually one he could make before he had time to breathe heavily. But not today.

He hadn't yet glimpsed the high tower of St. John's over the treetops, and already his side ached and his breath came in heavy gasps.

"Mary!" He searched along the hedgerow. "Where are you?"

Only the lone call of a warbler answered him.

What had happened to her? Nausea churned in his stomach. What if someone had accosted her, intent on taking advantage of her blindness? She was a pretty young girl. Any filthy vagrant could easily use her and dump her in a ditch or field. What if she was lying abandoned with a broken bone or bleeding gash, crying out for help with no one to hear her?

He *had* to find her, especially before it got dark. The rain would shear one hour, maybe two from the day, precious moments that could mean the difference to her survival. Once night settled, his search would be futile. She might end up lost to him forever.

His eyes scanned every willow and elm and every spot of grass and brush. When he finally turned onto St. John's Street, his lungs burned and his voice was hoarse from calling her name.

He barged into the meetinghouse, peered down the aisle and under each pew. Then with growing panic he banged on the rectory door. "Willie has already scoured the parish," Vicar Burton answered. "Several of the neighbors joined in the search too."

John blew out a shaky breath.

When he met Willie and the neighbors, they only shook their heads, having combed the streets and alleys of Bedford to no avail.

John turned his steps toward St. Cuthbert's and trotted the distance with the lingering hope that maybe she had somehow made it home.

"Mary?" he shouted as he ducked inside the dark cottage. Nothing but silence greeted him. The stomp of his boots echoed through hollow rooms. He pictured her lying unconscious, hardly breathing, unable to answer him.

Finally, after searching every possible spot in the cottage and forge, he stepped out of his forge and blew a frustrated breath.

She had disappeared.

He stared at the apple tree, where he had come upon everyone dozing yesterday. His racing heartbeat stumbled to a halt.

What if she had not been abducted nor merely separated from the group returning to Elstow? What if she had purposefully run off?

She had despised his decision to send the baby away. The rest of the afternoon and evening she'd spoken to him only when she had to. And when she'd returned to the loft and laid her pallet next to Betsy and Johnny, he'd heard her sniffling and tossing far into the night. He had left her to herself, reasoning it would just take time for her to accept his decision, to get accustomed to life without the baby.

But perhaps he'd been wrong to assume she'd come to terms.

He crossed toward the cow, his boots squeaking in the wet grass. The cow was tied to her post but had made her way out from under the lean-to shelter. He ran a hand across her flank, against the dampness of her coarse hair.

"What should I do, girl?" His voice trembled with all the help-lessness that swirled through him.

The cow turned and looked at him with droopy eyes, seeming to understand his pain. Slowly she chewed at her mouthful of grass and gazed at him.

"What should I do?" This time his cry was raised to the Lord. "Help me, Lord, to find this precious blind daughter of mine."

His mind clambered through his options and tried to make sense of where a girl of eight years would go if she had run away.

Sister Whitbread. His housekeeper's name entered his head as if the Lord had whispered her name.

He slapped the cow's rump, pulled down his hat, and started across the yard.

If anyone could help him find Mary, Sister Whitbread could.

She was an intelligent maid—she'd proven herself plenty of times to have a quick mind and tongue.

When he arrived at the bakehouse, its wooden shutters were pulled up, closed for the Sabbath like all of the businesses. He glanced around to the other buildings, most of which had been rebuilt after the raid on Bedford during the Civil War. The fire set by Royalist soldiers had destroyed much of the area.

John thumped on the door and waited. His eyes darted to

every trough and barrel, searching for any movement or sound. Time was slipping away, and if he didn't find her, he'd only have himself to blame.

He pounded his fist against the door harder.

The shutters of the second-story window above him rattled. "Who's there?" a man called.

The upper floor of the box-framed house projected outward from the main level. John had to step out from the jetty into the street to get a clear view of the window and make his presence known.

"It's I, John Costin." He pushed the brim of his hat upward and gave himself a better view of the upstairs window.

Henry peered down at John, his brows raised.

"I need to speak to Sister Whitbread."

"Which one?"

What was his housekeeper's Christian name? Surely after more than a month he knew her name? And surely Henry knew whom he was seeking.

Henry waited. His brows inched higher.

"I need to see my housekeeper," he finally mumbled. He knocked the brim of his hat lower to cover his embarrassment.

Sister Whitbread's face appeared next to Henry's. "Brother Costin?" Her tone held a hint of worry, as if she knew his unusual visit brought bad tidings.

"I'm sorry to bother you this Sabbath. But I need to speak with you. Can you come down?"

She disappeared. After a moment she faced him again and nodded. "I'll be right there."

The light mist gave his upturned face a cold bath. He nodded to Henry, who returned the nod before moving away from the window. Then John ducked under the overhang to shelter himself.

Sister Whitbread soon stepped outside and threw a cloak around her shoulders. Her gaze searched his face. "What's wrong?"

"It's Mary." His voice cracked. "She's gone and no one knows where."

The maid's eyes were an odd gray color, and at his words they darkened like rain clouds rolling in over the heath. "Where have you looked?"

"I've looked nearly everywhere." He couldn't keep the desperation out of his voice.

"How long has she been gone?"

"Methinks since after the morning service. No one has seen her since then."

She didn't say anything for a moment.

"She usually goes home with Willie's family when I have to preach. But she didn't go this time."

"Not surprising."

"It pains me to think of something happening to her. If you can help me find her, I'll be indebted to you."

"No, Brother Costin, you won't be in debt to me." Her face tightened with earnestness. "I want to find Mary too. I'll do everything I can to help you."

Relief washed through him. For the first time since she'd barged into his home, he was grateful for her—for her servant spirit, for her willingness to help, for her kindness. At the same time, he wanted to duck his head for the times he'd scoffed her help and taken her service to his family for granted.

"Let me explain to my father what's happening. Then we'll find Mary together. I think I may know where to start our search."

He gave her a nod, his throat too tight to speak.

She slipped back inside and was gone for several minutes. When she returned she carried a basket filled with a jug, a loaf of bread, and blankets. She tucked it under her oiled cloak before stepping into the drizzle.

They hurried through the nearly deserted streets, their feet sloshing in rain-slickened muck. John wasn't sure where his house-keeper was leading him, but he trusted her instinct.

When they reached the north end of Bedford and turned onto Bendhouse Lane, the wind from the open fields beyond the Friars had free access to them and beat them with its force.

She stopped in front of a low cottage, and then he knew. Even though he'd never been there before, somehow he knew whose home she had brought him to.

Mary was here. He could feel it in his gut.

Sister Whitbread knocked on the door.

It opened a crack, and a girl's face peeked through.

Distinct, unhappy cries greeted them. Even with the wind blowing in his ears, the wailing was familiar and strong. Always before he had blocked out the noise—not wanting to waste hope on the baby, not wanting to see the baby alive when Mary was dead. But at that moment the crying brought an ache to his chest.

"Tell your mother Brother Costin is here to see her," Sister Whitbread said.

The girl slammed the door.

"Sister Bird?" Sister Whitbread leaned into the door.

The door opened a second time, another crack. The same face appeared.

Again John heard the crying. Why was the baby distraught? What was the purpose in sending him away to wet-nurse if he wasn't satisfied?

"Is your mother coming?" Sister Whitbread asked with more patience than he was feeling.

Just then the door opened wide, and Sister Bird stood before them fixing her coif above untidy hair. One of her cheeks wore the imprint of a grainy blanket.

"Brother Costin." She bowed her head to him.

He nodded. Before he could say anything, Sister Whitbread

pushed past the matron and the handful of small children clustering around her.

"Sister Bird, I'm sure you won't mind in the least if I hold Thomas." Sister Whitbread had already set aside her basket and had started across the one-room cottage toward the wooden cradle. "I know he can be quite fussy, and I'm sure you could use a break for a few minutes."

Worry flashed across the woman's face, but she watched as if she had not the strength to move. "I was told not to let you near the baby—that it's because of you he's so whiny."

"Oh, nonsense." Sister Whitbread waved her hand.

John ducked inside the cottage. The odor of excrement assaulted him and forced him to breathe through his mouth.

"Truthfully, you mustn't touch him," Sister Bird said but without much force.

Sister Whitbread stooped and picked up the wailing infant. She pressed a kiss upon his head and crushed him to her bosom.

The ache in John's chest pulsed outward and constricted his throat. He swallowed hard to get past the tightness. This baby was a piece of Mary and himself. His flesh and blood.

Sister Whitbread smoothed a hand over the baby's head, over his face, and down his arms as if she was trying to get as much of him into her hungry soul as she could. She bestowed another kiss on his forehead and then put one of her fingers into his mouth.

Instantly he ceased crying, and the room grew quiet.

John swallowed hard again.

"How has he been nursing?" Sister Whitbread didn't take her gaze off the baby, who looked back at her with as much earnestness as she was him, sucking frantically at her finger.

Sister Bird sighed and picked up one of the whimpering infants at her skirt. "Truthfully, he's hardly nursed since he came. I've been tryin' real hard. But he's been turnin' from me and spittin' me out.

He won't take the spoon. He won't take the sleepin' cordial. He won't take nothin'.'"

Sister Whitbread's brow furrowed into deep lines as she again stroked a hand over the babe's head.

"He's been cryin' all the time. My husband couldn't take any more of it and left to stay with kinfolk." Sister Bird's shoulders slumped further at the admission. She turned to face John. "I'm sorry."

"It isn't working out, then?" A gentle breeze of relief blew through him. He didn't understand it, but somehow he knew God was giving him a second chance with this baby he'd given up for dead.

"My husband don't like crying babies. I know what happens when he gets himself angry enough. I'm afeared it wouldn't be safe for the baby—even if it is a Costin."

"Then we'll take the baby home with us."

Sister Whitbread gasped. Her eyes flew to his and locked there for a long intense moment. His heart began to thump with the conviction that he wanted his son to live, but he would need this girl to help make that happen.

Her eyes glistened with joy, and she gave him a wavering smile.

The ache pushed again at his throat.

"Mrs. Grew is going to be terribly angry." Mrs. Bird's voice shook. "She told me not to stop nursin' the baby for any reason."

"The child is mine. Last I knew I could still make the final decisions about his welfare." Mrs. Grew had gone too far. The woman didn't know what was best for his son—not more than he did.

He started to turn, but the truth socked him in the gut and nearly bent him over. He *hadn't* known what was best for his son. Instead, he'd ignored his son all this time, had let his own pain and the memories of Mary interfere with the care of the baby. Well, not anymore. "He's coming home with me. If Mrs. Grew doesn't like it, then tell her to see me."

John glanced around the simple cottage, to the sagging bed, the overturned benches, and the piles of soiled clothes. "Now, where's Mary?"

"Blind Mary?" Mrs. Bird raised a trembling hand to her forehead. "She's not here."

"Maybe she's outside." The worry in Sister Whitbread's eyes urged him back outside.

He stepped into the drizzle and pulled his cloak tighter. Though it was overcast, he prayed the long summer day would still afford him enough light.

He made his way around the side of the cottage and called Mary's name. When he came to the back, he scanned the small garden plot. It was overgrown with tall weeds and littered with scattered piles of twigs, broken slats of barrels, shards of pottery.

"Mary?" Her name trailed away with the wind.

He strained to hear any sound.

A faint cry near the back of the cottage sent his heart galloping.

"Mary!" he called louder.

He dodged the shallow piles and headed for a stack of boards next to the house. "Oh, Mary." He stumbled against a thin body crouched against the cottage.

She turned her face up to him. Tears made clear streaks through the grime on her cheeks. Her slender body shook with sobs.

John dropped to his knees and pulled her into his arms. Gratefulness poured through him. He leaned his chin on her head and tightened his hold.

"I only wanted Thomas back," she sobbed. "I only planned to stay until dark . . . sneak into the cottage . . . take Thomas . . . ."

He shook his head at the foolishness of her plan. How would

she have made it through the cottage without hurting herself, much less attracting attention?

"Then I was going to try to find Lucy."

"Then I'm just grateful I found you before you could try it." He couldn't imagine what she was thinking. Didn't she realize how helpless she was and the danger she could have brought upon herself? He kissed her silky hair.

"Thomas cried all afternoon," she continued between broken sobs. "Brother Bird yelled—threatened to silence the baby. Then he finally left."

For a moment she didn't say anything, and he just held her until her sobs began to subside.

"I was afraid for Thomas." Her teeth chattered and she clung to him with surprising strength. "I was afraid Brother Bird would hurt him."

The picture of the Birds' baby bundled in its winding cloth flashed into his mind. He'd attended more than one funeral for the Birds' dead babies. 'Twas true babies died all of the time. But what if Brother Bird's anger had contributed?

A shiver crept up his backbone. He'd placed his own baby right into the hands of danger. If anything had happened, he would have been just as guilty as Brother Bird.

One more reason to bring their baby home.

"Thomas is coming home." *Thomas*. The name stuck to his tongue. He couldn't remember speaking it before. But saying it somehow made the baby more real, more alive.

"You're letting Thomas come back home?"

"Yes. And I'm sorry, Mary, for not listening to you better. I should have tried to understand how you felt about losing Thomas." Apologies didn't come easily for him. But when she released a long shaky breath and melted into his arms, the tension slipped from his body, and he knew he'd done the right thing.

"We'll make it work. I promise."

John combed her tangled curls. "It won't be easy. He's weak and helpless. I want you to be prepared for the reality of his death." Without a mother, the baby's chances were still slim, even if they did everything they could.

"I know he would benefit from a regular wet nurse," his daughter said, "plenty of milk whenever he needs it. I won't deny this. But his chances of living are greater if he stays with us, even without the milk." Her tone was confident, and John could only pray she was right.

"He loves us. We love him," she continued, gazing up at him with her beautiful but blank eyes. "It's our love upon which he thrives."

John knew by *we* she meant his housekeeper. His mind returned to the picture of the girl embracing his son in the Birds' cottage, the fierceness with which she had hugged him. She loved the babe, even though he wasn't hers, even though she had no reason to.

Sister Whitbread was indeed a godly young woman.

"She's God's gift to our family. God brought her to help us in our need."

"Methinks you are sometimes a very wise child."

She smiled but then shuddered as her thin body gave way to the dampness that had shrouded it all afternoon. With the increasing winds, the temperate summer evening had turned chilly, especially against Mary's wet skin.

"Only *sometimes* wise." He swept her up into his arms and stood. "Sometimes you can be very foolish—like today, running off and sitting in the drizzle."

He carried her inside to Sister Whitbread, who hugged her, all the while scolding her for running away. She shed Mary's wet outer garments and wrapped her in one of the blankets she'd brought. She made Mary drink of the milk in the jug and eat some of the bread. Then, after bundling Thomas in an extra blanket, they left.

The baby started crying again. One look at Sister Whitbread's creased brow told him the situation was serious. The baby needed nourishment. When Sister Whitbread informed him she was taking the baby to Lucy, he insisted on accompanying her, even though she encouraged him to take Mary home out of the rain. In the fading evening Sister Whitbread would not be safe alone.

He carried Mary in his arms like he would a baby. She weighed nothing compared to the bag of tinker's tools he was accustomed to slinging. Sister Whitbread led the way through the muddy streets to the poorest area of Bedford, near the wharves along the River Ouse. Along the way he dodged the refuse littering the street.

Finally Sister Whitbread ascended a stairway and disappeared into a hovel. His body tensed as he waited. Mary tried to reassure him Sister Whitbread would be safe, that she came often with Thomas, and that she distributed bread to the poor here. But Mary's words did nothing to calm him.

He glanced around at the lurking shadows, and the back of his neck pricked at the thought of the danger that waited at every turn. What trouble lay behind the door at the top of the steps? What if Sister Whitbread was threatened even as he waited?

"That's it. I'm going in to get her." He pulled himself up to his full height, Mary still in his arms, and started up the steps. His boots clomped and the stairway shook. No matter what she wanted, he wouldn't stand idly by while she placed herself in jeopardy.

He made it only halfway when the door creaked open and she stepped outside.

Her face was alight with relief. With a smile she started down the steps. " 'Tis all settled. Fulke's gone—been gone for days. Lucy's desperate for money. She needs the wet-nursing job now more than ever." She stopped on the step above him.

He nodded, conscious that she stood at eye level. She met his gaze directly. Her eyes sparked and her cheeks wore a rosy blush. Her coif lay flat against her hair, the loose strands plastered to her forehead. She was drenched, but she had an air of confidence and vibrancy.

Life emanated from her, infusing him with an energy he hadn't felt in a long time. With Mary safe in his arms, and the babe Thomas in the care of a woman as capable as Sister Whitbread, he could almost believe the storm clouds hovering over his soul were beginning to dissipate.

Almost.

Chapter
II

*H*ow dare you interfere?"

The sharp voice of Mrs. Grew sliced through the cottage and pierced Elizabeth with dread. She took a step away from the boiling kettle of water and wiped the dampness from her forehead. Her muscles tensed, preparing for battle.

It had been over a week since Thomas came home, long enough that she'd begun to believe Mrs. Grew would forget about him.

The woman strode into the cottage, her skirt swishing in short, determined bursts. She held her chin high and looked down at Elizabeth from beneath the brim of her plain but fashionable hat.

Elizabeth splayed her hands over her stained apron and wished she'd donned a clean one earlier.

"You've completely disobeyed and disrespected my wishes." The woman's gaze lingered over her bodice, which was just as spotted as her apron. "I thought I made myself clear when I instructed you to stay away from the Costin baby."

"I have never intended to show you disrespect. I've only wanted to do what's best for Thomas—"

"You are a meddlesome, ignorant, presumptuous girl. Your father ought to whip you."

"Brother Costin made the decision to bring Thomas home. If you're displeased with the arrangements, then perhaps you ought to discuss it with him." Elizabeth wiped her sleeve against the sweat trickling down her cheek. The summer heat permeated the room, and the high flames of the hearth only made it worse.

"Where is Brother Costin?" Mrs. Grew demanded. "Once I speak with him, he will see the folly of your advice."

"He's not available right now." Elizabeth's heart began to thud. What if Mrs. Grew persuaded Brother Costin to let her take the babe again?

The woman glanced at the bedroom door.

"Mary's very ill," Elizabeth rushed to explain. "She's unable to get out of bed, and her feverish body is wracked with a cough. Brother Costin is praying for her with Vicar Gibbs."

"Tell him Mrs. Grew is here and would like to speak with him."

"Surely you wouldn't have me disturb these godly men, especially when Brother Costin has already made his wishes in the matter of the babe so clear?"

"Once he is aware of my presence, he will gladly speak with me."

A spurt of barklike coughing from the bedroom spurred Elizabeth back to the pot of boiling water. Mary needed more steam to keep breathing. And the girl was likely in need of chamomile water and another chest rub.

Elizabeth lifted the steaming kettle from its hook. "You'll have to pardon me, Mrs. Grew. But Mary is needing my attention."

The iron pot handle burned through the rag, and Elizabeth staggered toward the bedroom trying not to slosh the hot water.

Mrs. Grew stepped in front of her and forced her to stop.

"You need to learn your place, and you would do best to stay there."

Elizabeth met the woman's gaze straightway. "I do know my place, Mrs. Grew. My place is helping the Costins and the babe Thomas."

"You need to learn a lesson, and I'll make sure you do." Even though the woman was outwardly composed, an animosity burned in her eyes that sent a shiver of fear through Elizabeth.

"I'll be taking my lessons from God, as He sees fit. Now, if you'll excuse me." She sidled around the woman, praying she wouldn't try to intercept her again.

Once she stepped into the bedroom, she closed the door behind her and released a shaky breath.

Mrs. Grew's shoes tapped away from the bedroom back toward the front door of the cottage. When the door banged closed, the tension eased from Elizabeth's shoulders.

She hefted the kettle, made her way around the long legs of the men kneeling next to the bed, and positioned the kettle near the head of the bed. Mary gave her a weak smile, and Elizabeth forced one in return, even though her heart sank at the blue skin around the girl's mouth and the ribs that collapsed with each strangled breath she took.

None of her treatments were helping Mary, and life was oozing from her.

Vicar Gibbs's urgent prayer was a soft mumble against the bed.

I've served you well, Lord, Elizabeth added silently. *I've willingly sacrificed much of myself for you. Surely I've pleased you. Surely you will hear my prayers for Mary too.*

Didn't Scripture promise "Taste and see that the Lord is good"?

Wouldn't He be good to her when she had devoted herself entirely to Him?

She studied Brother Costin's boots. They were big, just like everything else about him—his presence, his personality, his grief, his fears, his loyalties. He was an intense man, and it was hard not to be drawn into his moods and emotions—especially now with his anxiety over Mary.

Vicar Gibbs lifted his head and said amen. John echoed him, and then they pushed themselves up, their faces haggard, their shoulders stooped.

Elizabeth wanted to say something—anything—to offer them a word of hope. But their gazes were fixed upon Mary's face, and Elizabeth was all but invisible to them.

A twinge of regret slid through her that she didn't elicit any more attention than the scuffed bed table against the wall.

What would it be like to be noticed? How would it feel to have John look at her, to really notice her? Keen longing twisted at her heart.

She had watched Catherine's coquettishness often enough to know one could work at drawing a man's attention. And yet, even as she pictured her sister's inviting smiles and coy glances, she shoved them out of her mind. She would never lower herself to such behavior. She scorned such wanton, imprudent conduct for gaining a man's attention.

Besides, how could she keep his regard once she had it? She had nothing arresting or beautiful about her. She was the plain one—the moth among the butterflies.

With a sigh of resignation, she lifted the bowl of broth she'd left at the bedside earlier. She held the spoon to Mary's lips. Most of the broth dribbled down the girl's chin; the rest she gulped past her swollen throat.

"It's a pilgrimage, John," Gibbs said softly. "Our way is fraught with many temptations and detours thrown at us from the ultimate deceiver."

Elizabeth wiped the liquid off Mary's chin.

The girl smiled again, and Elizabeth brushed her hand against the girl's cheek.

"There will be low valleys in the shadow of death, and there will be steep mountains to climb." Gibbs rubbed the stub of his left arm, his war wound. A small callused point was all that remained at his elbow. "Our foe will try to drive us off the true path, the hard path. But we must stay on it, knowing it will lead us to Him, to greater holiness."

John didn't respond.

The room was quiet except for Mary's wheezing.

Elizabeth's gaze drifted to John.

As if finally sensing her presence, he looked at her with an intensity that made her lungs close up.

"What think you now, Sister Whitbread?" He had jammed one hand into his hair, gripping it as if he would tear it out. His shirt was rumpled and his face scruffy with unshaven growth. "You have saved my son's life. Do you think you can save my Mary now too?"

"God will surely hear our prayers." She tried to take a breath. Didn't God promise to deliver them from hardships and work things out for the good of those who loved Him?

His eyes refused to let go of her.

"And I will do everything I can to aid her," she added. Her heart thudded louder, until she was certain everyone in the small room could hear the clamor. She didn't understand why, but she knew she'd give him the whole world if she could.

⁓

Elizabeth worked ceaselessly to keep Mary alive. Sister Norton and the other women of the congregation helped too. And finally, after days of coughing and wheezing, Mary began to breathe easier and to cough less.

The lines of worry across John's forehead went away. And Elizabeth was certain God was watching over them and answering her prayers.

Even Thomas began to gain weight. Lucy's frequent nursings sated him. For the first time, Elizabeth began to see him smile and coo with a contentedness that gave her hope for his survival.

"He's going to make it," Mary said from her spot in the wicker chair by the hearth. She didn't have the strength to walk, but John had carried her out of bed for the first time in over a week.

Betsy and Johnny hovered near her. They had stayed in Elstow to keep safe from the illness and had only returned the previous eve.

Elizabeth rubbed Thomas dry. "He does seem to be filling out quite nicely. Aren't you, little love?" She kissed his bare belly, and he burst into bubbly giggles.

Happiness swelled within her like rising bread dough. She smiled. If motherhood had more moments like this, she could understand why it was easy to settle for a loveless marriage. Marrying Samuel Muddle was preferable to turning into an old woman with no chance to experience these joys of being a mother.

She slipped a clean clout under Thomas and folded it into place. Samuel had developed the habit of appearing every evening to walk her home. He clung to the notion that she needed a chaperone. But Elizabeth sensed his real concern was that she might become too attached to the Costins.

She tugged Thomas's dress over his head. He managed to get two of his fingers into his mouth and began sucking them. His eyes widened in surprised delight at the new sucking sensation, and his lips smacked loudly.

Her smile widened. Samuel's fears were not unfounded. She was indeed growing fond of the Costin family. Already half the summer was over, and she couldn't bear to think of the rest of it passing. She resented Catherine's plans to assume the housekeeping duties in her stead. The girl certainly wouldn't be able to care for the children the way she could.

'Twas only a matter of course before she must leave the Costins and marry Samuel. But at the moment she couldn't imagine how she would ever be able to leave the children. Being away from Thomas for only a day had been torment enough. How could she leave them forever?

She brushed a kiss across Thomas's forehead. Then she laid him on the floor and began swaddling him in clean linen bands. She allowed his arms and hands to remain free from the tight bundle that enclosed the rest of his body.

"Lucy should be coming soon." She tucked the last wrap around the babe, picked him up, and cradled him against her chest.

"Lucy is too smelly." Betsy pinched her nose and grinned at Johnny.

Johnny giggled and pinched his nose. "Too 'melly."

"For shame, children." She narrowed her brows at them. "Lucy is a blessing. She's the lifeblood of your brother. If not for her, Thomas wouldn't survive."

Betsy dropped the hold on her nose, and her smile faded. Johnny watched her and then imitated.

"Moreover, Jesus showed love to the lowest, poorest, sickest people. As His followers, He calls us to do the same."

The children were quiet. Thomas began to squirm and fuss.

A knock sounded on the door.

"Good. 'Tis Lucy. And you're ready to eat, aren't you, little love?" Elizabeth stood up and stepped toward the door. Since Fulke had disappeared, Lucy had arrived at regular times of the day. She didn't know where Fulke had gone or when he might return, but Elizabeth decided they would take advantage of his absence as long as they could. 'Twas another blessing.

"Right on time." She swung open the door.

"Good day, Elizabeth."

She drew in a sharp breath and forced herself not to recoil.

The man who had threatened her and insinuated she should spy on John stood before her. She had put him out of her mind these past weeks; she'd never imagined she would have to face him and his horrible lies again.

With his cavalier hat tilted at an angle so that its feather touched his shoulder, he gave her a smile that was just as bent.

"Brother Costin isn't home." She shoved the door.

He rammed his boot against the planks. The force slammed it against the wall.

With Thomas in her arms, Elizabeth couldn't maneuver rapidly enough to close it. Instead, she planted her feet wide and barricaded the entrance with her body. "You cannot come inside."

But the man pushed against Elizabeth and forced her away from the door. She stumbled backward until she bumped against the table and scraped her shin against the corner of the bench. Her heart thudded against her chest, and she clung to Thomas, trying not to lose her grip on him.

"I'm not here to see John Costin." He kicked the door closed. "I'm here to see you."

"Who are you?" She wished John was working at his forge. But as most days, he had left after breaking fast and worshiping and gave her no knowledge of his whereabouts.

The man swiped off his hat. In his narrow face his eyes were like hen's eggs, bulgy and brittle.

"I'm here to collect what you owe me."

"I don't owe you anything."

"If you recall, I expect your cooperation in silencing our poor unlicensed preacher." With hard, calculated footsteps he crossed the room. His eyes glinted at her. "And I expect much, much more."

Her body tensed. What was he planning to do to her?

Her gaze flew to the children. She wanted to send them away, out of harm's reach. She certainly didn't want them to witness the man hurting her.

Mary sat pale, like a wilted flower. The other two cowered beside her. Without Mary's guidance, Johnny and Betsy wouldn't be capable of following any instructions to leave for help.

Elizabeth's mind whirled. What could she do to spare the children?

She had no doubt the man wanted information to defame John. But she had nothing, and even if she had something to pass along, she was certain she couldn't divulge it.

He stood near enough for her to see the splotchy redness in the whites of his eyes and to smell the staleness of his breath.

"Am I to presume you have failed to do what I asked of you?"

Should she lie? If she made something up, would he leave her alone?

For a moment the only sound in the room was Thomas's grumblings, the grunts and half whines that announced his hunger. Elizabeth absently pushed her finger into his mouth, willing her mind to think, needing all the quickness and persuasiveness her words could give her.

"Brother Costin is gone much of the time," she said. "How can I gain knowledge of his doings if I am rarely in his presence?"

The back of his hand crashed against her cheek and mouth with unexpected swiftness.

Pain shot through her jaw. The blow threw her off balance and thrust her against the table. Before she could catch herself, the sharp bones of his knuckles connected with her cheek again, then her eye. She cried out at the pain but couldn't escape the force of his fist against her mouth. She tasted blood and swayed with sudden light-headedness.

As if in a distance, through the drumming in her head, she heard the frightened whimpers of Betsy and Johnny and the startled wails of Thomas. She clung to the babe, knowing she couldn't let go or lose consciousness.

"I told you not to fail me." His rancid breath fanned against her face.

She blinked and tried to bring the room back into focus. She lifted her fingers to her lips and felt the sticky warmth of blood.

His hand enclosed her upper arm and pinched her skin. "You must do what I've asked."

"But, sir, how can I when he's gone—"

"Find a way. Take his sermon notes. Letters. Tracts," he hissed. "Get me something."

"I've seen only good in him."

With a fierce jerk, he smashed her body against his and crushed Thomas between them.

A new horror crashed through Elizabeth, and she struggled to pull away. She had to extricate herself from the luridness of his position before he suffocated Thomas.

"I always get what I want, one way or another." His voice was low against her ear.

She jerked against him. At that moment she knew he was capable of anything, even defiling her.

"Costin shouldn't be the only one having all the fun with you." The hand pressing against her back began to slip downward.

Revulsion choked her and the helplessness of her position threatened to strangle her, along with the thought that the children were witnessing everything.

A knock sounded on the door. The man cursed under his breath, released her, and took a step back.

Fear propelled her away, and she flung herself toward the children. With a half sob she knelt before Johnny and Betsy and gathered them into her arms next to Thomas.

The knock sounded again.

The man glared at the door and then at her before finally

donning his hat. "Don't fail me again. Get me the information I want or you won't fare so well next time."

Her body shook with trembling, whether her own or the children's, she knew not.

"Besides, I don't think you'd like the entire shire of Bedford to hear about what really goes on behind closed doors in the Costin household. You wouldn't want your *good* Brother Costin's name to be sullied, would you?"

Elizabeth didn't answer—she couldn't think past the pain in her head.

The knock on the door changed into an insistent pounding. The man stalked toward it and flung it open, but then pulled back. The rise of his brow told her the guest wasn't whom he'd expected.

"What do we have here?" His gaze slid down then up.

When there was no response, Elizabeth knew it was Lucy.

"Another of Costin's women?" The man pinned Elizabeth with another hard look—one that assured her he wouldn't hesitate to spread rumors if she didn't cooperate.

She forced herself not to break eye contact, even though her insides screamed in protest.

With a final nod the man left.

⁓

"There's more blood than pain." Lucy pressed a cloth against Elizabeth's lip. "And it always looks worse than it really is."

Elizabeth bit back a cry. Blood had trickled onto her large white collar, her sleeves, and even her apron. 'Twas indeed a great amount of blood.

"Fulke 'as given me more split lips than I can count." Lucy's firm hold had stopped the blood flow, but Elizabeth's cheek throbbed and her lip stung.

"A little pressure and it'll be as good as new in no time." Lucy's soot-streaked face was lined with compassion. Since Fulke's disappearance, the usual bruises and gashes had healed.

"Thank you, Lucy." Elizabeth took the cloth from her and handed her the squirming Thomas. "I'm surely grateful the Lord sent you to the door when He did."

She patted the scrap of linen against her lip and shuddered at what could have happened, horrified at the remembrance of the man's hands upon her.

" 'Twill be a bruise on your cheek." Lucy moved to the chair next to Mary. Without caution, she pushed aside her stained shift and exposed herself to the babe, who grunted for his meal.

Elizabeth touched the tips of her fingers to the throbbing bone in her cheek.

"Why did the man hurt you?" Betsy asked. She sat on one side of her lap and Johnny on the other.

"Man hurt you." Johnny sniffled and snuggled tighter into Elizabeth's hold.

"What information does he want from you?" Mary's voice wobbled. "What did he mean when he said you failed him?"

"Why did he hit you?" Betsy tugged at her arm.

"He hit you."

"What do you owe him?"

The children's voices made her dizzy. " 'Tis a complicated predicament in which I find myself, and I'm afraid I won't be able to answer all of your questions."

She removed the cloth from her lip.

"Keep it there a mite longer." Lucy patted Thomas as he sucked noisily. "The bleeding will be stoppin' soon enough."

Elizabeth pressed the rag back to her face. Out of the corner of her eye she could see her hand shake, and the quaking traveled to the core of her being.

"I 'ave to find a new place to live." Lucy scraped at her scalp with dirt-encrusted fingernails. "Mr. Dugar figured out I 'ave been lying to 'im about Fulke. He said if Fulke is gonna keep missing work, then we gotta move out."

Elizabeth willed herself to stop trembling. Shaking was for weak women. Strong women faced their difficulties fearlessly.

"Besides, I can't pay 'im rent. He said if Fulke doesn't work for 'im, then he got no choice but to charge us more."

"Do you have a place to go?" Even as Elizabeth asked the question, she couldn't seem to find the concern she knew she should have for Lucy.

"I'll find one soon enough."

Elizabeth nodded but placed a hand to her forehead. The throbbing in her cheek radiated outward and pounded through the rest of her head.

"The only problem I 'ave is Martha. She's gonna have to find her own place now, or I'm gonna get into some trouble."

"I'm surprised you haven't gotten into trouble already for having her with you."

"We've been careful. Martha only goes out at night."

The temptation to lie down and close her eyes overwhelmed Elizabeth. Morning had only begun, but she was as tired as if she had worked a full day. Perhaps the blows to her head had knocked all the energy out of her.

By noon she knew something more was wrong than her bruised face and swollen lip. When Sister Norton ducked into the cottage after her morning at the market to check on Mary, Elizabeth nearly fell into the woman's arms from exhaustion.

The widow gleaned information from the children about the strange man who had hurt Elizabeth. Sister Norton insisted Elizabeth go home and assured her she would stay the rest of the day to care for the children.

Elizabeth wasn't sure how she made it to the bakehouse, but she mustered all her leftover strength to pull herself up the narrow stairs to the bedchambers. She couldn't make it to the middle room she shared with her sisters but instead collapsed in the head room on the bed Jane shared with Henry and their children.

Then the world turned black.

Chapter
12

*J*ohn couldn't remember the last time he'd been so angry. The tap of his tinman's hammer against the thin layer of tinplate echoed the persistent thud of rage pulsing through his blood.

"Methinks even if I find out who attacked her, I'll be helpless to bring him to justice." John's face dripped with sweat. The forge was indeed sweltering, but the heat of his temper was no less cool.

For two days he'd attempted to discover who'd been behind the attack against Sister Whitbread, but he'd gotten nowhere in his inquiries. And even if he had, what could he have done?

John clenched his teeth and restrained his muscles from pounding the delicate tin too hard.

Gibbs leaned against the doorframe and watched him. "You're making enemies. That is true."

"They can attack the innocent and take advantage of the weak, but because I am a poor tinker there is naught to be done."

"I believe you have started the difficult uphill climb, my friend. The more successful you are, the more our great enemy will attempt to stop you."

"I won't let the devil stop me." Another billow of fire fanned through his blood and stoked his temper. And he wouldn't let a group of disconcerted Royalists stop him from carrying out God's calling. Not now, not when his ministry was growing so quickly.

"God is indeed working much success of late," Gibbs said.

John nodded. "Everywhere I go, large numbers of people are coming out to hear the Gospel." He ceased hammering and suspended the narrow tool in midair. "How can my adversaries deny that God is at work saving souls?"

"They only see that you are drawing people away from the Anglican Church and converting them to our Puritan ways." Gibbs glanced out the door toward the cottage.

"And they are jealous. They accuse me of blaspheming Scripture because I'm preaching without one of their licenses, but really they envy my success. They would not have a simple man like me prove more skillful than their university graduates of noble blood."

"Changes are in the wind, my friend. Even some of our own kind are growing dissatisfied with Cromwell—especially the generals."

John had been stationed with Gibbs at the garrison in Newport Pagnell during the war. Gibbs was now minister of the Independent Congregation there. Although the need for an army post no longer existed, the garrison was still a gathering spot for many of the officers who had served under Cromwell, and Gibbs was privy to their murmurings.

"I'm afraid we cannot count on Old Ironsides or his policy of religious tolerance forever," Gibbs said.

In the silence of the forge, the faint cries of Thomas and the squeals of the other children coming from the cottage sounded altogether too loud. Brother Whitbread had sent another of his daughters to replace Sister Whitbread, who was not only recovering from her wounds but also battling illness.

The replacement had neither the skill nor fortitude of Sister Whitbread—to say the least.

John tossed the narrow hammer to the floor and reached for the hand snips. He lifted the candlestick from the wooden mold and held it up. He turned it slowly. The crimping was finally taking the shape of a gentle wave.

He did not oft have the luxury to create tinware. His life was full of demands and his tinkering work spent repairing.

"It's beautiful," Gibbs murmured.

John rubbed his fingers over the smooth metal in the shape of a long cup.

"Which benefactor requested such a fine work?"

John ducked his head. A tinge of guilt and embarrassment added to the heat of his face. He spun the candlestick in his hand, wishing his friend hadn't inquired.

A crash and another loud cry from the direction of the cottage propelled John to his feet.

"I can wait, my friend." Gibbs nodded toward the door. "I believe you need to restore order to your home."

John set aside the candlestick, arose with a sigh, and started toward the cottage.

When he reached the doorway, he folded his arms across his chest and watched. The young Whitbread girl was attempting to swift the babe. The squirming infant squalled as if being tortured. The girl was flushed with the efforts of consoling him and seemed oblivious to the game of war Betsy and Johnny played behind overturned benches. Each behind opposite barricades threw newly picked beets at the other, screaming war cries while dirt and red dye from the beets splattered on the floor and walls.

Mary, meanwhile, stood in the middle of the war zone and yelled for them to stop, tears trickling down her cheeks.

The fire in the hearth was too high and too hot for midsummer and was overheating the room. The strength of the flames on the bottom of the kettle forced black smoke between the crack of the lid and sent a cloud into the room with the stench of burning pottage.

Mary turned her head in his direction. "Father?"

At her one word silence descended upon the room.

Thomas's cries faded. Johnny and Betsy cowered behind their benches. And the young girl turned to face him.

"Brother Costin," she said with a bright smile—too bright.

John didn't feel like smiling.

"Would you like a cup of ale?" She lowered her lashes and tilted her head. He'd seen that look often enough of late from the young maidens who wanted to catch his attention.

"How is your sister doing?" He bent over and picked up a battered beet.

"Elizabeth?"

He nodded, although he realized he still didn't know her given name.

"She's doing well enough," the girl said with little enthusiasm. "She's abed but no longer feverish."

"You can tell Elizabeth we'll welcome her return."

The sparkle of her smile diminished.

He narrowed his brow and hid his satisfaction at her reaction.

She stammered over her reply before finally settling with "Yes, I'll tell her."

With deliberate carefulness he placed the handful of beets onto the table next to the remains of the previous meal. Then he straightened to his full height. "It appears you need to attend to our midday meal."

She glanced at the smoking kettle and gasped. Her gaze bounced between Thomas and the kettle, as if she didn't know what to do with either.

"Give the baby to Mary. Have the other two clean up this mess, and then send them out to the forge to await my discipline."

John shook his head. He backed out the door and bumped into Gibbs.

"Methinks my housekeeper's return can't come soon enough," he mumbled as he walked with his friend into the deserted street.

Gibbs adjusted his hat. He met John's gaze directly. "I know it's not long since Mary's death, my friend. But perhaps it's time to consider taking another wife."

"Absolutely not!" The words roared out before he could stop them.

"Now, hear me out, John. It's soon to love again, that's for certain. But many a man marries for other reasons, especially a man who has children needing a mother."

"We're getting along fine." He paused and forced himself to speak more slowly and softly. "It's a misconception that children need to replace their mother. When my mother died, I didn't want a new mother, certainly not within a month's time, while the dirt was still fresh on her grave."

"You were much older, my friend. And your children are so young. They need the influence and guidance of a mature, godly woman. The presence of a housekeeper isn't enough."

John shook his head. Gibbs was older and wiser than he—and usually right. But John couldn't agree with him about remarriage. He couldn't think about taking another wife yet. Maybe not ever. God's call to preach had grown strong over the past years, and now he needed to focus on his ministry, not marriage.

Besides, his children were getting along fine without a mother—or would be when Elizabeth returned.

If Gibbs saw his housekeeper in action, he would surely have a different opinion. She was competent, his children liked and obeyed her, and from all he could surmise, she was a godly influence on them.

What more did they need?

⌢

Elizabeth sat in the four-poster bed, the mending idle in her lap. The stillness of her hands contrasted the spinning of her mind and the restlessness that had plagued her all day. When she'd been ill, she'd only wanted to sleep. But now, after over a week, she had too much time to think, and her mind was taking full advantage of the opportunity.

She couldn't keep from missing the children and wondering if Thomas was getting enough to eat, if Mary was regaining strength, or if Betsy and Johnny were staying out of trouble. She couldn't keep from worrying whether anyone had milked the cow or weeded the garden or picked the radishes.

Even though she had reminded Catherine before she left in the morning, she knew 'twould be a miracle for the girl to accomplish everything. Rather than listening to her, Catherine had been more interested in vanity. She'd pinched her cheeks to redden them, cleaned the spots off her apron, and pulled tendrils out of her coif to hang about her face in a wanton display.

Elizabeth sighed and picked up the petticoat she had been hemming. Certainly Catherine would accomplish her mission—to catch the attention of John. How could such a pretty, fair-haired young girl not capture a man's notice?

After so many days with Catherine, why would John want his plain and practical housekeeper back?

"Are you still in discomfort, Aunt Elizabeth?" Her niece on

the end of the bed looked up from the mass of wool yarn Jane had assigned her to untangle.

"No, love. I'm not in discomfort." Elizabeth tried to force more cheerfulness into her voice than she felt. "I am better—at least in body, if not in spirit." She'd likely contracted Mary's illness, although hers hadn't been as life threatening.

Her niece cocked her head and stared at the bruised side of Elizabeth's face. The swelling had diminished and her lip had healed, but the discolor remained and still attracted the gawking of her family whenever they joined her.

Her father hadn't allowed any other visitors to her room—not even Samuel when he'd brought her a gift—a piggin with a long stave shaped into a handle.

Elizabeth glanced to the far corner, where she'd instructed Anne to place it. 'Twas of good craftsmanship. Samuel had learned his cooper's trade well.

Her gaze came back to the narrow bedside table, to the candlestick. No matter how many times she lingered over it, wonder and warmth stole through her heart. Her gaze traced the intricate leaf pattern made of tiny holes pierced in the tin. It wasn't the workmanship that fascinated her, though it was crafted just as well, if not better, than Samuel's piggin. Rather what sent her mind whirling was the thought of the hands that had wrought such beautiful workmanship. For her.

When Anne had delivered the gift, Elizabeth had accused the girl of confusion. Surely the gift wasn't for her?

Even now, a part of her mind refused to believe anyone would want to bestow a gift upon her. Anyone but Samuel . . .

She tore her gaze from the candlestick and forced it back to the bucket. She ought to feel just as much gratefulness for Samuel's gift.

With a firm press of her lips she gathered the petticoat again and picked up the thread and needle. Why couldn't she muster the appreciation?

Surely she was just irritated that Samuel wanted her to stop working for the Costins and move up their wedding plans.

"Elizabeth!"

She raised her head at the urgent call. The stomp on the steps leading to the bedchambers grew louder.

"Elizabeth!" Her sister Anne burst into the room and gasped for breath. The girl, on the verge of blossoming into a woman, had assumed the responsibility of managing the home since Catherine had gone to work for the Costins.

Distress lined her sister's face and sent anxiety shooting through Elizabeth. She struggled to sit up higher on the feather mattress, which sagged within the crisscross of ropes that held it in the wooden bed frame.

"Elizabeth," the girl gasped again.

"What is it, Anne?"

Anne put a hand to her chest and dragged in a deep breath. Her gaze darted to the open window.

The heat of the July afternoon had permeated the second-story room, and even with the shutters open, Elizabeth could feel narry a breath of air. But 'twas better than the bedroom she shared with her sisters in the middle room, which had no windows at all.

"You must come, Elizabeth." The girl's tone was laced with panic.

Had something happened to Mary again? Or Thomas? "Whatever is the matter?"

"Come see."

Elizabeth scooted to the edge of the bed and lowered her feet over the side.

"Hurry." Anne pulled her up. "Sister Norton said you must hurry."

"Bear with me, Anne. I've hardly been out of bed in a week."

Her legs shook as she stood. "Tell me what's wrong. Is it one of the children?"

Anne took hold of her arm. "It's Lucy. She's in trouble."

"Trouble? What kind of trouble?" Had Fulke returned? Had he discovered Lucy's secret earnings from the wet-nursing? 'Twas only a matter of time until Lucy would be battered and bruised again—especially when Fulke realized Lucy had deceived him by hiding the coins.

"You must do something to help her." Elizabeth clung to Anne and limped across the room to the window. "Sister Norton said you would know what to do."

Anne pointed outside to the public greens north of the bakehouse on High Street.

A crowd from the nearby marketplace had gathered, and for a moment Elizabeth only saw the tops of hats and coifs.

Then her stomach dropped with a sickening thud. A woman was locked in the pillory.

"Lucy," she whispered. Horror spread through her.

Lucy stood behind the long rectangular wooden structure that was fastened to a tall beam. The Bedell had clamped her head in a crude circle formed between two hinged boards, and he had locked her hands into the smaller circles on either side of her head, which would prevent her from protecting herself from anything the townspeople might throw at her. Her bright red hair fell in a tangled mass over her face, hiding her eyes.

Elizabeth caught sight of the figure locked in the stocks next to the pillory. "Martha." Lucy's sister sat on the ground with her feet fastened into the small holes of another set of wooden boards. She slumped and her hair too fell in disarray in front of her face.

Elizabeth's already weakened legs turned as soft as cream and she grabbed on to Anne to keep from collapsing. "What happened? Why are they being punished?"

"Listen." Anne nodded toward the public green, where a man was stepping forward to face the crowd.

The patch on his coat signified him as the Bedell of Beggars. He limped, dragging one foot along behind him.

"I assign these vagrants to receive twenty lashes apiece and spend one hour in public disgrace for their crimes." The man's voice rang out over the gathering.

"No." Elizabeth covered her mouth to stifle a cry.

The man pointed at Lucy. "This one for harboring a vagrant without permission and for wandering the streets of Bedford as a vagrant herself in deliberate idleness and vice."

His finger shifted to Martha. "And this woman for her illegality in residing in this parish, her idleness, and vice."

"Oh, Lucy," Elizabeth moaned. Martha was only one vagrant among the many that passed through the parish. Surely the church-wardens would make better use of their money assisting the beggars, rather than paying the informants who drew their attention to the presence of the rogues.

"After their punishment for laziness and other vices," the Bedell of Beggars continued, "these slothful, sinful vagrants will be thrust from this parish and sent to a house of correction to learn diligence and work."

"No," whispered Elizabeth with a jolt of urgency. The house of correction, the bridewell, the workhouse. They were all names for the same place: the prison of death. She couldn't allow the Bedell to send Lucy there—or anywhere.

She grabbed Anne's arm with trembling hands and turned away from the window. "Take me down there, Anne. I must do something to stop this."

"Sister Norton was right." Anne gave her a shaky smile. "You'll make everything right."

Elizabeth didn't have the heart to tell her young sister she had absolutely no idea how to stop the horror unfolding before their eyes. What could she do when the Bedell of Beggars had already pronounced his verdict and was even now carrying it out while she stumbled down the stairs?

When they floundered to the bottom and shuffled outside to the front of the bakehouse, Sister Norton was waiting on the street. She rushed to Anne's aid and reached for Elizabeth.

Sister Norton slid her long strong arm around Elizabeth's middle and held her up as they stood under the parapet. Elizabeth strained to see through the crowd. Her father and Henry peered out the bakehouse window, its shutters open, the top one propped upward, providing an awning, and the bottom one forming a counter with only a few loaves and pastries left for sale.

Elizabeth caught a flash of Lucy, enough to see that the Bedell had slashed open her bodice and yanked it to her waist, leaving not only her back exposed, but her front as well.

Heat leapt to life in Elizabeth's face and made a burning trail through her body. Her innocent Puritan mind couldn't imagine anything more torturous than having to endure a public display of her bare body. She was sure a beating would pale in comparison.

"Ah, ah, the poor, poor dear." Sister Norton shook her head and clucked her tongue against the roof of her mouth.

"What will you do, Elizabeth?" Anne's voice was edged with agitation. "You must do something quickly."

Elizabeth's mind worked as slowly as her legs. She fixed her gaze on the muck on the ground. The slap of the whip against bare flesh and the agonized cry that followed tightened her body.

"Hurry! Hurry!" Anne's words ended in a sob.

Elizabeth glanced at Lucy long enough to see the Bedell of Beggars raise his arm for another strike. He thrust his hat back, and she glimpsed of his face. His thin but distinct smile carried a clear message: he took pleasure in his job.

"That man." Sister Norton shook her head. "He's not fit for such a position, even if he is a Grew and son of an alderman."

"Grew?" Elizabeth's stomach churned. "The Bedell of Beggars is a Grew?"

"Of course, my dear. He has been for some time now. It's only natural since he's the eldest son of a yeoman and in line to inherit his father's holdings."

Her thoughts sped back to the times on Calts Lane when she had felt eyes watching her. Surely the Bedell of Beggars hadn't stalked her.

Elizabeth drew in a sharp breath. Surely not. But if he had, would he have acted under the influence of an informer?

Elizabeth's gaze darted to the crowd and dashed from one person to the next. Her insides curdled and a sour taste settled in her mouth with the realization that Lucy's arrest by the Beddell of Beggars had likely been no accident.

Her gaze halted on the face she'd hoped she wouldn't find—Mrs. Grew's. The woman wasn't looking at the prisoners but was instead watching her, as if she were the spectacle to be observed, not Lucy.

Elizabeth wanted to groan at the trace of a smile on Mrs. Grew's face and the satisfaction it contained. The small curve communicated more than words ever could: the Beddell of Beggars was doing her bidding. She was in control. This was what she would do to her enemies.

Weakness spread through Elizabeth. She clutched at Sister Norton to keep from falling.

The slapping of the whip and Lucy's screams, the jeers of the crowd, Anne's sobs, Sister Norton's clucking—the noise hammered through her head until finally it seemed to pound through the daze.

She straightened with a burst of strength. "Anne, go fetch Brother Costin."

Anne turned to her. Tears streaked her cheek.

"Lucy is in the employ of Brother Costin. Perchance he will be able to save her from the bridewell."

Sister Norton's long neck bobbed awkwardly. "True, true. As the Costin wet nurse, she *is* gainfully employed, even if she is currently homeless."

"Begone with you, Anne." Urgency sharpened her tone. "Begone and make haste."

Anne wiped her eyes and cheeks with her sleeve, gave her a nod, then dashed away.

Elizabeth could only pray Providence would have John home that day instead of roaming about the countryside.

Chapter
13

The slap of Lucy's twentieth lash cut into Elizabeth's shredded heart, and she swayed with weakness. She had forced herself to stay and watch, even though each of Lucy's hoarse screams made her long to return to her bed, climb under the blankets, and pull them over her head.

Instead, she clutched Sister Norton and swallowed the bile that kept rising. The last thing she wanted was to give Mrs. Grew the satisfaction of seeing her vomit in her agony.

"Poor, poor Lucy," Sister Norton said. "Robert Grew is powerfully built. And with the strength he's using, you would never guess he was whipping that bony little woman. If I didn't know better, I'd have thought he was beating a man twice his size."

The Bedell of Beggars walked away from Lucy and left her standing in the pillory with her head hanging against the wood of the hole. He limped over to Martha. She cowered away from him and buried her head in her arms. With a jerk of his knife he ripped through her bodice and yanked it to her waist.

"Please, Lord." Elizabeth closed her eyes to shield herself from the shame but couldn't keep it from burning through her again. Why was such humiliation necessary?

"There's Anne," Sister Norton said.

Elizabeth raised her eyes to the breathless girl shouldering her way toward them. She searched behind the girl, willing John to appear. But she didn't see his broad shoulders or ruddy hair.

Anne's tears were answer enough that her mission had failed.

"Catherine said Brother Costin had been home all morning." Anne spoke in a rush and coughed as she fought to fill her lungs with air. "But now he's left for Newport Pagnell."

"How long ago?" Elizabeth straightened her feeble knees. She would run after him herself if she had to.

"Not long. She doesn't think they could be too far on the road out of Bedford."

"I must go after them." Elizabeth pulled away from Sister Norton.

Sister Norton reached for her. "My dear, you cannot possibly—"

Elizabeth stumbled to her knees and groaned with frustration. She banged her palms against the ground. Why did she have to be so helpless?

"Young lad." Sister Norton called quickly to a boy nearby, bidding him to chase after Brother Costin with the promise of reward should he deliver the man.

"Tell him it's urgent," Sister Norton instructed. "If he hesitates, tell him Sister Whitbread has need of him."

The boy scurried away.

Sister Norton lifted Elizabeth and helped her sit on an overturned barrel.

Elizabeth leaned her head against the bakehouse and closed her eyes, grateful to rest her weak body, even relieved she could no longer see the public green or the haughty tilt of Mrs. Grew's chin.

'Twas now during the next hour of disgrace, while the Bedell left Lucy and Martha in their awkward, defenseless positions, that the crowd would heap further humiliation upon the women. She had seen it plenty enough—the throwing of rotten food, muck from the street, feces, even dead animals. No matter the crime, she'd never understood how anyone could want to participate in the jeering and shaming.

As the hour dragged, hopelessness seeped into Elizabeth. She shuddered to think Lucy could very well die that day. 'Twas not an uncommon fate for someone subjected to the pillory.

What would Thomas do if Lucy died? He was nigh to three months, still too young to survive without the milk of a wet nurse. Would they have to return him to the Birds?

Sadness settled deeper within her. They would very likely lose him once more.

She was sure Thomas would be crying by now, hungry and ready for Lucy, who would certainly not be coming to feed him this day—nor perhaps ever again.

The thought of sending Anne back to the Costins with pap-making instructions for Catherine filtered through her weary mind, but before she could rouse enough energy to call Anne, the girl rushed to her.

"He's coming!"

Elizabeth sat up with a burst of renewed energy. "Brother Costin?"

Anne nodded and stood on the tips of her toes to see above the crowd. "He's coming this way."

Elizabeth smoothed her petticoat and pulled it over her ankles. Before she could make sense of the quivering of her insides, the crowd had parted and he stood in front of her, towering above her.

"Sister Whitbread." His chest lifted and fell in huge breaths and gave testimony to his exertion in returning to Bedford with all haste.

"Brother Costin." She tipped her head back to peer up at him.

His shirt strained against his broad chest. "The lad said it was urgent. That you were in urgent need of help."

" 'Tis very urgent." She took in the rough angles of his face and fought against a sudden rush of light-headedness.

John swiped off his large brimmed hat. His damp hair stuck to his forehead in a ring. His eyes were so blue and keen with concern that Elizabeth squirmed, especially when his gaze moved to the side of her face, to her bruise.

She wanted to turn away from him, to cover it, to hide the ugly color, but the intensity of his gaze immobilized her.

He lowered himself to one knee in front of her until they were eye level. With his focus on her bruise, he raised his fingers and poised them above the battered spot.

Elizabeth's breath caught in her throat. His face was near enough to see the stubble on his cheeks and the slight bend in his nose.

He hesitated only a moment before his callused fingertips brushed the edge of the bruise. "I'm truly sorry," he whispered.

She could think of nothing but the warmth of his skin against hers. "To besure, 'twas not your fault."

"I take full responsibility, Elizabeth."

His touch was as soft as the wings of a butterfly. Her stomach wavered not only at his touch but also at the intimacy of her given name on his lips.

"I came earlier in the week to see you, but your father said you were too ill to receive visitors."

So he had truly visited her? Perhaps Anne hadn't been confused about the gift after all. The fluttering in her stomach wanted to take flight. His fingers strayed to a strand of her hair and poised there for a moment.

She sucked in a breath.

Then his thumb caressed down.

The air stuck in her lungs.

He gently slid the strand back. His gaze traveled over the long tresses that hung loosely about her face and flowed over her shoulders.

Heat rushed into her cheeks. She had been in such a hurry to get downstairs and her mind filled only with thoughts of saving Lucy, she hadn't stopped to consider her appearance and the immodesty of her unplaited and uncovered hair.

She grabbed her loose hair and scooped it away from her face, away from his touch, to the back of her head. Her fingers, as brittle as kindling twigs, stumbled over each other as she began plaiting, trying to bring about a measure of decency.

John watched her awkward struggle. After a moment his eyes took on a glimmer, and a grin played at the corners of his lips. His gaze returned to her face, to the flames she knew danced on her cheeks.

His grin inched higher. Then his bright eyes finally settled on hers and swept her up until she was floating in the clear blue sky of them.

For a long moment his gaze held hers. The humor faded, and the darks of his eyes grew bigger.

Sister Norton cleared her throat.

Elizabeth glanced at the widow.

The woman raised her eyebrow and tilted her head toward the public green.

Elizabeth looked around, suddenly aware of the people surrounding them, watching John. Heat seared her face again.

She wanted to cover her cheeks with the coolness of her palms but clasped them in her lap instead. " 'Tis Lucy. She's to be taken to the bridewell."

Confusion narrowed his eyes. "Lucy?"

"You must stop them from taking her away."

His gaze again strayed to her bruise. "Then you're faring well? You're not in trouble?"

"No. 'Tis Lucy."

His brows came together in a puzzled furrow, as if he couldn't place the name.

"Lucy. Thomas's wet nurse."

Understanding as well as disinterest smoothed the lines of his face. He stood to his feet and raked a hand through his damp, matted hair.

"They've locked her in the pillory and nearly beaten her to death." Elizabeth scrambled to keep John's attention. "They're planning to take her to the bridewell."

He put on his hat, as though making ready to leave.

"We must save her." She fought through her weakness to argue for Lucy's case, to gain John's sympathy for the woman. "We cannot let them take her away. Thomas still needs her."

John peered over the crowd to the public green.

"No one deserves such punishment, no matter their crime."

"What was her crime?" he finally asked.

"She harbored her sister, the one in the stocks, without permission. And she was forced to leave her home after her husband disappeared."

"Where's the Beddell?"

"There. Yonder." Sister Norton pointed to the edge of the green, where the Bedell leaned against a cart, whip in hand, waiting for the hour to lapse before he loaded the women and drove them to the bridewell.

"Robert Grew?"

Sister Norton nodded.

John's eyes narrowed. "Alderman Grew is a decent, God-fearing man. Methinks the son does not take after the father."

Elizabeth knew very well whom the son resembled, but she wouldn't say the words aloud. "He'll have no cause to take Lucy to the workhouse if you make the case she is in your employ as wet nurse to your babe."

"If she is indeed homeless, he'll have cause."

"Then we must find a way to ensure she's no longer homeless," Elizabeth said.

"She cannot live with me," John said. "Even I know bringing her into my home would set tongues wagging."

"Lucy will live with me." Sister Norton straightened to her full height. "As long as the churchwarden permits it."

"Truly?" Elizabeth sat forward. "You would take her in along with her children?"

"I'd gladly help the poor dear. It's Sister Spencer that will need the convincing."

"We'll worry about her later. If indeed *you* are willing to house her, then we have no time to lose. We must save her."

"Very well." John tipped the barrel next to her and rolled it through the crowd. When he reached the middle of the street, he propped it on end, then hopped on top.

"Let's pray, Anne." Elizabeth clutched her sister's arm and rose to her feet. "Pray that Brother Costin's popularity and persuasive tongue will benefit him today."

"My brothers and sisters," John called.

A hush fell over the crowd.

"Methinks there has been no justice here today."

"Homelessness and harboring vagrants are crimes punishable by law," the Beddell's voice rang out.

"So one of the women has been whipped for trying to shelter another poor soul and for being homeless though she had no choice?"

"The parish doesn't allow vagrancy," replied the Beddell. "It's the law."

John raised his arms and spread them wide. "Then we, the church, are just as guilty. We all ought to be bound and likewise whipped for not extending our hand to assist these two women in their direst time of need."

"It's the church's duty to help the poor by driving the vice from their bodies and setting them to profitable work," the Beddell called.

"The homeless and beggars aren't filled with vice nor are they criminals simply because they are poor."

The authority in John's voice sent a tremor through Elizabeth's body. She swayed and tightened her grip on Anne. "Oh, Lord, please," she whispered.

"We, my brothers and sisters, are filled with vice when we can so callously and contemptuously spurn these helpless souls, rather than showing them the true love of God." The crowd had turned to face John, drawing closer to him as he spoke.

"They have lived the sinful lives of harlots," the Beddell shouted, "and now have only received their due punishment."

"Perhaps they have lived in sin and brought God's judgment upon themselves. But were they at fault for losing their home and resorting to vagrancy to survive?"

The crowd began to murmur and nod at John's words.

"We would all do well to remember the words of Jesus to the Pharisees, 'He that is without sin among you, let him first cast a stone at her.' "

Elizabeth smiled weakly. "He's doing good, isn't he?" she whispered to Anne.

Anne squeezed her arm.

John didn't need to speak much longer before the people began shouting out their agreement. And just as their calls to the Beddell turned angry, John jumped down from his post and approached the public green.

The rumors that wove through the crowd made her heart lurch and weakened her knees until she sagged against Anne. She closed her eyes to block out the dizzying sounds.

Finally one rumor broke through the clamor raging through her head: the Beddell of Beggars would release one of the prisoners.

The news was all she needed to hear before she collapsed.

⌐⌐

"Take her up to the bed." Her father's voice was distant.

Anne's sobs hovered above her in a dreamlike world.

Strong arms lifted and cradled her the way she carried Thomas.

Rough woven linen scratched her cheek and nose. She took a deep breath of woodsmoke and metal. The scent was unfamiliar, but not unpleasant.

Her face bumped against a hard chest, and the pounding thump of a heartbeat echoed through her ear.

She pried opened her eyes and lifted her head.

Bright blue eyes peered at her from between scraggly locks of rusty hair.

"John?" The name slipped out, unbidden, a whisper.

His gaze was solemn. "You're still not well. We must get you back to your bed."

He carried her up the stairs, his footsteps slow and hesitant. She knew she ought to protest. She was not petite nor light of stature—she would be no easy burden to bear.

Nor was the situation prudent. He had discarded his doublet. His coarse shirt was all that separated her from the heat of his chest. One of his powerful arms rested beneath her neck. The other was locked under her knees and inadvertently pressed against her backside.

He was touching her bottom? Her head began to swim with the indecency of her predicament.

"You must put me down," she whispered, unable to meet his gaze.

He stopped. The low rafters and narrowness of the stairwell forced him to stoop his head and shoulders so that his face was only a breath away. "Methinks you will like it much less if I put you down here. For then I will be compelled to pick you up once more. And this time I shall have to sling you over my shoulder like my sack of tools."

Her eyes, as if they had a will of their own, were drawn to his. "Then I shall have to beat my hands on your back like anvils."

A grin flirted at the corners of his lips. "Then we are agreed. I shall finish carrying you to the top this way."

She did not dare contradict him. The picture of being slung over his shoulders with her backside sticking into the air was a horrifying thought. And yet the nearness of his eyes, the heat of his breath, the power of his presence surrounded her, overwhelmed her.

He resumed his halting climb, and her breath wouldn't budge past her throat. "Lucy?" She squeezed out the word.

"They're taking her by cart to Sister Norton's cottage."

"She'll live?"

"Sister Norton will tend to her."

Elizabeth knew by his tone and what he left unsaid that Lucy was in danger of losing her life.

"You must rest now," he said as they came to the top of the stairs. "Your father has ordered it."

He carried her to the bed and lowered her to the sagging mattress. Instead of backing away he hovered over her. His breath fanned warmth over her forehead.

She sucked in a gasp of air and waited—waited for something she couldn't name.

At the echo of voices in the stairwell, he straightened and

bumped his head against the slanted ceiling. He ran his fingers through his hair and then glanced around the room. His gaze came to rest on the candlestick, only a hand's distance from her head.

"I see you got my gift."

She tipped her head and let her gaze caress the dotted pattern once again. "It's beautiful," she whispered past the lump in her throat.

"I made it for you." He looked from the candle holder to her face and then back again.

Her heart constricted with a tremor of delight. "Thank you."

He shifted his feet and glanced around the room again. "The children miss you," he finally said.

"Tell them I miss them too."

His eyes strayed to her bruised cheek.

She raised a hand and covered it.

"I despise whoever did this to you." He hesitated. "I realize working for me will put you in danger. But if you're willing, I'd like you to resume your duties once you're able."

Had Catherine failed to win John's heart as she had hoped?

He tilted his head and raised an eyebrow.

Relief slipped through her, and she smiled. "Are you actually admitting you need a housekeeper?"

A grin tugged his lips. "I know we didn't get off to a good start—I was proud and naïve. But I clearly see now what a help you've been. We can't get along without you. I need you to be my housekeeper."

She wanted to throw caution away and shout out that she desired nothing more than to return to her housekeeping position, that she'd been afraid of losing it and couldn't dream of doing anything else.

"If you're willing," he added.

She held her emotions in check and nodded. "I'm willing."

She was always willing to serve the helpless and needy, and the

Costins certainly fit those qualifications. She would serve them as she did anyone else in need.

Her willingness had nothing to do with John.

Nothing at all.

Chapter 14

*E*lizabeth grazed her fingers across the grainy paper, one of the many scattered on John's desk. Her hand quivered and she pulled back.

Dare she take one? Her pulse quickened, and she cast a glance over her shoulder to the other room. Silence stared back at her. No one would know if she slipped a sheet into her pocket.

Now was her chance to get something—anything—to give the dangerous stranger. She'd been back more than a week and hadn't seen him, yet she knew it was only a matter of time before he returned.

Her fingers hovered above the paper. Surely if she took it, the Lord would understand. She would only borrow John's writing, not steal it.

A quill pen lay on top of a stack that had been tied with twine.

The handwriting on the upper piece was small and sprawling, as if he'd been in a hurry to reach the end of each line. Even as her head screamed at her to stop, to flee from temptation, her heart pulsed with the fear of what would happen the next time the man came and found her empty-handed.

She brushed her fingers across the words, picturing John's strong hands forming each stroke—his callused yet gentle fingers. She could imagine the scratchy roughness of his fingertips caressing her cheek. Her stomach whirled, as it did each time she relived the attention he'd paid her—the closeness of his face, his penetrating gaze locking into hers, the solidness of his arms carrying her.

She traced his words again. Surely John would want her to take the paper—to protect herself.

She glanced out the oilskin window overlooking the garden and cottage plot. Mary held Thomas near the tree. Betsy and Johnny ran in the tall grass, taking a break from drying plums. They had helped her pit and lay them on coarse canvas frames she had erected in the sun. But now they were running in circles until they dropped with dizziness. Then they picked themselves up and did it again.

If she quit housekeeping as Samuel wanted, then she wouldn't have to worry any longer about the stranger. Certainly she'd make Samuel happy. And Catherine too. The girl still talked about becoming the next wife of John Costin, albeit less ardently after her week of vigorous work.

Elizabeth had no such dreams. God had already determined her place in life. She would become the wife of the cooper. Samuel made certain she didn't forget it. Nor did he let her forget summer's end was fast approaching.

She turned back to the desk and pushed down the irritation that had a habit of surfacing too oft when she thought of Samuel. She didn't need his constant reminders. Ending her housekeeping would be hard enough without them.

All the more reason to take one of John's papers. She'd ensure her safety until summer's end. Then she'd put it back. He'd never need to know it was gone.

Elizabeth studied the top paper. The gray was flecked with the imperfections of the paper-making process and the stray drips of ink that had dried. The letters and words were as foreign to her as if they had been another language. Since she could neither read nor write, how would she know if the sheet contained anything of value, anything the man would want?

She peeked over her shoulder again. John had left for the day, but that didn't mean she was safe in his study. Anyone could enter the cottage and catch her going through John's desk.

Anyone could enter the cottage. She was well aware of that now.

She shuddered and raised a hand to her cheek. The bruise was gone, but the memory of the attack was still vivid—his grip pinched the flesh of her arms, his fetid breath suffocated her, and the luridness in his tone crawled over her skin.

But it was the gleam of lust in his eyes that had birthed the deepest fear. She might be naïve but she knew enough. He would corner her and brutally steal her purity and innocence.

Would today be the day—the day he returned? Her heart thudded against her chest with a swell of fear.

She grabbed the paper. Her fingers fumbled to fold it and faltered at the drawstring of her pocket. She stuffed the paper inside, heedless of wrinkling it.

Then she took a step away from the desk and crossed her arms to still their trembling. She was only doing what was practical and necessary.

The next time her assailant came she must have something to give him, a paper, information, anything. She dared not fail again.

Wouldn't John be grateful she stopped any rumors about them? His ministry was more important to him than anything else. He would be glad she was taking steps to prevent his good name from being tarnished.

Yes. If he ever discovered what she'd done, no doubt he'd fall at her feet in thankfulness.

～

"Will we have enough bread for everyone?" Anne swung her basket at her side. "I would like to save a loaf for Lucy."

Elizabeth's basket, like Anne's, overflowed with the bread that had not sold that week. She suspected her father always made more than they needed. Each Sabbath, without fail, they had plenty to take to the poor, always enough to fill her basket and another.

"This bread won't last long," Elizabeth said, knowing that no matter the generosity of her father, they would never have enough to feed all those who had need. "We shall take Lucy and Sister Norton fresh bread on the morrow."

"May I take it to them?"

"Surely." Elizabeth smiled at her sister's eagerness.

Elizabeth lifted her eyes to the clear morning sky and gave a silent prayer of thanksgiving. Lucy's recovery was God's blessing. Although Lucy gave credit to her strong back, which had already survived many of Fulke's beatings, Elizabeth didn't doubt God was rewarding her for serving Him well.

They knew naught of what had happened to Martha, and Lucy didn't pretend she would ever see her sister again, especially if the Bedell of Beggars had taken her to the bridewell.

"I only wish we'd been able to rescue Martha too," Elizabeth said as they turned the corner away from the marketplace and headed south to the wharves along the river.

"Sister Norton could have taught them both bone lace-making," Anne said.

The Sisters were teaching Lucy many things, among them bone lace-making, a craft many unskilled women used to earn money. 'Twas laborious toil, involving hours of weaving intricate patterns with threads attached to bobbins made of bones. Even though the demand for lace had diminished over the years of Oliver Cromwell's protectorate and his conservative ways, the craft still provided a small income for poor widows like Sister Norton and Sister Spencer.

The clopping of horse hooves echoed behind them. Elizabeth edged Anne to the side of the street and glanced over her shoulder to see the lone figure of a man coming toward them.

The plume of his hat was long and bobbed up and down in rhythm to the horse's cantor.

Fear jabbed Elizabeth.

The dashing hat, the tailored clothes with their rich colors and fine laces—they could belong to any Royalist gentleman. But the plume, with its jaunty, almost arrogant tilt, reminded her of one man.

She halted Anne with a touch of her hand and scanned the cottages. Only a few shutters were open. Would anyone hear her if she screamed?

She peered down the street to the wharves, to the hovels and dilapidated cottages crowded close together. Several men loitered—the drunkards who hadn't yet made it home after a night of carousing. They would be of no help to her.

The clomp of hooves drew nearer.

"Run home." Elizabeth turned to Anne. "Run as fast as you can."

Anne gave a start but didn't move to leave.

"Go. Now." Urgency made her tone sharp. She grabbed Anne's basket of bread and tugged it from the girl's grasp. "You must go tell Father to send help."

"What's wrong?" Anne's voice rang with concern.

" 'Tis him, the man who hit me."

Anne gave a cry of alarm.

"Go!" Elizabeth shoved the girl. Anne would be in danger too if she stayed.

"I can't leave you," she whimpered.

"You must get help."

Elizabeth pushed her sister again, and this time the girl stumbled away as the man drew his horse alongside them. From his perch atop his saddle, he tilted up his hat.

"Well, if it isn't Costin's whore." Even from his position above her, the glint in his eyes was sharp.

The slap of Anne's footsteps echoed in the quiet of the street as she ran.

The man cast a glance at the girl, and Elizabeth held her breath and prayed he wouldn't try to stop her.

His fingers twitched on the reins.

" 'Tis the Lord's day." Elizabeth squared her shoulders and faced him, determined to distract him from chasing Anne. " 'Tis a day to put aside all quarrels and disputes and live at peace with one another."

His gaze fell back on her and contempt curled his lip. "We will have peace only when commoners learn to stay in their place instead of aspiring to be more than they are."

Out of the corner of her eye, Elizabeth saw Anne turn the corner.

"What do you have for me?" His gaze slid down her body and then up.

She forced herself not to shudder.

"I have given you more than enough time," he said. "I want information now."

Muffled voices came from within the cottage behind her. Elizabeth took a step backward. Could she make her way to the door and find refuge within?

"Well, what do you have for me?" He pulled his riding switch out of his saddle and with slow, deliberate motions laid it across one knee and lightly slapped it against the soft skin of his leather jerkin.

The strips of leather and willow braided together sent a shiver to the core of her body. She tried to swallow, but her mouth was suddenly parched. What could she tell him or give him? She'd left the paper tucked in the pocket she wore with her everyday apron. As she had donned her Sabbath garments that morning, she had never imagined she would have need of it.

Perchance she ought to stand up to him, tell him as she had last time that she had nothing, that she never would have anything for him, that he could hurt her if he wished, but she would not betray John Costin.

He tapped the riding switch against his knee again.

"I do have a paper for you." She forced the words out but despised herself for her weakness. "But I don't have it with me at this time."

"Then tell me something." His voice was as tight as the lines of his lips.

She slid back and noticed the coat of arms painted on an ornamental shield attached to the horse's leather strippings. The charge was a crane clutching a fish, its sharp bill poised to devour, set against a field of red and gold. Was she the fish, her flesh about to be pecked apart by this man?

"Well?" He lifted the whip.

Her mind scurried for something to say, some news of John she could share without having to disclose too much. But the plain truth was that she didn't know anything. His preaching took him away from home most days, and tinkering demanded the rest of his time.

"You are a stubborn one, just like him," he growled. "Give me the information I want, or you'll wish you had."

"I'm not trying to be stubborn." Desperation cramped her

stomach. "I don't know anything of value to tell you. He's rarely home. And he hardly speaks to me when he is."

With startling quickness he lifted his riding whip and brought it whistling through the air. Even before it struck her, she screamed and dropped the baskets of bread. She held up her arms to protect her head, and the thin strips sliced through her sleeve.

The sting of leather bit into her flesh, and she cried out again.

He raised his arm and put the force of his body into the next swing.

The whip slashed through the air, and Elizabeth jumped against the cottage. The leather strips swooshed through empty air and narrowly missed her.

Frantic to escape him, she turned and pounded on the cottage door. "Help! Help me! Please!"

The whip fell across her back like the blade of a knife and took her breath away. The piercing pain ripped another scream from her. Before she could move, slap after slap caught her, slicing away her bodice and searing her back with a quickness and intensity borne of skill.

The horse whinnied and reared away. Her attacker cursed and turned his whip onto the beast.

Her body sagged against the door. Was this how she would die?

Just as her knees gave way, the door of the cottage opened. She fell forward and sank to the dirt floor within.

"What's the racket?" a man's rough voice demanded.

Elizabeth couldn't speak past the tightness of her throat.

A woman kneeled next to her.

"What's this all about?" the man asked again, louder. He scratched his stomach with both hands and squinted into the bright sunshine.

"It's narry your concern," her assailant replied. Horse hooves tapped against the street. "If you know what's best for you, you'll speak not a word about this to anyone. Now, hand the wench over to me."

Fear pulsed through Elizabeth. She struggled to push herself off the ground, desperate to escape this madman.

The woman at her side took hold of her arm and helped her rise to her knees.

"This here is my cottage," the man bellowed. "Think you, just because you're a rich gentleman, you can come to my home and order me about?"

"I think I can do whatever I may please, you foolish old man. Now, give me the girl."

Elizabeth peered around the dark shadows of the sparse room. Where could she hide?

"I may be only a thatcher, but I don't take orders from arrogant young men such as you."

"You better do what I say. I have the power to make sure you never thatch another roof."

The old thatcher scratched his stomach again.

What if he handed her over? What would happen then? Fresh fear charged through her blood. "Please help," Elizabeth whispered to the woman.

"Do not fret, dearie." The woman patted her arm. "You're safe now."

Elizabeth gripped her hand.

"If this here's your wife, I'll give her to you," the thatcher said. "A man has a right to do whatever he wants with his wife."

"No," Elizabeth cried, answering before her attacker could lie. "I'm not this man's wife. I don't even know his name. Please, I'm only a poor woman he's trying to hurt because I haven't done his evil bidding the way he has wished. Please help me."

The thatcher squinted down at Elizabeth and studied her through the slits of his eyes framed by arches of untidy gray eyebrows.

The young man cursed under his breath and raised his riding stick. "You are a foolish old man." He brought the whip down hard and aimed it at the thatcher's face.

Before the strip made contact, the thatcher snatched it with bare fingers and yanked it out of the attacker's hand with a strength that nearly pulled the man from his horse. Then he brought the switch around and snapped it at the man, slashing him across his leg.

The attacker's horse whinnied and sidestepped, moving the young man out of reach just as the thatcher snapped the whip forward again.

This time the switch slapped only air, and the old man chortled. "Think you it isn't so pleasant to be on the other end for once?"

Her assailant steadied himself on his horse and clenched his jaw. "You will pay for this." His words were low and ominous.

"You might be able to ride around on that horse of yours and amuse yourself beating helpless girls. But you can't never bully me. I'm not afraid of the likes of you."

The young man spat at the thatcher's feet. "Someday you'll be afraid. I'll make sure of it." Then he turned to Elizabeth.

She clutched the thatcher's wife.

"And you—" He spat on her skirt. "I'm not done with you yet. Just you wait."

He jerked his hat low over his eyes. Then he dug his heels into the flank of his horse and galloped away.

Chapter
15

*J*ohn paced in front of the meetinghouse, each step heavy with the weight of his frustration. "None of it is true. Not one word of it."

"Calm down now, Brother," Vicar Burton said. "We shall learn the truth when she gets here." The vicar stood before the entryway with several elders. Their anxious eyes followed John back and forth.

John couldn't blame them. He was full of questions too. Heat burned through his blood and radiated through his whole body. He tugged at his doublet and wished he could shed a layer or two of his meeting clothes. The sun hadn't reached its high point, and yet his body was already sticky with sweat.

When he'd arrived a short while ago and made his way into St. John's, he'd tried not to notice the stares, the whispers behind hands, and the accusation on faces. But when the elders and Vicar Burton had approached him and asked to meet with him in private outside, he'd realized something was seriously wrong.

"We have heard that Elizabeth herself has claimed you are using her as your mistress," one of the elders said.

"Why would she say such a thing?" John shook his head. "It's not true—not in the least."

Disappointment roiled through his gut. After all the weeks working for him, surely Elizabeth wouldn't stoop to spreading rumors, would she? He didn't want to believe she'd merely been biding her time, waiting until an unsuspecting moment in which to tell vicious lies—lies to trap him into marriage. Maybe another maiden would attempt such deceit, but not Elizabeth.

He dragged in a deep breath of warm summer air and tried to calm the churning in his stomach. He'd believed Sister Whitbread was different, that she truly was serving his family out of her devotion to God and out of her growing fondness for his children. She had seemed genuine—a girl who spoke her mind and lived without pretense.

How could he have misjudged her? Certainly he hadn't.

"Come now, John," Vicar Burton said with a cough. "We're not saying the rumors are true. And we're not saying we don't believe you. We only want to hear what she has to say for herself."

"When she arrives, she will put these rumors to rest." At least he hoped she would. He dreaded to think how the rumors would damage his reputation if they spread—even now would put a blemish on him. Elizabeth needed to arrive quickly and tell everyone the truth.

The large wooden door of the church squeaked on its rusty hinges. Samuel Muddle lumbered out, followed by his uncle.

"We've heard the most disturbing of rumors." The uncle approached the elders. His forehead wrinkled underneath the brim of his hat.

"We're aware of what's being said," Vicar Burton replied. "And we hope to clear any misunderstandings as soon as the Whitbreads arrive."

Samuel puffed out his chest and glared at John.

"I don't know what you've heard." Indignation sprang to life in John. "But none of it is true."

"Elizabeth Whitbread is a chaste woman." Samuel's voice filled with accusation. "If anyone is to blame, it must be you."

"There is no wrongdoing!" John balled his fists and fought the urge to pummel them into Samuel's bulging belly. "Why must everyone assume the worst?"

"Because you're a rogue." Samuel took another step forward.

John stiffened. If Samuel Muddle wanted a fistfight, then he'd get one. Even though he'd put off the fighting ways of his past, he hadn't forgotten how to give out a few good punches.

"You have a past reputation, Brother Costin," Samuel's uncle said. "I'm sorry. But it still follows thee."

John straightened his fingers and tried to rein his frustration. He wouldn't help matters by resorting to a fistfight with Samuel. He'd only prove Samuel's uncle right. Besides, he'd brawled enough in his past to know it would only add fuel to his anger.

"I forbid Elizabeth from working for you any longer," Samuel said.

"Now, let's not be hasty." Vicar Burton waved his hand at the street. "Brother Whitbread is coming even now."

John swung his gaze to the bowlegged man walking toward them. His cane tapped a slow rhythm on the dirt street. Only Henry and Jane with their children attended him. Elizabeth was nowhere in sight.

Where was she when he so desperately needed her skillful tongue to smooth out the situation? John wanted to groan in frustration but instead blew an exasperated breath.

When they turned off the street onto the stone path, Brother Whitbread came to an abrupt halt, his face creased with worry.

"Have ye heard the news of mine daughter?" His gaze skimmed the crowd.

Vicar Burton nodded. "Indeed, Brother. That's why we've gathered."

"Something has got to be done, Mr. Burton." Brother Whitbread thumped his cane on the stones. "This cannot happen again."

"I think we can all agree with that," the vicar replied.

"We must put a stop to the attacks—" Brother Whitbread started.

"We must bring an end to the rumors—" John said at the same time the old man spoke.

"What rumors?" Brother Whitbread's eyes narrowed.

"What attacks?" John stared at the baker.

Except for the twitter of a sparrow in the scraggy elm near the street, silence descended over the churchyard.

"Perhaps you had better go first, Brother Whitbread," Vicar Burton finally said. "I daresay we're all perplexed."

Brother Whitbread's gaze traveled over the men, confusion in his kind eyes. "Have ye not heard, then? My Elizabeth, my daughter—she was attacked this morning whilst she delivered bread to the poor."

John's breath stuck sharply in his chest. "No." Not again.

"We had not heard." Vicar Burton's voice lowered with concern.

"How is she?" The words squeezed past the tight dread closing off John's throat.

"She's in pain. But she's of hardy stock, my Elizabeth."

"What happened?" Samuel Muddle stumbled over his words. "Who attacked her?"

Brother Whitbread wobbled. Henry stepped to his side and

braced him. "It was the same man as the last. Only he took his riding whip to my daughter this time."

John's mind flipped back to the picture of Elizabeth on her bed after the last attack, the purple and black welt against her pale cheek. His heart kicked against his ribs. What kind of brute would prey on his housekeeper? With a riding whip, no less?

Samuel pointed a trembling finger at John. "This too is your fault, John Costin. You've been nothing but trouble for Elizabeth."

John's skin bristled at the allegation *and* something more uncomfortable—something akin to guilt. He would take full responsibility for putting Elizabeth in danger because of her association with him, but Samuel Muddle didn't need to add to his public disgrace.

"Methinks you have never liked her working for me and are just looking for an excuse to have her stop."

"We'd be married by now if it weren't for you."

"Elizabeth is a grown woman. She made her own decision to work for me." John willed calmness to his voice. "Perchance she housekeeps because she is looking for a reason to postpone marrying you."

"That's not true." Samuel's face puffed with crimson. He strained forward, but his uncle's hand upon his arm restrained him. "She *is* ready to wed me."

"Then why does she continue to work for me?"

"She won't . . . I won't let her . . ." Samuel sputtered and pulled at his breeches.

John couldn't hold back a smirk. Samuel's tongue was no match for his—nor for Elizabeth's. She would easily tire of his witless words. She needed someone who could keep her sharp as well as in her place, and Samuel Muddle was not that man.

"I won't let Elizabeth work another day in your house, Brother Costin."

"That's not your decision."

"But she must stop." Samuel's tone turned into a whine. "It isn't safe for her anymore."

"I will find a way to keep her safe." But even as he said the words, the emptiness of them echoed through him.

"I think I have to agree with Samuel." Brother Whitbread shook his head sadly. "My Elizabeth is in too much danger working for ye, John."

John met the kind eyes of the baker, and deep in his soul he knew the old man was right. Fresh frustration pumped through him. He wanted to lash out at his enemies for hurting her again. He'd gladly take the stripes across his back if he could spare her the pain.

"If only mine enemies would attack me instead," he mumbled, but then stopped. What if his enemies *were* attacking him?

He reached for Vicar Burton. "The rumors. Elizabeth didn't spread the rumors. She had nothing to do with them."

Samuel rolled his eyes.

"Elizabeth once told me the attacker threatened to spread rumors that would destroy me. And now he has carried through."

"Who would want or have need to spread such rumors?" Vicar Burton patted his handkerchief across his damp forehead.

"I can think of many Royalists who would like to silence our Brother Costin," Elder Smythe said.

"By spreading vicious lies they hope to see me defamed and bespattered." John doffed his hat and ran a sleeve across the mop of hair sticking to his brow. "And they are right. Who will want to listen to a preacher charged with the grossest of immoralities?"

His heart dipped with the thought of the repercussions the falsehoods could have on his ministry. Surely no one would come to hear him preach now. People would shun him.

"Elizabeth, my daughter, will testify before the whole congregation that you have only been kind and honorable to her in every way." Brother Whitbread leaned heavily against Henry. "We can make efforts to refute the lies of your enemies, John. But my Elizabeth will still be in danger as long as she is working for you."

"I will post the banns," Samuel cut in, "and we will get married as soon as possible."

"If she marries Brother Muddle with all haste, then our enemies will have no more fodder for gossip," said another elder.

The elders murmured and nodded among themselves. John heaved a sigh and dug his fingers through his damp hair.

"If Sister Whitbread doesn't work for Brother Costin, then who will?" Elder Smythe asked. "Surely none of our women will be safe."

"I would not want to place my daughter in harm's way," said another.

"But I must have someone." A twinge of panic pushed John to his full height. "The preaching ministry is demanding more and more time away from home. How can I continue without help?"

Again the men spoke around him, their voices growing louder.

"John needs someone . . ." Vicar Burton started but then trailed off on a cough that wracked his body and left him speechless.

God had called him to preach. Surely he wouldn't want the ministry to suffer now—not when he was beginning to reach so many people. "Don't you see?" he shouted above the clamor. "This is exactly what the Anglicans want. They want to prevent me from preaching. And they think that by starting licentious rumors and frightening away my help, they will force me to stop."

The passion of his words brought silence.

"We cannot give in to their tactics to scare us from spreading the true Gospel of our Lord."

Several of the elders nodded.

"If I do not continue with my preaching, then our enemies will think they have won—that they can badger us into submission. This is what they want—to control us and to frighten us into doing their will."

More of the men nodded.

"My foes have missed their mark in their open shooting at me," he continued. "If all the fornicators and adulterers in England were hanged by the neck till they were dead, John Costin would still be alive. I call not only men but angels, even God himself, to bear testimony to my innocence in this respect."

He stood, his wide shoulders braced like his feet for battle. "No. I will not fear them or their slanders of the blackest dye. They will not scare me away from my preaching."

"How will you defend yourself, John?" Vicar Burton asked through a wheeze. "How will you uphold your reputation?"

"Sister Whitbread will give testimony. And I will defend myself with my preaching and writing, as I always have. The truth will be made known and will prevail."

He listened to the calls of agreement.

"Since we are all of the belief that we must stay strong against our opposition, then you will not object to Sister Whitbread continuing her housekeeping duties."

Samuel gave a loud grunt of protest, but before he could speak, Brother Whitbread held up his hand and silenced him. The baker's shaggy brows came together, and his gaze met John's, peering down into his very soul.

"I do not like the danger of the situation," Brother Whitbread said.

"And I don't like it either," John added.

Brother Whitbread stared deeper. John wasn't sure what he expected to find, but finally he sighed and looked at Samuel.

"Since we are unable to come to an agreement, we must let my Elizabeth decide." He straightened himself and hobbled forward with his cane. "When she's feeling better, she'll make the decision."

Samuel nodded. Brother Whitbread walked past them to the

church door, and only then did Samuel toss John a triumphant smile.

A sickening lump lodged in John's gut. What would happen if Elizabeth chose Samuel over him?

He'd surely have a difficult time finding a suitable replacement— if he could find one at all. His ministry would indeed suffer.

But for some reason that wasn't what bothered him the most.

Chapter
16

"Elizabeth cannot rebuff Samuel's wishes." Catherine's bare hands slugged through the dough their father would bake in the oven that night.

"We're not asking for your opinion," Elizabeth replied. She wished the girl would keep her mind on her task instead of giving foolish opinions.

Elizabeth perched gingerly on the bench and regretted that she was unable to join the rest of the family in the work. After a restless night and then day spent in bed, the pain in her back had started to diminish to a dull ache, but her father had prohibited her from her usual duties.

The wounds on her back would eventually heal; she wasn't so sure about the other injuries—the ones to her reputation. She couldn't even think about what people were saying about her and

John without shame searing her soul. Like every Puritan maiden, she treasured and guarded her chastity—she didn't know how she could ever go out of the bakehouse and face anyone again.

"So what will ye do, then, Elizabeth?" her father asked. He stood at the brake and held on to the long-hinged roller, pressing down with all his strength. He rolled it back and forth across the mass underneath. Sweat dripped from his face and slickened the dough. Jane stood at his side and constantly turned the lump so that he could knead it evenly, but her gaze flicked to the far corner where Elizabeth sat.

At the moulding table Henry's hands paused above the dough he had already kneaded but was shaping into loaves. His gaze wavered in her direction too.

"Samuel has been entirely too patient with Elizabeth as it is," Catherine said, spilling more flour and water onto the floor around the plank-kneading trough. 'Twas not an easy job to mix the maslin flour that was half wheat half rye into the old sourdough, which had been dissolved in water to form the yeast for the new batch. But Catherine never seemed to notice how much flour she wasted as she sloshed the ingredients together.

And she never seemed to realize when she was talking too much.

Frustration twisted through Elizabeth. "The decision is too difficult."

"You cannot tell Samuel no." Catherine paused, her arms up to her elbows in dough. "He's been very kind to you. Not many men would want a bride of questionable purity. You'd be a fool to spurn him now, since he's willing to still have you."

"He's willing because he knows I'm not capable of the things being said."

"But if you refuse him," Catherine continued, "no one else will ever want you. For who will know and trust you the way Samuel does?"

"Shush, Catherine," Jane said. The gentle reprimand was followed by a look meant to be stern, but Elizabeth doubted Jane could muster a severe countenance even if she spent time practicing.

Elizabeth's insides knotted tighter. She hated that Catherine was right. No one else would ever want her. Regardless of her tainted virtue, she had no other prospects besides Samuel. She never had. If she lost Samuel, would she lose her chance of marrying and having a family of her own?

Though none of the others would say it, she didn't doubt each of them was thinking the same thing.

"But what about Brother Costin?" Elizabeth couldn't dismiss her responsibility to his family, even if she was putting her life in danger working for him. "He cannot function without a housekeeper. If he has no one to help him, he will have to stop his preaching. And you told me this is exactly what our enemies want to happen."

Catherine shrugged her shoulders. "If he has no housekeeper, perhaps he will consider marriage. I overheard some of the elders say his enemies would not dare hurt his wife the same way they would a mere housekeeper."

"Brother Costin made the pronouncement that he wants Elizabeth to stay as his housekeeper, and now he has swayed most of the elders to his plan." Their father huffed as he spoke. The exertion of kneading the coarse dough took more energy with each passing year. "But Elizabeth must not let their desires sway her."

The *thump, thump* of the dough kept rhythm with their father's heavy breathing. "No, my Elizabeth must discover God's plans for her."

She released a long pent-up breath. "But, Father, how will I know what God wants?"

Before her father could answer, Samuel's bulky frame darkened the open doorway of the bakehouse and blocked the late afternoon sunshine.

"Come in, Samuel, my boy," her father greeted. "Ye are early today. We have not lit the oven fire yet."

Samuel stepped inside, carrying the basket of dough he always delivered for his aunt. He squinted through the dimness of the bakehouse. "How is Elizabeth? I was worrying and wanted to check on her health."

Elizabeth hid her face in her hands and wished she could slip upstairs before he noticed her. He would want her answer and wouldn't be satisfied unless it was an agreement to stop working for the Costins.

"She's here," her father said. "And we were just discussing the decision she must make."

Samuel's heavy steps clomped through the maze of bread-making equipment. His apologies followed the bumping and banging his body made.

When he finally reached her, his labored breath formed a cloud above her. His odor seeped around her—a day's worth of sweat mixed with the strong scent of wood shavings.

She had the sudden urge to press herself into the wall. But if she tried to wheedle away or ignore him, she would affront his kindness—for he truly had been kind to her. As Catherine had indicated, he'd trusted her. He hadn't believed any of the rumors, had stayed true to her. He'd even defended her reputation when it would have been easy to give up on her.

How could she refuse him now?

Tentatively she took her hands away from her face and opened her eyes to his stained cooper's apron pulled tightly across his bulging middle.

"How are you?" he asked.

"I'm faring better, thank you." She glanced upward to his face, but at the sight of his eyes, the anticipation within them, she dropped her gaze to her lap.

He stood mutely for a moment. His fingers scraped through

his beard. Then with several grunts he managed to lower himself until he knelt in front of her.

"I've heard more rumors this day," he huffed.

"They are buzzing about town like flies," her father said. "We've been hearing enough of them today, Samuel, my boy. We don't want to hear any more."

"I wouldn't repeat such rubbish, even if I was on the rack."

"Good, my boy, good."

Elizabeth bowed her head with the weariness of shame. How could she withstand additional rumors? Wasn't the humiliation already sufficient?

"I'm sorry," Samuel said.

"And I'm sorry for you, Samuel. You're a good man, and you don't deserve a wife with a tarnished reputation."

He reached then pulled back, reached again and pulled back. He groped until his sweaty fingers finally made contact.

Elizabeth stared at her hand swallowed in his fleshy one. The feel of his skin was cold and clammy and sent bumps up her arm. She fought the distinct urge to jerk out of his grip.

She hadn't wanted to pull away when John had touched her bruised cheek. Indeed, she'd liked it well enough that she'd longed for more.

What was wrong with her? How could she enjoy the touch of a man she could never have but feel revolted by the caring hold of the man she would have forever?

As if sensing her discomfort, Samuel let go. He cleared his throat and fumbled at his breeches, searching for a place to put his hands.

"I know the elders left the decision to you," he started. "But with the increase of gossip, I must insist that you cease working for Brother Costin. Immediately."

Even with his bumbling, his tone was firm and his eyes intense.

"Now, Samuel, my boy, let's not be hasty." Her father gave the bread dough the last punches. "We agreed to let Elizabeth make the decision. Ye cannot be making it for her."

"But the rumors are getting worse. My honor is at stake, as well as Elizabeth's."

Elizabeth looked back at her hand, the hand he'd held. Should she reach for his hand and let him hold her again? Surely she'd not given him a fair chance. His hold should give her as much pleasure or even more than John's.

Samuel grasped the bench and heaved himself upward. The bench wobbled and Elizabeth teetered. She grabbed it to keep from sliding off. When he finally stood, he hitched up his breeches underneath his apron.

Maybe she needed to try harder. Perchance she had been too busy for Samuel or hadn't spent enough time with him yet to welcome his hold.

"You cannot go back." Samuel's tone took on the obstinacy of a child. "If you choose him, then you will lose me. I will not marry you."

The room suddenly grew still and silent.

His words echoed through her head. *If you choose him, then you will lose me. If you choose him, then you will lose me.*

Samuel pulled on his beard.

If she didn't know better, she'd almost believe he was competing with John for her affection.

"What will it be?" he persisted. "Me or him?"

"Hold on, Samuel, my boy."

Her father wiped his hands on his apron and cast Elizabeth the kind of look that said he did not want her to lose Samuel. He had seven daughters to marry off. She would only burden his conscience if she didn't seize this opportunity for marriage when she had it.

"Ye cannot push this matter, especially when Brother Costin and the elders—"

" 'Tis all right, Father." There was no choice between Samuel or John. Samuel was all she had, and she couldn't toss away the chance of lifelong marriage for a temporal housekeeping job. "I'll do as Samuel wishes. I'll stop working for the Costins."

Samuel released a whoosh of air. The lines in his face smoothed into relief.

She wanted to laugh at the absurdity of his anxiety. He truly had nothing to fear. But the emotion seeping through her was not humor. It was resignation. She must marry Samuel, and she couldn't put it off any longer.

"Then I'll go to the vicar and ask him to read the banns on the coming Sabbath."

Elizabeth shook her head and reached out to the air as if to stop him. "All I ask is for one more day."

He started to protest.

"Please." She almost touched his hand but couldn't go through with it. "Please let me say good-bye to the children and explain to them why I won't be coming back."

He hesitated.

"They lost their mother. Now they are losing me too. Please let me go. It will be my last day."

He pulled his beard harder.

"Please. I need to say good-bye." Her voice caught on the sadness that had pushed its way into her heart. How would she ever be able to say good-bye to them?

Samuel nodded. "That's reasonable enough. One more day, then."

One more day. The ache inside swelled against her chest. How would she ever survive it?

Chapter
17

$\mathcal{N}$ow I know why you love the Costin baby." Lucy stepped back from the doorway and gave Elizabeth room to enter.

Something about the woman's simple statement undressed her and made her want to turn away and hide. "Of course I love Thomas."

She ducked into the one-room cottage where Sister Norton and Sister Spencer lived, grateful for the darkness of the early dawn. The glow of the fire cast flickering shadows and illuminated Lucy's children sprawled on pallets near the hearth.

Elizabeth stepped around buckets and benches and placed the basket of bread on the table. Sister Spencer stood across from her, sawing through the crusty end of their last loaf.

Elizabeth nodded at her.

The widow pressed her lips together in a tight frown that vanished into the folds of her face.

Did everyone in Bedford believe the rumors about her and Brother Costin? Her heart burned with mortification. Didn't they know her well enough to realize she was incapable of anything even remotely brazen when it came to men?

She lifted the warm wheaten loaves from the basket and placed them on the table. Then she slipped her arm through the basket handle and fumbled back toward the door.

Lucy lifted her eyebrows. "I always wondered why you were so set on savin' that baby's life."

"For the same reason I deliver bread—because I want to help anyone in need." She was tempted to remind Lucy of all the times she'd given *her* bread and assisted *her*. But she bit back the words. She'd have her chance on the Sabbath to defend herself. The elders wanted her to make a public statement in defense of John before the start of the service.

"I must be on my way to the Costins'," she said. "Are you leaving now, Lucy? We can walk together."

Lucy glanced at Sister Spencer.

The woman gave a slight shake of her head.

Lucy tucked a strand of her neatly plaited hair under her coif. She wore clean and mended clothes. Her face was unblemished, the lacerations and bruises a thing of the past. Except for a few scars, she had nothing left to tell the tale of her previous life with Fulke.

"I 'ave to shift the babe first, see?" Lucy looked down at her hands.

"Very well." Elizabeth nodded and stepped out of the cottage, wishing she could as easily shed her shame.

"Ah, good morning, my dear," Sister Norton said as she emerged from the corner of the cottage carrying two baskets laden with produce from the large garden she grew behind their home. The widow smiled, her eyes alight with her usual warm greeting.

Elizabeth's throat tightened in an ache of gratitude. At least one of her friends hadn't believed the rumors.

"Truly the harvest is more plentiful this year than I have ever seen," Sister Norton said.

"Praise be to the Lord," Elizabeth replied. "I believe He's blessing you for your generosity in caring for Lucy despite your own struggle to survive."

"Praise to the Lord is the truth. As I told Sister Spencer, if we are obedient to Him, He will provide. Moreover, I would rather starve in this short, temporary life and do what pleases Him, than starve for eternity in that place of judgment away from Him."

"I cannot but think He's pleased by the progress you've made with Lucy."

Sister Norton lowered the baskets of vegetables to the ground. Some she would sell at the town market. The others she would save for the winter, either by drying or storing.

Elizabeth pictured the bean plants in the Costin garden, bent under the weight of the harvest and ready for picking. Who would dry the beans for winter now? John would surely have trouble finding someone else to finish all she'd started.

"Ah, ah, poor Lucy. Would that I progressed more with the state of her soul. What benefit is the washing away of her outward filth when her soul languishes in the mire?"

Elizabeth nodded, but her thoughts were tied to the Costins. How would the children survive without the proper stores?

Desperation clutched her insides. It had plagued her all night, since she had acquiesced to Samuel's ultimatum. She reached a hand to her side, to the pain there.

Sister Norton clucked. "You poor, poor dear. Your back is still hurting?"

Lathered with salve and fresh bandages, her back was the least of her agonies at the present. "It does pain me a little. But 'tis the greater heartache at what I must do this morn that pains me most."

The tall widow tilted her head.

"Samuel has insisted I stop working for the Costins or he won't marry me. I go this morning to say good-bye to the children. 'Twill be my last day."

Sister Norton searched Elizabeth's face and eyes. "I didn't think you'd marry the cooper."

"You didn't?"

"Ah, ah, my dear. It's obvious you've grown to care about our Brother Costin."

"Oh no." Heat rushed into Elizabeth's cheeks. "No. Most certainly not."

Sister Norton smiled.

"I won't deny I've grown to love his children. But him? No. Most certainly not." She forced a laugh at the thought.

"You may not yet realize it, my dear. But I've seen the signs oft enough to know. You love Brother Costin."

"Absolutely not." Embarrassment steamed over her like vapor from a boiling pot. "I think you're mistaking me for Catherine or any of the other maidens in our congregation."

"Ah, my dear, I've seen the look in your eyes when Brother Costin is near. And I haven't seen that look when you're with Samuel. It's the look of a maid in love, to besure."

" 'Tis true I don't have affections for Samuel. Ours is a practical match, a partnership. But I certainly don't have affections for Brother Costin. I'm in his employ. Nothing more."

"Surely you have felt differences in your regards of Brother Costin from Samuel." She cocked her head, as if daring Elizabeth to contradict her.

'Twould be a lie to do so. She *had* felt differences, but it didn't mean she loved him. "I have admiration for Brother Costin. He is an appealing man in many ways."

The widow smiled gently and knowingly.

"But," Elizabeth continued, " 'tis only admiration you see in my eyes. That's all."

"Ah, my dear, but I see more than admiration in his eyes for you too."

"That can't be."

"I witnessed the concern he had for you when you were sick. And I was there when he rushed to your side the day Lucy was in the pillory. I saw the way he looked at you."

She didn't need to ask what Sister Norton was talking about. Her mind replayed the time outside the bakehouse on the day of Lucy's beating, when he'd kneeled before her. The intensity of his gaze had taken her breath away; the softness of his fingers on her cheek still made her stomach flutter. She would never forget. The sensations were burned into her memory forever.

But one moment of attention did not mean John cared for her. She was his housekeeper. That was all. He had grown to value her work. Had he not specifically asked for her to be his housekeeper, even after having the chance to have Catherine? He liked her work. And now he needed her help so that he could continue his ministry.

"Give him time, Elizabeth, my dear." Sister Norton reached for the baskets of vegetables and looped her arm through each one. "He is still grieving for his dear Mary. But he's shown there is room in his heart to love again."

Elizabeth shook her head with a rush of denial. "Even if he should love again, why would he ever want someone like me? I count myself fortunate that Samuel Muddle is willing to marry me."

"Ah, ah, my dear, you are a sweet child. But you're naïve and most certainly don't give yourself enough esteem." The widow moved toward the cottage door and bumped it with her elbow to open it.

"I only try to see my outlook truthfully."

With another bump, Sister Norton pushed the door open. "You are an attractive girl, my dear. It's time for you to see that."

A rebuttal formed on her lips.

Sister Norton gave her a sharp look that silenced any argument. "Far be it from me to tell you what to do, my dear." She hefted the baskets higher on her arms, the weight hunching her shoulders. "This I will say, though. You're a desirable young woman. Any man would be fortunate to take you as his wife."

⁓

"Any man would be fortunate to take you as his wife."

Elizabeth shuffled her feet, kicking up dust. The words pounded through her mind to her soul.

She knew what the words meant: Sister Norton didn't believe Samuel Muddle was her one and only prospect for marriage.

But how could the widow possibly be right? Plain Elizabeth Whitbread? Desirable?

Elizabeth's clutch on her bread basket was as tight as the agony that gripped her heart. No man had ever paid her any attention until Samuel. And anything John had shown her was just a fleeting moment of a dream.

What did the widow know? Elizabeth swung the basket in a burst of indignation. She was mistaken to think Elizabeth had grown to love John. 'Twas an absolutely absurd notion. More preposterous was the conception John might have feelings for her.

She reached up and tucked a stray wisp of hair back under her coif. Surely she was still as plain as she was always? She sucked in her stomach. The rough linen slipped lower on her waist. She had grown thinner in the past weeks, mostly due to her illness.

But that didn't mean she'd somehow grown more desirable,

did it? She lifted her hand to her cheek, then to her nose. Her features hadn't changed.

She dropped her arm with a short laugh. 'Twas vain to be thinking of such things. She would do best to focus on the difficult task of saying good-bye to the children.

When she arrived at the Costins', she stopped at the door. Her body tensed with the dread of facing the sweet little faces and kissing them good-bye.

Giggles from within the cottage tore at her heart and brought tears to her eyes.

She couldn't put off the inevitable. She'd come to say good-bye, and now she must do it. With a deep breath, she forced the door open and stepped inside.

"You're here!"

Before she could close the door or set her basket down, Mary flung her arms around her and buried her face into her chest.

Elizabeth bit back a cry of pain from the pressure against the wounds in her back.

"I was so afraid you wouldn't come back." The words trembled on the trail of a sob.

Elizabeth dropped the bread basket and wrapped the girl in an embrace. Unshed tears squeezed Elizabeth's throat, making it ache.

"She's back!" Betsy rushed to her and threw herself onto Elizabeth too, with Johnny following, wheedling his body into the melee.

With a choke, Elizabeth opened her arms to receive them. She pressed a kiss onto each of their heads, her tears anointing them with her love. Her embrace tightened as the anguish in her chest radiated outward. How could she say good-bye? How could she leave them when she loved them so?

"Father didn't think you would choose us," Mary said, her

tangled golden curls falling over tear-streaked cheeks. "He said Samuel would win."

Elizabeth smiled through her tears. Did men have to make everything a competition?

"I knew you would want us," Betsy said with a smile that filled her face. "I know I cannot call you Momma, but that's what you are."

"Momma," Johnny repeated, letting go and jumping up and down.

She couldn't speak past the constriction of her throat, and the agony of what she must do pierced her.

"We won't let anything else happen to you," Betsy said, stepping back and gazing at her with earnest eyes. "Father said we wouldn't let you get hurt again."

"That is very kind of you." Elizabeth swiped her cheeks, trying to dry them, knowing she would be safe but not because of anything John might do to protect her. She would be safe because she would no longer be with them. She would be with Samuel. And that would be the protected, secure life she wanted. Would it not?

"Good day, Elizabeth." John's voice came from behind her, from the open doorway.

Using her sleeve to finish drying her cheeks, she spun around. Flames spurted into her cheeks at the thought of John overhearing the children's declarations. Surely that one little word *Momma* would drum up his anger.

He filled the doorframe and leaned against the post, his arms crossed at his chest. In the shadows of the cottage, his eyes were dark and unreadable. For a moment she wished she could run to a place where she wouldn't have to face his disappointment and anger. For he would surely find no pleasure in her company once she shared her decision.

"Thank you for coming," he said softly.

"Good day, Brother Costin." But 'twas *not* a good day. 'Twas indeed a horrible day, as he would soon know.

"Methinks it could not have been an easy decision for you to make."

" 'Twas the hardest decision I have ever made." Even now she wondered if she had chosen correctly. Was she right to accept Samuel's ultimatum?

John shoved away from the doorframe and crossed the short span that separated them. When he stood in front of her, she saw the softness in his eyes. "I've had much time to think since the Sabbath meeting, and perhaps Samuel is right. My home is too dangerous for you."

His words toppled the precarious defenses she'd tried to build. He didn't want her? Was he letting her go that easily? "But I thought you needed help—"

He put a finger to her lips.

The warmth of his skin brushed against the sensitive fullness of her lips and silenced her words and thoughts.

"How can I leave every morning, wondering what will happen in my absence, worrying if you and the children are safe while I'm away?"

"I would never let anything happen to the children—"

The pressure of his finger stopped her. "You truly have a servant's heart and have only sought to help me in my time of direst need, without ulterior motives, with no thought of reward."

The feathery lightness of his finger sent finches to flight in her middle. At his merest touch she could think of nothing else, nothing but his nearness and the gentle cadence of his voice.

"Even though I know you would continue to sacrifice for me and the children, I don't want you to get hurt again, Elizabeth." His voice turned to whisper. "I truly don't."

"I am not easily downtrodden," she whispered against his finger. "Besides, since you are putting yourself in harm's way for the sake of the Gospel, should not the rest of us sacrifice our comfort as well?"

His eyes took on a spark. He moved a step back, lifting his finger, leaving her lips barren for his warmth. "I would expect the slanders and attacks against myself. But I cannot bear it against a helpless woman."

"Helpless?" She straightened her shoulders, the light in his eyes suddenly igniting a spark in her. "Brother Costin, I am far from helpless. My attacker may have caught me off guard these times past, but not again."

"Then you are not afraid of another attack?"

"I may not be much, Brother Costin." Her blood pumped with the passion of her words. "But if I am anything, I am a strong woman."

His flashing eyes locked with hers.

"I won't cower. And in this we are alike, are we not?"

He said nothing for a long moment. Then a smile tugged at the corners of his lips. "I don't deserve your help, Elizabeth. But I am beholden to you for choosing to come back, even against the danger, against the slanders, and against the possible ruination of your reputation."

Her next word and breath stopped short. What had he said? Did he think she was choosing to remain his housekeeper? "No. You're mistaken—"

"Methinks you are altogether too humble."

"No. You've misunderstood me."

Mary stiffened and released her.

Turmoil rolled through Elizabeth. She had come to say good-bye and had somehow made them believe she was back to stay. What had happened?

Mary stood by her side rigid and silent. But John had turned away. He scooped Johnny into his arms and tousled the boy's hair.

Elizabeth didn't know what to say, how to begin to explain the true nature of her visit that morning.

Mary's hand grasped her arm in a tight, biting grip, and Elizabeth realized the girl knew—this beautiful blind child could see what none of the others did.

"It's a victory for me to have you stay." John reached for a wedge of dry cheese on the table. " 'Twill not be what my enemies are expecting, and it'll teach them they can't harass me into doing what they want."

He took a bite of the hard cheese and gave the rest to Johnny. When he turned to face her, he looked at her too innocently. Had he realized her true plan also?

"By standing strong with me, you will fight this battle against those who would stop the Gospel from being preached."

She cocked her head at him. Now was it his turn to persuade her? After he'd goaded her to agree with him?

"Therewith, if we give in to our enemies, they'll continue to control the minds and wills of the commoner, and by so doing, effectively keep from them the truths of salvation." His voice echoed with passion. "We must, each one of us, take up the cause and stand firm."

How could she disagree now, when she'd already pleaded the very same case? Turbulence wove through her. "But I must think of Samuel—"

"And Samuel must do his part too." He set Johnny down and reached for Betsy, who stood before him with outstretched arms. "If he allows you to remain as housekeeper, then he will have a hand in the saving work of God. Surely you, Elizabeth, with your eloquent tongue, could convince Samuel of this?"

His tone dared her. She shook her head. "You are the one with the eloquent tongue today, Brother Costin. You have me talking in circles. But the truth is, I cannot defy Samuel."

John was quiet for a long moment before setting Betsy down.

He gave her a pat and then stalked past her toward the door. When he reached it, he stopped and pinned his gaze upon her. "Man's efforts shall not stop me from carrying on the work to which God has called me."

Elizabeth's eyes were irreversibly drawn to him. The fire within him spread to her, a powerful force. The Spirit of God was with John Costin in a mighty way.

How could she oppose him? Was she foolish to even try?

Chapter 18

*A*gony churned in Elizabeth's stomach. The day was almost over and she'd yet to say good-bye.

She straightened the kink in her back and glanced up from the gooseberry bush. Her gaze traveled around the yard, making a count of the children. She passed over John leaning against the doorframe of his forge. But then she looked back and her heart flipped. He had narrowed his eyes upon her and was chewing on a long piece of grass.

How long had he been watching her?

She wanted to squirm and at the very least smooth the loose hairs back under her coif. Instead, she turned away and reached back into the bush, hoping he wouldn't notice the sudden quiver of her hands.

Out of the corner of her eye, she could see him push away from the shack. He tossed the sliver of grass to the ground and started across the yard toward her.

She ducked her head, glad for the wide hat that hid the heat in her face.

"Are there many left?" Behind her his voice was low.

She leaned into the thickly set branches. "This will be the last picking."

The gooseberry bushes tangled with the hedgerows along the edges of the cottage plot and separated the Costins' from the neighbors'. Johnny and Betsy had helped her harvest the first ripenings, but now their hands couldn't reach past the sharp spines for the last of the crop. So she'd given them the task of cleaning the cow's pen and transporting her droppings to the garden to mix into the soil for the winter.

Elizabeth plucked the fuzzy green cluster brushing against her fingertips.

The intensity of John's gaze on her back sent a rush of warmth through her blood.

"I'm sorry about the attack, Elizabeth. When I find out who is responsible, first I'll beat up his face, then when I'm done with his face, I'll take a whip to his back."

" 'Tis not God's way to seek revenge. 'Tis not our Puritan way either."

"Methinks it will not be revenge. It will be the discipline he needs for his evil deeds." His voice hinted at humor, and when she glanced over her shoulder, he wore a half grin.

Her heart flipped upside down.

"You're a hard worker, Elizabeth."

" 'Tis nothing less than God desires." His praise warmed her and strangely added to the turbulence that had rumbled through her soul all day.

He knelt beside her and reached into the gooseberry bush. The thin linen of his shirt pulled taut across his arms—the same arms that had carried her up the stairs of her home and cradled her so tenderly.

She tore her gaze away from him and focused straight ahead. Her fingers fumbled to find another berry.

"Mary was never very strong." He stretched his arm deeper into the spiky branches.

Surprise jolted her, and the cluster at her fingertips slipped away. Would he speak to her of his late wife?

He stared into the thick hedge, his brow furrowed, his eyes filled with pain.

"She always struggled to accomplish anything." His voice grew tight, and he stumbled over his words. "When I started preaching, I had to be gone longer. And this left her with more to do than she could handle. She grew weaker."

Elizabeth sat back on her heels and savored the wonder of the situation . . . John Costin was baring his soul to her.

"I knew if I stopped, I could help her more, but she wouldn't let me. She said it was God's purpose for me, that he had gifted me in a great way, that I must do His will even if it meant more hardship for her."

"She was indeed a godly woman."

He nodded and took a deep breath. "After the baby was born, she couldn't regain the little strength she had left. She was just too frail."

He fell silent.

Mary's song to Thomas drifted through the branches of the ripening apple tree. The sweetness of the girl's voice tugged at the strong thread of compassion woven through every fiber of Elizabeth's body.

She gazed at the wrinkled fabric of John's sleeve. Did she dare reach out and touch him, to show him she truly cared? Her hand twitched, but she couldn't seem to make it move.

For a long moment they both sat motionless. Finally Elizabeth peeked again at John. He stared unseeingly ahead.

Her mind reeled. He'd unburdened his soul to her, and she had to say something. "Some are more fit for heaven than for this life. And no matter what we do to help them, therewith God brings them home to Him. He desires them more than we do."

As if sensing her gaze, he turned to her, his eyes dull with grief and guilt. "I did not wish her to be one of those more fit for heaven." His voice was low and raw.

Elizabeth nodded.

He jabbed his fingers through his wind-tossed hair and shook his head. "You are strong, though, Elizabeth. And you will do well."

"Do well?"

"You will do well as a wife."

Elizabeth ducked her head. Why was he talking to her about this now?

"If I were to marry again," he continued, digging into the mound of gooseberries in the basket. He lifted his hand and let the berries slide through his fingers. "I would choose someone like you this time."

Her heart lurched to a stop. Like her? Truly? Irresistibly, her gaze lifted to his.

"I know not when I will remarry—if ever." His eyes lit up with warmth but also crinkled at the corners with firmness. "I am too busy to concern myself with such matters right now. My focus is solely on the work of God."

She swallowed hard, trying to push down her rising anticipation.

"But if I ever needed to find a wife, I would favor a woman of your strength and diligence, as well as your honest and pure heart. And you have a way with the children . . ."

Something unspoken in his eyes reached out to her, as if he

were asking her something he knew he shouldn't. Was he asking her to wait for him?

Her heart fluttered back to life and propelled forward in spurts. He couldn't be. 'Twas only her imaginings.

He didn't linger for her response. He pushed himself off the ground and ambled back to his forge.

She could only stare after him, speechless and more confused than ever.

By the time she reached home that evening, her father and Henry had already made the loaves, molded them, and set them to their last rise.

She wasn't surprised to find Samuel waiting inside, watching her father and Henry filling the oven with the gorse, preparing to fire it up to the high temperature needed for baking the bread.

"I was just on my way to get you," Samuel said.

" 'Twas no need, Samuel." There never had been. But she hadn't been able to convince him of that, and now it was over.

Was it over, though?

She stood in the doorway and dragged in a deep breath of the rising yeast.

Trepidation besieged her anew, as it had all day. She had considered her surrender to Samuel's wishes permanent. Hadn't she given him her word that today would be her last day at the Costins'? Even though she hadn't said good-bye to the children, she couldn't let that dissuade her from doing what she knew she must.

She must marry Samuel Muddle.

And yet at the sight of his bulky frame taking up space in the middle of the bakehouse, she could think only of John, his intense blue eyes, which clouded with the depth of his passions but also cleared to sparkle with mischief. His entire being radiated energy and power. When he spoke, or worked, or even when he was just thinking, he was fervent and alive and interesting.

She couldn't deny Samuel was a good man. He had a kind heart and had always treated her with utmost consideration. But compared to John, Samuel was like flat bread—bland and lifeless. Could she partake of him the rest of her life, now that she had nibbled on a different kind of relationship—a relationship with a man like John Costin, full of rich texture and flavor—like rising bread?

John had told her she would do well as a wife, that he would choose someone like her, that he favored her strength and diligence. He liked her purity and the way she cared for his children. She had been mulling his words over and over, and the pleasure of them warmed her insides.

Had she been wrong to assume the only man who would want her was Samuel? If John Costin would have someone like her, then surely other men would want her too. After all, didn't Sister Norton tell her she was an attractive girl and to give herself more esteem?

In a secret place inside her heart, she had tucked away the notion that maybe, just maybe, Sister Norton had been right about the other things too. Maybe she was growing to care about John. And perchance he would eventually learn to think about another woman besides his wife. He wouldn't always be too busy with his ministry. Surely one day he would have time for another marriage.

"Now that you're home, perhaps you could help me convince Father to let me begin housekeeping for the Costins on the morrow." Catherine scraped the leftover dough into the trough. "He must have someone to help him. Why not me?"

"Shush, Catherine. It's too dangerous." Jane whisked the dough into some water, making yeast for the next day's bread. "Besides, think about Elizabeth. It must have been a difficult day saying good-bye to the children."

"I shall be on my way," Samuel said as he settled his hat onto his head. "I want to speak to Vicar Burton this evening about posting the banns."

"I didn't say good-bye to the children." The words blurted from her mouth before she could stop them.

Samuel's hand froze on his hat.

Everyone but her father turned to look at her. He continued poking at the gorse with his pitchfork.

"I couldn't say good-bye."

"You'll see them again," said Catherine. "It's not like you're sailing to America."

"I'm sorry, Samuel." Elizabeth stepped toward him.

First his eyebrows lifted in confusion, and then they came together in a dark scowl.

"I don't want to say good-bye to the Costins. Not yet."

His eyes filled with hurt. "So you're choosing *him*."

"I'm not choosing *him*. I'm not choosing *you*. I'm not choosing *anyone*. I'm just not ready to say good-bye."

"I knew I shouldn't have given you another day."

"She shouldn't have had any days to begin with," Catherine mumbled.

"If you go back, then I won't marry you."

Elizabeth took a deep breath and released her fear. "Very well, Samuel. If that's how you feel, then that's how it must be."

Catherine gasped. "Elizabeth!"

"I don't have peace about putting an end to the Lord's call. Perchance He has more work for me there. I cannot leave them yet."

"Fine." Samuel turned and stomped toward the door.

"Hold on now, Samuel, my boy." Her father tapped the handle of his pitchfork against the floor.

Samuel stopped and faced her father. Hurt and anger shifted across his features.

"There are too many elders who agree with Brother Costin that my Elizabeth should continue. Samuel, my boy, I cannot oppose them and gain their reproach. Ye know that, don't ye now?"

Samuel's scowl deepened into a pout. "They'll do anything for him. He convinces them to do whatever he asks. And now I'll look like the fool."

"Samuel, my boy, what if the Lord's hand is keeping her there longer? How can we meddle with that?"

For a long moment Samuel rubbed his hands on his beard, his gaze fixed on her father.

"Can ye wait for my Elizabeth, my daughter?"

Finally Samuel turned and looked at her, hurt still filling his eyes. "How much longer, Elizabeth? When will you be done with the Costins?"

"I must stay as long as I am needed." Was this truly God's answer to her prayers? Was His hand keeping her there? She could only pray it wasn't merely her emotions from the day.

"Will you give me a time, a day, anything?"

"I can't."

"I won't wait—not without a date." He huffed then turned again.

"Hold on, Samuel, my boy. Hold on," her father boomed. "If ye cannot wait for my Elizabeth, then perhaps ye will be happy taking another of my daughters to wife."

Samuel's back stiffened. He stopped and slowly turned around.

No! Her mind shouted the word. But she couldn't make her lips work to say it.

"What about my Catherine there? She would make a good wife for ye, wouldn't she?"

Catherine gasped and shook her head. "No, Father—"

His stern look silenced her.

Samuel's gaze alighted on Catherine, and his eyebrows lifted.

"My Catherine is younger, but she has been speaking of marriage and has been eager for it."

Dismay widened Catherine's eyes.

Elizabeth knew she ought to say something to thwart her father's plan, anything to keep from losing Samuel to Catherine. But she stepped back against the wall and let the shadows of the room swallow her.

Samuel took in Catherine's fresh young beauty. His eyes widened.

Catherine shook her head, but again their father stopped her with one look.

Elizabeth's heartbeat crashed against her ribs. Surely Samuel would not give her up so easily?

"Think on it, Samuel, my boy. And if ye want to marry my Catherine in place of my Elizabeth, then I will give ye my permission and blessing."

Chapter
19

*H*aven't I served thee well?" Elizabeth prayed. "Haven't I tried to do thy will?"

Her petticoat was damp from kneeling in the long grass wet with dew. But she bowed her head regardless. The dampness was the least of her concerns that Sabbath.

"Will thou not show me thy favor?" she whispered. After all she had done and was doing for God, surely He would bless her. Didn't Scripture promise He would work all things for the good of those who love Him?

"Be thou with me today, Lord."

The faint call of her name wafted through the early morning, but she kept her head bowed.

She oft struggled to find a solitary place. In her sanctuary in the garden, amongst the herbs, she was alone, and she especially needed the time this morn.

Each time she thought of having to stand up in front of the congregation and defend herself from the rumors, embarrassment and humiliation washed through her anew. She could speak about anything else, easily defend herself against anyone. But to speak of intimate relations, adultery, fornication—her face flamed just thinking about it.

She understood why people looked the other way when she walked by and refused to greet her or do business with her. Some said she was John's mistress, others said she was his wife—that secretly she'd married him when Mary was alive, that he'd had two wives at one time. Other rumors claimed Thomas was her babe, born of her womb, and that John had seeded other bastard children from her too.

"Lord, I need your strength. I cannot do this on my own."

Again she heard her name, louder this time.

She lifted her head and opened her eyes. A common blue butterfly flittered around the pink flowers of the hyssop her mother had planted many years before. In the sunshine of the early morning, the plain blue on the butterfly's upper wings looked almost lavender. It landed and folded its wings into their upright position, giving her a full view of the beautiful underside—the white-ringed black spots that contrasted with the brilliant orange marks near its edge.

Was she more like a butterfly than she had given herself credit? She'd always thought of herself as a moth. But maybe she was more like the common blue—ordinary, perhaps even plain from outward aspects. And yet from another view, deeper in, was she complex and colorful?

"Elizabeth!" Anne rounded the side of the bakehouse. The urgency in the girl's voice prodded Elizabeth to her feet.

"There was a fire."

"A fire? Where?" Her heartbeat slammed to a halt. Please, Lord, not the Costins.

Anne sucked in a shaky breath. "The thatcher's wife is dead."

"What do you mean?"

"The old man who rescued you last week. The place where we found you after the attack. His cottage burned to the ground."

Elizabeth's insides collapsed. "And his wife is dead?"

"Killed in the fire."

She stared at Anne's pale face and tried to make sense of what the girl was saying. The Costins were safe, but her relief evaporated in the heat of sudden fear.

"Did you see the thatcher?" Her heart thudded. "Do they know who started the fire?"

Anne shook her head. "The neighbors are claiming it wasn't an accident."

"Oh no." With growing horror she pictured the switch coming toward the thatcher's face, his bare hands yanking it from the cocky young man on the horse. The man's ominous warning that the thatcher would pay for his insolence echoed through her head.

"You think it was him, Elizabeth, the man who hurt you?"

"It had to be."

Elizabeth covered her face with her hands and wanted to groan. If indeed her attacker had taken revenge upon the old thatcher and his kind wife, then she was at fault. She had exposed them to the danger.

"I must go." The ache in her heart pushed her toward the bakehouse. "I need to see for myself."

Her father had already prohibited her from delivering the Sabbath bread today. Now with the news of the murder, she persuaded him to let her go, but only in the company of Henry.

"Henry, this cannot be." She pulled her brother-in-law to a stop in front of the low blackened walls of the thatcher's cottage. The chimney had crumbled into a pile of stones on the hearth, and a charred kettle sat alone among the smoking ashes.

Her throat tightened.

"I need to find out what happened," she said hoarsely.

Henry mumbled under his breath but accompanied her to the neighbor's cottage—its roof torn away, likely in an effort to prevent it from catching the floating sparks of the burning cottage next door.

Neighbors milled about, and when she approached, they greeted her with silence and dark, accusing eyes.

Her footsteps faltered. "Can anyone tell me what has happened?"

For a long moment no one spoke. Then finally a thin man with a soot-blackened face stepped forward. "What else do you need to know? You can see for yourself."

She straightened her shoulders. "Who is responsible?"

"Heard tell the gentleman William Foster paid a couple of no-goods to do in old Bud."

Elizabeth tucked the gentleman's name away. She wasn't familiar with it, but she could easily discover who he was. "And where is the thatcher—Bud—today?"

The thin man shrugged. "After he got home this morning, he didn't stick around too long. He looked real scared. Said something about being next if he didn't flee the town."

Elizabeth's gaze strayed back to the wisps of smoke curling like black fingers out of the ruins of the thatcher's house. Guilt mingled with a new sense of fear. Her attacker had threatened her too. Was it only a matter of time before he came after her again?

∽

By the time they arrived at St. John's, a large crowd had gathered to hear the testimonies. Elizabeth stated her defense of John and herself but wondered if anyone really believed her. Her face burned during the rest of the long service, and she kept her focus in front of her to avoid the curious stares and even disapproving ones, like Mrs. Grew's.

When the service came to a close, Vicar Burton read the banns. "I publish the banns of marriage between Samuel Muddle of the Parish of St. John's and Catherine Whitbread of the Parish of St. Paul's. If any of you know any cause or just impediment why these two persons should not be joined together in holy matrimony, ye are to declare it. This is the first time of asking."

Catherine squirmed next to her and her hands gripped the edge of the pew, her knuckles white.

Their father wasn't forcing her, but he'd made clear his strong desire for Catherine to marry Samuel in place of Elizabeth. Catherine had submitted, but not without the many tears she'd shed in the privacy of the bed they shared. She'd pleaded with Elizabeth every night to change her mind and marry Samuel.

But Elizabeth had turned deaf ears to the girl. She'd made the right decision. Even though she'd always told herself that her match with Samuel was a practical one, she couldn't marry a man who would so easily exchange her for another. And that's exactly what Samuel had done—he'd willingly given her up and now feasted his eager eyes upon Catherine.

Vicar Burton paused and his gaze swept over the congregation. Elizabeth held her breath until he finally nodded and smiled. "You're dismissed."

Elizabeth rose and fought the urge to run from the building. With bowed head she slipped into the aisle and started toward the door.

"Sister Whitbread, wait." John's voice stopped her. Her heart started pumping at twice its speed, and she turned to face him.

Dressed in his meeting clothes, a snug-fitting jerkin over a shirt with a wide falling collar, he looked less like a tinker and more like the famous preacher everyone talked about. His gaze was solemn, made more somber by the dark mulberry dye of his attire.

"Then you won't marry Brother Muddle, not even at summer's end?" he asked softly. He scanned the room with an apparent awareness that everyone was watching them.

She shook her head and realized this was probably the first time John, like many, had heard the news. "Samuel decided he couldn't wait for me. And now it appears he is not too particular about whom he marries. I'm sure he'll be pleased enough with Catherine."

"And you?" His gaze probed her. "Will you be pleased with the arrangement?"

"If he cannot wait, then perchance he's not meant for me." She said the words with a bravado she did not feel. Surely she hadn't thrown away her one chance of having a home and family of her own.

With a sudden gleam in his eyes and the tug of a smile on his lips, John's focus strayed to Samuel. "He most certainly was not meant for you, Elizabeth."

She couldn't smile. John might be able to revel in victory. But what about her? If not Samuel, then who? The question begged for an answer.

His gaze came to rest on her face again. As if sensing her unease, his eyes crinkled with gentleness. "Methinks Samuel had no hope of gaining your affection."

She searched the depths of John's eyes and longing tore at her heart. Could she ever hope to gain his affection?

"You've committed yourself to seeing the Lord's work done now." His voice turned brusque, and he looked away. "There is no greater calling."

"Brother Costin," her father greeted. The tapping of his cane echoed against the barren walls of the church. "I'm sure my daughter, my Elizabeth, is telling ye of the events of the morning. We think we may finally know the culprit behind all the attacks."

"Is that so? Who, then?"

"William Foster," she replied.

"The lawyer William Foster?" John's eyes began to burn like the hot blue flames closest to the fuel.

"The thatcher's wife died in the fire, and his neighbors heard it boasted that Mr. Foster was behind it."

John's jaw flexed. "Foster is smooth on the outside, but underneath he is full of poison."

"Ye said there was a sign on his saddle, did ye not?" Her father patted her arm.

"His coat of arms. A crane clutching a fish."

John's brows furrowed. "I can easily discover whether that is indeed the family emblem of the Fosters. But 'twill not prove he was responsible for the thatcher's fire. He's too shrewd to let any responsibility trace back to him."

"Surely we can make a case with all of the evidence." If she were a lawyer, she could make a case. "The neighbors could testify."

"Foster is a cunning man, married into a powerful family," John said. "We wouldn't be wise to bring such serious charges against him unless we have solid proof. The word of a commoner would hold no sway."

"Then we must find the thatcher?"

John tossed an impatient look at her, as if she ought to know better than to ask such a question. "If Foster is behind the murder, the thatcher would be a fool to stay. If he valued his life, he would be long gone, never to be seen in Bedfordshire again."

The embers of fear inside fanned back to life. "Then 'tis hopeless? He'll do whatever he pleases, torment whomever he wishes, even kill an innocent woman, and no one shall hold him accountable?"

Her father patted her arm again. "Now, Elizabeth, my daughter, I'm sure our Brother Costin will do whatever he can to rectify the situation."

John nodded. "The nobility would do what they can to keep the laborer in his place. They've always had more freedom to do what they wish. The laws that govern the privileged are oft different from those that rule the common man."

Elizabeth couldn't disagree. One was born into a life of wealth and comfort; one didn't choose it; neither did one choose the life of a laborer. Both stations were entered into and accepted as God-ordained.

"We aren't just fighting a battle for religious freedoms," John continued. "We're struggling for human liberty as well. The two go hand in hand. But this is the very issue the wealthy are afraid of. Methinks it's why they are fighting so hard to stop me. If they allow my preaching, then in essence they're allowing the laborer to elevate his position, to upset the status quo, to change a way of life that has existed for centuries."

"Our Brother Costin would do well to put these words to paper." Her father thumped John on the back.

"They're mostly down," John replied. "If not in the myriad of papers scattered across my desk, then surely in the pamphlet soon to be published."

Elizabeth's mind returned to the stolen paper still tucked in the pocket she wore with her everyday apron. She had wanted to confess taking it, to give it back to him, but she hadn't found the right moment. He trusted her as his housekeeper. He believed she was honest and pure. What would he think if he discovered she had lied? And stolen?

Guilt ate at her and would continue to do so until she confessed her sins—first to her heavenly Father and then to John. But how could she do it without ruining the goodwill John felt toward her?

And what if her attacker returned to hurt her again? Would she have need of the paper then?

"Even if we cannot link Foster to any of the attacks yet," John said, stepping back from them, "I'm most glad to have his name. I shall not rest until I've confronted the man and done what I can to learn of his part in the attacks and rumors."

"Very good, Brother Costin. Very good." Her father linked his arm through hers. "In the meantime, we shall have to do our best to keep our Elizabeth safe. Shall we not, Brother Costin?"

"Indeed, Brother Whitbread."

Elizabeth couldn't meet his gaze as he dipped his head and turned to go. Instead, she cast her glance the opposite direction, and it landed upon Samuel Muddle, who had managed to intersect Catherine's path. Now the two stood in the aisle together, Samuel bumbling and eager as he attempted to make conversation with Catherine, whose eye was on the door. No doubt she was wondering how she could make her escape.

Was it too late to switch places with Catherine and marry Samuel after all? Had she been a fool to spurn him? She'd thought she'd done the right thing by staying with the Costins. But what if she'd made a horrible mistake and only made matters worse for herself?

Chapter
20

I knew Father would find a way to keep you safe." Mary fumbled with the laces of Thomas's dress.

Elizabeth knelt with the girl before the hearth for warmth. The coldness of early November seeped through the cracks in the doors and shutters and slid along the floor throughout the small cottage like a phantom, swirling around them.

"Tie it like so." Elizabeth guided the girl's hand.

Mary followed her lead. "Father said he would keep you from more danger, and he did."

Elizabeth wanted to believe the girl. During the passing of harvest, she'd finally stopped looking over her shoulder everywhere she went. She wasn't sure why William Foster hadn't sought her out again. Perhaps he was too busy now with other matters. In September, the Puritans' invincible leader, Oliver Cromwell, had died unexpectedly. Even though his son had taken his place, she'd heard rumors the Royalists were plotting to take leadership away from the Puritans and regain control of England. Certainly Mr. Foster had little time to concern himself with John Costin and his unimportant housekeeper now.

Even the rumors regarding her and John had faded away. And now with winter's nearness, they only lingered in her mind like a bad dream.

"You made the right decision staying with us," Mary said.

"Of course I did, love." Elizabeth helped Mary wind the lace into a long loop. "Of course I did." She forced cheerfulness to her voice and tried not to think of the news Catherine had shared earlier that morning—she was with child.

'Twas no matter Catherine and Samuel had married before summer's end. And it was certainly no matter Samuel's ardent attention had so easily switched away from her and found a receptive home with Catherine.

"I'm learning to dress Thomas well, aren't I?" The girl finished the bow and plopped the baby into her lap.

"You're doing an excellent job." Elizabeth swallowed the lump in her throat, the one that had been squeezing to the surface since she'd seen Catherine.

"When will you teach me how to milk Milkie?"

Elizabeth smiled at the name Betsy had given the cow. To a four-year-old, an animal's name ought to reflect either its color or its purpose, and Milkie had covered both requirements.

"I shall teach you to milk Milkie just as soon as you learn to swift Thomas."

The baby gave a squeal of happiness and grabbed his chubby toes tangled in the flowing fabric of his dress. Elizabeth's heart swelled. She loved the children as if they were her own—especially Thomas. Every day he needed less of Lucy's milk and less of the pap mixture she still fed him. Her fears of Lucy's milk corrupting the babe had been for naught.

Her gaze strayed to Betsy and Johnny where they played with the small butterflies she'd constructed out of twigs and old rags dyed into varying colors. From the other room, John shuffled and thumped around his disorganized desk. He was rarely home, especially in recent weeks. Whenever he was home, he was preoccupied and busy, as he had been all that morning.

"I should surely like to learn to milk the cow," Mary said earnestly, her expression turning serious.

Elizabeth studied the girl for a moment and then brushed her cheek with the back of her hand. " 'Twas not your fault, Mary," she said softly, knowing the girl still blamed herself for her mother's death.

"But it is my fault." Her face constricted and tears formed in her unseeing eyes. "You don't understand what truly happened."

Elizabeth's fingers lingered on the girl's cheek. "What don't I understand, love?"

"I'm to blame for losing the cow."

"Your old cow?"

She nodded. "Mother wasn't feeling well, could hardly get out of bed. I wanted to help her in some way. So I tried to milk the cow . . ."

Elizabeth smoothed loose curls away from Mary's forehead.

"But I made a mess of everything. I couldn't find her udder, and I only made her angry. She tried to kick me. Then her rope came untied, and I didn't know it. When Mother finally realized the cow was gone, she tried searching for it, but she was too weak to go very far."

"You only tried to help."

"But it's because of me and my daftness that Mother became ill." Mary's voice cracked.

"You are not daft, Mary."

A line of tears slid down the girl's cheeks. "After Mother got back from looking for the cow, she came down with her fever."

Elizabeth reached for Mary and gathered her and Thomas into her arms. "Oh, love, you're not to blame for her fever. The fever had nothing to do with her search for the cow."

"But it made her weaker."

"No, Mary, she was already weak. She would have developed the fever whether the cow had gotten loose or not. She had childbed fever. This happens to some women after giving birth."

"But maybe looking for the cow made her weaker. Maybe if she hadn't gone out that day, she would have recovered. Maybe if I could have helped her more, she wouldn't have grown so weak."

Thomas wiggled and Elizabeth switched him into her other arm. Then she drew Mary closer.

"You're taking much upon your shoulders," Elizabeth said, "thinking you are equal to God, having the control of life and death."

Mary sniffed and looked up with confusion in her eyes. "I could never be equal to God."

"Then you must stop taking responsibility for your mother's death." Elizabeth bounced Thomas on her knee. "The power of giving life and taking by death belong to God alone. He won't allow what He hasn't already ordained. And since He fixed the number of days your mother would walk on this earth, neither you nor anyone could do anything to prolong it, not even if you helped in a dozen ways."

Mary was quiet.

Thomas made happy gurgling noises.

"I think I understand what you're saying," Mary finally said. "But I would still like to learn how to milk Milkie."

Elizabeth squeezed her and kissed the top of her head. "You shall learn. Indeed, you shall learn many things, for you are a smart, capable young girl."

"Methinks Sister Whitbread speaks rightly." John's voice startled them.

Mary stood up and smiled in the direction of her father.

Elizabeth's insides fluttered as she raised herself off the floor and turned to face John. She didn't see him oft these days, but when she did, her heart did strange things.

"Elizabeth is instructing me in many tasks and has promised to teach me to milk Milkie."

John stood in the doorway of his study. His gaze turned to Elizabeth, and an unspoken message of gratitude filled his eyes.

"She's already catching on quickly to swifting and dressing the babe." Elizabeth positioned Thomas on her hip. "She can learn much more that will help her get along better in this life."

"I'm indebted to you, Sister Whitbread. I don't know what we would do without you."

Warmth crept into her cheeks, and she tucked his praise into her heart, where she stored his other words. During the long periods when he was too busy to notice her, she would pull them out and savor them like precious jewels.

"Perchance you can help me now." He ran his fingers through his disheveled hair. With dark shadows on his unshaven cheeks, he looked tired, as if he'd had too many restless nights.

" 'Twould be my pleasure to help you."

"I seem to be missing several papers, one of particular importance."

His words hit her like a chill and blew through her, rapidly chasing away the heat. "What do you mean?"

"Either I'm getting more careless with my pages or the mice are eating them. I can never seem to find what I'm looking for anymore."

She must confess about the paper she'd stolen. She'd always had an excuse for putting it off: John wasn't home, he was busy, she was busy. She'd been afraid of Mr. Foster carrying through with his threat.

But she had no excuse now. If he hadn't sought her in these past weeks, surely he had no use for her at the present.

Even though she had smoothed out the sheet and returned it to John's study long ago, the guilt had stuck with her. Her confession to the Lord hadn't been enough.

She had to tell John.

"Maybe with your help, we could bring order to the bedlam of my desk and in the process find what I'm looking for."

Dread plunged through her. How should she start such a confession?

"You've brought order to the rest of the household. If anyone is capable, *you* are the one who could bring light into the dark chaos of my study." He smiled.

She couldn't speak.

He waited and his smile lost its shimmer.

Thomas squirmed. She hoisted him higher on her hip. What should she say?

"I won't be offended if you say no. It's not fair of me to expect you to do more when I have already burdened you with so much."

"No. You haven't burdened me. And I would willingly help you . . . I want to help you . . . But . . ." *Help me, Lord.* "But I don't think you'll desire my assistance once you've learned of my sin."

His smile faded.

She took a deep breath. She had to confess now or she never would. "I stole a paper from you."

He exhaled a low whistle. "You've been stealing my papers? That's why they're missing?"

"No. No. 'Tis nothing like that. I only stole one paper—"

"So I'm not losing my mind." The brows dipped into a scowl. "I haven't been misplacing the papers. You've been stealing them."

"No! You're wrong—"

"I trusted you."

"Please, let me explain. I took only one paper. I took it because I was afraid of Mr. Foster."

At Mr. Foster's name, John glared at her expectantly.

"He wanted information about you—told me to spy. He beat me the first time because I didn't have anything for him. After that I was afraid—afraid of what he would do to me the next time I failed to give him what he asked. So I took it."

"Why didn't you tell me he asked you to spy on me?"

As if sensing the mounting tension, Thomas began to fuss. Elizabeth hefted him around and began patting his back. "At first I didn't believe myself capable of such treachery. But then after I realized what a danger Mr. Foster truly was, I could see no other way to protect myself."

For a long moment John didn't speak. But the disappointment that clouded his eyes and deepened the grooves in his forehead reached across the room and shouted at her.

"You must believe me. I stole only one paper, and I never gave it to Mr. Foster. I returned it many weeks past."

"Perhaps you returned it only to take others."

Elizabeth crossed toward him and stopped when she stood in front of him. "I've no need of late to take any others. And even if I had, I surely learned my lesson with the first."

"I thought you made the decision to work for me because you supported my work."

"I do support you. I made the decision to stay with you because I want to help you." She had given up married life for him. Now Catherine was living the life that could have been hers.

"How can one who supports me steal my papers and give them to my enemies?" The sadness in his eyes made her heart ache. "Perhaps they are paying you to work for me and spy on me. Is that it, Elizabeth?"

"No," she cried out. "I would never do such a thing—"

"How can I trust anything you say now?" The hurt in his voice tore at her.

"You must believe that I don't know where your other papers are. I'll help you look for them—"

"No. Don't step into my study ever again."

"Please, John." Desperation added to the havoc tearing at her heart. Was there nothing she could do to make him see how sorry she was? "I was wrong to take it. I know now I behaved as a coward. I would rather face trials with a clean conscience before God than avoid persecution with sin in my heart."

He sighed and then raked his fingers through his hair.

"I don't deserve your forgiveness, but I'll covet it until you give it."

He was silent for a long moment. "I want to believe you, Elizabeth, I really do. But these are dangerous times, and I have gained many enemies. Even those I once called friends have turned their backs upon me."

Elizabeth wanted to cry out and defend herself. But somehow she knew that nothing she could say would convince him.

"I don't know who to trust anymore," he said. "Not even you."

Chapter
21

$\mathcal{W}$e all think it's time for you to remarry," Gibbs said.

John's stride faltered and he glanced at his friend sitting at the oaken table near the hearth holding one hand toward the low fire. The other arm hung useless, and the shortened sleeve revealed the blunt point of all that was left of his arm.

"So you've been a part of these meetings—the ones I'm not invited to?" John picked up his feet and paced faster. Tension radiated into each hard stomp of his boots.

"The elders of St. John's only invited me to one." Gibbs spoke quietly. Even though they were alone in the rectory of St. Peter and St. Paul, where Gibbs held vicarage, the troubled times urged them to caution.

"So you are turning against me now too?"

"None of us are turning against you, John. We are only discussing the best course of action to keep you and your family safe."

"We are safe." Even if the Royalists were growing more brazen over the past weeks, none of the turmoil had touched his family.

"We all know the Independents are losing power."

John couldn't disagree. Richard Cromwell was failing them. They had hoped once he was in authority, he would prove himself to be a strong leader like his father. But so far, he'd been a marionette in the hands of Parliament. "How many months does he have left?"

"Not many more. Perchance till spring."

"Are there speculations of who will rule the Protectorate then?"

Gibbs shook his head. "It's too soon to tell."

In the many meetings John had attended and amidst the dozens of hushed conversations, no one could predict what the future would hold for the Independents. But everyone agreed that nothing would be the same as when Old Ironsides had been alive.

"I do know it won't get any easier for you, my friend." Gibbs straightened and rubbed his warm hand against the stub of his other arm. "Even our own Independent clergy are grumbling about giving too much freedom to unlicensed ministers."

John had already heard the renewed surge of grumblings. "What can we do?"

"We must be prepared."

"You know I cannot cease doing what God has called me to." John stopped his pacing. "People are hungrier than ever before for the Gospel. Every day when I preach and teach, I see grown men fall to their knees in repentance."

Gibbs nodded. "Your ministry is more effective than ten vicars combined."

"Surely I cannot abandon God's calling, even during the worst of trials."

Gibbs reached his hand back to the low fire crackling on the hearth. He studied the flames for a moment. "You cannot cease. It's true."

John stalked forward again, pacing the length of the shadowed room.

"Should the Protectorate dissolve completely," Gibbs continued, "some are making plans to leave for America."

"I won't flee the tide of persecution. I will suffer aright."

"Perchance God would spare your life and have you serve Him best elsewhere."

"If the call to preach God's Word in America came during times of peace and prosperity, then I would not stand against it. But I could not in good conscience accept such a call during times of affliction, for fear that my desire to escape tribulations dictate my actions."

Gibbs was silent for a moment. Then he sighed. "What you say is true. The Lord surely uses His flail of tribulation to separate the chaff from the wheat."

"Would you leave for New England? If the Protectorate dissolves, surely you'll come under persecution as well."

"I wouldn't leave, my friend. I'm old and wanting." He touched what was left of his arm. "My place is here. My flock is here."

"If you aren't making plans to leave, then why would you suggest it of me? Aren't we made of the same ingredients, you and I?"

Gibbs gave a small smile. "In our hearts, we're brothers in the Lord. But besides that, our circumstances are entirely different."

A quick rebuttal formed on John's lips, but Gibbs silenced him by holding up his hand.

"John, you're young. God has given you a special gift with words and with writing. Your work is just beginning." He arose and then straightened with a wince. "I, on the other hand, have fought the good fight. I'm nearing the end. My wife is gone. My children grown. I don't fear what mortal man may do to me, whether it be prison or even death. I'm ready to be with my Lord, should He bring me home."

His friend's words stirred his blood with passion. "I don't fear what man may do to me either."

"But what of your family, my friend?"

The gentle words stopped him.

"You have young children who would suffer for losing their father. Who would take care of them should you be arrested? Who would provide for them should you die?"

John's first thoughts went to his brother Willie. Willie had always had a compassionate heart and would take his children as if they were his own, even if it meant he would go without to provide for them. Undoubtedly he would go without, for Willie was a poor man, barely able to feed and clothe the family he had. Adding four more would be a hardship—especially a babe and a blind child.

"If you won't plan for yourself, you must at least plan for your children. It's time, John. It's time for you to marry again."

"I don't have the desire for it, neither do I have the time."

"The elders are all agreed and asked me to help persuade you. If not for yourself, then for the children."

John forced his words of refusal down. He thought of his daughter Mary's angelic face framed by dangling golden curls, her beautiful smile, her crystal blue eyes, and her sharp, perceiving mind that saw what her eyes did not. What would happen to this precious blind child if danger befell him? The world would trample her, reduce her to nothing.

The image of her dirty, listless, and begging in the cold pierced his heart.

Gibbs watched him. "It would be best for the children to have a mother to look after them should something happen to you."

Deep inside John knew Gibbs was right. Last spring, before Mary had died, a Royalist judge had threatened him with imprisonment.

Even though his Independent friends had easily reversed the charges, the danger of his unlicensed preaching had become a reality. Mary had been large with child. Had he gone to jail, he would have hated being away from Mary and the children. And yet he would have had a small measure of comfort knowing his wife would take care of the children and home in his absence.

But what would happen now, especially when he was losing the support of some of the influential Puritans? If his enemies were to bring charges against him again, would he have any friends left to come to his aid?

"You are busy, but I think you must make time for marriage now too." Gibbs stepped to the hearth, reached for the poker, and stirred the fuel. The flames flickered higher and cast long shadows.

"You're rarely wrong about anything." Even as he said the words, his body tightened with resistance. "And it's likely you are not wrong about this either."

Gibbs turned and gave him a smile. "Then you'll consider finding a wife?"

John wanted to growl. Instead he began pacing again. "I suppose if the elders have asked you to speak with me, then they have finally grown serious about it." They'd murmured about wanting him to remarry, especially when his enemies had been spreading rumors. But since his confrontation with William Foster, there had been fewer rumors. The man had denied any involvement in the attacks on Elizabeth, claimed innocence regarding the slander, and feigned insult when asked about the thatcher and his wife. Except for the dark look of sin in the man's eyes, John would have believed the man's smooth talk.

"Surely your congregation has many godly young maidens," Gibbs said. "You should have no trouble finding one that's suitable."

John tried to think of the maidens who had vied for his attention, whose mothers had pushed them forward and tried to bring them into his favor. But he could picture only one—his housekeeper.

She was sturdy and strong. They had more provisions for the winter through her resourcefulness than they'd ever had in previous years. She was a hard worker, the kind of woman who wasted little time. Whenever he saw her, she was busy.

There had been times when he'd thought that should he *have* to remarry someday, he'd want to find someone like Elizabeth. Not that he wanted to marry or even planned to, but if and when he *must* marry, he had decided she would make a good wife. Especially because his children already loved her.

More importantly, Elizabeth didn't expect much from him—not his time, nor his attention, nor his affection.

Such a woman would make the perfect wife for a busy man like himself.

"If only . . ." His shoulders sagged with the same disappointment that had burdened him since he'd learned of Elizabeth's betrayal. Even though she claimed to have taken only one of his papers, he continued to lose them. If she'd stolen one, what was to prevent her from taking others?

The ache in his chest pulsed harder. If only she'd remained faithful. If only he could trust her . . .

He shook his head. He couldn't marry a woman he didn't trust, no matter how strong and diligent. Elizabeth Whitbread was not a wifely candidate.

If the elders and Gibbs insisted that he should remarry, then he would have to find someone else.

Too bad he couldn't think of any other woman who'd make a finer wife.

Chapter
22

"I have some delicious gossip." Catherine smoothed a hand over her rounded stomach.

Elizabeth paused in sweeping the crumbs from the table and narrowed her eyes at the girl. "For shame, sister. I won't listen to gossip. Saint Timothy instructs young women not to partake in idle talebearing."

"It's not idle." Catherine had grown more beautiful as the months passed and her body swelled with child. Now as February came to a close, her eyes were brighter, her skin creamier, her body fuller.

A weight of envy settled in the pit of Elizabeth's stomach. Samuel Muddle had been good to Catherine and had done everything he could to make her happy. Perhaps Catherine didn't yet reciprocate Samuel's love, but she had adjusted to being married to him and enjoyed his attention and flattery.

Elizabeth glanced to the hearth, where the men had gathered after finishing their late Sabbath meal. Samuel bent near the flames warming himself, along with her father and Henry. Would Samuel have been as good to her as he was to Catherine? Would she have been happy and expecting her first child?

She sighed and turned her attention to cleaning the long plank table.

Catherine leaned toward her. "I heard it only this morning at the meeting," she said quietly.

"I don't want to hear it," Elizabeth retorted more sharply than she intended. " 'Tis wrong to gossip."

As usual Catherine paid her no attention. Her eyes sparkled as she leaned even closer to Elizabeth. "Brother Costin has been in discussion with Elder Harrington about courting one of his daughters. Lizzie, I suspect."

Elizabeth froze. Ice crusted over her insides as though a snowstorm had blown through her suddenly and without warning.

Catherine smiled. "I knew you would be interested."

"John—Brother Costin is courting?"

"I don't know if he has started courting yet. But Sister Harrington told some of the matrons this morning that Brother Costin had called on them to get permission for courting."

Elizabeth's mouth turned dry, and she could hardly form the words of her question. "It is arranged, then?"

Catherine straightened and situated one hand on her lower back and one on her protruding belly. "To think I once wanted to be the next wife of John Costin." She gave a small laugh. "Now I pity the woman who must marry him."

"Pity?" Elizabeth felt anything but pity. Shock. Despair. And perchance envy. But never pity.

"They said that any woman who marries Brother Costin will find herself soon a widow."

"That's not true." Even though Richard Cromwell was becoming more and more unpopular, and it appeared his short reign as Lord Protector was doomed, Elizabeth could not believe much would change. Her father and Henry both said the Independents still held enough power in Parliament to hold the Protectorate together. They would appoint a stronger leader next.

"Either way, John Costin won't have need of a housekeeper much longer." Catherine's smile turned to a smirk. "What will you do then, sister?"

Feeling the pressure of tears in her eyes, Elizabeth ducked her head.

An intense longing deep inside welled up and burned against her chest and throat. How could John think of marrying Lizzie Harrington? How could he think of marrying anyone except *her*?

Sudden clarity pierced her. She had been waiting for him these past months, since the day he had come to her when she was picking gooseberries—the day he had hinted he would someday want to marry her.

Had she been wrong? Hadn't he said she would do well as a wife? Hadn't he said if he had to marry again, he would want to find someone like her?

That was what he had said, for the words had seared her memory, and she had reviewed and savored them many times since.

Had she perhaps misunderstood him? Had she read more into his words than he'd meant? Panic sent a cold chill through her body.

But he'd shown some regard toward her when he'd crafted the candlestick for her—surely a man wouldn't make so fine a gift for just any woman.

She swiped the last crumbs from the table and let them fall to the floor.

Catherine must be wrong. John could not be getting ready to court someone else.

Her sister said no more about it as they gathered for family worship. No one mentioned it as they reviewed the sermon and as Father taught them from Scripture. As much as she wanted to discover the truth, Elizabeth dared not ask about the rumor, for then she would be as guilty as Catherine of gossiping.

All night she tried to tell herself that Catherine had not heard right and that rumors were never true. The next morning, however, the moment she entered the Costin cottage, thick dread clouded around her. It took only one look at the children sitting at the table to know something was not right. And she had the feeling that *something* had to do with the rumor.

Mary's expression was pale and stricken. Tears lingered in her eyelashes. The muscles in John's jaw and cheeks were taut, and his hair stuck on end. When he saw her, he refused to meet her gaze. Instead, he pushed away from the table and mumbled about having to get an early start in the forge.

When the door closed behind him, Elizabeth didn't move.

"You know, then?" Mary finally asked, rubbing Thomas's back, as if by doing so she could bring comfort to herself.

Elizabeth fumbled with the cuff on her sleeve. "I'm not certain."

"Father's going to marry one of the Harrington girls." Betsy's voice rang with disdain. "And we told him we don't want her for a momma. We told him we want you."

"He is going to marry her?" Fresh despair paralyzed her. "What about the courting?"

"They'll court first." Mary spat the words as she would a bitter herb. "But he's determined to find a new wife."

"We told him we want you," repeated Johnny with sad eyes.

Elizabeth fought the growing panic winding through her body. Why wouldn't he consider her? Surely he remembered what he'd told her. He thought she was strong and diligent and would make a good wife.

"He said he couldn't marry you," Mary continued, "and that we're too young to understand his decision."

"He didn't explain himself?"

"I told him he's making a big mistake, just like when he gave Thomas away to the Birds."

"But did he give any reasons why he didn't want to marry me?"

"He wouldn't say." Mary patted Thomas as he began to fuss. "And I'm *not* too young to understand."

Elizabeth tried to push down the lump in her throat. Her one desire at that moment was to run, run hard and fast to somewhere she could be alone, throw herself down, and give in to the cries begging for release.

She had gambled and lost. She had given up Samuel Muddle, along with the certainty of marriage and a family, for the dangling hope she would be able to marry John Costin instead.

She wanted to marry John.

Moreover . . . she loved him.

Her heart constricted at the admission. She turned her back on the children and brushed tears from her cheeks. She loved the way his eyes lit with passion for his ministry. She loved his courage and his dedication and his zeal. And she'd hoped one day she would be the one to stand beside him and partner with him.

She couldn't imagine anyone else capable of helping him the way she could.

Sister Norton had been right about one thing. The widow had seen the love growing inside her long before she had.

"What will you do?" Mary asked softly. "Will you tell him how you feel?"

Elizabeth wiped her cheeks. She took a deep breath to steady her voice. "Your father is a godly man, children. We'll accept his decision as God's will. And we'll respect and honor it."

Mary scowled.

Elizabeth's throat burned with the effort to keep from crying. "And you know I'll always love you children. Nothing will ever change that."

The rest of the day passed in a haze of pain. She went through the motions of living. Somehow she managed to garner enough strength to gather gorse and roots. But all the while she worked, her heart bled with the anguish of knowing she wouldn't be there to see the fruit of her labor. She wouldn't be with the children to watch them grow. And she wouldn't be the one who claimed John's heart and affection.

When Anne appeared near the end of the afternoon, Elizabeth gazed at her wearily.

Her breath came in jagged gasps, and her face was creased with worry. "Sister Norton is on her way to Lucy's. She asked me to send you and to make sure you bring Brother Costin with you."

A wisp of uneasiness curled through Elizabeth as she realized Lucy had not come to nurse Thomas all day. He had fussed more than usual, but she had attributed it to the possibility that he was cutting a tooth.

Now that Thomas was in his ninth month, his need for nursing had diminished. Lucy came less frequently, but she still came for the small amount of money it brought her.

Elizabeth blew into her cold, red hands. "What is it, Anne?"

"Lucy's in trouble."

"The pillory again?" Elizabeth rose, straightening her petticoat. Had Mrs. Grew found another way to torment the poor woman?

"Fulke beat her," Anne said with a trembling voice. During the time Lucy had lived with Sister Norton and Sister Spencer, Anne had grown to care for the poor woman and her children. But a fortnight past, Fulke had appeared without explanation. After months of being gone, they had come to believe he was dead. Yet he'd tracked Lucy down and demanded she return to him.

They had attempted to convince her to stay with the Sisters. But Fulke had claimed to be a changed man, had promised to treat her better.

It hadn't taken much to sway Lucy back into his arms. When Fulke had secured a place for them to live, Lucy had taken the children and returned.

Elizabeth glanced toward the forge. The clinking of an anvil reverberated within. "We won't bother Brother Costin. I can handle the situation on my own."

"The constable wants him." Anne forced a smile at Betsy and Johnny, who waved at her.

"It must be serious."

"Sister Norton wouldn't say more. But she said it was urgent for you *and* Brother Costin to go."

Elizabeth looked again at the forge and hesitated. Her whole body resisted the idea of facing John.

"You must hurry. I'll stay with the children until you return."

Elizabeth nodded. She took a deep breath of the cool, damp scent of soil and made her way to the forge. When he saw her, he acted as though he would ignore her. But with the news of the constable's request, he laid aside his tools, untied his apron, and departed with her. He said nothing to her as they traversed the muddy streets.

She pulled her cloak tight about her and kept her gaze focused ahead, all the while chastising herself for wanting to look at him and let her heart dwell on his admirable features. With each squelching step her mind throbbed with the reminder she had loved him and lost him.

"Costin," the constable boomed from the dark interior as they approached Lucy's cottage. "There you be."

The crowd parted to make room for them. John ducked his head and entered but stopped abruptly.

Elizabeth pulled up short but couldn't keep from bumping into the broadness of his back. At the contact with his warmth, heat fired to life in her cheeks, and she took a step away.

John held up his arm, cautioning her, keeping her from sidling around him. "I don't want you to come in, Elizabeth." His command was soft yet terse.

She knew she ought to obey him, but annoyance fanned to life amidst all of the hurt that had collected in her heart during the day—annoyance that he had avoided her all day, chosen another woman over her, and now ordered her around as if he had some right over her.

"Sister Norton said I was needed too. You aren't my husband. You have no right to assume control over me."

With a huff, she slipped under his arm and pushed him aside. She squeezed through the doorframe into the crowded one-room cottage. She peered through the dimness and glimpsed Sister Norton holding Lucy's infant.

Then her gaze landed upon Lucy. With a gasp Elizabeth drew back. Nausea gurgled through her stomach and pushed up her throat. Weakness spread through her.

She swayed and the solid strength of John's arms caught her. He grabbed her shoulders and spun her around against his body.

She buried her face in the span of his chest, wanting to block the carnage from her view, from her mind. But the picture of Lucy's bludgeoned corpse sprawled on the floor was branded to her thoughts. Blood seeped from her skull. Matted hair hung in loose clumps away from the scalp. Her bruised and swollen face was almost unrecognizable.

She shuddered with the shock of the brutality.

John's arms wound around her middle, and he pressed her face into his chest. She dragged in a shaking breath of the metallic scent that permeated the fabric of his shirt.

He lowered his head so that his mouth was near her ear. "I told you to wait outside, Elizabeth. I'll handle this." The warmth of his breath tingled her cheek, and she closed her eyes. She was exactly where she wanted to be, in the protection of his arms. How could she ever think about leaving him . . . forever?

He pulled back and stared into her eyes with an intensity that burned down to her soul. "Don't come in again." The blueness of his eyes caressed her face with a gentle concern that made her want to do anything he asked.

She allowed him to guide her around him and out the door. The neighbors moved aside, and she staggered away until she braced herself against the crumbling wall of the cottage next door. She groped the wattle and tried to steady her uncontrollable shaking, not sure if her body was reacting to the chill in the air or the sight of Lucy's body.

It didn't take long for those milling in the crowd to give her the details of what had happened. Fulke had caught Lucy with another man. No one knew exactly who, but they had witnessed a gentleman's horse tied up outside the cottage. Some said they had heard the gentleman beating Lucy, that he was the one responsible for her murder. But others claimed they had heard Fulke raging when he found the man and Lucy together. After the man had ridden away, they'd heard more yelling and screaming and cursing—they were sure Fulke was the one to blame, otherwise he wouldn't have left as rapidly as he had.

As Elizabeth listened, her stomach curdled until she thought she would be sick.

Sister Norton soon stumbled out of the cottage, carrying Lucy's infant in one arm and holding the hand of another of her young ones. Deep lines creased the corners of the widow's mouth, and blue veins crisscrossed her pale skin.

When Sister Norton reached her, Elizabeth lifted the little one from her arms and tucked the babe under the warmth of her cloak. The infant's damp, sour clout left a wet ring on the old woman's bodice.

Elizabeth kissed the chubby cheeks streaked with tears. The child's wet clothes soaked into her too, but Elizabeth hugged her close anyway and brushed the child's tangled hair away from her face.

"The children were crying and wouldn't stop. The sound brought the neighbors in." Sister Norton laid a hand on the head of the small boy at her side. "Poor, poor dears. No one should have to witness such a scene."

"Where are the others?"

"One of the neighbors last saw the older children with Fulke." Sister Norton's eyes drooped. They had become the grandchildren the widow had never had. "I'm taking these poor dears home with me. Until the officials locate Fulke and decide what must be done, I'm prepared to keep them."

"Being with you will bring them much comfort to besure."

Sister Norton smoothed a hand over the infant's cheek. Tears pooled in her weary eyes. "If only I had been more insistent that Lucy remain with us."

"No, Sister." Elizabeth laid a hand on the widow's arm. "Don't blame yourself. You gave her a taste of God's love and goodness. You strengthened and helped her. No one could ask for more."

Sister Norton glanced back to the crowd surrounding the cottage. "If only I could know her soul was with our Lord."

Elizabeth could testify to Sister Norton's efforts to share the saving love of Jesus with Lucy. But the young woman had never shown interest, almost as if life had been too cruel for her to begin to grasp the concept of a God who could care about her.

The infant squirmed and let out a wail.

Elizabeth pulled her closer to her bosom.

Sister Norton would need help.

Elizabeth's heart squeezed with longing for the Costin children. But perchance God was giving her a new calling. The widows could certainly not take care of the young children by themselves and manage to earn the little they lived on. They would benefit from her help.

Her calling to help the Costins would soon end. That had become painfully clear that day.

Was God now providing an opportunity for her somewhere else?

Chapter
23

*J*ohn riffled through the papers the constable had given him. His fingers glided along the tattered crease of one stained sheet until he reached the scrawl of smudged words—his words written in his messy handwriting, and the constable had recognized them as such.

He tossed the sheets onto his desk. Then he leaned back in his chair and crossed his hands behind his head. The disarray of his study was greater than usual and matched the tumult that had ransacked his mind the past few days since the death of the wet nurse.

He didn't need to check whether any more of his papers had disappeared. Indeed, he wouldn't need to worry about his papers disappearing ever again. He couldn't find the energy to be angry at the wet nurse for having stolen from him these past months. All he could feel for her was pity. She'd likely taken them to protect herself, but in the end it hadn't helped.

His mind flashed to the image of her body, the awkward tilt of her head on the floor, her blood forming a sticky puddle in the dirt. His gut tightened. Could he have done something more to save her?

The tinkle of laughter outside tugged his gaze to the oilskin window. The children skipped around Elizabeth as she knelt with Mary near Milkie. She patiently positioned the girl's hands upon the cow's teats, then sat back on her heels to watch Mary, encouraging and instructing her.

His gut twisted. She was truly a godly and loving woman. And any man would be blessed to call her *wife*.

"Oh, Lord. What have I done?" The wrinkled papers stared at him and pointed an ugly finger of accusation in his face. He'd been a sot for refusing to believe Elizabeth's plea of innocence. He should have known he could trust her. Hadn't he learned that by now?

He sat forward and slapped his hands on his desk. And now he was all but married to the Harrington girl. He'd begun the courtship over the past weeks, and even though it had comprised of nothing more than partaking of a few meals with her family, he could not breach the agreement now.

With a groan he slid the returned papers underneath another stack. Then he picked up his pen and dipped it into the ink. If he worked on his pamphlet, perhaps he would be able to forget— forget his frustration with himself, forget about the young woman outside the window, and forget about the fact that she would soon leave their family.

He poised the pen above a fresh paper, but his mind was suddenly devoid of any thoughts save the one of Elizabeth's wide eyes filled with horror when she'd turned away from Lucy and let him gather her into his arms.

If he was completely honest with himself, he had to admit the bloodied corpse of the wet nurse had terrified him. He couldn't stop thinking *What if it had been Elizabeth instead?*

He fingered the tattered edges poking out from the stack. He couldn't shove the stolen papers aside and forget about them any more than he could shove aside his fears and frustration.

He turned and glanced out the window again.

William Foster was stalking across the yard toward Elizabeth.

A burst of anxiety and anger ripped through him, and he sprang to his feet. What did that evildoer want with Elizabeth now?

His blood pumped hard with the need to get to her. He tripped over the clutter littering his study and stumbled through the cottage. Foster had hurt Elizabeth before. And now that Lucy was gone, was he back to harass Elizabeth?

John slammed open the door and charged around the cottage, his blood pulsing hotter with each pounding step.

"Foster!" he called as he sprinted into the back.

Annoyance flitted across Foster's countenance before he had the time to hide it. More disturbing was the sharp lust in the man's eyes directed at Elizabeth.

"John Costin," he greeted with a thin smile that lacked warmth. "I didn't realize you were home this afternoon."

"What are you doing here, Foster?"

Elizabeth's face was pale and her body rigid. But she had lifted her chin and straightened her shoulders as if she would stand up to Foster and face danger without flinching.

The fire of his temper heated and combusted with all the worry and frustration he'd felt over the past days. Elizabeth would be no match for a man like Foster. He would do what he wanted with her and then beat her senseless, just as he had likely done to the wet nurse. Although the constable had no proof to link Lucy's death to Foster, John didn't doubt he played a role in it.

"What do you want?" John stopped before the man, and his fist contracted involuntarily with the desire to slam his face.

247

"No need for hostility." Foster tucked his riding whip through his belt. "I was merely delivering a message."

"Don't go near Sister Whitbread again. You have issues with me, not her."

"Possessive, are we?" Foster raised an eyebrow. "There will come a day when you won't be around. Then I shall have my turn."

"State your business, Foster." John braced his shoulders, ready for battle. If the man didn't leave soon, John would dishonor the Lord by his violence.

Foster tipped his hat back and revealed more of his face. Even though his expression was placid like the surface of a pond, a poisonous serpent lurked beneath and swam in the murkiness of his soul.

"Word has arrived that the Royalist Army is in London."

John had already received the news that morning. It signaled severe trouble—possibly the abolishment of the Protectorate, certainly the end of Richard Cromwell's leadership. The Puritans could only hope that somehow they could manage to sway the rump Parliament, still largely Presbyterian, to find a new leader supportive to their Independent cause.

"In good conscience I could not pass without warning you, out of brotherly concern, of course." The sharp swords in the man's eyes slashed at John. He had no doubt William Foster would rather see him suffer than save him.

"Instructing people to forsake their sins and close in with Christ is not a crime now and will never be."

"Very soon we shall find only those properly trained and sent forth by the bishop doing such instruction."

John lifted himself to his full height. If Foster wanted a verbal battle, then he'd get one. "A call from God and fire in the soul cannot be kept within the bounds of a bishop's license or statutes at large."

"What does a tinker know of such weighty matters as callings and fire in the soul?" Foster's gaze slid to his tinker shack and the places where the wattle and daub walls had fallen away. "If a tinker can preach, then who will stop the illiterate laborer in the field from preaching? Who will be able to stop anyone who says he has a *calling* from blaspheming and distorting the Word?"

"If such a man was to receive the gift, even so let him minister the same."

Foster's gaze lingered overlong on the cow's post and the boards falling to the ground.

Elizabeth had used the time of their interchange to move away and had gathered the children. Now they clung to her petticoat, watching Foster with wide eyes.

"God gave you the gift of mending pots, John Costin," Foster said. "You'd be safer to stick with what you know."

"And you would be safer if you took your leave now and never came back."

Foster glanced at Elizabeth.

John's fingers tensed into tight fists, and he took a step toward Foster.

The man backed up and started to stride away. "It won't be long, Costin," he called over his shoulder, "till you'll finally be forced to stay in your place."

John stared at Foster's back until he disappeared around the cottage. He could only pray the man wasn't right.

"What did that snake really want?" he asked, turning to Elizabeth. He uncurled and stretched his fingers, his body tense with anger.

"He didn't have the chance to say." She gave Betsy and Johnny comforting hugs and then nudged them back to their play. " 'Tis no doubt he wanted me to spy again," she said quietly, once they had run off. "I'm just glad you were home."

Sudden helplessness overwhelmed John. Elizabeth very well could have been home alone, and Foster could have done anything he wanted with her, as he'd done with the wet nurse. With a groan, he stuck his fingers into his hair.

"Please," she rushed. "I have not stolen again, nor will I. My life isn't so valuable on this earth that I would sin to save it."

"No, Elizabeth. I know you won't steal." Now he understood why she had taken his paper. She had needed something—anything—to try to protect herself from Foster. And once again she needed a way to stay safe. But how could he protect her?

"Truly, I promise you. I won't take from you again. I learned the lesson God had for me—"

"I know you learned, and I know you won't take again."

"I— What did you say?"

Shame washed over him. He'd been too hard on her; he hadn't listened to her. As usual, he'd let his temper have control. In God's eyes, his quick judgment had been no less sinful than her stealing. Perhaps his was worse, for he'd harbored pride and unforgiveness in his heart these past months when she'd shown humility and repentance.

"You weren't the one taking the papers," he said.

"I wasn't? I mean, you believe me now?"

"I know it wasn't you."

"How?"

"The constable found some of the missing papers on the wet nurse."

Elizabeth nodded, as if the news made perfect sense. "She would have been easy prey for Mr. Foster."

"His horse was at the cottage the day of her murder."

She shuddered. "Now I know why he has left me alone these past months. He had someone else doing his evil deeds."

John folded his arms across his chest and watched the play of emotions on Elizabeth's face. He was sure she was thinking the same as he was. Now that the wet nurse was dead, was today's confrontation with Foster a foreshadow of what was to come? Would he harass Elizabeth again?

She met his gaze directly. Her eyes filled with determination. "God is my shield and my protector. Whom shall I fear?"

He liked the color of her eyes. It was unusual—like the gray of stones, strong and unshakable.

" 'Twill not be much longer either," she said hesitantly. A rosy hue flushed the cream of her cheeks.

"Not much longer?" A breeze gently lifted the loose strands of her hair and caressed her neck with them.

"With courtship underway, you won't need me many more weeks. 'Twill not be long before you have a wife."

Her words splashed against his face like thawed river water on a spring day. He took a step back, as though somehow he could avoid the reality of what she'd said.

But reality stalked him as it had the past days since Lucy's death. He was bound to marry another woman. He'd already made an agreement with Elder Harrington. It didn't matter that he couldn't remember the girl's name, that he didn't know anything about her except that she was young and pious. He'd given his word that he would marry her, and now he must follow through or lose the respect of the community.

His insides twisted, and he tore his gaze away from Elizabeth.

He focused instead on Mary, holding tight to Thomas's leading strings, laughing as she followed slowly behind him. The infant toddled in the matted grass, held to his unsteady feet by the lengths of fabric attached to the back of his dress.

The boy's cheeks were flushed, his eyes bright, and his smile as wide as a sunlit meadow. A pang shot through John's heart. Thomas would soon reach the first anniversary of his birth—something he'd never dreamed would happen.

Elizabeth's steadfastness had saved the baby. Her devotion and determination had held his family together, made them stronger, helped his ministry thrive. How would they get along without her?

The aching swirl in his gut tightened. He'd been a fool to let her go.

"Methinks you will need to steal from me again."

"No. Never."

"Yes. Stealing is the best way to keep Foster from harming you." The least he could do was keep her safe in the remaining weeks.

She straightened her shoulders. The gray of her eyes had turned to polished iron. "I have promised, and I won't break my word."

"What if I steal papers from myself and give them to you? You wouldn't be breaking your word then, would you?"

She started to respond, then stopped and raised her brows.

He forced his lips into a grin.

Understanding dawned in her eyes.

"And I would know which are the best papers to steal, since they are my own. This might even be the occasion to write a few more especially convicting sermons about rich men abusing the poor. These would be the best to steal, don't you agree?"

Elizabeth smiled. " 'Twould be a good opportunity to preach to Mr. Foster about the sinfulness of his ways."

"Indeed it would."

Her smile was fresh and guileless and reminded him of the godly woman she truly was. Certainly she was not perfect—stealing his paper had shown that. But she was humble and upright in heart.

"I'm sorry for not believing you earlier." He couldn't keep his gaze from lingering on the tendrils of her hair dancing about her face.

"No, 'tis I that offended you. Though I don't deserve it, I still covet your forgiveness."

"I give it to you now and am sorry I didn't give it long ago."

"Thank you."

He nodded, feeling something inside that he shouldn't toward

Elizabeth—something he hadn't felt in a very long time—a warmth, a thawing, the beginnings of a desiring.

As if sensing that something in him, she ducked her head and focused on the cuff of her sleeve.

The strange stirring made him want to draw nearer to her. By the shy lowering of her lashes and the pink innocence of her cheeks, he realized she didn't know the effect she was having upon him. She wasn't trying to ensnare him nor was she flirting with him. She was completely unaware of the freshness and vitality of her womanliness, and that only added to her allure.

Elizabeth Whitbread was an appealing woman, and as his eyes drifted over her, he wondered that in the many months she had worked as his housekeeper, he had never noticed it.

He shook his head. It was neither fair to Elizabeth nor to the Harrington girl for him to entertain such desirings. He would do best to put such thoughts of Elizabeth far from his mind.

For the fraction of an instant, he pictured himself pounding on Elder Harrington's door, barging inside and blurting out that he'd changed his mind, that he no longer wanted the man's daughter.

But as quickly as the thought came, he shoved it aside—angrily. The repercussions would only stir up dissension, damage his ministry, and bring disgrace upon himself and Elizabeth.

He'd already made his choice. Now he needed to live with the decision—as frustrating as that might be.

Chapter
24

*T*he pungent smell of onion burned Elizabeth's nose and eyes. The knife made sharp chops against the table and the shriveled roots, the last of what she had stored from the previous fall harvest. With rapid slices, she diced them for the pottage of dried peas and barley bubbling in the pot.

"I'm past ready for fresh vegetables again," she said.

"Me too," Betsy replied from her spot on the floor with the other children.

The rumble of thunder sounded in the fields beyond the cottage, and Elizabeth glanced to the open shutter, hoping the rain would wait until Mary returned from milking the cow. 'Twould not be easy for Mary to carry the small pail of milk back to the house on slippery ground.

"Mary better hurry." Elizabeth chopped steadily. "If she wasn't so stubborn about doing it herself, I'd send you to help her, Betsy."

"She doesn't like my help with anything." Betsy flipped a cloth ball into a wooden cup. "Thomas doesn't know how to play the game."

Elizabeth had sewn together stuffed straw balls for each of the children. Then she'd tied string to the balls and to the handles of their mugs and shown them how to toss the balls up and try to catch them inside.

She smiled as Thomas stuffed the ball in the mug, then dumped it out, stuffed it back in, then dumped it out again, repeating the motion over and over. "Thomas is indeed having a grand time, even if he isn't following the game."

Elizabeth scooped the cut onions onto a wooden platter, turned to the boiling pottage, and scraped them into the pot. With a long-handled ladle, she stirred the onions into the thick greenish-gray gruel.

She would soon be finished with her housekeeping job. 'Twould not be many more days before her leaving—at least if Catherine's latest gossip was true. If so, John would trothplight to Lizzie Harrington by week's end and post the banns not long after.

With a sigh, she lifted a spoonful of pottage and blew on it. She'd tried to resolve herself to the inevitable, but she couldn't muster up fervor for helping the Sisters take care of Lucy's orphans. Nigh three weeks had elapsed since Lucy's death, and they hadn't seen any signs of Fulke. The widows would benefit from her help. Surely God was giving her a new calling.

Why, then, couldn't she embrace it with joy?

She sipped the pottage then dipped the ladle back into the pot and stirred.

The door, already open a crack for Mary, squeaked as it opened wider.

"How did you fare?" She banged the spoon against the edge of the pot and then moved the pot hook, swinging the kettle away from the flames to keep it from burning.

"How I fare will depend on you."

Elizabeth jumped and dropped the ladle. It landed on the floor with a clatter. Her fingers shook as she slipped them into the pocket under her apron and felt for the paper she had tucked there.

William Foster's boots tapped sharply against the cottage floor. Fear slithered through her, but she squared her shoulders and turned.

He swept his wide hat from his head, revealing his cold smile.

"Go away, Mr. Foster. You aren't welcome here."

"Now, Elizabeth, is that any way to treat someone who has the power of your life and death?"

She lifted her chin. "What do you want?" Her heart whispered a desperate plea to the Lord for strength.

"Oh, I want many things." His footsteps echoed as he slowly, deliberately, began closing the gap between them.

She slid toward the table, anxious to keep a barrier between them.

"With the other wench dead, someone has got to do my bidding."

She fumbled at the strings of her pocket and pulled out the sheet John had given her. With trembling fingers she shoved it across the table toward him. "There. Now leave."

Guilt seeped through her as she watched him pick up the paper and stuff it into his doublet without so much as a glance. Even though giving him the decoy had been John's idea, her heart agonized over the thought of giving the man anything.

Mr. Foster laid his hat on the table across from her and began tugging at the fingertips of his leather riding gloves.

"You have what you came for. I must insist that you take your leave."

One finger at a time he continued loosening his gloves. "I don't yet have everything I want." He raised his gaze to her, the lust in his eyes unmistakable.

Fear coiled tighter and pinched the breath from her.

"You're more comely than the other wench."

From the look in his eyes, she understood then the depths of his evilness, the vileness with which he had treated Lucy. She wondered that Lucy had never given any indication of the abuse she had received from Mr. Foster. She supposed Lucy was so accustomed to having one man hurt her that she couldn't resist another.

He slid a glance to the children, who watched him with wide eyes. "I suggest we conduct the rest of our *business* in the other room."

"We have no other business, Mr. Foster. You have all you'll get from me this day."

His smile faded. "If you knew what's best for you, you'd do as I say."

She took a deep breath to quell her shaking. Then she saw the knife lying on the table, bits of onion still clinging to its blade. Without thinking, she lunged for it, grasped it between both hands, and held it out before her.

The blade glinted. The tip was sharp, even if the long edge was dull.

Mr. Foster glanced around the room as if searching for another weapon.

"If *you knew* what was best for you, you'd take your leave." She tried to keep her voice and hands from quivering.

Fury darkened his eyes, and his lips pinched together in a tight line. "You are a foolish girl. A very foolish girl."

"I'm not like Lucy. You can't push me into immoral deeds."

"You're a fool to resist me."

"I'd rather die than submit to your evil intentions."

Again he searched the small room. This time he spotted the broom near the hearth.

He darted around the table toward it.

Elizabeth backed toward the children and held the knife out in front of her.

"You would rather die?" He grabbed hold of the broom. "Then I shall grant you your wish."

She stood near the children, her body tense, her mind whirling. She would be no match against him should he come at her with the broom.

He thrust the end of the broom into the low flames on the hearth and the fresh straw burst to life.

Her heart slammed hard in her chest, and she pointed the knife at him.

Strangely, however, he walked away from her, grabbed his hat and gloves from the table, and headed for the door. When he reached the doorway, he swung it open and turned to face her. "No one crosses me without paying for it."

The straw was burning fast, the fire leaping up. She cringed as the flaming end of the broom came within inches of the doorframe. If he wasn't careful, the fire would spread.

"I'm sure you remember what happened to the thatcher and his wife." He glanced sideways at the burning broom.

Her eyes were riveted on the crackling, sparking fire.

"No!" With a scream she rushed toward him.

But he was too quick. In an instant he was outside and slammed the door shut.

She yanked it and heaved on the handle. "Please, open the door! Please!"

The clinking of a chain scraped against the planks of the door.

Her frantic heartbeat sputtered. She glanced toward the window. It was high, but they could surely escape through it.

She started forward, but he slammed the shutters closed before she could reach them.

Darkness shrouded the room and descended over her soul.

"The children!" Her chest heaved and fear made waves through her. "Please let the children out! They've done nothing to deserve this!"

Thomas's cries were shrill and incessant.

The thump of something hitting the roof was followed by the sound of horse's hooves galloping away.

With pounding heart she stared up through the cracks of the floorboards of the loft. For an instant, paralyzing fear gripped her. She had the oddest feeling she had already experienced the situation and was reliving a nightmare. She imagined the scorching heat surrounding her and the long fingers of the flames reaching out to grasp her. She backed toward the wall, desperate to escape their grip.

In a daze she searched the room for a place to hide. Through the open door of the bedchamber, the bed beckoned her to the dark, shadowed place underneath. A dreamlike haze urged her to find safety in the black cavern there.

Somewhere in a distant corner of her mind she heard crying—the frightened, pitiful cries of a small child, endlessly calling for a mother and father.

The yanking of her petticoat wrenched her mind back to the present.

"Did he leave?" Johnny looked up at her with innocent, trusting eyes. His fist grasped the folds of her skirt.

Elizabeth looked first at him and then at Betsy, who was trying to console Thomas. She blinked hard and tried to understand what was happening.

Murder. William Foster was murdering her.

He had locked her into the cottage and had thrown the burning broom onto the roof. Though the thatch was damp with recent rains, the rye yelms would still burn and the flames would spread— albeit more slowly—and would eventually reach the mud-twig walls and easily burn the entire cottage to its foundation, taking them with it.

Just like the thatcher's wife.

They would be roasted alive. A cold shudder rippled through her.

"Lord, won't you spare these precious children? Take me, if thou must. But please spare these little ones."

Thomas's wails had grown wilder. Elizabeth dropped the knife on the table, hurried to the infant, and drew him to her bosom. She pressed her lips against the silkiness of his hair and then against the sweet roundness of his cheek. Murmuring words of comfort in his ear, she hugged him tightly and rocked from side to side.

His cries subsided and his body relaxed. He fully trusted her and believed she would protect him. He was too young to understand how fleeting his safety was, that ultimately he would die if she didn't do something.

She glanced through the ceiling cracks again and saw thin wafts of smoke filtering into the loft.

If only she could get help . . . get someone to open the door . . .

Her mind flashed to Mary outside milking the cow.

"Children, come with me." Her voice was sharper than usual, and their eyes grew frightened once more.

Mary could go to the neighbor's.

"Come with me quickly." She herded them toward John's study, and as she passed the table she picked up the knife.

The children hesitated at the door of their father's forbidden closet. Elizabeth didn't have the fortitude to explain that much more was at stake than their father's anger. "He'll understand," she reassured them.

She used the knife to cut through the oilskin covering bound tightly across the window. After a few minutes of jabbing and slicing, she opened a hole.

She peeled back the tear and peered toward the forge.

Mary's milking pail sat next to Milkie, but she didn't see the girl anywhere.

"Mary!" With each call her voice grew hoarse and the tension inside tightened.

Finally, in desperation she stabbed the oilskin, yanked it, wrenched it wide enough to fit the children through.

At last, with sweat beads slicking her forehead and her chest heaving from her efforts, she reached for Betsy. The girl offered no resistance when Elizabeth stuffed her through the hole. She was thankful the girl was obedient and daring enough to follow her instructions without questioning or crying.

"Go to the forge," she ordered from the window once all three were safely outside. "Go there and don't leave. Do you understand?"

Betsy nodded and pulled on Thomas's leading strings.

"Don't leave for any reason." With tears on their cheeks, they hastened to obey. "Betsy, you must watch Thomas and Johnny. They're your responsibility. You're to wait in the forge with them until help arrives."

She watched until they disappeared inside the forge. Then she stood back and stared at the hole in the oilskin. The window was too small for her to fit through. Even if she managed to chop away more of the skin, she wouldn't be able to squeeze through the opening. Her mind whirled at a dizzying speed and passed by all the possible escape routes again. Finally, her thoughts screeched to a halt.

Only one thing was certain.

There was absolutely no way to get out of the house.

She was trapped.

Chapter 25

*A*ll that mattered was that the children were safe.

Smoke from the burning thatch permeated the cracks in the loft floor. The haze was just a cloud, high and hovering. But Elizabeth's body shriveled at the thought that the smoke would begin to push lower until eventually she wouldn't be able to breathe.

She watched it swirl above her. Perhaps the smoke would kill her first. Then she wouldn't have to experience the pain of having her flesh burned.

A shudder made a trail to her knees and threatened to buckle them underneath her weight. "Lord, please send help."

She lived to please the Lord, to serve Him, to do His will. Would He let her suffer this way? Surely not. Surely He would reward her for her faithfulness. Didn't He promise to take care of those who served Him well?

With her back against the wall, she slid to the floor. The flames crackled in the thatch, and the scent of damp smoke permeated her senses. The neighbors would see the flames and smoke by now too. They would come to help.

She crawled to the door and banged it with her fists. "Help! Someone help! Please let me out!"

The shouts in the street were faint. Even if they saw the fire, would they be able to get past the chain on the door and free her from the burning inferno before it was too late?

Smoke poured over the rafters near the ladder and began to bathe the room with thick grayness. It rolled across the ceiling, and panic sprouted out of fear and urged her to hide.

Her mind screamed with the need to find a safe place. She fixed her eyes on the bedchamber door and the dark place under the bed, but she couldn't make herself move. Her arms and legs were paralyzed. For a long instant the room swirled before her. She was sure she was dying.

Then her raging heartbeat gave way to a shaky, unsteady feeling. A clammy sweat dampened her hands and head, and she found herself scrambling forward on hands and knees toward the bedchamber.

In seconds she made it to the bed and began shoving crates and baskets out of the way. When she had cleared a big enough space, she crawled underneath.

Clods of dust and cobwebs itched her sweaty face. Loose mattress feathers and dried insects stuck to her forehead. She rested her cheek against the cool boards and took a deep breath of the mustiness. The pounding of her heart echoed in the stillness.

She'd heard accounts of the day the Royalist army had ridden through Bedford during the Civil War, killing and maiming and setting fire to the town. She'd only been an infant, too young to remember anything. But the soldiers had murdered Robbie that day.

She'd heard her mother talk about that dreaded day often enough. Her mother had blamed herself for not better protecting Robbie when the Royalist soldiers had turned onto High Street. Their father had been away delivering bread to the parliamentary army, and her mother had been large with child and nearing birthing time. She'd had three young children to protect, and she'd been knocked unconscious during the rampage. But none of the excuses mattered. She'd held herself responsible for the soldier's blow that had taken the life from her son.

The bakehouse had been one of the businesses nearly burned to the ground. If it hadn't been for the quick thinking of neighbors, they all would have perished in the fire. A few brave men had pulled their unconscious mother from the flames and managed to find her and Jane under one of the beds.

Elizabeth choked on a sob. She prided herself for being a strong woman and not succumbing to fear and disaster. Her mind told her she ought to climb out from under the bed and face the fire with bravery and integrity instead of cowering like a child. But dread nailed her to the floor.

A sudden banging and shouting at the door startled her.

Her heart thudded forward with hope. "Help! In here. Under the bed. Help!"

The door cracked under the battering and shook the walls of the cottage. The fierceness of the pounding grew until at last a splintering noise reverberated through the dwelling.

"Elizabeth!" John shouted from the main room.

A sob slipped from her lips.

"Elizabeth!" His voice was frantic. "Where are you?"

"Here! I'm here!"

Footsteps slapped the floor and gave way to a fit of coughing.

She knew she should slide out from the bed and show herself, but she couldn't make her body work.

"Elizabeth! Where are you?"

265

She clawed at the floor to propel herself out of her hiding place, but her body wouldn't obey her mind.

His heavy boots stomped into the bedroom.

"John!" she cried.

A moment later he was down, flat on his stomach, his eyes probing the shadows. He reached out a hand and grabbed her arm. "Thank the Lord. Can you move?"

"I'm too frightened."

His grip tightened and he slid her out, even as everything within her resisted. He was too strong, and in an instant she was out.

The heaviness of the smoke assaulted her, and she could hardly see John through the haze.

Bright flames danced amidst pieces of falling thatch. She cowered and looked back to the dark recess under the bed. Fear urged her to go back.

He shielded her with his body, and his strong hold on her arm prevented her escape to her hiding spot. "Trust me, Elizabeth. Grab hold of my neck."

He bent nearer until his face was only inches from hers. The intensity of his eyes and the depth of his determination breathed life into her.

She reached her arms around his neck and buried her face in the safety of his chest.

He staggered to his feet, lifting her into his arms.

Immediately the thickness of the smoke surrounded them, and the heat of the flames above pressed down.

She held her breath and crushed her face against him.

He lurched forward, half running, half lunging toward the smashed door. He crashed through the splintered boards and would have fallen if one of the neighbors hadn't caught and steadied him. The man swatted burning wisps of thatch from John's back and helped him stumble to a safe distance down the street.

John gasped for a fresh breath and sank to his knees.

His arms trembled against her, but instead of releasing her, he pulled her against him even tighter. In an instant his lips grazed her forehead.

The softness and warmth of the pressure went all the way to her heart and set it fluttering with a strange longing. His mouth moved to her ear. "I thought I'd lost you." His hoarse whisper was threaded with desperation. The heat of his breath caressed the sensitive skin of her neck.

"Elizabeth!" Anne cried. "Oh, Elizabeth, you're safe!"

Anne and Sister Norton pushed against them, and neighbors surrounded them, but their voices and questions came to her from a distance. For a long moment John's rasping breath was the only sound in her world.

Her sister reached for her, but John tightened his hold.

"Are you hurt?" he asked, the bright blueness of his eyes racing across her face.

"No more than you." Her own breath came in heavy gasps.

His gaze stopped its frantic search and hovered upon her lips.

She couldn't keep her own gaze from straying to his mouth. She could almost feel the soft brush of his lips upon her forehead again, and the remembrance swirled that strange ache in her stomach, but this time into a current too fast for her innocent heart to understand.

"The neighbor's house is on fire!" The shout came from nearby and pulled Elizabeth back to the reality of the inferno raging behind them.

"The children?" Fear strangled her words.

"They're safe," Anne reassured her.

"It's a good thing Mary got help when she did," said Sister Norton, shaking her head. Their gazes followed hers to the thatch of the neighboring cottage. A crowd of men had begun ripping at it to keep it from burning the entire structure to the ground.

Their cries of alarm loosened Elizabeth's paralyzed tongue,

and she struggled to break free of John's hold. " 'Tis all my fault. I must help them."

"No. Don't go anywhere near the cottages." His harsh command halted her. When his gaze swung back to hers, the possessiveness in the depths of his eyes brought her heart to a stuttering stop.

Warmth seeped into her blood and gave her the sensation of flittering on a gentle breeze. She'd never had a man cherish her before, but what she saw in his eyes came as close as she'd ever seen to love.

Was it possible to believe John cared for her? Now, when it was too late to matter?

"Get the children and go to your father's house," he said more gently. His gaze caressed her face. "And stay there until I come for you."

Her throat constricted and tears stung her eyes.

Anne reached for her again, and this time John released her into the young girl's arms.

Only when he turned away and began to weave through the crowd did a tear slip out and make a cold trail down her cheek.

"Are you hurt?" Anne's hands fluttered over her and swept the loose hairs away from her forehead.

"No." The word was out before she realized how untrue it was. She grasped her chest and fought against the pain pulsing upward to her throat.

Oh, what she wouldn't give to have his heart for her very own.

⁓

Later, in the back room of the bakehouse, near the warmth of the hearth, Elizabeth cradled Johnny under one arm and Betsy under the other. Their eyes drooped in the first signs of sleep.

The hum of voices in the room and the patter of rainfall outside the back door had soothed her aching heart only a little. The darkness of the evening had settled. The glow of the candles and the fire bathed the room with soft light, and she tried to find solace in the thought that God had spared her life and protected the children.

From her spot on the floor with her back against the wall, she had the perfect angle for watching John without his knowing. He sat at the table with the other men—her father, Vicar Burton, and elders who had gathered to console John as well as give advice. John's brother, Willie, had also come and offered to make room in his cottage for John and his children.

Elizabeth watched the way the flickering candlelight enriched the red hues of John's hair and how it cast shadows over his cheek and chin, highlighting the strong angles of his face. Every time her gaze strayed to his mouth, to his lips, she imagined them against her forehead.

Even though John hadn't been chaste, she wasn't sorry he'd given her the feathery kiss on her brow. Whether he'd done it out of relief or gratitude or a momentary lapse of sanity, she didn't know.

Whatever the reason, she couldn't stop thinking about the brief moment of intimacy and the way he'd looked at her—the affection in the depths of his eyes. Surely she hadn't imagined it this time.

When finally Willie stood to leave, John rose with him. "You're sure I cannot convince you to come stay with Sarah and me?" Willie asked.

John shook his head and stretched his hands above his head. "Mayhap in time. But methinks for this night, the children would be better warm and dry here. They will feel secure with Elizabeth."

Her father had offered their home to John and the children. Although John had insisted on returning to the cottage remains and sleeping in the forge, he'd wanted the children to stay with her.

John glanced her way, to the faces of the children, to her fingers gently combing their hair. Then his gaze traveled up to intertwine with hers.

His eyes were dark and troubled.

The ache in her heart swelled again.

"This is the second time in her life my Elizabeth was pulled from the flames." With a grunt her father pushed himself up from his bench. His cane thumped hard against the floor. "I'm indebted to ye, John."

"No, I am indebted to you, Brother Whitbread," John said without breaking his gaze from her. "You've entrusted your daughter into my care these many months—despite the danger I've brought her."

"God has indeed protected her." Her father's voice trembled. "He has miraculously spared her life these many times. And I cannot help but think our almighty Lord has a special purpose for her."

Something in John's eyes reached out to her, and her heart pattered erratically.

Willie looked from her to John. He studied John's face before he broke into a wide grin. "I believe God is giving us a sign."

At his words, silence descended in the room, as if the voice of a prophet had spoken.

Willie thumped John on the back. "God's trying to show you that He wants you to be with Elizabeth Whitbread. Why else would He keep preserving her life, if not to be your helpmate?"

The steady tap of rain filled the silence.

His words sank to her core. Fear and hope swirled together, and she couldn't keep her body from trembling.

Willie looked around. His grin faded and confusion creased his brow. "What did I say wrong?"

"This is a very serious matter of which ye speak, my boy," her father said. "If the Lord is indeed giving us a sign, then we would be wise to discuss the situation further."

"It's obvious to me, Brothers," Willie said slower, probing John's face. "God has preserved John's life more times than I can count, and now he's done the same for Elizabeth. Certainly God is bringing the two of them together for a special purpose."

The others in the room began murmuring. Elizabeth didn't dare look at John to gauge his reaction to his brother's words, and she certainly couldn't look at Elder Harrington to see how he was taking such news. Instead, she focused on the silky strands of the children's hair as it slipped through her fingers.

She wanted to grab onto Willie's words and refuse to let go of them. Deep inside, she wanted to believe he was right, but she was too frightened to let herself.

Chapter
26

$\mathcal{L}$et us come to a consensus, Brothers." Vicar Burton thumped his hands against the table, and the men seated around it fell to silence.

John's stomach gurgled with nervous bile.

"What shall we say, then?" Vicar Burton glanced around at those who remained for their impromptu meeting—the elders and Brother Whitbread. "Are we agreed that God has given us a sign?"

John wanted to speak out, to add to the discussion that had been ongoing since Willie's proclamation earlier in the evening. But he forced himself to lean against the bakehouse wall, cross his arms behind his head, and pretend he was amiable—when really he just wanted to stand up and tell everyone he didn't care what they thought, that he was marrying Elizabeth.

For a long moment none of the elders spoke.

Finally Brother Whitbread sat forward. "Ye men are much wiser than I. But I'm inclined to agree with all that Willie said—that God has a special purpose for my Elizabeth. He's saved her from the bowels of death more times than most. After preserving her life these many times, God must have greater plans for her than most women."

Several of the others nodded. But Elder Harrington, at the far end of the table, folded his hands, a frown upon his face.

John's muscles tensed. What more could they say to convince Elder Harrington to release him from their agreement with his daughter? If he appeared overly eager to free himself, the man might grow more insistent. But if he did nothing, he might lose this heaven-sent opportunity to have Elizabeth.

He'd thrown away his chances with her once before, and he couldn't let it happen again.

John's stomach roiled with sickening steadiness, the same as it had done when neighbors had brought him news of the fire. Thankfully, Mary had managed to alert the neighbors, who had then sent word to him. Panic had overwhelmed him, and he'd sprinted from the rectory of St. John's all the way home. When he'd seen the chain on the door, he'd wanted to kill Foster. The intensity of his emotion, the force with which he had beaten the sledgehammer against the door, the anxiety he'd felt looking for her—he could remember thinking he would rather die than lose her.

That same feeling haunted him still.

"It appears to me," Vicar Burton said, "God has indeed saved Elizabeth Whitbread for a special purpose."

"What better purpose than marrying John and assisting him in his ministry?" Brother Whitbread asked.

"She would be dead if not for you, John," another said.

"It's true." Brother Whitbread banged his cane against the floor to emphasize his words. "As I said once and say again, I'm indebted to ye, John. I will do anything ye ask."

John had already tried to convince Elizabeth's father he didn't owe him anything, but he couldn't sway the man.

"What say ye? What will it be?" The baker held up his hands, as if surrendering the few possessions he claimed. "Ask what ye will. Shall it be my daughter Elizabeth in marriage? I would gladly give ye her along with her portion. Not a big portion. But I'll make it sufficient, especially for ye, John."

John wanted to tell the old man to keep his worldly wealth, that he only needed Elizabeth. Instead, he looked at Elder Harrington. The deepening creases in the man's frown stirred the panic rustling in the pit of his stomach.

"Who am I to deny the hand of God at work?" John sat forward. He must speak now or chance losing her once and for all. He took a deep breath and called forth all the powers of persuasion his tongue held.

"My dear Brothers." He pushed his palms against the table and made a show of rising to his feet.

Their eyes followed his move.

"This is indeed a difficult decision." He straightened to his full height and forced a gravity to his tone that belied the tremor that threatened to weaken him. "Elder Harrington has done me a great honor by offering his daughter in marriage. Any man would find himself fortunate to become a part of such a godly and esteemed family."

He stopped. Surely he could persuade them all. God had indeed gifted him with a skilled tongue. But . . . could he live with himself knowing he'd manipulated his way out of a binding agreement?

"No one could ever spurn such a privilege, least of all me." He paused and glanced to the other faces focused on him, and suddenly he knew what he needed to do, even if it came with great loss and heartache.

He swallowed the smooth convincing words that begged for release. "As much as we may all feel God has ordained Elizabeth to be my wife, I can do nothing less than honor my commitment to Brother Harrington."

The words burned his throat and threatened to cut off his breath.

Elder Harrington squirmed. The elders turned toward the man.

"What think you, Elder Harrington?" Vicar Burton asked.

"I cannot deny I would be disappointed to lose John as a son," Elder Harrington said hesitantly. "But I am wise enough to know I cannot interfere with God's will."

Hope sprang to life in John.

"Besides," Elder Harrington continued, "I cannot in good conscience force my daughter upon a man when he has affections for another. It wouldn't be fair to either my daughter or to John."

Murmurs of agreement rounded the table.

The tension in John's shoulders eased, and he wanted to drop back to the bench in relief.

"Then we're agreed. Today's rescue is a sign from the Lord that John and Elizabeth Whitbread are intended for each other?" Vicar Burton asked.

Again the men conveyed their assent. Even Elder Harrington nodded.

"Then what say you, John?" Vicar Burton asked.

The men turned toward John.

He forced himself to remain stoic, even though his nerves were sizzling with a new excitement. "Methinks I can do no other than take the advice of such a godly group of men. And I certainly cannot ignore so great a sign." He lifted his hands in surrender. "I'll accept Brother Whitbread's offer to marry his daughter."

Loud voices clamored with opinions.

"Let us dispense with their courtship altogether. We must not waste time."

"They must trothplight on the morrow and post the first banns on the Sabbath."

"The sooner married, the better."

John shook his head and tried not to smile. "Not so fast, Brothers. Not so fast." He was sure they didn't want to give him any time to change his mind and back out of the plans—especially now that he was finally cooperative. He understood their concerns. They wanted him to secure the future care of his children should any danger befall him. But they need not worry. God had graciously given him a second chance to have the woman he truly desired. He wouldn't spurn her again. "I must first speak with Sister Whitbread and gain her consent for such an arrangement."

"She is a good girl, my Elizabeth. She will obey me and will marry ye if I tell her she must."

"I'm sure she would, Brother Whitbread. But I'd like her to be agreeable to it nonetheless."

"It's reasonable enough," Vicar Burton said.

"If she's willing to marry me, then I'm willing to betroth as soon as we are able. But I must postpone the calling of the banns and the matrimony ceremony until I have fixed the damage to the cottage and restored order to my home."

The men quickly came to a consensus. John would speak with Brother Whitbread's daughter, and they would make arrangements for the repairs of his home. Then he would be married with all haste.

∽

The patter of bare footsteps on the floor awakened John. The hearth next to him was just a smoldering of embers and provided little heat and even less light. From what remained, he assessed that he'd slept for a few hours and dawn was nearing.

He shivered and pulled a thin blanket back over his bare arms. After the rain, the air had turned chilly, and he was glad he had accepted Brother Whitbread's invitation to sleep beside the fire, rather than in the cold, damp forge.

The footsteps crossed the room and would be upon him in a moment.

He closed his eyes and settled his back against the cold floor. If he pretended to sleep, maybe the early riser would let him rest in peace awhile longer.

But the footsteps came closer until cold bare toes tripped over his feet.

A womanly gasp filled the air above him, and in an instant he knew it was Elizabeth.

He scrambled to sit up.

But in the dim shadows, his movements only startled her more.

She gasped again louder, the beginning of a scream lacing her breath.

"Be still, Elizabeth," he whispered. "It's only I, John."

"Brother Costin? I didn't know you were here. To besure I wouldn't have disturbed you. I'll leave—"

"Wait." He reached for her and locked his fingers around her wrist. "Wait, Elizabeth."

For a moment the only sound between them was the soft rhythm of her breathing.

They were alone. This was the perfect opportunity, a rare moment of privacy in which to ask her about marriage. Who knew when he might have another chance?

"I must speak with you, Elizabeth." He loosened his grasp of her wrist but didn't let go.

She didn't try to free herself, and he took that as a good sign.

"You know I must remarry?"

"Yes." Her reply was a whisper.

"All of my friends have counseled me on this matter, and I know they're right."

" 'Twill be for the best, I'm sure." Her tone was uncertain. "Especially for the children."

"So I've been told."

"I suppose the fire will delay your plans?"

"Not too much." He didn't doubt the elders would do their best to get the cottage repaired as rapidly as possible.

"Good. Then I shall let Sister Norton and Sister Spencer know 'twill not be long till I'm available to help them. What think you? Perchance one month longer?"

He shook his head. The conversation had somehow taken a turn he hadn't intended. "No. Not one. Not any." He pushed himself up onto his elbows.

"You're releasing me of my duties now? 'Tis so soon. Will the children be staying with your brother?"

He shook his head, attempting to slow down her rush of words.

"Are you sure that is the best plan?" she asked. "Surely they will miss you and their home and . . . I would keep them here with me. My father would not object. Just for a little while longer."

"No, Elizabeth." His tongue, usually as smooth as butter, stuck like dry bread to the roof of his mouth.

She gave a deep sigh.

A small measure of relief whispered through him. Mayhap she would agree to his proposal—if he could get her to listen.

"Will you take them to your brother's this day?"

"Stop, Elizabeth." He rose to his knees and pulled her closer. Part of him wanted to draw her into his arms and hold her the way he had after he'd rescued her from the fire.

He'd only scare her away if he did that. She was a devout Puritan maiden in every way.

"I only have the best interest of the children in mind," she started. " 'Twill be hardest on Thomas and certainly inconvenient for you if the children aren't in Bedford . . ."

Through the darkness he reached for her lips and touched them lightly with the tips of his fingers, cutting off her argument. She gave a short burst of breath before catching it. The warmth spread over his rough skin, and the soft roundness of her lips beckoned him.

What he wouldn't give for just a small taste of the sweetness of her lips. The intensity of his longing flared out and heated the space between them. For a long agonizing moment, he could think of nothing but pulling her into his arms.

She trembled. From fear or desire, he knew not. He knew only that her youth and her naïveté formed an aura around her that drew him in further. He couldn't help relishing the thought that she was untouched, that as her husband he would be the first to savor her blushes and innocence.

"I would marry you, Elizabeth," he whispered, his fingers lingering, tracing the soft curves of her mouth.

"What?" she asked breathlessly.

"I want to marry you."

She gasped and moved away from his touch.

His hand hung in midair.

For a moment she said nothing.

Would she refuse him? He wished he could see her face through the darkness to read her emotions. She'd been chaste in all of her dealings with him, had never crossed the boundaries of familiarity to flirt with him as many young maidens had. Her behavior had always been above reproach. But surely he had sensed something there, an attraction of some kind.

"What of the Lizzie Harrington?" she asked hesitantly. "I thought you would troth—"

"Elder Harrington has released me from our agreement, and the elders and your father agree I should marry you."

"They do?"

"They have agreed with Willie's declaration—that my rescuing you from the fire is a sign from God that we are meant to be together."

"What do you think?"

"Methinks the providence of God has indeed been at work."

"Oh."

Did he sense gladness in her tone, or was he just imagining it? "The elders would like us to dispense with courtship and make haste to trothplight."

"They would?"

"I told them I would only do so if you were agreeable."

Again she was silent.

"The children would be excited," he continued, "Mary especially. After all, you said you have their best interests in mind. Wouldn't they fare best to have you, whom they love and know, as mother?"

"Yes. 'Twould indeed make life easier for the children."

He took a deep breath, willing himself to finish saying what he must. "You are indeed a godly young woman, Elizabeth. I have seen your kindness and compassion these many months. I've seen your strength and your determination."

Her hand shook.

He grasped it tighter. "I could find no one more suited for me and for my children, even if I were to search through all of the shires and cities of England."

"Truly?"

"Truly. I have been miserable these past weeks, thinking I could not marry the woman I cared for most."

Her breath hitched.

"Then what say you? Are you agreeable to marrying me?"

She was silent for a long moment. "Yes," came her breathless reply.

He smiled and then brought her hand to his lips. He pressed a tender kiss against her fingers, satisfying himself with the thought that soon he would be able to give her their first kiss—as his bride.

Elizabeth took a deep breath of the brisk morning air. She wanted to reach up and pluck a pink ribbon from the dawn sky and then throw her arms wide and twirl round and round until she dropped to the ground.

Instead, she pressed her hand against her stomach and smiled. The law forbade any form of dancing, so the swirling and twirling of her insides would have to content her.

"There he comes," Anne said, watching the narrow pathway that led to the bakehouse garden from the street.

Johnny and Betsy squealed and ran toward their father. When they reached him, he dropped his tool sack, bent low, and scooped them into an embrace.

Elizabeth's insides quivered with fresh delight. He *was* coming—just as he'd promised. Then he truly did wish to marry her? He'd meant what he'd spoken in the bakehouse the previous morning?

He set the children back upon the ground and then moved toward Mary. He gently cupped her cheek and pressed a kiss against her coif. Thomas reached a hand to his father's scruffy chin, and John kissed the boy's fingers, earning a giggle of delight.

Elizabeth's heart thudded until it ached. She couldn't deny she loved this man with all her being. But did he feel the same? Had she truly seen affection in his eyes, or had she only dreamed it?

As if sensing her questions, he lifted his gaze and met hers directly. The brightness of the blue, like the early morning sky, took her breath away.

"Good morn, Elizabeth." He walked toward her, giving her father and Vicar Burton nothing more than a passing nod.

When he finally stood before her, he stretched out his hand. A bouquet of wild purple hyacinths and yellow daffodils glistened with dewdrops. "For you," he said softly.

Her breath vanished and her heart refused to beat. She reached for the flowers, and her fingers brushed against his. Warmth flooded her cheeks. She buried her nose in the sweet perfume, letting the cool petals bathe her face.

If she was dreaming, she didn't want to wake up. "Thank you," she said, lifting her chin and letting her joy spill forth from her smile. "They're beautiful."

His lips curved into a smile that lit his eyes.

Her joy swelled until she knew she could never again be happier than she was at that exact moment.

"Are you ready to pledge yourself to me, Elizabeth?" he asked.

"Oh yes."

With a smile just for her, he lifted his hand. "Then shall we?"

She placed her hand in his. The strength of his fingers closed around hers, wrapping not just her hand but her entire heart in a cocoon of warmth.

The few that had gathered to witness their early morning betrothal stepped nearer. Vicar Burton prayed, then smiled at them. "You may trothplight."

John squeezed her hand and met her gaze. "I will take you as my wife."

The sun's light beamed brighter, and the last traces of dawn slipped away. John's presence surrounded her, and no one else existed. "I will take you as my husband."

"Your pledges to each other are true and binding in the sight of God and these witnesses." Vicar Burton's voice sounded far away.

John's gaze made a slow journey over her face, lingering on her lips, before finally traveling back to her eyes.

She sucked in her breath. He wanted to kiss her. His eyes spoke the message just as if he'd said the words aloud. Her stomach fluttered with anticipation. Would he dare, in front of the witnesses, even though 'twas not customary for their Puritan betrothals?

His gaze went back to her lips, and he swayed toward her.

"Ye shall stay to break fast with us, John?" Her father clapped him on the back.

John let go of her hand and stepped away, putting a safe distance between them. "Ah, it would be a pleasure, to besure," he said to her father, clearing his throat. "But methinks I must get a start on my work. I have a long hike ahead to Lower Samsell. It will be a full day of teaching and tinkering."

"Then ye shall have some fresh bread for your trip."

"I would be grateful." John walked back to where he had dropped his bag. He slung it over his shoulder.

Elizabeth watched him and her heart raced after him, unwilling to let him go, longing for another moment together, no matter how short.

But he patted the heads of his children before tossing one last smile in her direction. Then he hefted his bag higher, the linen pulling taut against the thick cover of his Bible within.

She smiled in return, forcing her wistfulness away. When he turned away, she buried her face in the velvet blanket of flower petals, soothing her hot cheeks and reminding herself that John cared about her.

They were pledged to be married. 'Twould not be long before they would be together, and she would get her fill of him to her heart's content.

Chapter
27

*Y*ou wouldn't believe what I heard this morning at market."
Catherine patted the back of her newborn babe, and his tiny grunts
of complaint took on the rhythm of her thumping.

"I don't wish to hear any gossip." Elizabeth turned away from
her sister. With one last tin mold of candles to pour, she was sticky
and tired and wished to finish without Catherine's prattling. "Are
you not capable of speaking of anything else?"

The girl had too much leisure. If she took her responsibilities
more seriously, then she would have less time to partake in idle
tale-bearing. And if Samuel didn't spoil her so much. . . .

With a frustrated breath Elizabeth blew the loose hairs out of
her eyes. Deep down, what really bothered her was that Catherine
knew more about John's doings than she did.

In the weeks since their betrothal, she and the children had lived at the bakehouse while John stayed at the forge. On occasion he joined them for a meal, but most of the time he was either gone preaching or laboring on the cottage.

"I heard both good and bad news." Catherine lowered her babe back to her breast and pushed him against it. His grunts turned into hungry gulps.

Elizabeth held a long-handled dipper, filled with melted wax, above the candle molds. She was sure Catherine felt it was her duty to share every rumor she heard about her and John. The most recent was that they had to get married because she, Elizabeth, was carrying John's child. 'Twas a rumor that left her feeling soiled, like all of the others. She had no doubt William Foster was behind it but was thankful he had otherwise left her alone.

"Which do you want me to tell you first? The good news or the bad?"

Elizabeth examined the tall tapered tubes, the wicks already threaded through a narrow hole in the far end and looped over small sticks laid across a pan at the top of the mold. She wanted to tell Catherine to hold her tongue, to shame her for gossiping. But whenever the rumors involved John, she couldn't make herself say the words. She saw and heard so little of him that she was eager for any news at all.

"I suppose I shall start with the bad." Catherine's voice lacked the regret one would expect in the bearer of bad news.

Elizabeth began pouring the melted wax into the first tube.

"They've agreed to the king's return."

Elizabeth's hand trembled and splashed wax. She looked up from the candles to Catherine's face. "Truly not."

Catherine nodded. The ruff of her new bodice outlined the womanliness of her nursing figure. Samuel was indeed pampering Catherine and the new babe. Whatever Catherine wanted, he gave, including linen for new clothes. "They are talking about recalling King Charles from Breda."

"That cannot be." Elizabeth poured the next candle and steadied her hand, even as her heart quaked at the news. At the beginning of the spring, Richard Cromwell had finally resigned as Lord Protector. That news had been a blow to the Independents but not unexpected.

They hadn't known what would happen next or who would rise to leadership to replace Richard Cromwell. Certainly they hadn't expected Parliament to consider having a king again, especially Charles.

Why would they do such a thing? Everyone knew Charles was Catholic, having been indoctrinated by his French mother. He'd fled to France and the Netherlands after Oliver Cromwell had beheaded his father, King Charles I, and he had lived there during the days of the Protectorate. Now Parliament was considering his return?

Elizabeth poured the last of the hot wax and then stood back. Having a Catholic king would bring trouble to the Puritans—to John.

"A king won't tolerate the Independents," Catherine continued. "He'll certainly come down hard on our preachers."

"Whatever shall we do?" She was on the brink of marriage, at the start of a life with the man she loved. Would she miss her chance after all?

"We shall all have to be prepared for the worst." Catherine's words were too unfeeling. The girl was only repeating what she had heard, but nevertheless, Elizabeth wished Catherine was capable of sympathy.

"Now the good news. Or would you rather not hear any more of my *gossip?*"

Elizabeth met Catherine's self-satisfied expression and pinned her with a hard look.

Catherine rearranged her nursing babe and raised her eyebrows in sweetened innocence.

"Matron life and motherhood are a means of maturing most young girls. You have not benefited from either."

"Then you shall need neither, for you are already the saint of maturity."

Elizabeth turned away. Sparring words with Catherine would fuel her anger and lead them both to sin.

She ran her fingers over the dried splotches of wax on the table and picked at one with her thumbnail. If she waited long enough, Catherine wouldn't be able to resist sharing the rest of her news.

"Very well," Catherine said finally. "Since you are so insistent, you leave me no choice but to tell you what else I heard."

Elizabeth scraped at the cold wax.

"The banns will be posted this Sabbath."

"Banns?" Elizabeth's breath stuck in her throat.

"Seems the bad news has put more haste into Brother Costin's marriage plans."

"Then we shall be married in a month's time?"

" 'Tis what they say."

Elizabeth's heart rolled forward like a carriage hurrying toward its destiny. She would finally wed John. 'Twas not just a dream.

Only one month and she would belong to John. No more smiles in passing. No more separations. She would be able to linger with him by the fire at night and listen to him talk about his busy day.

"You may end up married." Catherine lifted her babe to her shoulder and thumped his back. "But you won't have wedded bliss. If you don't find yourself a widow, you'll find yourself alone—with Brother Costin in prison or banished."

The wheels of Elizabeth's heart lurched, bumping and jolting over rocky ground. She narrowed her eyes at Catherine, cheeks flushed from the heat of her nursing, and she fought a sudden and unholy surge of malice. Why must Catherine discourage her at every turn and find pleasure in it?

"Perchance your hope lies in convincing Brother Costin to

forsake his preaching." Catherine wiped spit off her babe's chin. "After all, when you're his wife, you'll have great influence over him. You may be just the one to save him from certain destruction."

"Forsake preaching? How can I sway him to do such a thing? Am I the Lord that I should even attempt it?"

"You'll be able to sway him more than you realize." Catherine smiled. "At least Samuel is very agreeable, especially when we are in bed."

"For shame, sister!" Flames sprang to life in Elizabeth's cheeks. "Say no more!" She turned away from Catherine to the cooling tins of candles. The girl was foolish, and Elizabeth knew she would do well to pay no heed to her advice.

~

True to Catherine's word, the banns were read the following Sabbath, then for two consecutive weeks after that. Hearing her name linked with John's filled Elizabeth with warm pleasure that grew each time she heard it.

'Twould be the usual simple ceremony the Puritans had practiced since Cromwell's Marriage Act, which had banned marriages from taking place in churches.

A short wedding ceremony before the justice of the peace was enough for Elizabeth. Royalists, and even some Puritans, had never accepted the marriage law and had continued the practice of marrying in the church. But she was content with simple Puritan ways.

As a girl who'd never had much of a chance of attracting anyone, she was happy enough to have the opportunity to experience marriage.

She was marrying the man she loved, and that was the important thing.

When the day finally arrived, Elizabeth's heart fluttered with excitement.

Late afternoon sunshine poured through the glass windows of the guildhall chamber and filled every corner of the big room with light. The murmur of voices surrounded her. She brushed a hand over the smooth linen of her Sabbath meeting clothes, her best apparel, and then glanced at the doors.

They were still closed.

She surveyed the room and recounted those already gathered—her family, the witnesses, the magistrate. Everyone was there, except John.

Sister Norton met her gaze. "Don't fret. He'll be here."

Elizabeth nodded and attempted a smile. But her heart couldn't muster enthusiasm past the sudden fear. What if something had happened to him? The Royalists were growing more daring in their defiance of Puritan rule.

A rampage of thoughts assaulted her and wouldn't let up their siege.

Only when the large doors squeaked open did her thoughts finally capitulate with relief. John barged inside and his breath came in heaving gulps. He leaned over and grabbed his side.

"Is everything all right, Brother Costin?" the magistrate asked.

He nodded. "Just out of breath is all."

"We need to commence. You're late, and I have another appointment following this."

John took a deep breath and pushed away from the door. "I'm sorry I'm late." He tossed Elizabeth an apologetic smile. "I was preaching south of Elstow. I lost track of time and had to run the last three miles."

She released the breath she hadn't realized she was holding and gave him a wavering smile as he took his place next to her.

His hair hung in a sticky array against his neck and forehead.

Elizabeth fidgeted with sudden self-consciousness. Perhaps she'd made a mistake cleaning herself and putting on her Sabbath dress.

"I'm sorry, Elizabeth," he whispered, catching her gaze. The warmth in the depth of his eyes went straight to her heart, and she was helpless to do anything but forgive him.

When he reached for her hand, nothing else mattered. He was there.

His fingers surrounded hers but then slowly maneuvered until he intertwined them with hers in an intimate hold like nothing she'd ever known.

Her breath hitched.

His palm pressed against hers, and she couldn't focus on the magistrate's examination of her father regarding his consent to the union. She chanced a sideways glance at John. He winked at her.

When the magistrate had sufficient proof that her father supported her underage marriage, he turned to them.

"Now you may state your vows."

John turned to face her. "I, John Costin, do here in the presence of God, the searcher of all hearts, take you, Elizabeth Whitbread, for my wedded wife." His smile softened, and his earnest words brought joyful tears to her eyes. "Also, in the presence of God and before these witnesses, I promise to be unto you a loving and faithful husband."

Elizabeth took a deep breath. Could she speak her vows past the tightness of her throat? "I, Elizabeth Whitbread, do here in the presence of God, the searcher of all hearts, take you, John Costin, for my wedded husband." Her voice strengthened with each word. "In the presence of God and before these witnesses, I promise to be unto you a loving, faithful, and obedient wife."

The magistrate closed his book and stepped back. "You are now husband and wife."

The ring, along with the elaborate ritual that accompanied its giving, was no longer permitted. Neither was the conjunction for kissing the bride. Indeed, the ceremony lasted only minutes and was over before it had the chance to begin.

The men of the congregation who'd come to witness the wedding surrounded John. As he turned to greet them, his hand slipped from hers. In an instant, her own friends and family enveloped her with warm hugs, and she found herself separated from John.

Her gaze followed him, however. When he filed out of the guildhall chamber ahead of her, deep in conversation with the men, she reminded herself that these were troubled times. No one could stop debating who would lead their country next, not even on a wedding day.

Her father invited everyone to return to the bakehouse to join together in a meal. He had prepared extra pasties and pies and had baked a special cake with almonds for the occasion. As the evening wore on, well-wishing friends and congregates joined them until the small rooms of the bakehouse were crowded and many had to gather outside in the cool dusk of spring.

Elizabeth lost track of John and only occasionally spotted him deep in conversation with one elder or another.

When the hour had finally grown late and most had taken their leave, she helped her sisters clean up the meal and debated whether to search for John. She released a relieved sigh when he stepped into the room and nodded to her.

" 'Tis time for us to be going," he said quietly.

Both Anne and Jane grew motionless and turned curious eyes onto her.

She ducked her head, knowing what everyone would now be thinking. She would be going to her new home and would become John's wife.

Slowly she wiped her hands on her apron and then reached for a large bundle wrapped in a linen sheet. She didn't have much: a flaxen pillowbeer, a table sheet she had woven, a bolster, a blanket, the tin candle holder John had given her, and the few clothing items she possessed.

With an encouraging smile, Jane handed her a basket filled with leftovers from the evening.

"Thank you, Jane." Elizabeth's voice caught in her throat. She was leaving home, leaving her family, never again to be one of them. Her life would forevermore change.

As if sensing the same thoughts, Jane reached for her and hugged her, and then with a sob Anne did likewise.

She squared her shoulders and turned to face John, too embarrassed to meet his gaze.

He slid the large bundle from her shoulder. Then, with his tinkering bag over one shoulder and her parcel over the other, he led her through the farewells to her father and the rest of her family, until finally they were away from the smiles that whispered of secrets she knew not.

When they arrived at the cottage, John deposited her belongings on the table and spoke with her for a few moments about the last of the repairs he had recently finished. Elizabeth tried to focus her thoughts on what he said and give the appropriate responses, but her mind was as jumpy as a frog catching flies.

"The children will be glad to be home with you," she said as he bent low before the hearth and stirred the embers.

"And I with them."

Willie and Sarah had taken the children to Elstow for the night and offered to keep them for several days, until the Sabbath. Willie had elbowed John and proclaimed that John would need time with his young bride.

John had grinned in return but had shaken his head and remarked that he had a gathering near Elstow on the morrow and would retrieve them on his way home.

" 'Twill be quiet without them." Elizabeth fingered her sleeve cuff and looked around the room, the stillness of it making her insides do more flops.

Finally he stood, crossed his arms, and looked at her. Something in the dark depths of his eyes sent her heart scurrying wildly.

She quickly busied her shaking hands by reaching for her bag and fumbling with the drawstring. "Think you William Foster will try to harm me now that I'm back at the cottage?"

His footsteps thudded against the floor toward her. "Foster won't dare," he said behind her.

She pulled open the bag, drew out a handful of clothes, and tried not to think about John's nearness.

"He knew he could get away with harassing you when you were my housekeeper." John's voice was low. "But he would never try manipulating you now that you are my bride."

She dumped the rest of her belongings into a pile on the table. Her hands fluttered from one item to the next.

John stretched past her and picked up the tin candlestick. "I see you still have my gift."

Her hands stilled on the half-folded blanket. "Of course. It's my most treasured worldly possession. . . ."

For a moment John fingered the pierced leaf pattern. She stared at his strong callused fingers and remembered their strength and warmth as they'd intertwined with hers during the wedding.

He lifted his hand from the candlestick and touched her arm. Gently he turned her away from the disarray on the table until she faced him.

Before she could object, he caressed her cheek and then made a trail down her jaw, across her chin, and up her other cheek.

The softness of his touch took her breath away.

His fingers didn't rest. He drew them across to her lips until the callused tips brushed them.

A sigh slipped from between her lips, an echo of the delight he was stirring within her. And when he bent his head nearer, she closed her eyes and held her breath.

In an instant, the feathery caress of his fingertips vanished, replaced by the most exquisite tender warmth, the gentle pressure of his lips against hers. For an eternal, heavenly moment, his lips melded against hers, softly, sweetly.

When he pulled back, he smiled. "I've wanted to do that since the day I rescued you from the burning inferno."

She touched her lips, reeling from the sensations his kiss had brought to life.

His fingers moved to her coif, and in an instant he'd tossed it to the table and pulled her hair out of its neatly coiled wrap. Her hair rippled around her face in long waves.

She gasped at his brazenness.

"And I've wanted to do that too." He reached for her then and slipped both of his arms around her, drawing her to him.

"You are so beautiful, Elizabeth," he whispered, sliding his fingers through the thick strands.

Her heart stopped. She pulled back and searched his face, desperate to know the truth of his words. Certainly no man had ever thought her beautiful. Did he truly mean it, or was he merely spouting flowery prose in the emotion of the moment?

She probed the darkening blue of his eyes, needing to know.

His gaze was clear and guileless. "You're beautiful," he whispered again, caressing a strand of hair away from her cheek.

Her heart sputtered forward. She couldn't think past the swell of new emotions. She could only let him draw her along. When his lips descended upon hers again, she melted against him—her husband, the man who thought she was beautiful.

Chapter 28

At the barest light of dawn Elizabeth slipped from the bed and moved as soundlessly as she could. The shifting of sheets drew her attention back to the bed, back to John's face. Her gaze lingered over the peacefulness of his features, to the smooth lines, to his lips parted with his slow, even breathing.

Her heart thumped with a sudden quickening. A swath of his ruddy hair had fallen over his forehead, and she had the sudden urge to climb back next to him and smooth it away.

With a lurch of unexpected longing, she blushed and turned away. The night had brought a deluge of new emotions and sensations, and she needed a few moments to gather her thoughts before John awoke.

After dressing silently, she tiptoed through the cottage and made her way outside to the fields behind the garden plot. Dew glistened on the long grass and dampened her leather boots and the edges of her petticoat. The morning air was cool, but it was the bath her chafed skin needed.

Gathering dead gorse branches for fuel was a task she could accomplish in her sleep. Even though the gorse was damp and saturated her apron, it provided a useful source of fuel, since it would burn when wet. It also proved an important food for the cow now that its winter fodder had been depleted. Already that spring she had cut and crushed gorse for Milkie and had begun to see an improvement in the milk supply.

The morning sun had not yet risen, but its faint glow tinted the sky with hues of pink and orange. She breathed in the scent of freshly plowed soil of the nearby farm field and looked back at the dark outline of the cottage. Her heart swelled with sweet joy.

He had introduced her to the mysteries of married love with a tenderness that still left her breathless.

And he had said she was beautiful.

She smiled. He had said it not just once, but twice.

The flutter of a small moth in the yellow flowers of the gorse caught her attention. By its thicker, fuzzier abdomen and duller colors she knew it was a moth and not a butterfly, lingering from its escapades of the night.

She watched it flit and then land, leaving its wings down in rest. How oft she had compared herself to a moth, had believed herself plain, had considered herself unattractive and unlikely to gain a husband.

But after last night . . .

She gave a small sigh of delight.

She picked up another stick and placed it in her bulging apron.

Of course he hadn't yet told her he loved her. But surely a man couldn't hold a woman the way he had and not love her.

Her thoughts returned to the intimacies they had shared, and her face grew hot at the remembrance.

She glanced again at the cottage. How would she ever be able to be near him again without thinking of what they'd done, without blushing in embarrassment, or without her heart racing with desire for more?

Yet even as her heart flushed at the thought of looking into his eyes, she made her way back into the cottage, wanting nothing more than to spend the waking moments of her day with him, laboring alongside him, sharing secret smiles, and maybe even stealing kisses.

She tiptoed into the cottage, to the hearth. Working quietly, she emptied the gorse from her apron, then added sticks to the coals before straightening.

She sensed his presence behind her even before she felt his thick arms slide around her waist. "My bride, already hard at work this morn." His low voice rumbled against her ear, and the warmth of his breath grazed her neck.

A sweet delicate heat blossomed in her middle. "Someone must do the work. Not all of us have the luxury of sleeping late."

His arms tightened and pulled her back against his chest.

"Methinks I can find my wife more satisfying work than gathering gorse." The grin in his voice brought a smile to her lips.

She leaned against him, letting him envelop her. "And what kind of work would my husband have for me?" Her hands folded over his, and she skimmed her fingers up the silky hair of his arms, blushing with the realization he hadn't yet donned his shirt.

"Hmm . . ." His lips brushed against her neck in the spot behind her ear.

The merest touch spread fire through her blood.

"I would have you kiss me until you can't breathe," he

murmured, pressing his warm lips against her ear, then against the top of her jaw.

She gasped and arched into him. " 'Twill not be hard work, then," she said breathlessly.

"Then I would have you kiss me until *I* can't breathe." His lips made a trail down her jaw.

She tilted her head back, eager for him to reach his destination. When his lips finally descended upon hers, she met him with the passion the night had birthed within her.

His arms tightened, and she wanted nothing more than for him to scoop her up. She could imagine nothing more pleasant than spending the day together in each other's arms.

He groaned and pulled away. "You have accomplished your work much too quickly." His chest heaved and his breathing came in deep ragged gasps.

She smiled. "I would work longer for you, my husband. You need only command it."

He grinned, then released her. "There is no doubt about it, Elizabeth." He sat back on the bench and grabbed his shirt from the table. "You are a hard worker."

He wrangled to pull it over his head, exposing the broad expanse of his chest to her. She turned her face in hot embarrassment, glad for the shadows of the cottage that hid her blushes.

Elizabeth wanted to reach out for him and press herself into the warmth of his embrace. But when he finished with his shirt, he put on first one boot and then the other.

"I will bring the children home before dark." He stood and slipped on his jerkin.

"Are you leaving already?"

He nodded and reached for his tool bag. "I have a long walk ahead of me this morn."

She swallowed the disappointment creeping up her throat. "Surely you have time to eat before you leave."

He slung his pack over his shoulder. "I'll take something with me."

She moved to the basket of leftovers from their wedding banquet. "There's plenty here." She lifted the basket toward him.

As he stuffed bread into his bag, her mind scrambled to find a way to make him stay. Now that they were finally man and wife, she wasn't ready for him to leave. Life would demand much of them. She knew that to be true already. But surely they could face it together, hand in hand and side by side.

He clomped across the room to his study. Through the rustle of papers and thump of books he called, "I am certain Willie will insist we eat with him tonight."

Her mind whirled. Since the day he'd proposed to her, she'd pictured herself helping him in his ministry. Everyone had agreed God had a special purpose for her, had ordained her as John Costin's helpmate. Surely God did not mean for her to sit at home while her husband traveled the countryside preaching. If she accompanied him, she could not only support him, but they would be together.

He wouldn't want to be away from her any more than she wanted to be away from him. Not after the night they'd shared.

"What if I came with you?"

The study grew silent.

Her stomach twisted. "I'd love to hear you preach and meet the people you shepherd."

He didn't make a sound.

"I want to be there to help you in any way I can." This time she waited, the thudding of her heart the only sound.

Finally he stepped out of his study, slowly. "They are mostly simple, hardworking farmers, Elizabeth."

"They have wives, do they not? Perchance God would have me help you bring the Gospel to their wives."

He shook his head. "The distances are too great, the weather too severe, and the days much too long. I would not subject my wife to these conditions."

She straightened her shoulders. "I am not a weak woman."

"My enemies conspire against me." His jaw clenched. "The danger has grown severe these past months, and I would not impose upon you any more than you have already borne."

The tautness of the lines in his face mirrored the tightness of disappointment in her throat. "I would just like to be with you, John."

He stared at her for a long moment. The frustration in his eyes reached the length of the room and pricked at her heart. "You know I like being with you too. . . ."

"Then take me along." She hated that her tone had an edge of desperation to it.

He sighed and started toward the door. "I can't."

"Just for today, then?"

"No."

Her heart plummeted.

When he reached the door, he took his hat from the peg and slapped it on. He put his hand to the door but stopped and looked at her. "Not today, Elizabeth. Not ever."

She wanted to keep trying to persuade him, but something in his eyes halted her attempt.

"You will help me best by staying here at home. Just as you have always done." The firmness of his tone made clear what he desired.

She managed a brief nod. Then he was gone, the clank of the closing door echoing through her head.

Tears flooded her eyes, and she sagged to the bench. She pressed a fist to her mouth, but a sob refused the stifle and slipped into the silent cottage.

Her heart and throat burned. What had happened? What had she done wrong?

A tear dripped out and slid down her cheek.

Was she to have no more place in his heart than she'd had when she was his housekeeper?

Chapter
29

*E*lizabeth hefted the squirming Thomas and used the movement as an excuse to peek at the men's pews to John's bowed head, to his strong fingers twisted into his thick hair, as if he would pull it out if he could.

Fresh longing swirled through her. If only she could sit next to him and smooth her hand across his forehead and ease his distress.

Thomas whined and she quickly stuffed a bite of bread into his mouth to content him until the next piece.

If only she could find contentment as easily.

She swallowed a sigh and forced her eyes closed. She could blame her melancholy upon the deteriorating political situation. The news out of London did not bode well. Parliament was negotiating with the king. 'Twas almost certain he would return.

Such news was enough to depress any Puritan. She shuddered to think of the hardships it would bring for all of them. Already the elders had called two fasts and prayer meetings in the past week. Prayer was the only weapon the Independents had left.

But Elizabeth knew her discontentment went much deeper than the shifting political climate. Ultimately she longed for John. After only two weeks of marriage she'd begun to understand the reality of her new life. There was no laboring side by side, no passing smiles, no long conversations by the hearth. After his busy days, he had little left to give her, even in the bed they shared.

She did as he asked, carried forth her responsibilities in the home just as diligently as she'd always done, but her heart ached with the weight of disappointment that grew heavier every day.

When the noon meeting ended, her gaze sought John again. He'd already slid from his pew and was making his way to the door. Surrounded in her row by other matrons, Elizabeth could only watch him and wish she had the power to make him turn around and smile at her before he left for the day.

But he disappeared outside with nary a backward glance, and a weight settled on her shoulders, making her want to sit down and cry.

Thomas whined again, this time louder, and she absently broke off another piece of bread for him.

Her own stomach rolled with the pangs of fasting. She lifted her face toward heaven, and as she had been taught, she used the moment of personal discomfort and self-denial as a reminder to pray. *"Pray often,"* she'd heard John say, *"for prayer is a shield to the soul, a sacrifice to God, and a scourge for Satan."*

If only she could pray for something besides more time with her husband.

"The constable is waiting in the churchyard," a voice announced.

"They're arresting him," someone else shouted.

The whispers zigzagged through the small meetinghouse and crashed into Elizabeth. For a long moment she stood unmoving, her mind trying to decipher the words and the worried looks cast her direction.

"John?" Her heart picked up speed. "Are they arresting John?"

In the flurry of the commotion and eruption of noise around her, no one answered.

Mary tugged her sleeve. "Hurry. We must go find out what's happening."

Elizabeth gathered the children and pushed her way through the crowded nave until she reached the door and stepped outside into the cool drizzle.

She stopped short at the sight of the men gathered on St. John's Street. Her gaze swept over the crowd and alighted with cold fear on the thin face of William Foster.

She hadn't seen him since the day of the fire. John had reassured her that Foster wouldn't threaten her once they were married, and he'd been right.

Even so, Elizabeth shrank back.

"I just be following the orders," came the booming voice of the constable. "I just be doing me job, Costin."

"He's under arrest for preaching at the Burgess farmhouse near Lowell Samuel," said a tall man Elizabeth recognized as one of the Anglican ministers whose parish had been sequestered by Cromwell.

"That was in the fall," John replied. "That was many months ago."

"It doesn't matter when you broke the law, only that you did," the minister snapped. "It was unlicensed preaching, and you're under arrest."

The minister's words seemed to unleash the tension that had been building—hostilities that had been growing for years. The swaying of the political tide had given the Royalists a new freedom, and they were beginning to liberate themselves from the oppression they'd been under since the war. Amidst the shouting and arguing, Elizabeth couldn't hear John's reply.

Finally John raised his hand. "Enough!"

Angry voices trailed into silence.

"We cannot resolve this battle of differences here with irate words. Methinks 'twill only lead to enraged fists." He admonished the men with his glare. "Let us work together to find a peaceable solution."

"They want no peace," someone shouted.

John shook his head and turned to the constable. "I don't know by whose authority you bring these charges against me. But I know you are a God-fearing man, Bigrave. You wouldn't bring malice where none is due."

The constable pointed at the Anglican minister. " 'Tis him that be bringing the charges, Costin. 'Tis not my doing."

John looked at the minister, but then switched his focus to Foster.

As if sensing the mounting tension, Thomas began to fuss in her arms. Elizabeth absently pulled his blanket over his hair and hugged him. Johnny and Betsy shivered on either side of her. She tugged the hoods of their cloaks over their heads.

"I know what these charges are about and who is behind them." John gave Foster a last penetrating look. "Nonetheless, Bigrave, I don't wish to stir up trouble. Since I've done nothing for which I'm ashamed, I'll accompany you without guilt of conscience."

Mary gave a stifled gasp.

Elizabeth rubbed the girl's fingers.

"If you must arrest me, Bigrave, then let's get on with it."

Again there was a rush of shouting and pushing.

Mary's fingers dug into Elizabeth's sleeve.

"Brothers," John shouted, "I'm not a coward, and I will face these charges without fear." He turned toward the constable and allowed the big man to take hold of his arm.

"Father!" Mary turned her face toward the commotion.

The sound of her voice penetrated the noise. John stopped and glanced over his shoulder. He searched the crowd until his eyes alighted upon Mary and filled with heartbreaking pain. "Mary. You help Elizabeth."

The girl nodded and choked back a sob.

John's gaze lingered on the girl only a second longer before flicking to Elizabeth. For the briefest moment his eyes met hers. Amidst the sadness and resignation in the depths of his eyes, his message to her was clear. He didn't know when or if he would return. He wanted her to take care of his children—especially his blind daughter, who would be lost in the world without him.

Elizabeth nodded and hoped he would read the promise in her expression that she would not fail him.

Then the constable led him away.

Mary sobbed quietly, her thin body shaking.

"Alderman Grew, will you not go?" one of the onlookers asked. "Your influence will be needed."

Alderman Grew stood in the doorway of the church with Mrs. Grew next to him, her shoulders straight and her chin lifted high.

She peered at Elizabeth with narrowed eyes. 'Twas the customary response she elicited from Mrs. Grew, and she had decided it would never change. The woman would always bear her a grudge.

"Alderman Grew, surely you won't let the past stand in the way of helping Brother Costin?" Elizabeth asked. "He doesn't deserve your censure on my account."

The alderman hesitated and cast his wife a sideways glance.

Mrs. Grew slipped her arm through his and pulled him down the path to the street.

"Whether or not you like me, can't you help John? He is a godly man who has done this congregation much good."

"I don't see how I could be much influence." The alderman's voice was filled with regret, and he tripped along next to his wife. "I'm sure others are much better qualified than I to offer him assistance."

Mrs. Grew tossed Elizabeth a half smile, one void of all but the coldest spite. The hardness of her eyes declared that she was in control and had the power to withhold favor and make life miserable for those she disliked.

Elizabeth gave the woman what she hoped was a pleasant smile. She didn't want her to know she had succeeded. Elizabeth *was* miserable knowing it was her fault Alderman Grew wouldn't help John.

Sister Norton and others tried to comfort her. Jane invited her to the bakehouse so she wouldn't have to be alone. But Elizabeth wanted to be home.

It was late in the afternoon by the time they trudged to the cottage. Elizabeth heated water and scrubbed most everything she could find. She swept and dusted the dormer loft. She fed the children and tucked them under blankets on their pallets in the loft. Then she scraped and polished the blackened kettle.

Long after the children had fallen asleep, she worked at washing crusted stains off the plank of the table. Her back ached, her hands were red and raw from the heat and water, and her eyes smarted from working by the dim light of the fire.

All the while she labored, questions roared through her mind. What would happen to John? Would she ever see him again? If authorities forced him to leave England, to where would they deport him? If they imprisoned him, how would she provide for the children? How could she earn enough money to pay the rent and buy food?

She desperately wanted to deny what was happening. But she'd been in denial long enough. She'd heard the rumors—Catherine had made sure of it. John and other Independents like him would face persecution. Up to this point she hadn't wanted to hear the truth, but now she had to face the reality that maybe she'd end up being a widow, just as Catherine had predicted.

A sob pushed against her chest. She'd had so little time with him.

With a heavy heart she sank to the bench. She laid her head on the table and rested her cheek against the coolness of the plank. Weariness overwhelmed her, and unbidden tears slipped down her cheeks.

The ache swelled into her throat. She wanted to be with him. She understood how important his calling was. But surely God did not need so much of her husband that he didn't have anything left for her or the children.

When she'd had so little of his time and attention, was she now to be denied all of it?

"I love you, Lord. And you've promised to work things out for the good of those who love you. If I've pleased you, Lord, with my sacrifice and service, won't you help us now?"

She closed her eyes. Did she need to do more? Perhaps of late she hadn't done enough to serve unceasingly and diligently. She still took bread to the poor every Sabbath. She helped Sister Norton with Lucy's children whenever she could. But did God want her to do more?

Confusion rolled through her. The stress of the day clouded her mind. She could only conclude she needed to be holier, needed to try harder to keep sin at bay. And if she loved and served Him more, then surely He would be willing to deliver John back to her.

She wasn't sure how long she slept, only that she awoke to a gentle touch on her cheek.

"Elizabeth." A whisper came from above her. Work-worn fingers caressed down her cheek to her chin and then up the other side.

It took a moment for her sleep-lulled mind to awaken. Then she gasped. "John?"

"I'm home."

Joy shot through her and pushed her to her feet.

"Praise be to God," she whispered, drinking in the sight of him. His hair was disheveled, and tired lines creased his forehead and the corners of his eyes.

But his expression was one of relief. "I'm glad to see you, Elizabeth." He lifted his hand to her face and touched her cheek again. "I didn't think I would be back."

The tenderness of his stroke sent a warm current through her. "I didn't know either. I could only pray." She lifted her hand to his cheek. "I'm truly glad to see you too." She grazed her fingers against the dark stubble that shadowed his cheeks and chin.

The scratchy roughness of his skin sent a shiver through her.

His hand stilled against her cheek. The warmth of his breath fanned against the thumping pulse in her wrist.

She leaned her face into his hand, longing for more of his touch.

In that moment he wound his other arm around her and pulled her toward him into a crushing embrace, one that took her by surprise with its force. In the same movement, his lips descended upon hers.

She wound her arms around him and returned the hungry feast upon his lips.

With a half moan she pushed against him, wanting, needing more. His arms tightened and his kiss deepened.

She didn't want the moment to end. His heart pounded against her chest the way it was supposed to be between a husband and wife, and she wanted him to stay that way all night and every night for the rest of their lives.

As if he'd heard her thoughts, he suddenly broke away from her. His heavy breathing mingled with hers, and he pried her arms loose. Then he rammed his fingers into his hair and stalked to the fireplace.

She hugged her arms to her chest and fought off a strange coldness.

"An arrest could happen again at any time," he said in a jagged, almost harsh voice as he picked up a poker and stirred the dying embers of the fire. "It was almost the end of me today and would have been if William Dell of Yelden hadn't arrived and spoken on my behalf."

What had she done wrong that he had walked away from her? "Mr. Foster was there," she said with choppy breath. " 'Tis clear he had his hand in the proceedings."

"Indeed. Methinks he was the master behind the charges."

"Will he try again?"

He jabbed the ashes. "I have no doubt he will. But next time he won't have me arrested so publicly. The pressure was too great against him. He'll have to find a more guileful way to strike."

She shuddered. "Next time? Must there be another?"

"Whether we like it or not, I have no doubt there will be another."

Her heart gave a cry of protest. "Oh, John, surely not. Surely we can find a way to protect you. What if you stayed home more—"

"Would you have me cower behind your petticoats?" He stood, a scowl creasing his forehead. "I have never let my enemies dictate my calling, and I won't start now."

"But you are gone so much." She fumbled to find the right words to express the longing that had been building within her. "Not only do I want you to be safe, but I want to spend more time with you."

"I thought you understood how important my ministry is to me—"

"I do understand. But must you spend so much time at it? Must you leave so early and come home every day so late—"

"I can't believe you're saying this." His voice was thin with frustration. "You've never complained before. You've always supported my work. Why are you questioning what I do now?"

"I was merely your housekeeper for these many months past. How could I demand your time and affection?" Her voice was growing whiny, but she couldn't stop herself. "Now I am your wife. Don't most wives wish to spend time with their husbands—over a meal, or in their work, or even in quiet reflection?"

He was silent for a long moment. His jaw ground together as he stared at her. "I did not think you would be like other wives," he finally said.

The words cut through her. "What did you think? That I would be your wife at night but your housekeeper the rest of the time?" Her angry words spilled into the room before she could bridle her tongue. She clamped a hand over her mouth and fought back sudden hot tears.

John turned away from her and kicked a loose stick into the hearth.

She sucked in a wavering breath. "I'm sorry, John—"

"It's late." His voice was low and terse. "Go to bed."

She stared at his broad back for a moment. The tears in her eyes turned into heavy pools. She'd only wanted to be with him and to love him. Instead, all she'd managed was to make him angry.

"John—"

"Go to bed, Elizabeth. I don't want to talk about this anymore."

Her heart squeezed painfully, forcing the tears out. She turned and staggered away, not wanting him to witness the wetness on her cheeks or to know how deeply his words had hurt her.

⌒

Elizabeth tucked her hair into her nightcap and lowered herself to the edge of the bed. She folded her hands in her lap, then unfolded them and held on to the bed frame.

The door was open a crack and allowed in only a sliver of light from the hearth. She couldn't see into the main room but knew from the silence that John was still in his study.

Her tears were dry and now all she wanted was to be in his arms and to hear him whisper in her ear how beautiful she was.

'Twas only natural for all couples to disagree. Surely John's arrest had scared both of them and stirred their emotions to unnatural tension.

Once he joined her, everything would be as it should between them.

And if he wouldn't take heed to protect himself, perchance she ought to consider what *she* could do to protect him.

Catherine had alluded to the influence a wife could have over her husband and had suggested she may be able to sway him to abandon his preaching. At the time, Catherine's words had seemed sacrilegious. But now—she had witnessed the power her touch had exerted on John. Did she dare use that power to influence him to stop his preaching?

Was there the remotest possibility that God had placed her in John's life for this purpose? Did God have a new mission for her—to save John and by so doing save all of them from hardship?

Minutes passed. She waited until her fingers grew stiff from gripping the bed frame. She stood, tiptoed to the door, and peeked out. The door to the study was closed. With a soft sigh, she returned to the side of the bed to sit. Finally, her eyes grew heavy, and she lowered herself back onto the feather mattress.

She breathed in the woodsy, metallic scent of him in the blanket and smoothed a hand over his imprint next to her in the sagging mattress.

The warmth of memories slipped through her as she let her mind wander back to the intimacies they had shared.

She didn't realize she had fallen asleep until the coolness of the night awoke her. With a start, she sat up. How long had she slept? Her fingers skimmed the mattress next to her and sensed the emptiness before she felt it.

A mixture of curiosity and worry propelled her from the bed. Perhaps John had come, saw that she was sleeping, and then left. Her bare feet met the cold floor. She padded to the door, widened the crack, and peered through.

John was unrolling a straw-filled mat in front of the hearth. At the creaking of the door, he halted his preparations. His gaze swung to her.

Through the darkness of the room, lit only by the dying embers of the fire, Elizabeth couldn't make sense of the mat or what John was doing with it.

He straightened and fidgeted with a blanket.

Her eyes ricocheted from him to the mat to the blanket and back. Then slowly her mind began to comprehend his intentions. Her heart stammered to a standstill. Surely he wasn't planning to sleep by the hearth? Surely he wasn't still angry with her?

He stared at the mat.

Words of invitation stuck in her throat, unable to squeeze past the nervousness and fear. With each passing second of silence, the trepidation grew until she felt as if she would burst with the pressure of it.

Finally he lifted his gaze and met hers directly. The message in his dark, brooding eyes was clear. He wasn't planning to join her.

"After today and then tonight—" he started.

Anguish sliced through her. She bit her lip to keep the pain from escaping. Tears filled her eyes and blurred her vision. She was thankful for the darkness of the room hiding her pathos.

She hung her head and turned away.

"Things will be better this way for both of us," she heard him say as she nudged the door closed.

With tears streaming down her cheeks, she leaned against the door and covered her mouth with her hand. Sobs begged for release, but she stifled them, knowing she couldn't humiliate herself any-more. She'd made a fool of herself by going to look for him. If she let him know how much he had hurt her, she'd be a bigger fool.

Her throat ached and her chest burned. Her head pounded with a jumble of crashing thoughts. Never before in her life had she felt so low.

Chapter
30

*J*ohn gripped his axe and leaned into the door.

The revelry in the streets of Bedford had grown louder with each passing hour of the night. The lutes, the voices raised in song, the dancing—at some point the celebration had changed into shouts, smashes, and screams.

His body tensed at another roar of laughter on the street outside the cottage and the accompanying cries of fright. His fingers tightened around the handle of his only weapon—one he wouldn't hesitate to use if the drunken revelers attempted to break into his home.

He glanced to the corner near the smoldering hearth. Elizabeth's arms surrounded the children, and they cowered soundlessly against her. Through the darkness their wide eyes watched his every move.

Sweat trickled down his temple, to his cheek, and dripped onto his shoulder. Even though the night was sultry, he had bound the shutters hours ago, not long after the news had reached them that the king had returned.

Even though Bedfordshire was mostly of Puritan Independent sympathy, there were still many who had grown tired of the strict Cromwellian laws and now embraced the return of King Charles II. John had heard enough rumblings among the laborers to know they longed for their drinking and gaming and dancing—and even if they didn't support the Royalists, they would welcome a new leader who would restore England to her former ways.

Someone rattled the door and pounded on it.

John dug his shoulder into it and raised his axe.

"Wake up!" A man shouted from outside. "If ye don't join the celebration, we'll break down yer door and make ye!"

One of the children whimpered, and John shot Elizabeth a hard look. She clamped her hand over Betsy's mouth and drew her closer.

His blood pumped with fresh energy. He'd die defending his family if he must.

The door shook again.

He wedged his boot against it. He could tolerate his enemies bullying him, but he wouldn't let anyone touch his family—especially not a handful of drunken townsmen.

The door rattled again, and this time shook the cottage. John heaved his body against the planks and grunted in his effort to keep out the intruders.

More laughter came from the street, along with the crash of pottery. The heavy breathing of the man on the other side of the door slurred into a slew of curses, and finally his heavy steps thudded away.

John blew out a long breath and turned to look at Elizabeth and the children.

"Are we safe now?" Mary whispered.

"Don't worry, love," Elizabeth said quietly. "Your father is a strong man. He'll protect us." She pressed a kiss against the girl's head.

In the danger and heat of the night, John suddenly couldn't think of anything he wanted more than Elizabeth's kiss.

The past nights sleeping in front of the hearth had been agony, knowing she was only a room away from him. Whenever he heard the soft squeak of the bed, he couldn't keep from picturing her long thick hair splayed across the sheets, glistening in the moonlight.

He had to sternly remind himself that he was only doing what was right for both of them. Who knew how many more days he had left, especially now that King Charles had returned to power? Elizabeth obviously wanted more from their relationship than he was capable. He would only continue to hurt and disappoint her if he went to her at night.

Besides, he was busier now than ever, and he needed to keep his focus on his ministry. This wasn't the time to cut back on his preaching.

Frustration surged to life again. How could she even suggest it? She knew how important his ministry was.

He rubbed his forehead against his shoulder and wiped away his sweat. Yes, he'd made the right decision.

If only his gut didn't ache so much with the longing to hold her.

~

Elizabeth waited. Deep inside she knew it was only a matter of time before John would come to her again. He would put their disagreement aside and realize how much she loved him.

But in the days and weeks following the king's return, the tensions between the Royalists and Puritans only increased, and John was gone from home for longer stretches. The Royalists, who had faced oppression, suffered fines and losses of homes and liveli-hoods, had grown bold. Even after the week of revelry that had accompanied the king's return, Elizabeth continued to hear rumors of attacks against Independents, of beatings in broad daylight, of theft, of malicious revenge.

Her worry for John followed her every waking moment, and she wished more than ever he was only a simple tinker at work in his forge.

It wasn't until she had missed her monthly courses for the sec-ond time that Elizabeth allowed herself to hope she might possibly be with child. She had none of the sickness or tiredness Catherine and Jane had experienced. She felt no different, except an occa-sional tenderness of bosom.

She didn't share her suspicions with anyone. But every so oft, she would catch Mary's face turned toward her, a puzzled expression creasing her dainty features, as if she sensed something different.

As the summer days lengthened, Elizabeth waited for John night after night in her bed, her ears alert to his every move. Disappoint-ment crashed through her each time she heard the muffled thump of his straw mat unrolling onto the floor in front of the hearth. Her heart grieved that yet another night would pass without him.

By midsummer she knew she had to face the possibility that he wouldn't take the initiative to seek her out.

"Perchance he will find affection for me again if he knows I am carrying his child," she whispered into the sticky air of the dark night. She lay on her back and smoothed a hand over the gently expanding roundness of her abdomen.

With a push against the sagging mattress, she peered through the crack in the door, hoping to catch a glimpse of him. The urge to understand his rejection rose inside her like a swift summer storm. How could she live another night not knowing why he stayed away from her?

She swung her feet over the edge of the bed and sat on the wooden box frame. Should she go to him? Did she dare?

Her heart pattered with an unsteady rhythm.

Before she lost courage, she slipped her bare feet to the floor and made her way across the room. Her hand shook against the door, but she pushed it open and tiptoed to where he lay.

He was tangled in a sheet. Her face flushed when she realized he wore nothing underneath the thin covering. His back faced her, and as she lowered herself to her knees, her breath caught at the sight of the splotchy scars pulling his skin taut.

Slowly, carefully, she skimmed her fingers along the edge of one of the scars. He had suffered agonizing burns during the war to dethrone the last king. He'd nearly lost his life to put the Puritans in power—all for the sake of the Gospel. Would his scars be for naught now that a new king ruled England?

The uneven skin was hot underneath her fingertips. She let the outline of the burn mark lead her fingers through the maze on his back.

His breathing grew heavier.

She ignored the urge to retreat and glided her fingers to his shoulder and down his arm. Then tossing aside all caution, she lowered her face and pressed a kiss between his shoulder blades.

He didn't move.

Growing bolder, she brushed aside his thick hair and moved her lips to the back of his neck.

He gasped and turned. His thick arms wound around her and pulled her down to him. His chest rose and fell against her pounding heart. Then his lips chased after hers until they met in crushing passion.

"Elizabeth," he murmured against her lips.

Pleasure rippled through her. This was what she wanted. This was where she wanted to be. "I love you." Her declaration came out unbidden, soft and breathless.

His movements, even his breathing, ceased. He was still for a long moment, and then he struggled to sit up, pushing her away from him.

In confused desperation she reached for his hands, for his arms, for anything to keep the connection. But he strained away and shook his head. "I cannot do this, Elizabeth. I cannot."

She sat back on her heels and bit her lip to hold back a cry of frustration.

"Go back to bed." His voice was hoarse.

"Why? Why can't we be together as we were before?"

"I wasn't fair to you before—taking from you, but having nothing to give in return."

"We can let that be a part of our past. Surely we can start again?"

"No."

"If only you would talk to me. Please tell me what I've done wrong to make you loathe me."

"Loathe you?" He gave a short laugh. "I don't loathe you."

"You must surely find me disagreeable to reject me this way." Her breathing was labored as she tried to hold back the sobs that wanted releasing.

"You are not disagreeable. The problem lies the other way around. You are too agreeable, too pleasing, too tempting."

" 'Tis a problem? Shall I make myself unpleasant, then?"

He gave a groan. "No."

She gulped hard and pushed down the ache in her throat. "What then? Tell me what I may do to please you."

"You can do nothing to please me. I'm a marked man. My days are numbered. It's only a matter of time before they plunge the arrow into my breast."

"Perhaps. But what has that to do with us? Can we not be husband and wife while God gives us the chance?"

"When the time comes, it will already be hard enough. Let's not make it more complicated than we must."

She was beginning to understand. " 'Tis better not to love than to love and to lose it?"

"Methinks that sums it up."

She thought back to when Thomas was a babe and John's resistance to loving his son for fear of losing him. "Do you not think we would be wiser to cherish each moment we have as God's gift? I would say 'tis better to love and be loved, if only for a day, than to have not loved at all."

"The matter is complicated."

A lone cricket's chirping somewhere in the room suddenly chorused as loud as a hundred of them.

"You came to me before," she said softly, shyly. "Why must that change now?"

His sigh was ragged. "I must continue to be steadfast in sharing the Gospel as long as God wills it. I can't sacrifice more of my work, not now. I'm busier than I ever was before. I can hardly keep up with my tinkering, much less your demands—"

"Are not my *demands* only what God intended for marriage? Surely He would have more for us than mere coexistence."

"I did not think you had demands of me, Elizabeth. And that is one of the reasons I believed you were the right wife for me."

"I am the right wife for you. If you would only let me help you—"

"I've said it before—you must help me by taking care of the children. That is the primary reason the elders pushed me to remarry, and you know that."

"But must it change us?"

"Don't make this harder than it must be, Elizabeth. I cannot give you the time you crave."

The weight of pressure inside her chest was rising. She held her breath to keep back the sobs.

"And I wouldn't want the worry of having another child. It would be nothing but a burden."

"Burden?" she choked out the word and resisted the urge to lay a hand on her stomach.

"I would not wish to leave you helpless and with child."

"Would God not take care of me—of us all—just as He has always done?"

"Go back to bed, Elizabeth." He rolled onto his mat and turned away from her. "You would argue with me all night, but I will not let you persuade me otherwise. I have made my decision in this matter, and it is final."

Elizabeth scrambled to her feet, her legs tangling in her night shift. With tears blurring her vision, she stumbled away, desperate to get back to her bed, where she could bury her face and let her sobs loose.

In the following weeks Elizabeth couldn't hide her sadness. As much as she tried, she knew Mary could sense it. And the girl seemed to know the source as well.

"Father is gone altogether too often these days." Mary sawed through an apple with a dull knife on the wooden block Elizabeth had arranged before her in the grass.

Elizabeth's sharp blade methodically clanked as she made swift work of slicing. Without a pause she grabbed another apple from the pile next to her, her knife making neat, even slices, thin enough for the stringing and drying process.

"He's too strong-willed," Mary said, as if the expert in such matters.

Elizabeth didn't respond. Even if she had the words, she was in no mood to discuss John. Of late, her tears flowed easily, and thinking of him and his refusal to love her was a sure way to rouse all of the hurt she carried in her heart.

A glance at Thomas told her he still slept. In the shade of the apple tree, with the gentle breeze fingering through his red hair, not even the sight of his sweet face brought her joy as it usually did.

She finished her apple and laid down her knife. Then she put a hand on her lower back, arched it, and tried to work out the ache that came much more quickly in recent days. Her gaze darted to Johnny and Betsy in the field, chasing each other instead of gathering nuts as she had instructed them.

She didn't have the energy to reprimand them. She sighed and shifted her sore hindquarters. Her movement awakened the life inside her with a sudden flutter of thumps and taps. The sensation was becoming more common, especially at night when she lay motionless in bed.

It was getting harder to hide her condition. She hadn't told anyone, but lately Sister Norton had begun to look at her differently, and she'd seen others whispering and casting glances toward her swelling middle.

The excitement she had initially felt upon realizing she carried John's child had long since deserted her. John's one word haunted her. *Burden.* A babe would only be a burden to him.

Mary stopped working and lifted her face toward the cottage, her keen senses alert. "Father?"

Elizabeth's heart gave a lurch. She struggled to push herself off the ground, stood, and fluffed her petticoat to hide the babe, as had become her habit.

She turned and saw John striding past the garden, coming toward them. His eyes were riveted to one place, her stomach.

She took a step back under the shade of the low-hanging branches and wished she could disappear. Sooner or later the confrontation was inevitable. She had just hoped it would come later.

He stopped in front of her and stared at her midsection. "Mary,

I need to talk with Elizabeth—in private." His voice was terse and left no room for disagreement.

Mary cocked her head as though she wanted to say something.

"Go."

Mary pressed her lips together and then shuffled off, making her way toward Milkie's lean-to. When Mary was a safe distance away, John took a step closer to her. Branches caught in his wind-tossed hair.

"When were you going to tell me?"

"Tell you what?"

"Methinks you very well know *what*."

She *did* know *what*. She just needed more time to figure out how to answer him. "What is *what*?"

"You know *what*."

"What?"

He growled. He ducked his head and stepped under the canopy of branches, closing the distance between them. He grasped her arm and drew her toward him.

She didn't want to resist him.

"This is *what*." He splayed his hand across her stomach, stretching his fingers, feeling the fullness there.

She couldn't hide from him any longer. She bit her lip, as emotions bubbled up from the pool of anguish deep inside.

"I had to find out today from Elder Harrington that my wife is going to have a baby." His grip on her arm tightened. "My wife is with child, and I'm the last person in the whole of Bedfordshire to know."

She cringed at the hurt in his voice. "I didn't tell anyone. Truly I did not."

"You should have told *me*." He pulled her closer.

"I'm sorry," she whispered.

"Are you well?" He searched her face, the fear in his eyes making them almost wild.

She couldn't stop herself from cupping a hand against his cheek. "I am as well as always."

His gaze locked with hers and searched deep inside her, seeming to test the truth of her words.

"I have had no problems. I'm as healthy as I have ever been."

"Truly?"

She smiled, her heart warming at his concern. "Truly."

His breath swooshed, and the warmth fanned over her lips. She only had to tilt her face upward, and he could not resist her nearness. His lips quickly claimed hers. At first soft and tender, the pressure of his kiss awakened a longing deep inside her, and she couldn't keep herself from responding with all of the passion that had lain dormant in her heart. For a moment she forgot about everything, and she let her love for him swell up and overtake her.

"Why didn't you tell me?" He wrenched himself away from her and dragged in a shuddering breath.

She touched her trembling lips. "I was going to when I first suspected it. But then you told me you didn't want another child. You said it would be a burden."

"A new baby won't be easy for either of us and is certainly not what I would have planned. If I am gone, you will find yourself poor and alone with another child to care for. And I will only worry all the more about the family I've left behind."

"Then don't leave us, John." She reached for his jerkin and grabbed it in both hands. "Please, you don't need to leave. If you would but abandon your preaching, then we could live together as husband and wife without fear. We would have no worries over this new babe."

It took a moment for her to realize his body had grown rigid. He started to pull away from her.

She leaned into him and wound an arm around him. She nuzzled her face into the bare spot above his collar. A quiet desperation urged her on and gave her uncharacteristic boldness. She must sway him. This was her chance to convince him to give up the preaching that was putting him in danger.

"Wouldn't you want to be with me and the children?" She brushed her lips against his neck and made a trail of kisses to his ear.

He trembled and his grip on her arm tightened.

She arched into him and stood on her toes to reach his ear. "God wouldn't have you neglect your family in order to serve Him." She kissed his ear. "Most surely God wouldn't have you place yourself in danger when it can so easily be avoided."

His breathing grew louder, and his heart hammered against her chest.

Again she kissed his neck, savoring the saltiness of his hot skin.

With an anguished groan, he pried her away and took a step back. "You don't understand God's call on my life, Elizabeth, or you wouldn't speak this way."

She reached for him, but he stepped out from under the tree, putting distance between them.

"God's calling may change. Mayhap He's now calling you to something different than preaching. More writing?"

"He wouldn't have me quit the fight when it gets rough. It's not His way to give up."

Her mind darted, frantically searching for the argument that would persuade him to renounce his dangerous way of life so he would be free to stay with her and love her. "What if it is merely your pride standing in the way? What if you don't want to stop because you don't wish to concede victory to your opponents?"

Anger flared to life in his eyes again. "Say no more."

"The work of preaching in Bedfordshire doesn't rest on your

shoulders alone. God could accomplish His purposes without the help of John Costin."

"Enough, Elizabeth."

"Or perchance you have grown so puffed up with your ministry that it's become more about your fame than about God's—"

"Enough!"

His roar was loud enough to draw the attention of the children and waken Thomas, who sat up with a wail.

John's jaw was tight with the strain of keeping his voice low. "You don't know me. You shouldn't presume to understand more about my motivations than I myself do."

Elizabeth clenched her fists at her side. Holding up her chin, she refused to cower from the lightning flashing in his eyes. She was losing her chance. She could feel the moment slipping away. "Please, John. All I want is for us to be together, to be a real family. Truly, that is all."

His face was dark with anger. He spun away from her and then gave her one last look. "I take my preaching orders from God and God alone. I cannot and will not listen to the prattle of a foolish young girl."

Elizabeth watched him stalk toward the cottage. Frustration and hopelessness swept through her like the aftermath of a storm, leaving debris scattered painfully throughout her heart.

She plucked an apple from a nearby branch. Then with a cry she hurled it to the ground and stomped it with her foot. She mashed it again and again, until all that remained was a mush of soggy pulp.

Her chest burned. Tears stung her eyes and ran down her cheeks. Her breath came in large heaving gulps as she stared at the flattened remains of the apple.

John Costin had done the very same thing to her love. He had thrown it down and trampled, until he had broken her heart and destroyed her last hope of ever gaining his love.

Chapter 31

*T*here is a warrant for your arrest, Brother Costin," Brother Burgess said in greeting.

John ducked inside the farmhouse and dropped his tool bag to the floor. "Methinks there is hardly a day that goes by without word of threat against me." John cupped his hands at his mouth and blew on them, trying to bring back warmth. The air had finally grown too damp and cool for them to meet outside, and after the long walk, he was grateful to be inside on this November day.

Brother Burgess peered outside, scrutinizing the road before he closed the door.

John strode to the long table in the center of the room and took the mug of cider Sister Burgess offered. He gulped down half of the sweet liquid before the silence of the others in the room began to haunt him.

He licked the froth from his lips and glanced to the somber faces of those already gathered for their meeting. Unease settled in the pit of his stomach. He thumped his mug on the table. "My enemies may rant, but they have no just cause against me."

Brother Burgess sniffed several times and rubbed his sleeve across his red nose. "We have reason to believe it's not merely a threat this time."

"Word reached us that Mr. Wingate has issued the warrant. He's made it known that if you preach, you're to be arrested."

"I should have known." Francis Wingate was a staunch opponent of the Independents. His family had suffered heavy fines during the Protectorate, and it was no secret he was eager to avenge the past. Moreover, he was William Foster's brother-in-law. That alone was all John needed to grow pensive.

"I think it would be wise to postpone our meeting to another day," Brother Burgess suggested.

Throughout the summer and fall, John's enemies, along with most of England, had been too busy celebrating the king's return to take any measures against the Independents. But in recent weeks Parliament had restored the Anglican Church and the Book of Common Prayer. The exiled leaders had moved back into their parishes and forced the Puritans out.

Parliament assumed that everyone would return to attending the Divine Service, but none of the Puritans had made any effort to participate in Anglican services. Rather, the Bedford Independent Congregation had resorted to gathering in farm fields and barns.

No one had prevented them from meeting yet. And so far John's enemies hadn't had any basis for keeping him from preaching and teaching.

He had no reason to think Foster would succeed this time. Even with the help of Mr. Wingate, what reason did they have for his arrest? Parliament had not yet enacted any new laws that would prevent him from preaching.

"No," he said, "by no means. I won't stir, neither will I have the meeting dismissed for this."

The men began to murmur.

"Come, be of good cheer. Let us not be daunted." John reached again for the mug of cider and took a long drink. "Our cause is good, and we need not be ashamed of it. To preach God's Word is so good a work that we shall be well rewarded even if we suffer for it."

"Yes," Mr. Burgess said in a hushed tone, "but Mr. Wingate has already called upon the constable." He glanced at the door.

"We think you should flee while you still have the chance," another said.

The odd feeling churned in John's gut again. Foster was a snake—sly and unpredictable. What if this time he was able to finally sink in his fangs?

"Very well," he said after a moment. "Since we still have time before the others arrive, I will pray about the matter."

The men nodded their assent.

John retreated to the field behind the farmhouse, away from the fearful gazes, away from the anxious pressure.

He paced under bare elm branches. The dry leaves crunched under his feet, and the coolness of the day permeated his woolen cloak. He shivered and took a breath of the woodsy damp air.

He'd always known his unlicensed preaching carried the possibility of arrest. Even under the protection of Cromwell's rule, there were too many, even among the Independents, who believed only the properly trained and educated should preach.

Yet, in all the many months of his ministry, he had never let their threats sway him. God had given him skill with words and had called him to preach. Therefore, he'd obeyed God's call, not man's prejudiced dictates.

Why would he do any differently now?

Elizabeth. He could picture the way she'd looked when he'd left the cottage that morning. In the dim light of the hearth, he'd glimpsed the swell of her stomach and the soft lines of her full figure—and his entire body had ached with the longing to hold her again. When she'd turned her sad gray eyes upon him, he'd wanted to rush to her and wipe away the dark shadows from her tired face.

He'd tried to convince himself over the past weeks that he'd done the right thing by shutting her out of his life. He'd tried to remind himself of her demands and of how she'd asked him to abandon his preaching. But lately, whenever he was near her, he couldn't quite remember why those things mattered so much.

His gaze turned toward the road, the narrow path that would lead him back to Bedford. It would be so easy to slip away now. No one in the farmhouse would fault him. Instead, they no doubt would be pleased if he did. Then he could be with Elizabeth, really be with her, and stop fighting the longings for her that overwhelmed him at times. He could be with her when their baby was born. Maybe they could be the *real* family she wanted.

With a long sigh that blew a cloud of white moisture into the air, he hung his head. If he turned and ran now, what message would that send to the new converts—that he was not as strong in action as he was in word? If he, their mentor and teacher, fled from persecution, wouldn't they follow his example when threatened?

"Lord, I covet your wisdom. What would you have me do?" He paced quicker, as if in so doing he could think faster. "Surely you don't give a calling only to take it away at the threat of hardship."

The clamor of voices signaled the arrival of more people from the surrounding countryside, from Pulloxhill, Westoning, and Flitwick—earnest, hardworking tradesmen and laborers who had languished in the dead ritualistic religion that had ruled in England for so long.

Now that they had heard the truth of the Gospel, that God could save them and would invite them to an active and personal relationship with Him, they couldn't go back to their empty way of living. They were starved for someone to give them the solid food of the Word of God.

How could he give up the fight now? If he and other unlicensed preachers gave in to the pressures, they would concede defeat, not just to Foster and Wingate and others like them, but ultimately to the devil.

The old enemy of man's salvation was working hard to keep the purity of the Gospel message from spreading, just as he had worked in the days of the early apostles and saints. But they had persevered through persecution, even if it meant death. Was he willing to do the same?

Slowly John walked back to the farmhouse. Expectant gazes riveted to him when he stepped inside. "I won't run from danger." He shed his cloak.

The voices of the men rose in argument. Some of the new arrivals wanted to resist Wingate and had complaints of their own against him. Others wanted peace at all costs.

John pulled his Bible from his bag and took his spot at the head of the gathering. "I don't know what the outcome of this day may bring. But nothing will happen that our Lord doesn't ordain. If He's chosen me to suffer arrest for Him, then He has a purpose in it. And if my time for it has not yet come, He will make that clear too."

He flipped open the pages of his Bible.

Suddenly a thundering knock on the door broke the quiet.

His body tensed and his thoughts flashed to Elizabeth. He envisioned her face the day he'd discovered she was with child, when she'd stood under the apple tree, flushed and beautiful, arguing with him more convincingly than any man. What would she feel when she learned he'd been arrested?

"John Costin, I've got a warrant for yer arrest." The

constable banged the door open and stepped inside. Two brawny men accompanied him.

"What's he done?" A big farmer jumped to his feet and put a hand to the hunting dagger sheathed at his belt. "The king hasn't made any law against meeting together for prayer and Bible study— at least not yet."

The constable spread his feet apart, and his cloak fell away to reveal a long rapier. The two men with him did likewise, their hands already thrust through the hilts. The room grew quiet enough to hear hens cackling in the yard behind the house.

"All we want to know is what Brother Costin's done wrong," another man said.

"Why would I have a warrant if he weren't guilty of something? Now, let's get on with it. I've been waiting outside long enough for your foolhardy meeting to start."

"Well, this 'ere *foolhardy* meeting isn't open to you or Wingate's men." The big farmer took a step forward. His fingers worked at unsheathing his dagger. "You're gonna have to wait outside until we're finished."

"You're finished now." The constable stepped toward the farmer and pulled out his rapier. "I'll make sure of it."

The farmer jerked his dagger out.

"Brother Lyte," Burgess cautioned. "This is a peaceable gathering."

"It'll be peaceable soon enough, when I usher our unwanted *guests* back outside."

John closed his Bible. "There will be no fighting here. I'll go with them." He nodded at Brother Lyte to put away his dagger. Brother Lyte, along with several others, was still new enough to the ways of the Lord that he could easily be tempted into bloodshed, especially against Wingate's men.

The stocky farmer didn't move except to puff out his shoulders and arms into the kind of stance that shouted defiance.

"I don't want to be apprehended for being a thief or a murderer." With a calmness that belied the tension squeezing his muscles, John picked up his tool sack and stuffed his Bible inside. "No. If I must go to prison, it will be because I am innocent."

With even steps he walked toward Brother Lyte. "It's better in God's sight for us to be the persecuted than to be the persecutors." He reached for the farmer's dagger and pried it from the man's grip. Then he flipped it upside down and motioned it toward the sheath. "You must fight with your prayers, Brother Lyte. They are your strongest weapon now."

The farmer hesitated and then replaced his dagger into his belt.

Brother Burgess released a heavy breath.

"Let's go, Costin." The constable backed toward the door without taking his focus from the gathering.

John slung his pack over his back and nodded assent. But he turned to Brother Burgess. "Get word to my brother Willie in Elstow. He'll know where to find the Bedford elders."

"Let's go. Now." The constable opened the door and motioned for John with his head.

"And get word to Elizabeth and the children. Tell her not to worry." But even as he said the words, he had a feeling deep inside that this time she had every reason to worry.

~

When they arrived at the large double gates of Harlington House, the constable told him Francis Wingate was otherwise engaged. John was sure the delay was intended to put him off guard, to instill fear of the unknown, to make certain he knew who was in control.

After a sleepless night, John was finally ushered into the parlor. Even though he had spent much of the night praying, the moment he stepped into the dark room, the paneled walls and low ceiling closed in upon him and stole his last shreds of peace.

Gloomy fog enveloped him and shrouded his soul. He hesitated and blinked his eyes to adjust to the dismal lighting. One of Wingate's men gave him a shove that sent him stumbling into the room.

In the shadows, lit by a single candle, Mr. Wingate reclined in an upholstered chair, his legs crossed at the knees. One finely leathered boot tapped at the air, and long smooth fingers drummed on the carved armrest. The darkness of the room shadowed his face, but John could feel the man's eyes coldly regarding him.

"Do come in, Costin."

John straightened his shoulders and bristled under the man's haughtiness. "With the hospitality that's been extended to me, how can I resist?"

A sharp blow to his lower back caught him off guard, nearly knocking him to his knees with the pain. John gritted his teeth and struggled to hold himself upright.

"Costin, do you know why you are here?"

"Methinks I can guess—"

"You are here because you are guilty of plotting revolution against His Majesty King Charles II."

"Then you've got the wrong man, Mr. Wingate. I assure you I was leading a peaceable Bible study with not a thought toward rebellion."

"A likely excuse, I'm sure. Gathering your kind under the guise of Bible study but then using it as an opportunity to speak politically, arguing for yet another revolution."

John's temper fired to a hot flame and spread through his body like a spark upon thatch. "You can ask any man in that gathering yesterday or anywhere else, and they'll all attest to the same—I've never spoken against the king."

Wingate waved his hand. "I've read your works, Costin. Your writing is full of sedition."

"Then it's not my writing you've read—"

"I've read it. And *if* I so desired, I could prove sedition."

If. The word hung in the air, and suddenly John knew the charge of plotting revolt was not the real issue. Rather, it was the threat, the sword to prod him into submission.

John caught a movement in the corner behind Wingate. He could distinguish the outline of a thin man with a narrow face. Was it Foster?

John squared his shoulders. The battle was about to get rough. "So what is it that you really want from me?"

Wingate sat forward in his chair and stomped both feet against the floor. His face, now visible in the light of the candle, revealed features as hard as chiseled marble. "You are a tinker. Follow your own trade. Stop troubling everyone by usurping your place."

"I instruct people on forsaking their sins and closing in with Christ." John worked hard to keep his words even and calm. "I can do such exhorting without confusion or compromise to my tinkering trade."

"It's time you learned your place, Costin." Wingate stood and reached for the slender walking stick that rested against his chair. "God Almighty ordains some men to be leaders. The rest are followers. You are poor and ignorant. Your place belongs among the dumb sheep."

Heat pumped through John's veins. Wingate was just like the others—threatened by a laborer like himself who had dared to upset the balance of power. The hierarchy of rich and poor had been the same since the days of William the Conqueror—the few nobility and gentry held all the power and wealth, while the rest of them struggled to survive with the little they could scavenge. Men like Wingate didn't want the system to change.

"Doesn't Scripture say we are all like sheep gone astray?" John couldn't keep the sarcasm from his voice. "If the Shepherd and Overseer of my soul considers me a dumb sheep, then that must make you one too, Mr. Wingate."

The man raised his walking stick and swung at John's gut. The force of the hit knocked the wind from John and doubled him over with pain. Immediately Wingate's men were at his side. Each jerked one of John's arms behind his back in an upward movement that ripped his joints into a blinding anguish. The hold exposed his stomach and stretched it taut.

Wingate swung his stick again. The blow connected with his ribs with a crack. He grunted, dizzy with the searing heat that burned through his skin.

"You need to learn your place, Costin." Wingate tapped the walking stick on the wooden floor. "And you need to stay in it."

John struggled to breathe. "What do you want me to confess?" His voice was ragged. "You're privileged and I'm not?"

John knew what was coming even before the words were out. "I want you to confess that you'll stop all preaching." Wingate lifted the stick and pushed the end of it into John's neck at his windpipe.

The pressure cut off the flow of air, and he choked like a drowning man.

The room swirled before him. This was it—his time to die. He'd prepared himself for the possibility of martyrdom. He'd just not expected it so swiftly.

If only he'd had one last chance to see Elizabeth, to kiss her good-bye.

What would she say when she heard of his murder?

John shook his head and wrenched away from the men, away from Wingate's deathly grip.

The men grabbed him from behind and tried to wrestle his arms behind his back again.

John knocked them away.

The cold point of a rapier sliced into his jerkin and skimmed the skin of his back. The burning trail brought him to a standstill.

"Tie him up," Wingate said in disgust.

The man pierced his skin deeper with the rapier before pulling it away. Then they jerked his arms behind him again. They wrapped the rope tight, chafing the skin of his wrists.

"You must agree to leave off preaching." Wingate stalked back to his chair and sat down. "Or I will break the neck of these unlawful meetings."

John's breath came in deep raspy gulps. "If you want me to admit I am of the lowest rank of men, of the most despised of all families in the land, I will do so. I have naught to boast of noble blood or of a highborn state." Blood made a slow trickle down his back. He pushed down the pride that threatened to rear itself. "I can admit you are better than I. But I cannot, I will not, abstain from preaching. This I cannot do."

Wingate stared at John through narrowed eyes. "I was told you were stubborn. And I believe a lesson in humility is in order." He nodded to his men.

He quickly realized the nod was the signal to begin their work of beating him into submission. With his hands tied he had no way to defend himself as they took turns at him, slamming their fists into him, until finally he sank to his knees in agony.

He hung his head. The room flickered. Blood dripped from his nose onto the floor.

"Enough," Wingate finally said. "He'll ruin my rug."

Blessedly, the beating ceased. But the roaring in his head grew louder, and blackness wavered before his eyes. He didn't want to die yet. Not before he could tell Elizabeth he was sorry.

Chapter
32

The *thump*, *thump* of a fist against the cottage door brought Elizabeth to the edge of her chair. Her heartbeat echoed the urgent pounding.

She'd waited hours for news, yet now that it had come, she wished it would go away.

She heaved her aching body out of her chair. With one fist pressed into her back, she lumbered to the door and opened it far enough to peek outside. The face peering at her was surrounded by a shock of red hair. She couldn't remember the boy's name but recognized him as one of Willie's children.

"Got news about Uncle John," he said breathlessly, clutching his side. He had likely run the whole distance from Elstow to Bedford to bring her the tidings.

With trembling hands she swung the door open. The cold

darkness of the November dawn stepped inside with the boy. It took a grip on her belly and squeezed. She gasped with the intensity of it.

The boy greeted Mary, seated near the warmth of the hearth. Of the children, only Mary was awake at the early hour, or perhaps she'd never gone to sleep. She was sure Mary sensed something had happened, although neither of them had talked about it.

The boy didn't wait for an invitation, nor did he think to render his message gently. "Uncle John's been arrested. He's gonna be transferred to the Bedford gaol today."

Elizabeth's stomach tightened again. 'Twas what she'd feared but prayed would never happen. Her thoughts raced back to the last time John had been taken in. He'd been released then. Was there a chance he could go free now too?

"Is it for sure, then?"

"As sure as the cock crows."

Another sharp pain clenched her like a chain and pulled tighter and tighter until she couldn't breathe.

"Here tell they got all manner of charges against him." The boy eyed the bread and cheese on the table. "He ain't gonna get out of them this time."

Elizabeth bit her lip to keep from groaning—whether from the news or the painful cinching around her middle, she wasn't sure.

"My father wanted me to make sure yer okay before I head back home."

Elizabeth nodded, unable to speak through the pain. She'd had a few contractions from time to time, but nothing like this. Surely she ought not to have them so quick and hard. The babe was not due for two months.

"Have a fill of bread and cheese," she managed. A chill crawled through her with such force she shuddered at its violence. She clutched her back and fell to her knees. A cry slipped from her lips before she could hold it back.

"Mother!" Mary screamed.

The boy rushed to her.

A wet trickle made a trail down her legs—the birthing waters escaping from her womb where there should be none—at least none yet. Panic rose up within her.

"Is everything okay?" the lad asked.

She shook her head, and her belly began to constrict again. "Go get Sister Norton."

The boy's eyes widened, and he ran to the door.

She heard Mary banging into benches and knocking things over in her haste to get to her. She ought to pray, but she had an overwhelming feeling of being abandoned—by both God and John. She thought she had done everything right. She had labored to please them, had worked to earn their approval, had desired their love. But somehow, whatever she had done had not been enough.

They had left her anyway.

⁓

John had broken his nose often enough in the past to know it was broken again. Cracked ribs, bruises, cuts—his body ached just as it had during the war after he'd been wounded. When he'd told the gathering at Samsell that he would face whatever God ordained, he hadn't anticipated Wingate would beat him senseless.

He wouldn't change the decision he'd made to stay and preach. But the more time he had to think about what lay before him, the empty days, the separation from his family—the more he wished he could go back and change time and be with them, even if just for a day.

Wingate turned him back over to the constable and ordered him taken to Bedford and locked in the gaol. They'd only just started down the road when Brother Smythe and Brother Wheeler arrived breathless from Bedford, having heard the news of his arrest. They convinced the constable to return with them to Harlington House, certain they could do something to gain John's release.

Even though they were Puritans, they were too wealthy and prestigious for Wingate to ignore. He allowed them into his office, while John waited with the constable in the dark hallway.

John leaned against the wall, trying not to put any pressure against the burning cut in his back.

At the clomp of approaching footsteps, he straightened.

The man lifted his candle and revealed his face. It was William Foster.

"What? John Costin?" His voice was so amiable that an observer would have thought him pleasantly surprised to find John there. "Why, John, what are you doing here? I suppose you've gotten yourself in trouble again?"

John eyed him warily. Did Foster think him an ignorant sot? "You know why I'm here, Foster."

The man's face widened with feigned innocence, but the light of the candle gleamed against a dangerous glint in his eyes. "Have you finally gotten caught at one of your unlawful meetings?"

"Last I knew there was no law against meeting together to edify one another with God's Word."

"Oh, but there is. Haven't you heard of the Acts of Elizabeth, specifically the statute of '35?"

John glared at the man. The Acts of Queen Elizabeth? Was Foster so desperate as to stoop to unearthing ancient, outdated laws to persecute him?

"The law states that all who refuse to attend public worship in their parish churches will be subject to fines. And those who resort to a gathering of five or more shall be imprisoned until they submit. If they refuse to submit, then they are to be banished from the realm."

"If it is a sin to meet together to seek the face of God and exhort one another to follow Christ, then I shall continue to be a sinner."

"But, John," said Foster, as if talking to an old friend, "don't you think you can seek God's face at the parish church? Have you received a gift so far above others that you cannot come to the public worship like everyone else to hear the Divine Service?"

"I'm as willing to be taught as to teach, and I look upon it as my duty to do both."

"Now, John, you know no man ought teach or preach Christ's Gospel unless he is sent forth by the bishop and Parliament."

"The epistle of Peter encourages everyone to minister as he has received the gift."

"You, a lowborn, uneducated man have been given the gift of tinkering." His tone was quickly losing all pretense of friendliness. "You're a nothing, a nobody, and should not presume to be more than you are."

"God's gifting does not depend upon man's prestige. One need only look at Scripture to see that the Lord often works through humble *nobodies*."

Foster passed his candle to the constable, who stood nearby. He made a move as if to walk away, but instead reeled back and swung his knuckle into John's eye.

The pain and force threw John against the wall. The impact against the open flesh on his back took his breath away.

"I should have had the men finish you off earlier," Foster snarled. All efforts at pleasantries vanished like the mirage they had been. "Maybe I ought to put an end to your miserable life right now."

He took another swing, but John raised his arms and deflected the blow. He grabbed Foster's fist and twisted the man's hand like a piece of tin. Foster grunted and struggled against him, but John squeezed harder. He wanted nothing more than to inflict pain on this man who had hurt Elizabeth and nearly killed her.

Foster's breath came in short huffs, and the stench of it assaulted John.

He took a step back and dropped Foster's hand. The snake deserved a beating like the one he'd given the wet nurse. But John would not be the one to give it.

Foster stumbled backward.

"I refuse to do anything that might dishonor the Lord or wrong my own soul," John said.

The look in Foster's eyes was venomous. "I might not be able to kill you now. But someday I will take great pleasure in seeing you stretched by the neck, drawn and quartered." He retrieved his candle. "In the meantime, I will make sure you rot in prison."

⁓

Day turned into night and night into day. Elizabeth couldn't tell when one ended and another began. At times the labor pains made her delirious, and at other times she slept with utter exhaustion. Different women came and went, always with the same anxious looks, all with the same words: "The baby is coming too early."

She wanted to scream at them to go away. She didn't need help. She was a strong woman and would make it on her own.

But she knew she could die on her bed giving birth to her babe. She had watched her mother die that way.

"It's been a full week."

Elizabeth heard the whispers as though her mind were no longer attached to her body. Someone pressed a cool rag to her forehead and forced sips of water into her mouth.

"We need to do something today," came another urgent whisper.

The hushed voices argued around her.

When the labor pains began again, she knew that something was different. It took her a moment to realize the women had raised her into a sitting position and tied her hands to the bed frame. It took only another moment for her to realize why.

Intense agonizing pain ripped her body into two. She screamed with the little energy that remained. The torture burned, and she wrenched upward trying to free herself from the midwife who had forced her hand inside and groped for the babe. The ripping pain made her nearly delirious. Hands shoved on her womb from the outside. She screamed again and writhed with the agony.

"Push now, Elizabeth," the midwife commanded. "Push hard."

Elizabeth strained against the ropes and gasped for air. Darkness wavered through a dizzying haze. She suddenly longed for oblivion, where she would find relief from the torture.

"Stay with us, Elizabeth." Sister Norton's voice spoke gently near her ear. The woman's cool hands smoothed Elizabeth's hair away from her face. "It's almost over, you poor, poor dear."

"Push!" the midwife demanded.

"You can do this, my dear," Sister Norton urged. "You *must* do this to live."

Elizabeth roused all of the strength left inside her. A hoarse scream filled the air around her, too inhuman to be hers.

The command to push came over and over, until she was listless with the effort. Then finally, with one last excruciating effort, it was over, and she sank into darkness.

John paced the length of the dayroom of the gaol. Eight steps up. Eight steps back.

Two prisoners sat on a bench against the wall, and their eyes followed him back and forth. Two others sat at a small oaken table in one corner near the hearth. They tagged laces and pretended not to watch him.

John had given up trying to sit three days ago. Now he was going crazy.

The clanging of the locks on the gates outside the gaol stopped him midstride.

"Someone's a-comin'," said one of the prisoners on the bench, the one who'd been in the gaol the longest and didn't have front teeth. He'd lost them to scurvy. John prayed he'd be out before the same fate could befall him.

John held up a hand for everyone to be quiet. If they listened carefully, they would be able to hear the visitor enter a second locked door and then gain entry to the building.

"It's gots to be for yous." The prisoner spoke again, even though John scowled at him to be quiet. "Yous gets all the visitors."

John wanted news of Elizabeth more than he wanted his life. He prayed this time they'd finally tell him she was safe. He didn't care anymore whether the baby lived or died. He just wanted Elizabeth to live.

After the creaking and groaning of more locks, John heard voices in the long hallway—and one of them belonged to Gibbs.

The restoration of the monarchy had been hard on his old friend. His congregation had been forced out of the Church of St. Peter and St. Paul in Newport Pagnell, and he'd lost his living as rector.

As the gaoler's shuffling footsteps neared the dayroom, John's body tightened like a hangman's noose. Heavy keys clanked in the lock, and as the door swung wide, the old gaoler offered him a kind smile.

He led John to the small room that sufficed as an office, a plain room, void of all but a desk, chair, and a few crates.

"Take as long as you need, John." The gaoler's look was one of sympathy, one that set John at further unease. He nodded his thanks and then turned to Gibbs, whose eyes widened at the sight of him.

"You look terrible."

He still suffered from the bruises of Wingate's beating. But worse was the grime after just one week. He didn't doubt he looked as bad as he felt. He was equally certain he stunk. He was only just beginning to tolerate the stench. It permeated the men's cell, which was unheated and dark, save for a small window in the door and a few small holes near the ceiling. It was only three feet wide and six feet long, affording him and the other prisoners little room to maneuver or stretch out at night. If it had ever been cleaned, it wasn't in his lifetime.

He was grateful for mornings when the gaoler would unlock the cell and allow them into the men's dayroom, where they could stretch their stiff, numb limbs. The dayroom was small and dirty too, but at least it was heated by a fireplace and had a barred window that afforded light. With the onset of winter, neither the heat nor the light seemed sufficient, but it was something.

The news of his arrest had spread rapidly. Friends had visited him to bring him paper and ink, along with a change of clothes and food. Even though the prison rations were meager—bread, cheese, onion, and suet pudding—he'd had no appetite.

Gibbs held out a small crock. "It's stew. From Sister Wilson."

John ignored the outstretched hand. "How's Elizabeth?"

Gibbs hesitated and then placed the crock on the desk.

"Is she alive?"

His friend nodded but avoided his gaze.

The tension inside him mounted. "Tell me everything."

Gibbs studied his boots, then lifted his eyes. The sadness in them sucked the breath out of John. "The baby, your son, was born dead."

"But Elizabeth will live?"

"They tell me she's fine, that only a strong woman could have survived such a birthing."

A torrent of emotions poured through him and pushed against his chest, making it ache until he felt it would burst with the pressure. He rubbed his sleeve across his eyes to hold back the threatening mist.

A small part of him grieved the loss of the baby. A man never wanted to lose his flesh and blood, especially a son. But babies died all the time. There seemed no way to prevent that.

But to lose Elizabeth?

His legs began to tremble. He sank into the chair and lowered his head into his hands.

"You've grown to care about Elizabeth, haven't you, my friend?"

"I love her." With sudden clarity he knew he loved her.

He wasn't sure when he had first started loving her. But sometime, somehow, he had fallen in love.

"If only I'd realized earlier." He rubbed his face with his hands. Weariness settled over him. She had offered him her love, had given herself to him wholeheartedly. And he had spurned her.

Shame fell over him, and he groaned again. Instead of accepting Elizabeth's love and the time they could have had together, no matter how long or short, he'd pushed her away. He should have done as she'd suggested—love and be loved, if only for a day.

"It's never too late to let her know how you feel," Gibbs said.

"All she wanted was for me to be her husband the way God intended in marriage. She was right—I got too caught up in my preaching and thinking how important I was and how much God needed me to preach."

Gibbs was silent.

"And now look at me. My ministry is gone. My preaching is over. I'm truly a nobody."

"God will still use you, my friend. But in His way and His time."

"Perhaps. But He doesn't *need* me. The burden of sharing the Gospel does not rest upon my shoulders. And I don't know why I thought it did."

"God has gifted you mightily, and we all put a great deal of confidence in you and still do."

John studied the haggard lines in his friend's face and then sighed wearily. "I am tempted to give in to their demands, Gibbs. If I forsake preaching, they'll let me go free. Then I can be with Elizabeth and the children."

Again Gibbs was quiet for a long moment. "I don't believe God is asking you to give up your calling, my friend." His voice was gentle. "He gave you the gifts and will not revoke them. He would have you cling to them even if you must suffer."

John nodded. Deep inside he knew he could not give in to the demands of his enemies, no matter how much he longed to be with Elizabeth and the children.

"No," Gibbs continued. "You must hold fast to your gifts—but at the same time you must learn to use them more wisely."

"How so?"

"God would not have us use our gifts to the detriment of our families. I have heard it said: 'Fathers, first reform your families, and then you will be fitter to reform the family of God.' "

John bowed his head. Gibbs was right.

If only he could go back and give Elizabeth the time she'd wanted while they'd been together. And if only he could go back and take pleasure in spending time with his family.

Heat seared his chest and into his throat. But he'd thrown it away, and now only God knew if he'd ever have the chance to do it over and do it right.

Chapter 33

*W*hat had she done wrong to deserve such punishment?

Elizabeth dug her hands through the sticky trough of bread dough and pushed it around listlessly. She didn't have the energy to give it the heavy mixing it needed. She couldn't seem to find the strength to do much of anything. Her body had healed, and she had survived without illness or complications. But she felt as if her lifeblood had drained from her drip by drip, until only an empty corpse remained.

"Henry is ready for the dough." Jane came alongside her. "Perhaps I should finish?"

Elizabeth shook her head and pummeled the dough harder. "I can do it."

Jane regarded her with the sympathetic look she was beginning to despise—a look she received too frequently from everyone.

A tiny wail from a wooden cradle in the far corner drew Jane's attention away from her and to her babe born only a fortnight past. The babe's cries dug deep inside Elizabeth and ripped at the ravished flesh of her heart. It should have been her baby.

He would have been over six weeks old.

She bit back an anguished cry and pounded the dough with new energy borne of pain. She should have been the one feeling the fullness of her milk, ready to press him against her bosom and breathe in the sweet newborn scent of his head.

Instead, her arms and womb were empty, utterly barren of the life she had carried for those many months.

She beat her fists into the dough, and tears began to slip down her cheeks. She hadn't been able to see him or touch him. By the time she'd recovered enough to know what had happened, they'd already buried him.

The door to the bakehouse rattled.

Elizabeth brushed at her tears with her sleeve. She was sure it was her father returning from the quarter sessions at Chapel of Herne. Her heart lurched with the foolish expectation that by some miracle they'd let John go.

"That was no trial," her father boomed as he swung open the door. The cold winter air swirled past him, rushed at Elizabeth, and extinguished the flicker of hope she'd harbored all afternoon.

Her father shed his heavy woolen overcoat and his hat. "It was more of a bear-baiting contest, if ye ask me. Nothing more than a pack of spiteful, ravenous dogs tearing to bits a shackled bear."

Elizabeth's hands came to a standstill in the dough. Even though she was trying to convince herself not to care, she couldn't keep from inclining her ear every time John's name was mentioned. As much as she despised herself for it, she longed for news about him.

"They've indicted him for not coming to the parish church to hear the Divine Service." Her father limped with his cane to the oven that Henry had lit in preparation for the baking. "I say we're all guilty of that charge. Since King Charles came back, none of us have gone to the Divine Service."

She hadn't wanted to think about John's trial, but Catherine had made a point of telling her all of the rumors surrounding it, and none had been favorable. The judges were staunch Royalists who had suffered much during the Protectorate. They hated the Independents.

"And they're accusing him of holding unlawful meetings, to the disturbance and distraction of the good subjects of the kingdom." Her father gave a wry laugh. "*Disturbance and distraction* from their Book of Common Prayer is all."

He added more gorse to the oven, needing to bring the masonry to the right temperature before they could bake the bread. Henry pricked the loaves across the top with the sharp bodkin and then stamped them with the Whitbread mark.

Her father had asked her to help at the bakehouse and in exchange was giving her bread for her family. It wasn't enough to survive on, but it was something. Others in the congregation had been kind enough to bring her the things she could no longer buy at market: eggs, fish, fowl.

"Brother John did nothing to win their favor by telling the judges that he, for his part, could pray very well without the Prayer Book. They weren't too pleased with his remark and accused him of being possessed with the spirit of delusion and of the devil."

Elizabeth could picture John standing tall, his wide shoulders stiff with defiance and passion. He wouldn't cower from the fight. He was too skilled with his tongue and would surely thrash them back no less than they deserved.

"What's his judgment, then?" Henry asked quietly. He darted a glance toward Elizabeth before meeting Jane's gaze in the corner, where she nursed the babe.

"He must endure three more months of prison." Her father

turned to look at Elizabeth, his eyebrows furrowed over sad eyes. "After that, if he doesn't submit to go to the parish church and agree to leave off preaching, they'll banish him."

"Do you think he'll agree to what they ask?"

"Ye know John." He sighed. "He's a stubborn man. He told them if he were let out of prison today, he would preach the Gospel again tomorrow."

Elizabeth looked blindly on the dough in front of her. It was hopeless. John was as good as dead to her.

"He asked about ye, my daughter." He paused, as if waiting for Elizabeth to say something. When she didn't, he continued. "He asked if ye were well enough yet to visit him."

She shook her head. Tears sprang to her eyes again. "No. I'm not well enough."

"He sounded concerned about ye."

She ducked her head and squeezed the dough, wishing she could hide. She'd never shared John's rejection with them. It was too painful to think about, much less discuss.

Elizabeth gulped down the sobs that came all too easily these days. He'd wanted a strong woman. And that's what he'd gotten. She didn't want or need John's concern.

⁓

The three months until John's next trial dragged. Elizabeth tried not to think about it, but the question always lingered somewhere in the recesses of her mind: Would John submit and go to the parish church and leave off preaching, or would he choose to leave England forever?

When the time finally came, she learned the justices sent the clerk of the peace on their behalf in an attempt to try to reason with John, to extract a promise from him that his preaching would come to an end. 'Twas no surprise to hear he had refused again. But it was another blow, and it hit her harder than she wanted to admit. The justices gave him three more months in prison to reconsider, and by the midsummer assize expected him to yield to their authority or face worse consequences.

Part of her was glad for a little more time in which John might possibly be convinced to change his mind. The other part was weary of the waiting and the worrying about what would happen.

Most of the time, however, she was too busy to think. In addition to spring sowing and helping with the bread-making, Sister Norton had instructed her in bone lace-making. Elizabeth struggled with the intricate patterns that took hours of work for only four, maybe six pence a yard when it sold.

The demand for it had increased with the return of King Charles. England had gladly adopted the king's lavish tastes and had readily thrown off the simple, plain clothing styles that Oliver Cromwell had enforced during the Protectorate.

On warm spring days she sat outside to do her lace-making. Sometimes Sister Norton joined her and brought Lucy's children with her. The sister had grown to love the two she had taken in, and they adored her and called her Nana. If they did remember Lucy or Fulke, Elizabeth was sure it was only a distant nightmare.

"Your work is very beautiful, my dear." Sister Norton leaned over and studied the pattern beginning to emerge on the pillow in Elizabeth's lap.

Elizabeth sat forward on her stool and arched her back, ready for a break. Pulling the linen thread tight for too long cramped her fingers. And staying focused on the pins she had pricked into her pillow to make a pattern wearied her eyes.

She carefully laid the bobbins in a neat row. 'Twould waste precious time to have to detangle the thread wrapped around each small fish bone.

She looked in the direction of the heads bobbing among the tall grass, Johnny and Thomas and Lucy's children. Elizabeth had sent Johnny to collect any edible greens he could find and hoped he would return with enough dandelion leaves for soup and possibly burdock taproots or watercress to add more substance. 'Twas the hungering season, when the food stores were low, and this year Elizabeth could not silence the rumbling in her stomach. She was having to feed a family with a pittance and was sending John food every day too.

"We have been blessed, haven't we, my dear?" Sister Norton followed her gaze to the children.

"Blessed?" What could the old woman possibly mean?

"Blessed, indeed." Sister Norton rolled her neck.

"I do not see the fruit of a blessed life." 'Twas a barren, dry life of late. Anything that could go wrong had. Where was the blessing in that?

"Ah, ah, my dear. Maybe you're not looking for fruit in the right places."

"No, Sister Norton. Somehow I've failed to please the Lord. He's withheld His blessings from my life and given me only hardships to endure."

"My dear, do you think hardships are the sign of His displeasure?"

"Doesn't He promise reward to those who faithfully serve Him? I've tried. I've done everything I could. But it hasn't been enough."

"Elizabeth." Sister Norton's eyes filled with compassion. "Do you think only the *good* things that happen are blessings?"

Elizabeth's throat tightened, and she couldn't answer the widow. The pain in her heart threatened to overwhelm her, as it often did.

"Our troubles themselves are blessings."

"No. They can't be." Elizabeth shook her head. "How can troubles ever be a blessing?"

"Hardships are the Lord's greatest blessing to the believer.

Without them we would love the Lord only for what He does for us. Our troubles teach us to love Him for who He is."

Elizabeth bridled her response. Had she been serving the Lord for what He would do for her?

"We're back!" Mary's voice called to them.

"I think I shall try it on my own next time." Mary rounded the cottage with Betsy skipping along beside her.

"You've memorized the route?" Elizabeth asked.

"I didn't let Betsy help me at all today."

Betsy dashed off to the field to join the others.

"Father told me to tell you he appreciates the soup." Mary relayed the same message every day. "And he wants you to deliver it next time."

"No, Mary." Her answer was the same every time. She wanted to bury her feelings for John. Seeing him again would only dig up her longings and drag them back to the surface where they would taunt her.

No matter how adamant Mary was about John's desire to see her, Elizabeth wasn't willing to subject herself to the misery of being near him.

Mary was silent for a long moment.

Elizabeth could tell by the girl's thoughtful expression she had more to say.

"I overheard the gaoler speaking about the king's coronation," she finally ventured.

"Yes. 'Twill be on the twenty-third of April."

"They say it will be a big celebration," Sister Norton added.

Mary nodded. "The gaoler said the king will set some prisoners free to show his kindness and goodwill."

Elizabeth's heart lurched.

The girl hurried to speak. "Maybe you could appeal to the king. If you went to the king and told him about Father's arrest and how you're working so hard to take care of four children . . ."

Elizabeth shook her head. "I could never do such a thing. Why would the king listen to me?"

"But that's just the point. You're the poor wife, left alone to struggle to survive. Surely he will hear your story and have pity."

"It would be a good story," Sister Norton said.

"No. I could never go to the king. That would mean traveling to London, and I've never ventured beyond the bounds of Bedfordshire. It would never work."

With passion transfixing her dainty features, Mary reached for Elizabeth.

Elizabeth caught the girl's hands.

"It would work. Truly it would. You know how to argue just as well as Father. If any woman could convince the king, you could."

"Mary's right about that, my dear."

Elizabeth's mind began to spin slowly, like a wheel stuck in mud. Could she, a mere peasant woman, go to the king to beg for John's pardon? Did she have a chance to help win his freedom?

Mary squeezed her hands. "You could be just the one the king will listen to."

A flicker of hope rekindled in Elizabeth's breast.

"Besides," Mary said, lowering her voice, "this might be just the way to make him finally love you."

Elizabeth could only stare at the beautiful girl in front of her. Her blind blue eyes, with the color so like John's, sometimes saw everything. Was now one of those times? Would an appeal to the king for royal clemency be the key to unlocking John's love?

Perhaps it was worth a try.

⁓

When the elders came to her the next day with the same suggestion, Elizabeth knew she had no choice in the matter. They'd decided that Elizabeth, the helpless, lonely wife who'd lost a babe and had four remaining small children, one of which was blind, would be their greatest asset in the battle for winning John's freedom.

The men made all the arrangements for her travel and lodging. They wrote out the petition for her and rehearsed what she needed to say.

She made herself do what she knew she must. She withheld her complaints during the uncomfortable three-day carriage ride to London and tried to stifle her surprise at the massiveness of the city itself, the crowds, the stench, the noise, the commotion.

When the time came for them to make their visit to the king, she lifted her chin and went forward, praying she could hide her trembling, reminding herself she was doing this for John. If she succeeded in securing his release, she might—just might—earn his favor again.

"I would like to help you," Lord Barkwood said after he'd finished reading her petition. "But I'm afraid we must have a recommendation from the local authorities to consider your husband a candidate for the royal clemency."

Elizabeth wanted to melt into the thick rug and disappear. Everything about Westminster Palace and the House of Lords made her feel small—the high ceilings, the grand staircases, the extravagant paintings. From where she stood at the foot of the long polished table, even the lords were unapproachable, too important for someone as insignificant as she.

One of the elders behind her poked her back. She straightened her shoulders and forced air into her lungs. "The local authorities are prejudiced against him, my lords. He has broken no law, yet they are determined to keep him in prison or banish him from the kingdom."

Lord Barkwood perched his spectacles on the end of his nose and peered down at the paper in front of him.

Except for the thud of her heart, the room was silent.

Finally Lord Barkwood laid the paper onto the table and folded his hands over it. A lord next to him leaned to him and whispered words Elizabeth could not hear.

Lord Barkwood nodded and then tilted his head toward Elizabeth. "If the local authorities do not recommend him, then we cannot involve ourselves with your husband's case."

Elizabeth wanted to shrink under the gazes of the important men in their opulent clothes—if she but had the lace from one of their shirts, she could sell it and feed her children for months.

Instead, she lifted her chin. "If the king cannot grant him clemency, perhaps my lords would be so kind as to send me away with a petition of your good graces and will toward my husband."

The lords whispered together again. "Very well," Lord Barkwood said, taking off his spectacles. "We will give you a petition to present to the judges of Bedfordshire at the summer assize."

She bowed her head in gratitude, as was expected of her, but labored to swallow the bitterness at the back of her tongue. When they had the power to give her a feast, they instead offered her crumbs?

Even as hopelessness swirled through her, she knew she dare not shun anything they were willing to give. No matter how slim, it was still one more chance to win John's release.

And one final opportunity to secure his love.

Chapter
34

*E*lizabeth wrinkled her nose at the overpowering scent of tobacco smoke. It filled every corner of the Swan Chamber Inn and hung like a cloud over their heads. The practice of smoking had returned with the restoration of the king and now permeated every fashionable gathering of men.

Her gaze swept over the crowded room of wealthy gentlemen—gentry of the surrounding shire, along with the traveling justices of the midsummer assize. Panic shoved at her insides and threatened to dislodge the remnants of her last meal.

She took a step backward. Who was she to enter uninvited into the court meeting? How had she ever thought she could speak to these men, much less enter their presence?

A firm grip on her upper arm propelled her forward. "God be with you, Sister Costin. God be with you." Elder Harrington and the others of the congregation stood outside the door of the upper chamber on the staircase. Their presence blocked her escape. She had nowhere to go but forward.

The Independents knew more was at stake in this case than just John's future. If the justices of the assize convicted him, they would soon face persecution themselves.

Elizabeth swallowed the rising bile and forced one trembling step in front of the other toward a table of gentlemen, who puffed on pipes and sipped mugs of ale. The light from the tall, oblong-paned windows that faced the River Ouse displayed the ermine and scarlet robes of the judges.

Silence descended with each step she took. She was certain the appearance of a woman, especially a mere peasant woman, in the hallowed sanctuary of these elite men was a sacrilege not soon to be forgiven.

With a deep breath she searched for the face of Sir Matthew Hale. The elders had instructed her of his appearance and the need to speak directly with him. He was perhaps their only hope, the last of the judges who had any history of kindness toward the Independents.

"My lord." She tried to steady her voice. "I make bold to come to your lordship."

The distinguished judge sat up. His startled but kind eyes came to rest upon her.

"I've come to your lordship to know what may be done with my husband, John Costin." She spoke the words the elders had instructed her to say.

"You are not welcome here, woman," snapped Judge Twisden, the other presiding judge of the assize. His pompous expression, framed by loose cheeks and bulbous nose, dismissed her.

Elizabeth focused on Sir Matthew Hale and rushed to say what she must before they thrust her out of the chamber. "I have been to London, sir. I delivered the petition to Lord Barkwood. He entrusted me to your care, and I come now with the warrant of the peers to make my appeal."

"It is of no use for you to waste our time with your petition," Judge Twisden said. "Your husband has been duly convicted."

At the choruses of agreement from the other men sitting with the judges, Elizabeth wondered if she would have the chance to say anything at all. She had an odd sense of empathy for what John had gone through time after time with these proud nobles who scoffed at any who would challenge them.

Sir Matthew Hale puffed on his pipe. "So you are the wife of John Costin?"

"Yes, my lord. I have four small children that cannot help themselves, of which one is blind, and we have nothing to live upon but the charity of good people."

Her statement did as intended. Sir Matthew put down his pipe, and his eyes filled with sympathy. "Four children? You are too young a woman to have four children."

"My lord. I am only stepmother to them. I have been married to my husband less than two years. Indeed I was with child when my husband was first apprehended." She pushed aside the pain the remembering brought and made herself continue. "Since I was young and unaccustomed to such things, I, being dismayed at the news of the arrest, fell into labor. I continued for a week and then was delivered. But my child died."

"Alas, poor woman!" Sir Matthew sat forward.

"Don't listen to her," came a voice Elizabeth recognized at once, one that sent fear racing through her. She looked upon the thin face of William Foster, who was seated next to Judge Twisden. He regarded her with contempt, one that said he would finally destroy her.

"This woman is not one of repute, your lordships," Mr. Foster continued. "The rumors surrounding her have always been less than favorable. She was Costin's housekeeper and bed warmer before she became his wife."

His words elicited muffled coughs and a few guffaws.

Heat made its way into her cheeks and burned them with embarrassment.

"Costin is a pestilent fellow as well," Mr. Foster said. "There is none like him in the county. His reputation, like this woman's, leaves much to be desired."

The rumors had spread wide. Mr. Foster had made sure of that. "And yet time has indeed proven many of those rumors false," she said, looking directly at Mr. Foster. " 'Tis because we are poor laborers that we must endure the lies and attacks without the true culprit being brought to justice."

Mr. Foster smiled.

" 'Tis widely known that this man—Mr. Foster—set fire to my husband's cottage with the intent to burn me within." She turned again to Sir Matthew Hale. "But he will not be brought to justice for the wrong he's done, while my husband languishes in gaol, though he is innocent."

"This woman makes poverty her cloak," Mr. Foster declared, raising his voice. "As I understand, her husband finds it much better to run up and down preaching than to follow his calling."

"What is Costin's calling?" Sir Matthew asked.

A chorus of voices replied, "A tinker, my lord."

"Yes," she said loudly, to be heard over the commotion. "He is a tinker and a poor man, therefore he is despised and cannot have justice."

"He does not abide by his tinkering," said Mr. Foster. "He preaches and does whatever he sees fit, regardless of the Book of Common Prayer."

"He preaches nothing but the Word of God," said Elizabeth to Sir Matthew, refusing to look at Mr. Foster.

"*He* preaches the Word of God?" Mr. Foster rose to his feet, his face puffed with growing rage. "He runs up and down and does harm. That is what he does!"

"No, my lord." Elizabeth tried to keep her voice calm, even though her body was tense and ready for a battle of words. "God has owned him and has done much good by him."

"God?" Mr. Foster's voice was laced with contempt. "His doctrine is the doctrine of the devil."

"My lord, when the righteous Judge shall appear, all will know John Costin's doctrine is not the doctrine of the devil." Her words rang through the room, reverberated off the walls, and penetrated deep into her heart.

God *did* own John. And John's true calling was not his tinkering. They were wrong. *She* had been wrong. His true calling was his preaching—just as the disciples had been fishermen by trade, but their true calling had been teaching.

"Send her away," Mr. Foster demanded.

"Sit down, Mr. Foster." Sir Matthew Hale's command echoed through the chamber. "I think we've heard enough of your blustering."

Mr. Foster slid back into his chair, but his glare slashed into her.

With a shiver she turned once again to Sir Matthew. "My lord, I only ask that you consider my husband's case according to the law and not by prejudice. He has not been lawfully convicted. The king and Parliament have no law against meeting to exhort one another for Christ's sake."

"He is convicted. It is recorded," came the quick reply of one of the justices.

"How can there be a conviction when there has been no law for him to break? Surely you cannot hold a man accountable for an outdated law of which he had no foreknowledge." While she didn't understand the full ramifications of the law, she had heard enough of the talk about the statute of Queen Elizabeth to know the Royalists had twisted even the old laws to suit their purposes.

"What does a wench like you know of such things?" Mr. Foster said. "It's not your place to speak to this group of distinguished men in this manner. Leave the thinking and deciding to those of us who have been given the right by God—"

"Mr. Foster," Sir Matthew Hale's voice rose. "You will either hold your tongue or leave this gathering."

The words upon Mr. Foster's lips died away. He nodded at the judge and then clamped his lips together with a brittle smile—a smile that said he would murder her if he could.

Elizabeth pushed aside her fear and slid Lord Barkwood's letter across the table in front of Sir Matthew Hale. "My Lord, if you would but consider this petition . . ."

The judge glanced at it, then reached for his pipe. He took a deep puff and regarded her for a long moment. "Certainly John Costin is well aware of the law now—a law that has always been in effect—only it has been ignored these many years. Would your husband leave off his preaching now that he knows its illegality?"

The men fell silent.

Elizabeth lifted her head high and straightened her shoulders. The answer was clearer to her than it ever had been before. "My lord, he dares not leave preaching as long as he can speak."

As she said the words, the room erupted into chaos. Inside her heart, however, in the deepest part, she was filled with peace. He would preach until the day he died, or he would no longer be John Costin, the man she loved.

⁓

Elizabeth's hands shook so that the soup inside the crock sloshed dangerously close to spilling. "I will go today, Mary," she told the young girl.

It had been one week since the assizes, since her complete failure to secure John's release. All that week she'd struggled, reviewed each word she'd spoken, wondered if she could have done or said anything different that might have secured his freedom. She was sure the only way she could have gained his release was to extract a promise from him that he would stop preaching. And she knew now she could never do that.

Preaching was his calling. And John must face his hardships and go through them in much the same way she needed to face hers.

It was past time to apologize to John for what she had said about his preaching, for discouraging him in it, for asking him to stop. She couldn't rest until she did. And as much as she dreaded visiting him and facing his displeasure over her failure, she also realized she must see him one last time.

"Do you want me to go with you?" Mary steadied the crock.

"I must do this, Mary." Elizabeth willed her hand to stop shaking. "I regret that I have not done it sooner."

"He will be glad to see you."

" 'Tis no matter," she said, trying to convince herself. She'd let him down. Why would he want to see her now?

"He has never stopped asking about you." The girl's voice was soft.

Elizabeth tucked a stray piece of hair back under her coif and took a deep breath.

"Don't worry." Mary's hands patted the air until she made contact with Elizabeth's cheeks. Then her fingers gently glided over Elizabeth's face, her nose, mouth, and eyes. "You are beautiful, the most beautiful woman I know."

"Mary's right."

Elizabeth gasped, and her heart slammed to a halt.

Mary jumped back and screamed. In an instant she streaked across the room to the sound of his voice. She threw herself with abandon into the arms she knew would be outstretched for her.

For a moment Elizabeth could only watch in speechless shock,

373

not daring to move lest she lose sight of the apparition of John that stood within the doorway.

Mary's arms wound around her father, and she burst into heavy heartrending sobs.

The wails brought the other children pattering barefoot into the room.

Betsy squealed and ran to her father. Johnny approached more slowly, but John knelt and swept all three against his chest in a crushing embrace. Tears dripped from his cheeks onto the tops of their heads, followed by his kisses.

Elizabeth absently picked up Thomas, who clung to her, his eyes wide with fear for the man who had become a stranger to him. She didn't realize her cheeks were wet until Thomas wiped them with his fingers.

"Momma cry?"

Elizabeth smiled through her tears. "Momma is happy." This moment in time, watching John love his children—it was enough to feed her hungry soul for many days to come.

But then John's gaze lifted from the children and found her. The longing and love in his eyes swept the breath from her body.

She clutched a hand to her throat. Was he really there? Or had she finally grown so desperate that she was now dreaming during her waking hours too?

"Elizabeth," he said softly. He stood then and let go of the children. His gaze refused to release hers as he started across the room toward her.

When he finally stood in front of her, her breath came in shallow, erratic bursts.

Somehow Mary managed to extract Thomas from her arms and usher the children outside.

John didn't say anything, but he scrutinized her face, devouring her as if he needed to get as much of her into his soul as he could before they were ripped apart.

"Are you real?" she whispered, lifting her hand—wanting, needing to touch him and reassure herself that he truly stood before her. Hesitantly she grazed her fingers across his cheek.

He leaned into her hand. "I'm home," he whispered. "Now I'm most definitely home."

A choked sob escaped unbidden. She stepped away from him and pressed her fist against her mouth, holding back the flood that suddenly swelled for release. Home? For how long?

He thrust out a hand toward her. Purple hyacinths and yellow daffodils danced in a wild array of color. "For you," he said softly.

Her heart lurched with the memory of another bouquet and the same words on their betrothal morning.

"Can we start over? At the beginning?" His eyes probed hers.

She swiped at the tears slipping down her cheeks but couldn't keep them at bay.

"If you'll give me another chance, I'd like to be the kind of husband you deserve." He reached out and touched her tears.

At the gentleness of his fingers, another sob slipped out.

"I will take you as my wife."

His earnest pledge tore at her heart and stripped away the little resistance left.

"I truly take you as my wife, Elizabeth."

"Yes, but for how long?"

His fingers followed the path her tears had left. "A very wise young woman once told me 'tis better to love and be loved, if only for a day, than to have not loved at all."

She smiled through her tears.

"I love you, Elizabeth."

His soft words wrapped around her. She read his eyes and saw the truth in their depths.

"I promise to love you for as long as God shall give you to me—even if it is only for a day."

She took the flowers from him and buried her face in them, washing the petals with her tears.

"But it's my hope I have longer than a day to love you," he said, reaching for her and drawing her to him.

"What is the verdict?"

He shook his head and a shadow crossed his eyes, and she could see then the lines that the months in prison had added to his face.

"Sir Matthew Hale gave me no guarantees."

"You are here now." She brushed a hand across the crevices near his temple. "And that's all that matters."

A sudden grin played at his lips. "They told me you argued with those judges better than I could have."

She couldn't keep back a smile of her own. "I doubt anyone could argue more convincingly than the preacher John Costin."

His grin broke free. "Anyone except the preacher's bride."

Author's Note

$\mathcal{T}$he Preacher's Bride is inspired by the real-life story of one of history's greatest heroes of the faith, John Bunyan, writer of the classic Pilgrim's Progress. While history gives due laud to John, it fails to recognize the woman who stood by his side and helped shape him into the hero we all know and love. It is my sincerest hope that in telling this story, I have brought to life Elizabeth Bunyan and have given her the recognition she deserves.

While I have attempted to remain true to the recorded facts, I have taken liberty with a few dates, as well as John's final release from prison. As with most historical fiction, an author must use his or her imagination to fill in the framework of what was left untold by history, to patch up the gaps and add details to the real story. Thus, most of The Preacher's Bride is true fiction, the runaway creativity of a writer's mind.

However, you may be wondering which things within the story actually happened.

We do know John lost his first wife and was left with four young children, the oldest of which, a daughter, was blind. He received help from the women of his congregation in caring for his motherless children so he could continue preaching and teaching. John's enemies spread many vicious rumors about him, and I have tried to accurately portray the nature of what was being spread. William Foster was one of the staunchest persecutors of the Puritans in Bedfordshire. John was arrested by Francis Wingate, and the dialogue during his time at Harlington House is based on John's writings. Elizabeth fell into labor for an unbelievable seven days, and the baby she birthed died. She traveled to London as well as petitioned the judges at the assizes for John's release. The words during that trial are taken from transcripts. Characters like Gibbs, Sir Matthew Hale, Sister Norton, Mrs. Grew, Vicar Burton, and other members of the congregation were real people, as recorded in documents of their church. I have also attempted to use many of John's famous quotes throughout the book.

While I have taken liberty to have John released from prison at the end of *The Preacher's Bride*, in reality, John and Elizabeth faced twelve long years apart while John languished in the Bedford prison—twelve years of incredible hardship and the struggle to survive. They were indeed pilgrims on a difficult path. John steadfastly refused to give in to the Anglican Church's demands to stop preaching. Although they did not banish him from the country as they'd threatened, they did confine him in prison indefinitely.

During his twelve years of imprisonment, John was allowed occasional and brief periods of freedom. In 1665 the deadly bubonic plague swept through England, and John was allowed to go home. Then in 1666 after the Great Fire of London he was given another respite from prison. Neither of his breaks was long, and he ended up back in the same jail for six more years.

In 1672 King Charles II, in an effort to reduce tensions, issued an indulgence that permitted Puritans and other Independents to obtain licenses to worship freely. John was finally freed from prison and received a royal license to preach. He was named minister of the Bedford congregation, winning the right to share the good news of the Gospel anywhere and to everyone. The tinker had truly become preacher.

John and Elizabeth were finally reunited. They had two more children together, as well as a long and satisfying marriage. God used their hardships to strengthen their love for Him and their love for each other. If John had given in to the demands to stop preaching, then quite possibly the world would not have known one of the greatest pieces of literature ever written. For it was during John's dreary days in jail that he wrote *Pilgrim's Progress*, a testament to the persevering of faith in the midst of hardships.

So who was Elizabeth Bunyan? Near the end of his life John wrote these words in a deed of gift, and it describes Elizabeth better than I ever could: ". . . the natural affection and love which I have and bear into my well-beloved wife, Elizabeth Bunyan."

She was the *well-beloved wife* of one of the greatest heroes of the faith. May her story encourage and strengthen you in your pilgrimage.

Acknowledgments

As a mother of five young children, I often struggle to find writing time. I try to schedule it in six days a week, usually in the early mornings and also in the afternoons after I'm done teaching my children. But each day is full of challenges, distractions, and activities that often cut into that writing time. Some days it's a wonder I write at all!

But thankfully, God provided some incredible support during the writing of *The Preacher's Bride*, and I'd like to take the opportunity to thank all those who helped me.

I need to first and foremost thank the Lord for giving me the type of personality that can work through interruptions and chaos day after day! Secondly, I want to thank my husband for his support of my writing passion and for his willingness to help me find that illusive uninterrupted time.

I'm grateful to my older children for taking turns babysitting and playing with their younger siblings in the afternoons so that I could write. Without their help, I would have had innumerably more distractions. They sacrificed for me and cheered me on day after day.

I also want to acknowledge the fantastic organization ACFW (American Christian Fiction Writers). Every year ACFW sponsors the Genesis Contest, a national fiction-writing contest for unpublished writers. My double final in the 2009 contest helped me gain recognition and helped propel my writing career forward.

So many other people have come alongside me in my writing journey. My agent, Rachelle Gardner, championed my books. My freelance editor, Tiffany Colter, provided insightful and challenging feedback. All of my blogging writer friends have encouraged me every step of the way. My writing journey is so much richer because of each friend I've made.

Finally, I would like to thank the staff at Bethany House for their hard work on *The Preacher's Bride*. In the production of a book, much goes on behind the scenes, and I want to thank every single person for working so hard—initial readers, the cover and design team, marketing, and everyone else who had a hand in shaping this book. I especially want to thank my editors, Dave Long and Sharon Asmus, for their wisdom and dedication.

Thank you, Readers, for joining me in the story of John and Elizabeth in *The Preacher's Bride*. I would love to hear from you. Here are several ways you can connect with me:

Mail: Jody Hedlund
P.O. Box 1230
Midland, Michigan 48641

Web site: JodyHedlund.com
Blog: jodyhedlund.blogspot.com
Email: jodyhedlund@jodyhedlund.com
Facebook: http://www.facebook.com/AuthorJodyHedlund
Twitter: @JodyHedlund

If you enjoyed *The Preacher's Bride*, you may also like...

A dangerous secret, an overheard conversation, and a woman who is not what she seems... Will hidden pasts ruin their hope of finding love?

The Silent Governess by Julie Klassen

In a community where grace is unknown, what price will she pay for embracing love?

Love's Pursuit by Siri Mitchell

In a world where wealth and image are everything, she is loved by all. But at what cost?

She Walks in Beauty by Siri Mitchell

A world at war again. A horrific accident. And three lives forever intertwined. In the midst of God's silence, can faith and hope survive?

While We're Far Apart by Lynn Austin